Winning Wyatt

Football Heartthrobs Book Three
Cliff J. Cavender

Cavender Books

Contents

Dedication   1

Content Warning   2

Prologue   3

Chapter 1   7

Chapter 2   14

Chapter 3   22

Chapter 4   30

Chapter 5   38

Chapter 6   45

Chapter 7   60

Chapter 8   68

Chapter 9   79

Chapter 10   95

Chapter 11   115

Chapter 12   129

Chapter 13   137

Chapter 14   150

Chapter 15   167

Chapter 16   183

Chapter 17 195

Chapter 18 210

Chapter 19 224

Chapter 20 232

Chapter 21 240

Chapter 22 251

Chapter 23 262

Chapter 24 273

Chapter 25 277

Chapter 26 282

Chapter 27 287

Chapter 28 289

Chapter 29 294

Epilogue One—Six Months Later 309

Epilogue Two 315

What's Next? 320

Dedication

To those who have been baffled by their own sadness and feel like love is a drug—may you find the healing you deserve

Content Warning

Winning Wyatt dives heavily into the topics of depression, codependency, and suicide. I have chosen to include these topics to show how prevalent these things are, especially amongst men in the LGBTQ+ community. These issues are resolved, and there is an HEA, but please read at your own caution. I hope you enjoy the third book in the Football Heartthrobs series!

Prologue

Wyatt Nelson

AFTER PRACTICE, SEVERAL REPORTERS linger on the edges of the Salt Lake football stadium. As my fellow players and I make our way to the locker room, snow begins to fall on this chilly December day, and the reporters hurry to meet us there. Usually, when I talk to reporters, they ask about my ambitions as a tight end. But this time, I plan on leading the conversation.

I've got something special to share.

I make my way to my locker and begin undressing next to our quarterback, my good buddy Blake. He's on the shorter side—just below six feet—but his body is solid muscle.

"Don't tell me you're really going to do it," he says.

I let out a sharp laugh. "What's the worst that could happen? I wouldn't be the first."

As reporters flood the locker room, Blake closes the distance between us.

"Yeah, but those guys are done with their career. You haven't even reached your peak."

After I strip off my gear, I put my hand on my chest. "My, you flatter me."

He whacks my chest. "Stop it—you know what I mean. You're on track to be one of the best tight ends the NFO has ever seen. You can't throw all that away."

I get clean clothes ready to change into after my shower, but I plan on talking to the reporters before then. I'm not delaying this any longer.

"Trust me," I say. "I've thought about this." And thought, and thought, and thought. I don't want just want to be legendary. I want to be legendary while showing the world who I truly am. I'm doing this for all those kids who look at us and think that professional sports aren't for them.

Shirtless, Blake scratches his furry chest and shakes his head. He puts his hands on his hips and sighs.

Slightly distressed by his discomfort with this whole thing, I'm tempted to criticize him—tell him that just because he's too afraid to show who he truly is doesn't mean I should have to keep hiding.

But it's not that simple. And I know Blake. He's being as authentic as he can be.

He puts his hand on my shoulder. "I'll support you," he says. "You're helluva lot braver than me."

I put my hand on my his—my best friend's. "Maybe one day this will be you."

He scoffs and resumes changing. "Yeah, we'll see," he says dismissively.

As one reporter approaches us, I now see my chance. I stand up and put my foot on the bench, making myself open to talk.

The short male reporter stops right in front of me. "Wyatt Nelson—you got a sec?"

"I do," I say, resting my elbow on my propped knee.

He extends the microphone. "Statistics show that you're one of the best blocking tight ends the NFO has seen in a while. But is it true you're also trying to improve your receiving to the same level?"

I nod. "It is," I say. Then I take a deep breath. "But there's also something else going on with me."

I hear Blake sigh behind me as he makes his way to the showers. The reporter adjusts himself and moves the microphone closer to my face.

"What's that?" he asks.

Here goes nothing.

"I also finally wanted to put this out there: I'm gay."

Suddenly, the entire locker room goes silent. All the reporters and players in the room stop to gawk at me. Except for Blake of course. He's pretending not to care.

"You're..." the reporter stops himself, almost as if he doesn't want to say the g-word. Come to think of it, he probably doesn't. But that's okay. I'll say it for him.

"Yep," I say. "I'm gay."

The tension's so thick in the room that I could slice it like pie. But I prepared for this. I'll be okay. My skills are too good to be dismissed so easily, especially now that it's been slightly more normalized to be gay in the NFO thanks to Kyle Weaver and Tanner Bash.

"Well," the reporter says, lowering the mic. "That's interesting. Congrats to you."

"Thanks," I say, grabbing my things. "Just thought that as I'm improving my skills, the world should know who I really am."

And as I make my way to the shower, I swear I can hear a pin drop in the locker room. But I don't care. I don't just plan on being the best tight end of the 21st century. I'm gonna be an openly gay one, too.

* * *

It's a snowy day in the Salt Lake stadium a few days later, and I'm at the top of my game. We're playing against the Arizona Sparrows—the score 21 – 21—and we have one minute to secure a win. Which I plan on doing. Blake and I, along with the coaches, planned this next play as a Hail Mary. Since I'm typically known as the tight end who blocks rather than the one who receives—of course 'cause I stand at 6'5" and weight a good 250 pounds—teams never expect to me catch and run. But I've been practicing, and I sure as hell know I can do it. It also helps that since I came out, I've received so much love and support. It feels like the whole country's on my side.

We get into position. But suddenly, across the line of scrimmage, I hear the word I hate the most.

Faggot.

Chills run down my spine. Guess I don't have the whole country on my side after all. But I take a deep breath and steel myself. I knew that coming out in the middle of my career wouldn't be a walk in the park, but I didn't do it for nothing. People need to know that queers like me can thrive just like any straight man can.

Our center snaps the ball to Blake, and I juke out the Sparrows defensive back—the very one who I think called me a slur. I can see the fury in his eyes as I pass him, but it doesn't matter. I don't have to deal with him anymore.

As I run, I turn back to see the ball hurdling toward me. Out of the corners of my eyes, I see two Sparrows coming at me from either side, that fury I saw in the defensive back burning in their eyes.

Running as fast I can, I leap into the air to catch the ball. But just as I do, both of my legs are grabbed simultaneously by the two Sparrows. As I fall, they pull in different directions, making my knees splay outward and causing me to lose complete control over my descent. My arms clutching the ball, I prepare to meet the ground.

But my left knee hits first.

With a sickening pop, I shout as the rest of my body hits the ground, completely losing hold of the ball. And my world goes white.

Chapter 1

Silas King

Linda Higgins, the woman I'd like to call my adoptive mama, is hosting Christmas Eve. She has a massive tree up in her living room. Her cat, Miss Beautiful, is constantly trying to scale it, and we all have to yell at her to keep her down.

Kyle and Michael, two of my very best friends and scheduled to be married this next year, are cuddling on the couch. Next to them are Martha and Llewellyn, the women who took me in like their own little brother after I moved here from Alabama. Jimmy and Tanner, my newly engaged buddies, sit on the floor next to the tree trying to keep Miss Beautiful entertained and off the tree.

Linda walks in with a plate of her famous sea salt caramel brownies.

The whole room explodes with excitement, jumping up to grab one. I stay put on the nearby chair looking out the window at the lake in the distance. Around it, all the cabins are decorated with all sorts of Christmas lights. I wish I was in the mental state to appreciate it more.

"Silas," Linda says.

I look to her.

She walks over with a brownie. "Don't you want one?"

"Sure," I say, putting on a smile. I take it with both hands and take a bite. The sweet, gooey, yet crunchy texture with the nuts almost lifts me out of the funk I'm in.

Almost.

"How about we play some board games?" Kyle asks. "Settlers sounds fun."

"Oh, that would be perfect," Linda says, her arms raised. The others agree while she rushes to go get the game.

I sit forward, trying to muster all the enthusiasm I can. But it feels like I'm stuck below the surface of a frozen lake banging on the ice to free myself. And it's as hard as steel.

When we get the expanded edition of Settlers of Catan all set up, Jimmy and I decide to sit aside and watch, which leaves the rest of my six friends to play.

"You sure you two don't want to play?" Linda asks us.

"You know me, Linda," Jimmy says. "I get too competitive."

And I would explain myself, but Jimmy's got a large enough personality to cover for both of us. I'm used to staying quiet, anyways.

"Alright," she says. "Next game."

As we watch, I get that itch I usually get—not technically an itch, but a desire to just get up and get moving. To be away. Ever since I left the ranch I grew up on in Alabama, this feeling has stuck on me like a leech and occasionally makes itself known—usually in dark, quiet times. I've talked to Martha and Llewellyn about it, and they describe it as wanderlust, but that feels too romantic. In reality, I don't feel a rush to explore. I feel a rush to hide from something. It's never been easy to put this thing I'm hiding from into words. Sometimes, I imagine it as a big humanoid figure made of pitch-black smoke. Sometimes it's just the thoughts in my head. But regardless, this desire overwhelms me, and when I get it, I gotta do something to calm it down. And a walk sounds like the perfect thing.

"Hey, y'all," I say, grabbing my cowboy hat. "I'm gonna go on a walk to the lake."

"Alright," Linda says. "Be safe."

"I'll be back," I say, walking to the door. After I put on my jacket, I step outside and shut the door behind me. I take a deep breath, relishing the chilly air in my lungs. I'm wearing a henley, a jacket, and jeans. It's about forty out, which feels nice. Usually, it gets pretty cloudy and foggy around the lake at night. But

I can see the stars clear above, which is perfect. Looking up into space always calms me down.

I step down onto the gravel trail that leads down to the lake, enjoying the way the rocks crunch underneath my boots.

But that's really all I can say I enjoy at the moment.

As I stroll along, I'm haunted by all the 'shoulds' that float in my head: I should own a house; I should have a boyfriend at twenty-eight; I should lose this belly and get skinnier; I shouldn't have as much student debt as I do; I should have just gone straight into the workforce instead of physical therapy residency. I should just move back to the ranch and do what I've always been told I would do: live a small, empty, boring, lonely life. Funny thing is that I already am living such a life. I'm just not on the ranch.

By the time I reach lake, my mind is completely submerged in the 'shoulds', so I pull out my earbuds to unbury myself. As I lean over the deck railing, I put on my favorite musician for these somber moods: *Eluvium*. His dark, haunting melodies always seem to mirror how I'm feeling. Whenever I talk to others about music, I like to tell them that my favorite musicians are the ones who create music that seems to listen to me just as much as I listen to it. *Eluvium*? I feel like his music depicts the hulking wraith in my mind that's constantly searching me out while I hide. *Slow Meadow*? I feel like it pulls emotions out of me before I even know I'm feeling them. And *Alaskan Tapes*? I fucking feel like I see new colors when I listen to them.

Beneath me, I can feel the dock vibrate from steps that are not my own. I remove one earbud and turn around to see my buddy Jimmy approaching me. He's the quintessential bear: hairy, bearded, muscular, manly, and sweet as a peach. He used to use that to his advantage, sleeping with everything under the sun that had a penis. Until he met his now fiancé, Tanner. And now they're as happy as a December night is long.

"You doin' alright?" he asks, taking up his place next to me.

I stop my music and put my headphones in my cowboy shirt pocket. "You know me," I say. "Just enjoying the cold air."

A breeze blows by, smelling of smoke with a hint of something sweet. Someone in Glamour Springs is having a bonfire.

Jimmy clears his throat and spits into the water. "You don't feel left out, do you?"

I look at him, my brow furrowed. I tilt my hat upward to see him more clearly. "No. Why do you ask?"

He adjusts himself, putting one foot down and the other up on the wooden ledge. Nearby, some ducks are wading through the calm waters that reflect the Christmas lights around the lake.

"I just thought since, you know. You've always had Martha and Llewellyn together. Then Kyle goes and gets himself engaged to a hot pornstar."

I laugh. "Yeah, that was a crazy one."

"And then I somehow get sprung," he says. "Well, a lot more then sprung. I fucking fell head over heels for Tanner. And I still love him."

I smile to myself. Jimmy's like a big brother to me, just as caring as Martha and Llewellyn have been. So usually, I'm as transparent as I can be with him. But there's a part of me—the darker part—that not even him or Martha or Llewellyn know about.

"Jimmy, I'm not jealous of you or Kyle or anyone else," I say. "I'm happy for y'all."

"I mean, it should be any day now," he says. "You're a stud. You're a beefy, muscular cowboy type. You've got that sick mustache. You're thoughtful and intelligent. Any guy would be a sucker not to fall for you."

I sigh. "You may be right about all those things, but I'm okay. I'm alright single right now."

He adjusts his elbows and looks at me, and I can feel my cheeks heat under his gaze. I've never been attracted to Jimmy, but he always seems to read me a little better than everyone else, which gets me all flustered.

"Then why does it seem like lately you've got a cloud hanging over your head?"

I sigh through my nose, enjoying the way the hot air creates steam that sails into the air.

I've always had a cloud over my head, I want to say. No, I fucking want to scream it. But what good would that do? It wouldn't make the cloud go away. It would just make people pity me. Even Jimmy.

"Just the time of the year," he says. "I know people love the holiday, but Christmas always gets me feeling so somber and melancholy."

Jimmy laughs. "I love the words you use," he says. "Like a walking book."

I smirk at my good friend. "Thanks for coming out here, Jimmy," I say, leaning further onto the rail. "But I'm good. I promise."

Jimmy taps the rail, standing up. "Alright," he says. "You promise?"

I sigh, hating that I have to lie. But even if I said no, nothing would change.

"I do," I say again.

As he walks away, I turn to call out to him.

"I think I'm gonna retire early tonight," I say. "But tell Linda I'll be there tomorrow morning for the presents."

"You got it," he says with a silly salute. "And I mean when I say this that you can tell me anything. You know that, right?"

He's only about a quarter illuminated in the dark, but I can see his earnest expression all the same.

"I do," I say.

"Alright," he says. "You have a good Christmas Eve. And know that even though I have sexually wild and wonderful boyfriend doesn't mean I'm still not your best friend."

"I know, Jimmy," I say with a laugh. "I know."

"Take care, okay?" he says.

"You too."

He turns around and makes his way toward Linda's house.

I turn back to the lake, feeling a deep pit in my stomach. Part of me wishes I just spilled it all to Jimmy right there. But what would I spill? That I'm sad and have been for years? Everyone gets sad sometimes. I'll be fine.

I put back in my headphones, and once the first *Eluvium* song is over, the next one plays, and it's one of my favorites.

"Happiness".

I find it ironic that so many musicians I know release the most depressing-sounding music with the title of 'happiness'. Hell, even Taylor Swift. Well, I don't think they're all depressing, but people like Jimmy or Martha or Linda would think they are. I think they're deep, poignant, and emotionally exploratory. I feel like listening to this music when I'm sad helps me explore parts of myself that I otherwise couldn't with anyone else. I just hope that one day in these explorations I find something besides the black and blue.

On my drive home, the lyrics to the song haunt me. Usually, his songs are just instrumental, so this song nearly knocked me on my head when I first heard it. But I love the words. I relate to them more than anything else. I, too, feel that the world is unsafe. And when this unsafe world becomes too much, I, too, want to hide and sleep.

And sleep.

And sleep.

When I get home to the basement underneath Martha and Llewellyn's place, the lyrics are over, but the haunting, yet calming waltz-like melody continues, almost carrying me to sleep.

I pet my black cat, Cheshire, and then get ready for bed. Once under the covers, the music has ended, which means it's time to watch my space videos. Before bed, I like to watch stuff about the universe. Helps calm me down, and tonight's video is about magnetars. But once my eyelids grow heavy, I know it's time for sleep. I set my phone on my nightstand, and as I let sleep take me, I hear the echoes of Eluvium's haunting melody. It causes me to wonder if I'll ever have any lasting happiness.

Then I shoot my eyes open.

How could I forget? If I hadn't wondered about my lasting happiness, I would have neglected to do my most important nighttime ritual.

I turn on my nightstand lamp, bathing my whole basement apartment in a pale glow. Just as Cheshire's settled himself at the foot of my bed, I disturb him by crawling out and kneeling on the floor in front of my nightstand. I pull out a wooden container the size of a shoebox from underneath and undo the lock.

When it clicks open, my heart grows heavy as I assess the contents inside. I set the box on the bed to see it more clearly.

Inside, there are three things: multiple bottles of Everclear, a bottle of painkillers, and a small journal. I open the journal, the song "Happiness" still playing in my head, and pick up a pen from my nightstand.

"Is today the day we do it?" it reads at the top of the page. On this page, there are date entries for the past week, all saying something along the lines of 'no, not today'. Tonight, even though my heart feels heavier than ever, I just write today's date and a small x next to it. It's not yet time. With that, I put the journal back into the box, shut and lock it, and slip it back underneath my nightstand. This ritual may seem inconsequential to many, but it's calming for me. It helps me feel like I have some control over life's unpredictability. And God knows I need such a boon.

To Cheshire's annoyance once again, I disturb his sleep by slipping under the covers. But as I drift off into mine, I'm somewhat relieved for him. Because, at the very least, he'll wake up with an owner.

Well, at least tomorrow he will.

Chapter 2

Wyatt Nelson

WHEN I WAKE FROM the anesthesia, I'm a garbled mess.

"Mr. Wyatt," my friend Blake says. "How are we?"

I stare at a fixed point in the wall, feeling a dull, yet growing pain in my knee. "I feel like I lived three and half a lifetimes," I say. "All on different planets."

"And a half?" Blake asks, rolling up the wheelchair to the bed. "How do you live half a life?"

Immediately, my swirling mind immediately goes to when I was sixteen years old. I had finally admitted to myself that I was gay, but I knew I had to keep it secret if I wanted to go professional. Keeping that secret until now sure has felt like a half-life.

But thinking about all this just makes my head hurt more. I tore my ACL after I got tackled, and I'm just waking up from surgery. I need to focus on my healing.

Blake helps me slide into the wheelchair as the nurses explain to him the recovery, and most of it goes over my head. But I know the drill. Lots of physical therapy, rest, et cetera. Which is bullshit. That means I'm out until basically next season, if I'm fully recovered by then. How the hell am I supposed to become the best tight end like this?

"Alright," Blake says, squeezing my shoulder. "Let's get you home and rested."

After I manage to get inside Blake's car, he drives me to my penthouse. He'll be staying with me the next couple days to help me out, thank God. He and I met back at Miss U. I sang in their opera program, while he sang in their jazz one. Of course, we played football together, and we quickly jumped into the team's gay little sex club. We even fucked once, but it felt weird. So that was the moment when we decided we'd just be friends. And it's stuck since.

"Can I pleaaaaaase," I say, dragging out the word.

He laughs. "What do you want?"

"For the love of God," I say, putting one arm on his shoulder. "I want Swig. Dirty Diet Coke. You know, with the coconut?"

He can't keep a straight face. "Alright, and what else?"

My eyes widen. "Fuck. One of them Crumbl cookies?" Here comes the Texas accent. "Oh, and Café Rio."

He huffs out a breath, shaking his head. "You sure do like Utah food."

"Might as well call me a Mormon at this point. Did you know that you can get your own planet if you're Mormon? That's cool as hell."

"Yeah, but I don't think they like gay people," he says. By now, we're pulling into my parking garage. "So I don't think we'd get one."

I let out a loud gasp. "Are you serious?"

"Yeah, man," he says, playing along with my bullshit. "We'd go to their hell."

I collapse my face into my hands. "I thought Mormons didn't believe in hell." I let out a fake wail. "We're doomed."

"Alright, Wyatt," he says, laughing. "Let's get you to bed."

He manages to get me in my wheelchair and onto the elevator all while my fake wailing turns into genuine distress that I can't own a planet. By the time we reach my room, I'm in real tears, but this time I think it's a mixture of the lingering anesthesia and pain.

Blake helps me into bed. "Alright," he says, adjusting my pillow. "Get some rest, and I'll go get your food."

"Thank you, kind sir. Kiss me goodnight?" I ask, effectively black out drunk.

Blake kisses me on the forehead and pulls my blanket up. He closes the blinds, then stands at my door. "Holler if you need anything," he says.

"Aye aye," I say, closing my eyes. "I love youuuuuu!"

He laughs. "I love you, too."

"Yay!" I yell as he shuts the door. And then I fall into deep sleep.

Even with all my Utah food, the next couple days are hell. I wake up every couple hours either too hot or too cold, gradually processing what the hell happened to me. I was on the field jumping for the ball, and then, I swear, the two Sparrows players who came in for my tackle were trying to injure me on purpose. They pulled my legs so I would fall at a weird angle. I haven't really talked to anyone about it, not even Blake.

There's a knock on my door, then Blake opens it. Speak of the devil. He's wearing a tight tank-top with his thick black chest hair poking out the top with short shorts, showing off his hairy legs. If he wasn't gay, I swear he'd be married with five kids right now. And he's only twenty-five. I'm not exactly ugly either. I'm tall and built. I have a short, dirty-blonde hair with a ginger beard, which is really my winning feature. I've been told I have a killer smile, too, but I think what's most attractive about me is my attitude. I'm a positive, charismatic guy. Oh, and I have thick thighs. I think that helps, too.

"How we feeling?" Blake asks, opening the blinds.

I wince as the bright sun hits my face. "Fine. Not as groggy as usual."

"Well that's good," Blake says. He sits down in the chair in the corner of my room, and he sets his hands in his lap. "Now that you're a little better, we need to talk about the elephant in the room."

A pit forms in my stomach as I sit up in my messy bed, wincing from the movement. My knee is in constant dull pain, but every time I move it, I feel like I'm being stabbed with tons of needles.

"And that is...?" I ask. I think I know, but I don't want to be the first one to say it.

He shakes his head. "Come on, man. You know. You can't tell me you don't."

I fold my arms, which makes me realize how rank I smell. I could use a shower.

"You'll have to tell me," I say.

"Fine," Blake says, rubbing his knees. "I don't think it was a coincidence that you got violently tackled just after you came out. And I don't think you think it is, either."

I recall the play where I was tackled—where I suspect the two Sparrows were trying to injure me. But that can't be right. They would have been penalized for that.

I shake my head. "Injuries happen regularly. I got tackled and tore my ACL. Big deal. There have been worse injuries this season. It's the way things go. And you know how much public support I've been getting since coming out. I'm good."

Blake scoffs. "But I swear. I saw the way they tackled you. Something was off, man. Way off."

Shivers run down my spine as I recall the slur I heard just before the play. 'Faggot', they said. I guess I was the only one who heard it, or else Blake would be mentioning it now. So he may be right. This detail makes it much more likely that I was targeted.

But this is the last thing I want to be true.

My whole life, I've wanted to be out and authentic, and I've wanted to show that there's nothing stopping me from being just as good as any straight player. Yet if I'm being targeted as an out gay NFO player, then that turns this idea straight on its head. If this really happened, then there's so much more holding gay people back than just arbitrary stereotypes. If I was targeted, then there's real danger in being authentic. And I don't know if I'm ready to admit that this is case.

"Blake, my head's hurting," I say, rubbing my temples. "I can't talk about this right now."

He rolls his eyes and stands up. "Okay. I'll get some lunch started in a little bit. But this isn't the last time we talk about it."

I'm about to refuse this, but my phone starts ringing on my nightstand—a perfectly timed distraction.

I reach for it, but it's too far. Blake comes over and hands it to me. My chest tightens when I see it's my mom. Not quite the distraction I would wish for.

"Hello?" I say, answering. I give a Blake a terse thumbs up, and he gives an annoyed shrug in return, then turns to leave. I would be nicer, but I don't want to keep talking about my injury with him, especially now that he believes I was targeted. But knowing him, this conversation is far from over.

"Wy!" my mom yells through the phone. "It's so good to hear your voice. How did the surgery go?"

Right. I forgot to call her.

"It's good—just recovering now," I say, getting in the right headspace to have a successfully uneventful conversation with her. "They say it's a nine-month recovery."

"Oh my God," she says. "What about your playing? It'll be nine months until you can play?"

I squeeze my free hand into a fist. When I worry about my prognosis, that's normal. But when she worries about it, it feels oppressive. Like always, my mother seems to only care about my football career.

"That's what the doctor said," I say, trying not to grit my teeth.

"My goodness," she says. "And what will you do in the meantime?"

"Rest and follow the doctor's orders," I say. "As well as go to physical therapy and such."

"And the Pioneers—your contract with them is still good?"

"Yeah," I say. "Injuries are normal. I'll be okay."

"Okay," she says, not satisfied. "But it's still intact after...?"

Now I'm squeezing my phone. So much for an uneventful conversation.

"Yes, my contract is not under threat despite me coming out. Times are different now. It's normal. Plus, there are some newer gay players getting drafted. It's not so weird anymore. Most people have been nothing but kind in person, and even on the internet."

"Alright," she says, conceding. But I'm not convinced she is. "It was very brave of you to do what you did."

Don't patronize me, I want to say, but I stop myself. My mother was the first person to whom I confided my sexuality. Though she ultimately discouraged me from coming out as to not jeopardize my potential football career, she never once made me feel I was lesser for being gay. In fact, she would even ask me about boys or celebrities I thought were attractive, making me feel normal in my sexuality. And that counts for something. But I still wish I could find someone who could just see me—Wyatt—instead of Wyatt Nelson, rising tight end.

"I know it was," I say. "And I'm glad I did."

"Sure," she says.

There's a silence, and I'm starting to wonder if she called to ask about my surgery or talk about my coming out.

"Well, thanks for calling," I say. "I—"

"Wyatt," she says, more emotional now.

I freeze, feeling my stomach churn. "Are you okay?"

"Yeah," she says, and I can picture her shaking her head. "Look. I know I haven't been the best mom."

My chest starts to ache. Are we really having this conversation?

I sit up straighter. "What's wrong?" I ask. "Is Dad okay?"

"Oh, yeah," she says. "He's out playing golf right now. I just—" she sighs. "I feel bad. Ever since your father and I retired, I've been looking at my life in a new light, and I'm learning things about myself."

I rub my aching chest. "Alright."

"I know we haven't talked in ages," Mom says. "And I didn't even call you when you came out. And I'm sad to say it took me this long to call after your surgery. I haven't been a good mother, and I'm sorry."

There's a pain right in my sternum, and I feel my eyes heating up. "Awh, Mom," I say. "That's real sweet of you."

"I know it's been a while since I've seen you, and I know you're not fully to blame for that," she says. "But your father and I just moved to Glamour Springs, Mississippi—you know, where Kyle Weaver's mom lives? Linda Higgins."

"Mhm," I say. I already know about her move.

"Maybe you could come visit while you're recovering," she says. "It would be great to spend some time with you."

The pain in my chest sinks to my stomach. Stay with my parents? I haven't done that since high school, and there's a reason for that. As kind as my mom sounds now, I still remember her as the woman who pushed me into the NFO—for better and for worse.

"I don't know," I say. "I need to be working with physical therapists and trainers and stuff. To heal, you know. And I know I can't travel on a plane for at least a few weeks."

"A therapist? Well, Linda—she has a little friend about your age. He's a trainer physical therapist. Athletic trainer, too. He's a cute little cowboy man. He works over at Miss U, but he lives in Glamour Springs. He could help you out. I've only met him once or twice, but I think he's gay just like you."

I open my mouth to respond, but then I freeze.

A cute cowboy man? Who's gay? Who's also a physical therapist and knows how to maneuver a body? I don't know—that sounds risky. I remember growing and seeing all those hot cowboys in downtown Austin. I swear, when they wore those hats and jeans, it turned a five to a ten in an instant.

But if I work with him, we wouldn't be able to date, even if he's gay. As far as I know, physical therapists can't date or sleep with their clients.

"And you don't have to come right now," she says. "But I'd love to see you soon."

There's silence, and I'm playing with a loose threat coming off my comforter. Beyond my door, I hear Blake fumbling with some pots in my kitchen.

If I stay in Salt Lake, I just know Blake's gonna be on my ass about the tackle and how I was 'targeted'. I can't handle that.

But I could go back home. Sure, my mom's controlling, but there's some good in her, too. I don't think living with her would nearly be as bad as being constantly prodded to talk about the possibility of people out to get me. And who knows. Maybe she's genuine about wanting to be a better mom. Maybe staying with her could be the beginning of a better relationship between us.

"Take some time to think about it," she says. "Maybe it can—"

"I'll do it," I say. "I'll come visit. You'll just need to give me some time before I can fly."

She takes in a breath, and I can practically hear her smile. Which makes my heart warm. I always loved making my mom happy.

"Wonderful," she says. "We can pay for your flight and everything. Obviously, you can stay at our cabin. And..."

As she talks, the warmth spreads throughout my chest. Maybe this will be a good thing. My relationship with my mother has always been complicated, so I'm excited for us to potentially start healing. She's willing, after all, so I don't see why I shouldn't be.

And it wouldn't hurt to get to know a hot cowboy either.

Chapter 3

Silas King

BEFORE I EVEN WALK into work, I'm already dreading it. It's the first day of spring semester, and I'm sitting in my car, bracing myself for all the college athlete shit I'm about to deal with: huge egos, unnecessary skepticism, and blame for injuries these kids haven't been taking care of.

Back when I graduated from Miss U's dual PT-ATC program—physical therapy and athletic training—I thought it would be best for me stay for a residency. Even though it's not necessary for physical therapists, I wanted to do it because I thought it would give me a leg up.

But boy was I wrong.

All my peers went off and immediately got jobs. Most of them, having received financial help from their parents, didn't even have student loans, and now they're already making over 100K. But me? My residency pays a meager stipend, and I'm barely putting a dent into my loans. Plus, I'm not gaining much experience beyond what I did in school, so it feels like a waste. Because I grew up in bumfuck nowhere in Alabama, I didn't possess a knowledge of the educational system like my peers did, and now I'm paying for it. Quite literally.

Maybe, if this job wasn't so unbearable, I wouldn't mind the pay as much. But I've just about had enough with douchey college players who think their torn rotator cuff can be healed on their own with a couple stretches and an iron will.

I grab my cowboy hat from my passenger seat and get out of my car just as I receive a text.

"Hey Silas," it reads. "It's Linda."

I can't help but smile. Linda always introduces herself even though I have her contact info saved.

"Can my friend Joan reach out to you? She was at Thanksgiving. She has a son in the NFO recovering from ACL surgery who's coming to stay in Glamour Springs for a bit. She wanted to ask you about helping him out. She'd pay, of course."

More money? I'll take that opportunity.

"Of course," I send. "Give her my number and tell her she can call any time."

"Thank, love!" she replies. "Hope all is well."

"Likewise."

I hang up and grab my things, wishing to myself that all would be well with me, too. But maybe with this new opportunity, I have a chance.

I went into physical therapy and athletic training so I could eventually work in the sports setting, ideally football. That's a big reason why I took the residency in the first place. Experience working with a high-level college football team? I thought that would surely give me a shot at the NFO. Growing up, I've always loved football and what it's meant for the country. Sure, there are a lot of bad things that come wrapped up with masculinity, but I think American football is one of the few things that unites most of us. I hold on to that. And maybe helping a football player out will be my chance to break into the NFO.

When I make my way inside the PT building, I take a deep breath and steel myself. Let the fun begin.

I greet the other residents and then see what I have on the books today: two Miss U football players, and then a baseball player with an over extended shoulder preparing for his upcoming season. After that, I have lunch and nothing else, which I guess is nice. But it just makes me wish I went ahead and got a job. I don't just want to sit around doing nothing. These loans won't pay for themselves.

The football players are just as I would expect. One is a lineman with an ankle injury that he neglected over the break. We try to do some exercises, but he says the pain is too great to put any pressure on it. When I tape it up, he hisses at the tension it puts on his skin. I tell him to keep it on, but I don't have a lot of faith in him. The other guy is a wide receiver, and he doesn't show up to his appointment. When I call the patient's number—the Miss U football team is adamant about their players showing up to their medical appointments—he answers and tells me that he saw someone back home. Which makes me bristle just a little. A lot of these football players are rich and always have been. They probably have access to some of the best doctors in the south. And here I am, a licensed PT, struggling to get by.

When I go out into the waiting room for my last appointment before lunch, I find the baseball player waiting patiently for me. I call him back to the small patient room.

"That's a nice cowboy hat," he says, sitting down in the chair.

"Thanks," I say, blushing slightly. He has that typical baseball body: thick in all the right places with a huge ass. Out of the corner of my eye, I think I see him checking me out, too.

"Where you from?" he asks. "I sense an accent."

"Alabama," I say, not looking up from my clipboard.

"No way," he says. "Me too. Roll tide."

I chuckle and glance up at him. Like me, he's got a tasteful mustache, and he's staring at me with piercing blue eyes. If I were a couple of shades more confident, I'd believe he was flirting with me. But I doubt it. I'm probably a little too stocky, and men this handsome usually want nothing to do me. Plus, it's not like we could do much. I'd be liable to lose my license if I did anything with a patient.

I ask him to sit up on the table. Without asking, he takes off his shirt, and I have to use all my strength to focus on the task at hand instead of looking at his muscular baseball body. I run my hand along his shoulder blade, asking if he feels any pain. He winces slightly when I press into his muscle. He looks up at me, pain in his eyes. But when we lock eyes, his gaze drifts down to my lips.

Okay, maybe I don't have to be so confident to see that this man is flirting with me.

But we can't have that.

I pull away and clear my throat. I pick up my clipboard, and the baseball player looks at the far wall.

I tell him his shoulder looks good, that he should take over-the-counter painkillers as needed, and that he should be ready for the season come this spring. All the while, I keep my gaze focused on anything but him. And it's not just because it would be unethical to sleep with a patient.

But just because lust, and love, always end badly for me.

I don't know how my buddy Jimmy did it. In his 'whore' days, he would find at least one man to sleep with a night. But me? I swear, it's like once men start talking to me and getting to know me, they find something wrong—like they can sense the wraith living in me and want nothing to do with it. We may sleep together, but we'll never talk again. Or the relationship ends after an early date. Hell, I've never even had a long-term relationship. Best I just don't even try. I'm tired of rejection confirming to me what I already know: that I'm a sad fella, and I'll never get better.

When the baseball player leaves, he looks slightly disappointed. Good. Better I disappoint him now.

At lunch, since I have no more patients for the day, I decide to eat lunch with my friends Martha and Llewellyn. I drive from Fordsville over to Glamour Springs, no more than a twenty-minute drive, and park in the gravel lot of the Book Corner.

Knowing Jimmy's working today, I text him if he can make some sliders for me, Martha, and Llewellyn. He says they'll be ready in fifteen, so I decide to chat with them as I wait.

Inside the Book Corner, there are a few customers browsing, looking like they're from out of town. While Martha is helping check someone out, I sneak up to Llewellyn while she's stacking books.

"Can you recommend something..." I say in a deep voice from behind her.

She jumps a bit then turns her head slightly to give me a nasty side-eye. With a smirk, though.

"...with cowboys?" I ask, exaggerating my accent and placing my boot on the edge of the bookshelf. "Oh, and, uh, make it spicy."

She laughs. "Man, I wish we had some gay cowboy romances."

I break my posture and adjust my hat. "Even better would be some lesbian ones."

She clutches her chest. "A hot lesbian cowgirl? Sign me up."

"We just need to get Martha dressed up in some chaps and on a horse and then we'd be good to go."

Llewellyn laughs, moving her dreadlocks out of her face. "Now that would be insane."

I lean against the bookshelf and fold my arms, happy that the laughter briefly takes me out of my thoughts.

"How's the shop doing without me?" I ask. "I can help y'all out today. Got outta work early."

"You don't need to do that," she says, putting a shelving what looks like a dark thriller. "You got your residency now."

I resist a sigh. *Yeah, a residency that doesn't pay me shit*, I want to say. But I feel like I've been really negative today. I'm tired of my own problems.

"How's your mom doing?" I ask.

Her shoulders sag, and her face hardens slightly. "The same," she says. "She won't leave him."

I bite my lips and lean my back against the bookshelf. Llewellyn's mom has fallen in love with a man who loves insulting her almost as much as he loves drinking. And Llewellyn is reasonably concerned. I try to check in with her about it every once in a while, even though there's not much either of us can do. I think she just likes to know that someone else cares.

"We just gotta find her someone better," I say.

"Well, if Jimmy didn't have a boyfriend..."

I laugh. "And if he was straight."

Llewellyn's mom also developed a crush on Jimmy when she came to visit a while back. She was devastated to discover that he was one of the gayest men on the planet.

"Maybe she'll break up with his man and find someone just like him," she says.

"I'm praying for it."

My phone buzzes in my pocket, and I expect it to be Jimmy saying our burgers are ready. But when I pull it out, I'm receiving a call from an unknown number.

I gesture to Llewellyn that I gotta take a call and step outside the store. "Hello," I say, putting the phone to my ear.

"Is this Silas?" a harried female voice asks.

I immediately remember Linda's text from this morning. I think this might be Joan.

"This is he," I say.

"Oh, great," she says, relieved. "I get stressed with receiving numbers via text sometimes. I get worried I'll put the number in wrong."

I let out a small laugh. "Sure, I get it. How can I help you?"

"My son," she says. "He's in the NFO, and he just had ACL surgery." She goes on to explain that he'll be visiting home and staying with her in her cabin. "He really needs treatment from someone who has experience with athletes, and I heard you had that experience."

I stand up a little straighter. Maybe this residency wasn't such a bad idea after all. At least I can say that I do have such experience.

"He's going to be flying down in a few weeks. Would you be able to come help him recover? We'll honestly pay you whatever you ask for. I'm just grateful to be having my son in my home."

Her words make my chest tighten just a bit. I haven't spoken to my mom—or my family—since college. When I attended my first semester at Miss U, I was blown away by all the things I was learning. And it wasn't just in my classes. I made friends with kids who were rich and grew up with lots of opportunities. I made black friends, Mexican friends. I soon saw the world in a whole new way, much broader than how I understood everything back on the ranch. And when I came back home for the first time, I wanted to talk to my family about it.

But they wanted none of it. They insisted I was getting too big for my britches, that I was forgetting my roots. And that I was better off moving home and being the farm boy I've always been. I tried to reason with them, but they shut me out and said they wanted nothing to do with me.

So I decided I wouldn't have anything to do with them. I left and never came back.

And my whole family knows that it wasn't just this conversation that caused the fallout. It was everything that led to it—the neglect of me and my brothers, their bigotry toward me, and their close-mindedness. But I didn't completely close the door on them. I gave them a chance to reach back out to me, if they choose. I wonder if any of them will ever take it.

"Silas?" Joan says.

"Sorry," I say, shaking my head. "I think that sounds good. As his arrival gets closer, contact me, and we can work the logistics out."

"Wonderful," she says, relief audible in her tone. "I'll be in touch with you soon."

And just as she hangs up, Jimmy texts me to say that the burgers are ready and that he'll bring them over. I walk back into the bookstore, and Martha and Llewellyn have a rare moment of downtime. When Jimmy arrives, we all sit down at a table in the café and just chat it up. Jimmy makes a joke, and the rest of us laugh. I take a bite of my burger and look out the window as rain steadily begins to fall. And while Jimmy and Martha are talking about the state of business in Glamour Springs, while I'm enjoying Jimmy's delicious Cajun fries, there's a prick in my chest that feels like a needle going through my heart. Gradually, the pain extends to my whole chest, then spreads throughout my body, numbing all of me. And suddenly, it becomes alarmingly clear.

Today is the day.

For months—years—I've been waiting for some sort of confirmation. For permission, almost. For me to end things. For all this to be finally over. Which,

I know, makes no sense. I have people in my life who love me—Jimmy, Martha, Llewellyn, Linda, and so many more.

But I'm so, so tired.

Ever since I left my family for good, I've felt this gnawing loneliness inside me growing like cancer. Of course, it existed before, but cutting myself off from them accelerated the growth exponentially.

This loneliness is like an amplifier to all my emotions. Anger isn't just anger—it's fury. Sadness isn't just sadness—it's deep melancholia. Happiness, though? It's high euphoria.

But that's almost scarier than the sadness. Because once the happiness is gone, I feel like an empty husk of myself, unable to feel at all. And these are the times that I've been closest to ending it all.

I don't know why the confirmation is today, though. It could be seeing my friends all happy around me, making me believe I'll never be like them. It could be that they're making me happy, and my brain already knows it can't bear the depression I'll feel when I'm alone again. Or it's a mixture of both these things. Regardless, I feel, in my bones, that it's time.

But there's a problem.

I just got the opportunity to take care of a professional NFO player. This might be my ticket to a job that I've always wanted—working in the NFO—with pay that I can actually live on. Since I left them, I've just wanted to stick it to my parents that I could be the person who got a big boy, high-paying job despite their discouragement. And as I've been stuck in this residency, that has felt less and less like a possibility. But now I have a chance at it, and I can't just give that up. I know I got my confirmation that it's time to end things today, but who knows—maybe this job will lead to bigger and brighter things.

Or not.

But a little voice in my head tells me to wait and give this little physical therapy gig a try.

So I will.

Chapter 4

Silas King

I ADJUST MY COWBOY hat as I step onto the porch of Joan's cabin. It's an uncharacteristically warm day for February in Glamour Springs, so I'm wearing boots and jeans with my cowboy button up. I was sure to leave a couple undone at the top. I may not be trying to find any partner or whatever, but it doesn't hurt to impress.

I knock on the door and step back with my hands on my hips. When the door opens, a woman with short, gray hair answers, and she's almost surprised to see me.

"My," she says, her voice almost husky. "I almost forgot what strapping cowboy you were."

I chuckle and step forward, extending my hand. "It's nice to see you again, Joan."

She puts one hand on her cheek and extends the other. "So good to see you, Silas. If you'll come in."

I step inside and take my hat off as I wipe my boots on the welcome mat. To my left, there's a giant U-shape couch in front of a fireplace. Above it hangs a TV, and there are two massive windows just above it with the sleepy winter sun shining through them. On either side of the fireplace, there are doorways that lead out onto the back porch. To the right of the couch is a large wooden table just in front of the doorway to the kitchen.

"If you'll come this way," she says. "He's down the hallway."

I follow her down a narrow hallway, various rooms on each side. As I walk, I swear I hear someone singing. I try to listen to the words, but the song sounds like it's in a different language. But it sounds cool. It's bouncing and robust. The man singing it is talented.

We turn a corner and reach the end of the hallway. Joan knocks on the door, then gently opens it. The singing increases in volume just as Joan opens the door, but then it immediately stops. And I'm kinda disappointed. That shit sounded awesome.

"What's up?" the man asks. Oh, his voice is nice. It's not deep, but it's confident and smooth, like gelato. Not ice cream, but gelato. Thick and creamy, but light enough you'll want more.

"It's Silas," she says. "Your physical therapist is here."

I stand just behind her, ready to walk in and introduce myself.

"My physical therapist?" he asks, almost scoffing. "What do you mean?"

So I stop myself. He seems angry. But his voice sounds... almost familiar, too. I've heard it somewhere before.

"You know," she says. "Linda's friend. The physical therapist who I said could help you while you're here."

"Mom," he says, exasperated. "I told you I would contact him. You didn't need to do that."

"Well I knew you wouldn't be in the best of shape after your flight, so I took it on myself."

He sighs loudly. "Come on, mom," he says. "You shoulda given me his info. I would have reached out to him."

"It was faster this way," Joan says.

"It's not going to make a difference if I delay my physical therapy here a day or two. Let me handle it on my own."

"Well," she says, opening the door wide. "He's already here, and I'm paying for him. So you might as well take advantage of the opportunity."

Joan gestures for me to step into the room, and I do so awkwardly, taking too big of a step and nearly losing my balance.

"Silas, I'd like you to meet my son, Wyatt," she says. "Wyatt, this is Silas, your new physical therapist."

I stare at the strong football player sitting up in the king bed before me, and I feel my knees go weak. This is Wyatt Nelson, the first NFO player to come out in the middle of his career. He just did so like two months ago. That's why I recognize his voice—I watched the damn video. And I'd heard he'd been injured, but I never watched the game where it happened. And I guess in my depressive funk I didn't recall that Joan's son is the rising star tight end.

He's shirtless, and his muscular torso is carpeted with sexy, curly chest hair—so thick that my hands would get caught in it. His pecs are huge, and his pink nipples look like candy. Even thicker are his arms. Man, this dude is huge in person. His red beard is slightly overgrown, giving him a gorgeous, scruffy look. But his blonde hair is freshly buzzed, and I have to say that this suits him better than his longer hair. Fuck, this man is beautiful.

And I can't help but wonder what he smells like. Whenever I see a hot man, the first thing I want to do is smell him. I know that sounds weird. My buddy Michael is really the only one to get me here. But it's true. And boy do I want to take in Wyatt's natural scent.

"Mom," Wyatt says, still frustrated with Joan. "Let's—"

"I'll leave you both to it," she says. Joan hurries out the door and shuts it, leaving me alone in the room with an openly out and injured NFO player.

"Uh, it's a pleasure," I say, my accent Alabama accent stronger when I'm nervous.

He sighs. "Yeah. Nice cowboy attire you got."

"Thanks," I say, flattered. I set it down on the back of a tall white wing-back chair and gently sit down, my legs spread.

Now, I knew I was gay at the ripe age of thirteen. How did I know? Football uniforms. Goddamn does it make a man's behind look fire. And Wyatt Nelson in uniform? The man has thighs and ass for days. Sometimes, when I get especially sad, I don't really feel sexual at all. But a man in a football uniform almost always gets me going. So I gotta keep my thoughts pure while I'm working with this man. We have a professional relationship. I can't do anything with a patient, and I wouldn't want to jeopardize my relationship with the man who can probably get me a permanent position in the NFO.

"So, you're the physical therapist?" he asks, lifting up his thick arms to scratch underneath. "You look more like a cowboy to me." I shift my legs so I'm not putting any undue pressure on my dick. I don't want any help redirecting blood to that area.

I let out a short laugh. "I work over at Miss U as a physical therapist and athletic trainer. Help mostly the football and baseball guys."

He huffs out a short breath. "Ever helped out someone after an ACL surgery?"

I sit up a little taller. "I have, actually. Recovery can be a bit brutal, but as long as you work at it, it doesn't have to be so bad."

He nods, staring down at his leg underneath the covers. Judging by the two long lumps, the left one larger than the other, I can guess that that's the injured leg.

"So," I say, standing up and approaching the bed. "Is this something you really want to do? I overheard you with…" I point to the door, referring to his mom. "I don't want to do something you're not wanting to do."

He grunts and presses his head back into the wooden headboard. "I'm sorry you had to hear that." He lowers his head and shakes it, rubbing his eyes. "I sorta moved back here to get some more time with my mom." He lowers his voice. "Don't have the greatest relationship with her. Thought this would be good for us. But she's still stepping all over my toes."

I nod, folding my arms as I press one of my knees into the bed. "I get it," I say, thinking of my own family struggles. "I know how mothers can be."

He looks up at me and squints slightly, almost as if seeing me for the first time. "I really like your voice," he says.

My chest squeezes, and I look up at him. "My voice?" I ask, running my hand through my short hair.

"Yeah," he says. "It's soothing. You talk so… calmly. Like you got a good head on your shoulders."

I nearly scoff at that. *A sad head is what I really got*, I'm tempted to say, but that's TMI. "Well, thank you," I say, rubbing my mustache. "You got a really nice voice too. I, uh, heard you singing."

His eyes widen and brows raise. "Fuck, you did? Man, these walls are thin."

I can't help but laugh at his surprise. "Don't worry, it sounded good. But I couldn't tell what you were singing. Was that another language?"

He nods, rubbing his beard. "German. God, that's so embarrassing. I haven't sung in—"

"So you really sing?" I ask, fascinated. Without a thought, I sit down on the edge of the bed.

"Used to," he says, folding his arms. "I'm a trained opera singer."

I swear my face lights up because I can see the enthusiasm reflect in Wyatt's face. "Opera? Man, that's cool. I'm a big music guy myself. Mostly post-rock, but I love what music does to me. It's like a whole other language. So underrated."

"Yeah?" he asks, sitting up a little bit taller, which only makes me see how just how big his shoulders are. "I love it, too, man. Music just—"

He thins his lips, staring down at the covers, then shakes his head. "Yeah, music means a lot to me. Wish I could sing more than I do. I've been singing in bed because it passes the time. But now that I know my parents can probably hear me, I might stop."

"I don't think you should," I say. "If it helps you express yourself."

He gives me a thoughtful look, and it suddenly feels like there's a live wire connecting the two of us—that if I reached out to touch this invisible link, I'd be shocked. And I'm not sure if that's a bad thing. I can't remember the last time I felt connected to somebody like this. And the dude and I just met.

"So you're a physical therapist, cowboy, and mental therapist," he says. "Looks like I hit the jackpot."

I shoot up from the bed, suddenly realizing how intimate it was for me to sit there. This relationship needs to stay professional.

"I'm definitely not that kind of therapist," I say. *But I could probably benefit from seeing one.*

"I'm kidding," he says with a laugh. Then he sighs. "Well, I guess we better start working on my leg. I don't want to keep you waiting."

"Sure," I say, looking around. "Do you have any sort of treatment table? I know your mom was expecting me, so maybe she has one."

He shakes his head. "I don't know. You could go ask her, but if you don't mind, I'm pretty sore today, and I don't really want to get up off this bed."

He throws off the covers, revealing that he's just wearing some loose gym shorts, leaving very little to the imagination. I have to keep my gaze fixed on his knee brace to keep my thoughts pure.

"Alright," I say, approaching the bed. I sit down on the side of it, careful to look as professional as possible. I don't want to look like I'm goddamn crawling on the bed toward him. Eventually, I slide close enough to him to where I can get a better look.

"Have you been working with other therapists for this?" I ask, taking hold of his leg.

"Yeah," he says. "Some exercises and stretches."

"How long has it been since the surgery?"

"Five weeks."

I nod. "Looks like you're progressing nicely," I say. "I notice some swelling. Mind if I take the brace off?"

"Be my guest," he says. "But mind the smell."

I gently remove the brace, which helps me fulfill my fantasy of smelling an attractive man. And he doesn't smell bad at all—just sweaty, which I love. That earthy, pungent scent. It's heavenly. Plus, he smells no different than if he were working out or having sex.

Having sex. Why is that on my mind? It's been over a year since I've done anything. And there are so many things barring that from happening between me and Wyatt—most notably, losing my license. So my mind shouldn't even go there.

Once the brace is off, I put one hand on his huge thigh and another on his ankle. I gently raise his leg up into the air, keeping it straight.

"How does this feel?" I ask.

"Fine," he says, only wincing with his eyes.

My hands in the same place, I gently bend his knee and start moving upward towards his face.

"How about this?" I ask.

The wince spreads to his whole face. "More painful, but manageable."

I stretch it back and forth for a bit, feeling his leg loosen up underneath my grip. As I set his leg back down, I gently massage his lower thigh and upper calve just around his knee. He sighs, closes his eyes, and puts his hands behind his head, revealing his strong, hairy pits to me.

Part of me wonders what would happen if I slid my legs over and straddled him. If I just started kissing him right here. If I stuck my face in his pits. If he took off his shorts and stuck his dick—

I let out a sigh, hoping to dispel my horny thoughts with it. That will never happen. And that's not only because I'm trying to stay professional.

Men don't like me. I'm too sad. I like weird music. I'm too quiet. I'm on the huskier side. And Wyatt seems like a pretty cool guy, much cooler than me. I doubt someone like him would ever take interest in someone like me.

"Alright," I say about to release my hands. "Let's—"

And that's when my eyes catch something unbelievable.

Just underneath those loose gym shorts, I spot something hard—and this something is getting bigger.

Wyatt opens his eyes. "What's—"

And then he stares down at his boner in mortification. He grabs hold of the comforter and pulls it to cover himself up. But I'm sitting on the comforter, so such a quick movement threatens to pull me on top of him just like I was fantasizing. I manage to jump up just before that happens, though, and that leaves both Wyatt and I to stare at each other for an achingly long moment.

And then I rush to grab my cowboy hat off the wing-back chair. I need to leave before this gets any more unprofessional.

"Well, good session," I say, making my way to the door, not even daring to look in his direction. "I'll be seeing you."

But as I make my way down the hallway to leave this cabin, I don't know if that will ever happen. I can't risk losing everything.

Chapter 5

Wyatt Nelson

THE DAY AFTER THE world's sexiest cowboy shows up as my physical thera-pist—the day after I get a boner right in front of him and scare him off—I lay in my bed, refusing to get up. Not because I don't want to. But because I refuse to.

What the hell is wrong with me? All I did was publicly come out. Then I tear my ACL and get a boner right in front of the man who's supposed to be helping me recover? I doubt he'll ever want to come back after that. I probably creeped him the hell out. Plus, he could stand a lot to lose if it was discovered he was doing anything remotely sexual with a patient. God, I need to be more considerate.

There's a knock on my door, and for a minute I think it's Silas returning. I pull the covers and bury myself beneath them all the way, double-checking to ensure I don't have a boner. Yep, we're good.

"Wyatt, honey," my mom says, opening the door. And I breathe a sigh of relief. But then I tense right up. This is still my mom we're talking about.

She steps inside the room. "How did the session with Silas go?"

I think back to the way that man touched me. Fuck. It felt like he had the hands of an angel the way he handled me. It hurt getting my leg to mobilize but in a good sort of way. And the way he massaged my sore muscles after he stretched me. Lord Almighty above. It was like I melted into the bed, and my body didn't know what to do besides pool blood into the one area that it does when I'm that relaxed. When I opened my eyes, I swore I was going to die. I didn't know if I was more relieved or embarrassed that Silas ran out of there before I could think of what to say.

"It was... fine," I say, sitting up. "But I don't think he's coming back."

My mother furrows her brow. She's just showered, I can tell, because her gray curly hair is wet. "What do you mean he's not coming back?"

I grimace as I try to think of what to say. "I just don't think we hit it off too well."

"You don't have to hit it off well," she says, putting her hand on her hip. "He's your physical therapist, not your boyfriend."

Boyfriend. Now that I'm out, I could technically have a boyfriend. And that Silas guy isn't just cute. What attracted me to him most was how emotionally intelligent he was. When we talked, I really felt heard. Like he was understanding 100% of what I was saying and really giving thought to how he responded. He was also interested in my singing, and I can't think of the last person besides Blake that's taken an interest in my classical experience. My parents sure as hell don't care about that.

But it doesn't matter because I definitely scared the cowboy off.

"Yeah, well you can tell him that," I say. "Because I doubt he'll return."

My mom puts her hands on her hips. "Wyatt Nelson, what did you do?" she asks in that same scolding tone she used on me as a kid.

I rub my eyes. "Mom, can we please just drop it?"

"Drop it? You have to go to therapy while you're here. Don't you want to recover?"

"Of course I want to recover," I say. "I just don't think it will be with Silas again."

"Boy," she says, shaking her head. "This guy has experience treating men just like you. And he's close to a dear friend of mine." She pulls out her phone. "I'm going to send you his number. And today you are going to call and ask him to return. I don't care when, but you're doing it."

Dread and anger swirl around in my chest, creating an uncomfortable tightening sensation. "You can't make me do that," I say.

"You're under my roof, and you're recovering, so you're under my care," she says. "Please call him back."

I clench my fists under the covers. I feel just like I'm a teenager again back in Austin, arguing with my mom about wanting to sing in my recital that was the same time as an important game. I wanted, more than anything, to do it, but I knew my wants could never supersede my mother's.

And it's no different now.

My phone vibrates on my nightstand with her text—the contact info for Silas, the hot cowboy physical therapist I scared off.

"There," she says. "Breakfast is ready. Do you want me to bring it to you, or do you want to join us?"

"I'll join you," I say. I lift the covers, move my legs off the bed, and grab the crutches on the side.

"I'll get a seat ready for you," she says tersely. And then she's gone.

I curse to myself as I get to my feet, partly due to the pain of the crutches but mostly because of my mom. When is she going to get off my ass? I'm an adult now. I can take care of myself. I deserve the dignity to make my own choices.

My armpits already sore from the use of the crutches, I make my way out to the dining table just next to the kitchen. My dad is eating some eggs while watching ads about the Championship Game coming up—one the Pioneers didn't make it to. Likely because I'm not playing.

Fuck, I need to get better.

"Hey, bud," he says, lifting his glass of orange juice to me.

"Hey, Dad," I say. He's wearing his golf outfit, pants, shirt, hat and all. "Headed out?"

"Yeaaaah," he says drawing out the vowel, looking at something on his phone. "Just after I finish. How you feeling?"

"Improving slowly but surely," I say. "Pain here and there, but I'll be okay ."He nods as he begins typing on his phone, and I'm not even sure he heard me. Just like my mom, he hasn't really changed. But at least my mom said she wanted to.

My mom comes out with a plate and sets it down in front of me. It has bacon, eggs, sausage, and hashbrowns. This is her kind side—serving me without strings attached.

"Thanks," I say. "Looks great."

"Just want to make sure you're getting your protein in," she says. And I have to resist rolling my eyes. Guess there were strings. I just wish I could have one interaction with my mom that didn't allude to football. Just one.

My dad's phone rings, and he immediately picks it up. "Rachel, my girl," he says, setting down his napkin on his plate.

"What's she saying?" my mom asks him, but he doesn't hear her. Or at least he acts like he doesn't hear her.

"Mhm," he says. "Oh really?" he asks, folding his arms. "Hey," he says with a chuckle. "Good for you."

And I just squirm in my seat. Rachel, my oldest sister, is the apple of my dad's eye. After my dad retired, she took charge of his law firm in Austin, and she's only improved it. With how proud my dad was of his career, I thought he would be jealous, but he's loved to see his firstborn take his company and expand it in ways he could have never imagined.

"How's Maddie?" I ask my mom.

My mom dots her mouth with her napkin, pretending like she doesn't want to know what my dad is saying to her daughter. It's not like my mom doesn't have a relationship with her. It's just that law has always been their thing. And I think my mom feels left out.

"Maddie's doing wonderful," he says, nodding. "I still don't really understand what it means to work in finance in New York City, but whenever I do get the chance to talk to your sister, she says she's thriving. But that's all I get."

I nod, not knowing if it's me or my mom who's more uncomfortable with this situation. I don't talk to my siblings much either, and it's always intimidating to hear how well they're doing. "And Tyler?" I ask, feeling obliged to bring up my brother.

"He says his marketing firm has picked up a lot more clients," she says, moving her egg whites around on her plate. "And they're expanding to TikTok now, apparently."

I raise my brow. "Impressive. TikTok is intimidating."

"That's what he says," she says with a sigh. "But I can't remember the last time we talked either. He's busy as ever, too." She looks up at me. "I'm glad we're able to spend this time together."

I squirm under her gaze, not knowing if I should be honest about how I feel being here or try to make her feel better.

I'm about to respond when Dad gets up, beaming as he's talking to Rachel.

"You picked them up as a client?" he asks. "How'd you manage to do that?"

On the TV, another ad for the Championship Game comes on. This year, it's the Vanguards against the Sparrows. But I know we coulda had a shot if I didn't get injured. And I know I woulda been one step closer to becoming the best tight end in the world if those Sparrows hadn't thrown my knee into the turf.

"You know, maybe I'll call Tyler," my mom says, pushing away her plate. "It'll be good to hear how he's doing."

And suddenly, I feel small—smaller than my seventeen-year-old self. Here I am, injured and months away from doing anything remotely helpful for my career as an NFO player. Meanwhile, all my siblings are thriving, and the TV's just reminding of where I could be—and where I'm not.

"I'm gonna step outside," I say, grabbing my crutches.

"Do you need help?" my mom asks, phone in her hand but still trying to grab the crutches for me.

"I'm good," I say, pulling the crutches before she can reach them. "Just need some air."

With some pain, I quickly make my way to the back door and trot my way onto the back porch, making sure to shut the door behind me. I want to be alone.

It's about fifty out, but I'm okay in just a T-shirt and sweats for now. I inhale a deep breath, taking in the cool air, and let it out.

I don't know if I can do this. Nearly eight more months of just recovery? What if I lose my skills by then? What if the Pioneers decide they no longer want me now that I've come out? What if I just fade into obscurity as a pretty good tight end? Not the best?

I sit down on one of the porch chairs and wipe my hairy face. I know I need to shave, but I kinda like how shaggy I'm getting. Makes me feel more manly I guess.

Speaking of manly, I can't get the image of Silas out of my head, his thick arms massaging me so well I get a fucking boner. Fuck.

I know I said that I probably scared him off, but I think my mom is right. I should call him and invite him back. Because if I don't work on my recovery here, I may not be ready to play by next season. Which means my goal of becoming the best tight end of the 21st century—a gay one—is only farther away. And with how successful my family is—and especially with how much my mom is on my ass—maybe I'll finally get some peace of mind with that achievement. So if I want this, I think I'm gonna have to suck up my embarrassment.

I sigh. Here goes nothing.

I pull out my phone and dial the number that my mom sent me. While it's ringing, my heart begins to race, but I don't care. This is the only way I'll get back out on the field.

"Hello?" a thick, soothing, country voice answers.

I swallow my spit. "Is this Silas?"

"This is," he says. "Is this, uh—"

"Yeah, it's Wyatt," I say. "Hey, listen. I'm, uh, sorry about what happened yesterday."

He clears his throat. "It's, uh, all good." He sounds awkward, but he also sounds genuine.

I clear my throat. I swear the act is contagious or something. "Thanks," I say. "Well, you know, I still definitely need a physical therapist while I'm staying here. And I can tell you know your stuff. So I was hoping you still wouldn't you mind seeing me—as my therapist, that is. Physical therapist." I hold the phone away from my face and grimace. Could I be fucking this up even more than I am?

There's silence, which makes me regret ever picking up the phone. And I'm about to say something to cover my ass until Silas speaks.

"I can do that," he says, and my chest lifts.

"Really?"

"Yeah," he says. "I'm assuming Joan—your mom—would still be paying?"

I nod, even though I know he can't see me. "Yeah, she would."

"Then it's settled," he says. "I'd, uh, be happy to help."

"Perfect. Thank you."

"My pleasure," he says, nice and low, which stirs me nice and low, too. There's some more silence, and I know I should say something, but I'm out of words. This call has taken a lot out of me.

"When do you wanna meet?"

"Tomorrow would be fine," I say. "Honestly, as many sessions as possible would be good. I need to heal quick."

"Fine by me," he says. "Curious—would you mind traveling to me? You say you wanna heal quickly. I wanna get you in some water. I think that'll help."

"Yeah," I say, sitting up. "I can do that."

"Great," he says. "Come by the Miss U physical therapy facility around five? I can send you the address."

"I actually know where it is," I say. "I went to Miss U."

"Well alrighty then," he says, and it sounds like there's a smile on his face, which puts a smile on mine. "I'll see you then."

"I'll see you," I say. And when I hang up, I can't help but get butterflies. I'm going swimming with a cowboy tomorrow.

Chapter 6

Silas King

It's 4:30PM, and I can't wait for my day to be over.

I sit in the physical therapy lounge, finishing up some paperwork for a student athlete who is continually questioning my treatment of his sprained ankle even though he's the one neglecting it. I keep telling myself that I won't have to deal with this if I make it to work for the NFO, but I've heard enough horror stories to believe that NFO players could be just as bad.

I sigh to myself, rubbing a pain forming just between my eyebrows. Maybe making it to the NFO isn't something to hope for. Maybe the entire sports physical therapy world is just a crapshoot, and I've spent all this work and money for nothing. I can feel the gravity of my parents' ranch pulling me from here. I try to put my mind at ease by saying I have a backup—going back to work at the Book Corner. But what kinda loser works retail for the rest of his life? It's not like I own the bookstore. Martha and Llewellyn do. I wanna make it at something—to prove to my parents that I'm bigger than where I'm from. But it just feels like the more that I try, the less likely it seems.

Once I finish up the paperwork—which, of course, takes me ages to do—I collect my things. I put my earbuds in and start listening to "Crown of Amber Canopy", a song by Slow Meadow that always sweeps me up like a river and keeps me emotionally buoyed for its entire six-minute duration. I say goodbye to my colleagues I hardly know—even after being in this residency for six months—and make my way out of the facility. I just want to go home and take it easy.

When I make it out into the chilly February air, I spot someone getting out of their car in a disabled spot. They slide on a backpack, fish their crutches out of the passenger seat, then stand up straight, then I immediately recognize that red beard and those broad shoulders.

That's Wyatt Nelson.

It takes all my strength not to audibly groan.

I completely forgot I promised to treat him today. This damn fucking sadness brain fog.

It's not like I hate the guy, but there are so many reasons why I do not have the energy to deal with this. For starters, I fucking gave the man a boner. I was surprised he even called me and asked to set up another appointment. At the time, I said yes—he's my ticket to the NFO, and I'm making some more money helping him. But a busy day filled with stubborn patients completely erased this from my mind, and I've not mentally prepared myself to be in such close quarters with a hot man. I cannot do anything to jeopardize my license.

The second reason is that, because he's in the NFO, he's probably more insufferable than these student athletes. Hell, he's on track to be one of the best tight ends of the century, if not the best. I do not want to deal with an ego the size of Texas. Sure, he was kind when I first met him. Thoughtful, too, with his asking questions about me. But that's just the tip of the iceberg. I bet after a while of working together, I'll discover, unsurprisingly, that he's an asshole.

He makes eye contact with me, then waves. Putting on a happy façade like I always do, I take out my headphones, smile, and wave back.

I can't turn him away. My current residency is a dead end. I haven't gotten any good job prospects, and my money's only going down the drain the longer I'm here. But if I get on Wyatt's good side, a career in the NFO is very possible. I know NFO players can be even bigger assholes than student athletes, but what other options do I have? I'm on a sinking ship. I've spent all this money becoming a physical therapist and athletic trainer, and my skills are specifically with athletes. I can't start over my career anywhere else, and I need to be in a job that's as professional as possible. So, helping Wyatt is really the best choice I have.

Wyatt ambles up the sidewalk with his crutches and, even hunched over, he's a giant man. "Silas," he says, making his way to me. "Sorry, I'm a little early. Didn't want to have to rush with these crutches." He sounds out of breath.

Now standing in front of me, he eyes me curiously. "Did we still have our appointment today? I didn't catch you when you were leaving, did I?"

I put my headphones in my bag and shift it behind me. "No, man—not at all. Was just, uh, getting something from my car." I turn toward the building. "Why don't you come on in? Let's get us started."

I hold the door open for Wyatt and usher him through our waiting room. I take him back into the physical therapy lounge just as the remaining physical therapists are leaving. I'm worried they'll recognize Wyatt, especially because Miss U is his alma mater, but I think his beard is too overgrown for him to be noticed. And honestly, the beard doesn't look half bad on him. He's wearing a green flannel shirt, which just makes him look like a sexy lumberjack.

But I can't be thinking that way. Gotta keep it strictly professional so I don't screw up my chances of making it to the NFO. Or worse—lose my job altogether.

Wyatt sits down on a chair next to a round table. He's already sweating, and he's got dark pit stains, which makes some blood rush to my groin. Does it make me a pervert that seeing him like this turns me on?

No, but it does make me doubt my ability to stay professional. Focus, Silas.

Wyatt airs out his shirt. "Sorry, just did a home workout. And don't worry, no legs involved," he says before I can ask how he did that with his knee like it is. "And crutches are not a cool down. But we're doing some pool action today?"

I stare at my tablet as I huff air out of my nose, a fraction of a laugh. I need to keep my eyes off this man, or else my body will betray me.

"Yeah, some pool action," I say, taking off my cowboy hat and setting it on the table. I don't want it to get wet.

"I brought a suit," he says, taking off his backpack and setting it aside. "I can go change now."

"Sure," I say, working hard not to look at him. "Bathroom's right over there. I'll get the water ready."

Wyatt sits there for a beat, sighs, and then stands up with the crutches. From behind, I can see just how perky his ass is. It makes me curious to see what he looks like in uniform.

He turns back to me, and I immediately look away.

"There a chair in there?" he asks.

I look him up and down and realize how difficult it may be for him to change. "Yeah, there is." I pause for a second, asking myself if I really want to ask this next question. "But do you need help?"

He shakes his head. "No, I'll use the chair," he says. And I'm relieved.

"Alright," I say. "Holler if you need me. I'll be in the pool room."

While he's changing, I make my way to the pool. Using the digital interface, I open the covering, get the water flowing, and make sure the bar is in place so Wyatt has something to hold onto. Luckily, one of my colleagues just used the pool, so the water is already warm.

As the bar in the water moves, I try to reassure myself. People say they're not the relationship type. I would say that I'm not even the romantic type, especially with how much it seems like guys only want to use me—if they're even interested at all. But I can't remember the last time I was really attracted to somebody to the point where I wanted to be around them all the time. I did date one guy back in college for a little bit, but nothing much came of it.

Now, that isn't to say I have needs. I do get myself off on occasion, though it rarely is with other guys anymore. But Wyatt—there's something about him that gets me going. Even as he's recovering from his injury, there's a spryness about him that makes me want to linger my gaze on him. It's like he's eager, attentive, thoughtful—and it shows in the way he holds himself and the way he's taken care of his body. I've watched athletes let themselves go when they can't workout. Which is fine. To each their own. But Wyatt really hasn't let himself go—besides his beard, of course, but it looks great on him. And all this—I don't know. It comes off as thoughtful to me. And all this makes me question if I am, indeed, the romantic type after all.

I hear the bathroom door open, so I make dismiss my ludicrous thoughts and my way back into the lounge. Wyatt's my patient—not my love interest.

"You ready?" I ask just as I open the door. But then I freeze when I spot him.

Wyatt didn't just change into trunks. He's *only* wearing trunks. Sweat makes the forest of his hairy torso glisten, and my little observation about him taking care of his body is true. Because, somehow, even though I only saw him a few days ago, it looks like his chest has gotten bigger and his abs have gotten more defined. Maybe it's 'cause he just worked out. That's so hot. Part of me just wants to run my finger through the muscular creases of his body, then my tongue, grabbing hold of the hair with my lips and—

"Yeah," he says, tossing his clothes and backpack on the table like he lives here. "I have to admit, though—I'm kinda nervous."

I let out a small sigh through pursed lips, relieved that Wyatt can't read minds. "What are you nervous about?"

He looks at me, almost boyish, then down at the ground. "My recovery—it's, uh, really important to me. I just don't want to do anything to set myself back."

"Well, don't worry," I say, putting my hand on the pool room door, trying to keep my gaze off of him even though his body feels like it has the polar opposite magnetic charge from my eyes. I open the door and get hit by the warm humidity from the running pool. "I've treated many athletes with leg injuries," I say, holding the door open for him. "And some after their ACL surgery just like you."

He walks through and sits himself down on the bench just in front of the small pool, setting his crutches to the side.

"That's good," he says, rubbing both of his arms, almost making himself smaller.

I don't know how to describe it, but I can just tell by the way this man moves his body that he's emotionally intelligent—thoughtful. I work with a lot of athletes, mostly male. And many just hold themselves like the world owes them something. They'll come into the room, sit down, splay their legs, fold their arms, and stare lazily at the wall. They often won't even look me in the eyes when I speak to them. And they only move when I firmly request it, and I'm sure it's only because they realize they have to listen to me to get better. And of course, these are only the few who have egos small enough to actually listen.

But that's clearly not Wyatt.

As I move around him to check if everything's good on the pool interface, his body acknowledges mine, not unlike the way I know that binary stars orbit each other. He's always facing me, his body calm and open, not closed or arrogant like so many of my other patients. He holds his head in a poised way, almost silently communicating to me that he will happily respond to anything and everything I ask of him. I have to say that this was not what I was expecting of a high-profile player in the NFO.

"Should I get in the water?" he asks.

Once I know all the settings are good, I walk to the edge of the pool right next to the stairs and hold out my hand. "Yes," I say.

He reaches out and grabs my hand with a force that is somehow both strong and tender, two traits I never really thought could simultaneously exist in a man. But as he holds my hand steady while I guide him down the pool stairs, I start to wonder what could possess a man to have such a gossamer light yet steel-like grip—especially when going through the trauma of an injury. Of which, I actually know little about. Maybe I can get some more information during this session.

Without me even needing to tell him, Wyatt grabs hold of the bar and moves to the middle of the small pool. It's about three times the size of an average hot tub, and it has jets to keep the water flowing and to provide a little bit of resistance.

"How are you feeling?" I ask him.

"Okay," he says with a breath. He looks up at me with a piercing lucidity. "What do I do, doc?"

"I'm not a doctor," I say shyly. "Well, not technically."

"Regardless," he says, adjusting his stance a little wider. "I'm under your medical guidance. Take it away."

It takes all my strength not to gawk at the beautiful man just below me. And him handing over the reins of the session completely to me doesn't make it any easier to resist, especially with how humble he is compared to the average athlete. We need to speed through this session. The less time with him, the less tempting he'll be.

I decide to start with some basic exercises.

"Plant your right foot—your good foot—firmly on the ground," I say. "And keep your grip on the bar."

He nods and gets into position.

"Now, have you ever swung on a swing before? Like on a playground or something?"

He smirks and nods, looking like he's got memories flooding to his mind. I don't like how curious I am to know what he's thinking about, so I continue on.

"You're going to be doing a similar motion," I say. "Swing your leg forward, but be sure to keep your leg bent until it's fully extended."

He does so perfectly the first time.

"Wonderful," I say. "Now move that leg back like you're coming down backward on the swing."

"Alright," he says, moving it back.

"Good," I say, impressed by his comprehension and cooperation. "How's that feel?"

"Little stiff," he says. "But I'm feeling okay."

"This will help you get some of your mobility back," I say. "Strengthen your muscles, which will hopefully shorten your recovery time."

He looks up at me with a raised brow, and my stomach tingles.

"So let's keep doing it," I say. "Let's say twenty reps."

As he starts his reps, the tingle in my stomach lingers. Was it from the way that he looked at me? I want to say that look got me all giddy because that means he trusts me, which also means I'm closer to getting a job with the NFO. But really, I think I'm giddy because he just looked at me like I was the rising sun after a long ice age. And to think I could be that bright to anyone...

"Feeling less stiff?" I ask after he's done a few reps.

"Yeah, actually," he says, his movements a little swifter now. "Feels kinda satisfying, actually. Like I'm dusting off the cobwebs."

"That's a good analogy."

He turns and smiles at me with his lips only, and my stomach tumbles over itself. It's like everything he does is purposeful—like so genuine and sincere. And he's so handsome doing it.

You know—since I'm not completely unfortunate looking—I do know I have been flirted with. Asked out even. It helps that I'm generally a big guy—6'1" with a belly, a little smaller than Jimmy's, but with some muscle too. I got a smooth face, besides my mustache, and I've been told I have legs like a stallion. But whether the guy is asking to fuck or a date, I never feel enthused enough to say yes. Because so often, they're just in it to fuck. Or they get to know me, and they're not interested at all. So it's best to spare my heart.

But Wyatt? If he asked me out, I think I might be tempted to say yes. He doesn't seem like other guys. But I doubt he would. Even though he's gay, which would make him asking me out possible, he's a looker—much more attractive and built than me. I'm sure now that he's come out he's practically swimming in dick. And besides, he's my patient now. Nothing can happen—not if I don't want to lose my license.

Which reminds me. He did tear his ACL right after he came out. I wanted to ask him about that.

We move on to the next exercise—squats—and I make sure he's watching himself on the monitor above the pool.

"Keep your heels down," I say. "And stay focused on your form."

"Aye aye," he says. And as he does his reps, he's not the only one focused on the monitors. Because as he squats down, I'm able to see just how round his ass is. When he's even in the lowest position, his big ass stretches his tight trunks, making both cheeks plainly visible.

Man, what the fuck is wrong with me? I don't need to be objectifying another man like this—especially one who seems so aware of himself. I guess I gotta distract myself by talking.

"So," I ask. "Torn ACL. Musta been pretty bad, huh?"

He nods as he squats, and his mind seems distant. Probably focused on his form.

"How'd it happen?" I ask. "I didn't see the game, but I heard the tackle was pretty nasty."

He winces as he squats low.

I'm not huge into video games like Jimmy is, but I have played The Sims. In that game, when your sim is talking to another and says something that the other doesn't like, a little red negative sign appears above their heads, signifying that the relationship has weakened. So, I bet if Wyatt and I were sims right now, I'd see a big red negative sign floating just above the pool.

"Sorry," I say, shaking my head. "Figured that's personal. My apologies."

"It's all good," Wyatt says, standing tall after finishing his reps. "I just—" he wipes his face and looks down at the water. "Still processing it."

"I get it," I say, thrusting my hands in my scrub pockets, embarrassed. "Forget I asked."

He smiles up at me again, and something possesses me to not look away.

"You're a good guy," he says. "Don't' worry about it."

My stomach tumbles over itself so badly I'm afraid it'll fall out of me right into the pool. But I manage to collect myself and move us on to the next exercise. This time, I'm having him jump from one leg to the other. So I don't have to watch his pecs bounce, I keep my gaze focused on the monitors, but that isn't much help considering I have a full view of his ass. Yet it's not like I can keep my eyes off of him as his therapist.

Or really want to.

So I decide to talk about something else to keep us both occupied.

"So you speak German?" I ask. "That's the language you were singing that day I met you."

He chuckles as he bounces, which gives me a funny feeling in my dick.

"You could say that," he says. "I wouldn't say I'm fluent. I can just read it and pronounce it pretty well. And understand a few things. Same with Italian, French, and Spanish. And a little Russian, too."

"Russian?" I ask, surprised.

"Yeah," he answers, smiling, still focused on the monitors. But this time he doesn't seem as preoccupied as he was before. He feels present. Aware.

"It's one of the most beautiful languages to sing in."

I pull over a nearby chair and sit down. "Okay, but you sing. And from what I heard, you sing well."

He laughs, and I swear I see him blushing this time almost as red as his beard. Then he stops, standing on one foot, and turns to me. "If I tell you something, could you promise to keep it a secret?"

My chest gets tight, and I sit back in my seat. "You wanna tell me a secret?"

He nods, still looking at me—still on one foot. "You seem like a trustworthy guy."

I laugh, blushing now too. "Alright," I say. "Tell me your secret."

"In another life," he says, continuing his jumping. "I would have been an opera singer."

My mouth forms a small 'o' as I look at with a furrowed brow. "An opera singer? You did tell me you were trained as one. Is opera like 'Hallelujah'?" I sing the word poorly, referencing Handel's *Messiah*.

"No," he says with a short laugh. "Like—" he belts out a high, full note, and for a second, the acoustics of the pool room make me feel like I'm in an opera house.

He closes his mouth, stops jumping, and looks at me. "Sorry, I think I startled you."

"No, no," I say, sitting up straighter. "That was—how did you do that?"

He shrugs and turns to me, wading in the water like he's a little kid. "I told you—I'm trained," he says. "And I love singing."

"How do you play in the NFO and sing at the same time?"

He laughs again, but there's sadness behind it. "I don't sing as much as I wish I could."

There's a moment of heavy silence between us, but it doesn't feel like bad silence. It feels like were strangers at a station about to board the same train, basking in the comfort of the other's presence. I want to ask him more about how he doesn't sing as much as he'd like, but something about his face tells me that's not a good idea.

"I'm big into music myself," I say. "But not so much the classical or opera stuff. Not that I don't like it of course."

Wyatt walks to the side of the pool and leans over it facing me. I would stop him and tell him to start another exercise, but I can see him putting weight on one leg, then the other, which is actually one of the exercises I was going to ask him to do anyways.

"That's cool," he says, propping himself up with his arms, showing how hairy and bulgy they are, too. His beard is slightly wet from the water, but his eyes shine, and they're a radiant hazel—no, green I think. He's got green eyes. The rarest eye color.

"What do you listen to?"

I shift back in my chair a little, feeling the need to put some distance between us.

"I listen to a lot of post-rock and ambient musicians," I say quietly. "Not sure if you've heard of any of them."

"Try me," he says, still moving back and forth.

And I can't stop the smile forming on my face. "Alright," I say, leaning forward until we're only about a foot apart. I expect him to pull away slightly, but he stays right where he is, almost daring me to close the distance even more. But I decide to stay right where I am for now.

"Well, some of my favorites include: *Eluvium, Alaskan Tapes, Slow Meadow,* and *Jónsi.* And then there are a lot of other musicians in the genre where I like one or two of their songs."

"Interesting," he says, nodding. "I don't know any of them, but I've heard good things about post-rock. I could give it a try."

Fuck.

Whenever I've told any guy about what I listen to, they'll give me a lukewarm nod and look around, as if waiting for me to stop talking. In fact, it feels like when I talk to any man, that big red negative Sims sign appears above us as soon as I open my mouth.

But this time, I think there's a green plus sign.

"You'd listen to my music?" I ask with a raised brow.

He shrugs. "I don't know. You seem like a cool guy. So figure what you listen to could be cool, too."

I blush and laugh, looking away.

Is Wyatt Nelson from the fucking NFO flirting with me? And worse—is it actually working? Judging by my fluttering heart and turning stomach, I'd answer in the affirmative.

"I could make you a playlist if you're curious," I say. "Only if you want though."

He leans even further toward me, the corner of his mouth turned up. "I do."

I let out an embarrassed laugh. "Yeah, alright. I can do that." Okay, yeah, he's really fucking flirting with me. But why? What's so special about me?

"You have my number," he says, standing up straight. "You have Spotify?"

I nod, trying to keep my eyes on his face and not anything below. I have to remind myself that I made this man hard. By accident, of course. But I did. And I don't want any more unprofessional business happening. Not if I want to keep my license and secure a job with the NFO.

He stretches his arms, which from my perspective just looks like he's purely flexing them. And I think that's on purpose to impress me. Or something. If I'm worthy of being impressed.

"We, uh," I say, looking away. "I think we're good for today." I stand up and put the chair back in its place.

"Done already?" he asks.

I stare over at him, and he's fucking pouting his lips. Is he trying to sleep with me or something? I don't want to presume. And I don't even know what that would be like. It's been forever since I'm slept with someone, let alone someone as goddamn tantalizing as Wyatt Nelson.

But that won't happen. He's my patient, for Christ's sake.

"Y-yeah," I stutter, making my way to the interface to turn shut down the pool. "Do you need help out?"

"I think I'm good," Wyatt says, grabbing hold of the bar.

As I turn off the monitors and all the other machinery, Wyatt walks up the pool stairs. But then he lets out a startled hiss.

"Are you alright?" I ask, whipping around. He's standing at the top step, but his injured leg is still in the water.

"I think I'm a little tuckered out," he says. "My knee, that is."

"Of course," I say. "I'm sorry. Let me help."

I walk over to the stairs and get on his week side. "Put your arm around me," I say.

He does, and I help him out of the water. He's limping, barely putting any weight on his injured leg.

"Forgot to mention it'll feel like a lot the first couple times," I say. "But you'll get stronger."

He looks at me as he hangs on my shoulder, dangerously close—his face only inches away from my face. He smells like chlorine, but I catch a hint of his sweat—my favorite smell in a man.

"Sorry I'm too weak to hold myself up," he says. "And for getting you all wet."

I look down and notice that the entire right side of my body is drenched, turning my scrubs a dark blue. That's okay. At least I'm not hard. But if his smell was stronger...

"You're good," I say. I grab a towel off the nearby wall and then set him down on the nearby bench. "Here."

I hand him the towel, and the moment our hands touch, something feels electric. He grabs it with that same gossamer light yet steel-like grip, and as he pulls away, I find myself wanting to reach out and grab his hand again. This session has felt like a date—a date so good that one of us should be coming home with the other.

But that's definitely not what this is.

"Send me a playlist," Wyatt says, drying off his body, and I love the way his pecs bounce as he runs the towel over them. "I definitely wanna listen to your post-rock."

I blink twice. For a second, I swear he said 'hard cock'.

I shake my head and lean against the far wall, my hands behind my back. I know I should be keeping this professional, but what's the harm in sharing some music together? It's not like we're fucking. In fact, I don't even just want to send him my stuff. I wanna hear his, too.

"You should send me some of your opera stuff, too," I say. "Some of the stuff you sing. If you want."

He smirks up at me. "Original recordings of me or just general opera stuff?"

I widen my eyes. "You have recordings of yourself?"

"A few," he says. "If you're interested."

"Yes to both."

"Alright," he says, standing up with one leg, which is impressive considering how tall he is. His thighs are huge, though, so it makes sense. He wraps the towel around his trunks and grabs his crutches.

"Mind if I take the towel for the night? I'll bring it back the next time."

"Sure, that's fine," I say, trying not to look at the way his body hair sticks up off his belly after drying himself.

We walk into the PT lounge, and he grabs his things. Outside, it's already dark.

"When can we do this again?" he says, turning to me, backpack in hand, as if we're setting our second date. Which we're not.

"Friday works for me," I say, which is two days from now. "Same time."

He lazily salutes to me, still shirtless. Fuck, if these sessions are gonna be him always shirtless...

He grabs his crutches, and we walk out into the dark together. "Friday at five it is," he says.

"Perfect," I say. "I'll get you that playlist."

"Likewise," says.

After I help him get in his car, he drives off, and I can't ignore the heat building in my chest. As I walk to my own car, putting my headphones in to listen to some music on the way home, I think about what I'll be writing in my journal tonight.

And I conclude that Cheshire will definitely be waking up with an owner tomorrow. At least until Friday, most likely.

Chapter 7

Wyatt Nelson

I SIT AT THE dining table in my mom's cabin eating some late lunch or early dinner, depending on how you want to look at it. She's sitting across from me eating some salad while reading either a thriller or historical fiction—I can't tell from the title or cover. Meanwhile, I have my phone under the table, hiding it from my mom like I'm twelve years old and trying to text my crush in secret. But instead of texting my crush, I'm trying to hold back a grin as I make him a playlist of classical voice music.

I'm going to see Silas in an hour, and I can't wait. He sent me his playlist of post-rock and ambient music last night, and I've been listening to it every moment I can. It's wonderful. His music is so thoughtful and profound, which makes me think he's just as thoughtful and profound. I took note of some of my favorites, and I can't wait to tell him my thoughts.

But now I need to whip myself into shape and finish mine. I've just had a hard time picking the best things for him. I obviously had to put all of Ralph Vaughn William's tenor stuff in there, but the arias have been giving me trouble. Besides the playlist, I'll send him links to stuff I've posted on a private YouTube channel. If he likes my singing, he'll love these videos.

I know I *should* be focusing on my recovery—not flirting with my physical therapist. But Silas did send me some exercises to do on my own time to build up strength, which I've been doing religiously. So what's the harm in having a little fun? He's a looker, and he's so interesting. I love the way he holds himself. And

God, when he handed me that towel—it felt watching Rodolfo encountering Mimi for the first time in *La Boheme*. Like I was Rodolfo, and he was Mimi.

"What are you doing?" my mom asks, eyeing me above her reading glasses.

My heart skips, and I turn my phone over on my leg. And that's when I realize that this table is made of glass, and my attempts at keeping my actions hidden are useless.

"Just making a playlist," I say.

"A playlist?"

"Yeah, is that not allowed?" I ask, then fork some chicken and put it into my mouth. God, I thought that being here with mom would be nice, especially after all that she said to me on the phone. But she's hovering over me as much as she used to when I was under her roof in Austin.

"It is," she says with a seemingly innocent shrug.

She goes back to reading, and I continue eating the chicken and rice that she made, not even bothering to pick up my phone again.

"So, that Silas," she says. "Are you sure it's not him you're texting? Or are you really making a playlist?"

"Mom," I say, almost whining.

"What?" she asks, putting her book down and taking off her glasses. Great. Now I know we're in for a conversation.

"I literally am making a playlist."

She folds her arms. "Then why was there a big smile on your face while you were typing on your phone?"

I scoff. "Am I not allowed to smile?"

"You are," she says, shaking her head. "But you just—you have that look in your eye like you got a crush on someone." She sighs through pursed lips. "And I just want to say…"

"Say what, mom? I'm allowed to find love," I say, a little more heat behind my words than I intend.

"I'm just concerned," she says, looking down at the table. "That you might get distracted from your career. That's all."

"My career?" I ask. "I'm working on my recovery. And I'm doing good. That's pretty much all of my career right now." I shake my head. "And besides—how would love stop me? There are plenty of my colleagues who sleep around or get married. Why can't I?"

She opens her mouth, then closes it, hesitating.

"Mom," I say. "What is it?"

"Don't you just think," she says. "That it might be best to not date—of course, you can date eventually—but wait until your career is over? Just so that…"

I drop my fork on my plate, and my mom flinches, as if the sound alone is making her regret her words. Which I hope it does.

"And why would you think that?" I ask, already knowing the answer.

She scoffs. "You can't blame me for thinking this way," she says. "I'm from a different generation. We didn't accept—" she pauses, no doubt thinking about her words "—gays like they're accepted today. But not everyone accepts them. I'm just worried that you could compromise your career by not toning yourself down until it doesn't matter."

"Doesn't matter?" I say, adjusting myself in my chair to face her squarely, causing my phone to clatter to the wooden floor. "You think my love doesn't matter?"

She sighs. "Your putting words in my mouth. I said—"

"No," I say, cutting her off. "That's exactly what you said."

"No," she says, raising her voice. "I meant to say that after you retire, there wouldn't be any repercussions for you being gay."

I don't say anything, my chest heaving.

"I mean, look at Kyle Weaver and Tanner Bash," she continues. "Sure, they came out, but they did so at the end of their football careers. When it was no longer of importance if they were gay or not. But you—" she gestures to me "—are at the top of your career. Are you willing to throw that all away just because you think your physical therapist is cute?"

I fold my arms tightly. "He's not just cute, Mom. He's interesting. He's got this special aura about him."

She rolls her eyes and takes a sip of her wine. "Of course, here we go. Just wait until the attraction dies down."

"What?" I ask. "Straight people can have love? But when I do, it's just an empty, vapid crush? Just attraction alone?"

"That's not what I'm saying. Of course your love is real. But—"

"Just stop," I say, putting my hand up. "It doesn't matter what you're trying to say. Because what you are saying is hurtful. I made the decision to come out—me and me alone—because I was tired of living in the shadows. I saw Kyle and Tanner come out and thought that this might be my chance. You know hard it was to live a life of secret at Miss U? So many crushes on boys who I tried to pursue but were too afraid of who they were to let it happen." I shake my head. "I'm tired of living in fear, mom. I'm so fucking tired of it."

She sighs, her shoulders deflating with her exhale. "I can imagine you are," she says. "I'm sorry. It's just—I want the best for you and your career. And I don't know if that best can happen if you're with another man. Sure, you came out, and that's great. And maybe that's enough. People were ready for that, but maybe they're not ready to see you with another man. That's why I say don't risk a relationship until it doesn't matter anymore. Until you've proven to the world the caliber of player that you are."

My arms still folded, I stare out the big cabin windows at the pouring rain. Suddenly, I hear some buzzing, and I peer down at the wood floor to see my phone ringing.

"I'm not being—" she pauses to think "—homophobic as some might say. I'm just trying to be realistic."

I ignore her as I reach down to pick up my phone. It's Blake calling me. He's taking care of my condo while I'm gone, so maybe there's something wrong.

"I gotta take this," I say, grabbing one of my crutches.

"Sure, go ahead," she says, and there's definitely guilt in her voice.

I hobble down the hallway to my bedroom. By the time I get there and shut the door, I answer my phone just in time.

"Hey, Blake," I say, trying to be as quiet as possible. I learned from Silas that these walls are thinner than I'd like them to be. "Everything alright?"

"We got a problem man," he says, low and serious.

I fall back on the bed, my stomach twisting itself in knots. "Problem? What do you mean?"

"I've been talking to a friend who plays for the Sparrows," he says. "He has some info about what happened that day you got injured."

The chicken I just ate threatens to make a reappearance. I turn over onto my belly, hoping that will calm my stomach down.

"What are you saying?" I ask.

"I really think there was foul play that day," he says. "That you were targeted."

My chest tightens. "Not this again, man. I'm telling you: accidents happen. People get injured all the time."

"And I'm telling *you*," he says, more forcefully. "That this was no accident."

"And how do you know?" I ask, struggling to keep my voice quiet. "I was the one who was tackled."

"Because this buddy of mine knows the guys who tackled you. And he says they were scheming."

I turn on my side and prop myself up. Rain patters against my bedroom window, and this sound feels like the only thing keeping me sane right now.

When I came out, I knew that not everyone would be supportive of who I was. That's been true for any queer person that has gone before me. But I refused, and still do refuse, to believe that it would affect my career, let alone put a target on my back.

"Scheming to do what exactly?" I spit into my phone. "Purposefully injure me?"

"Yes," he says emphatically. "That's exactly what they were trying to do. My friend said he caught them lingering in the locker rooms after a practice one morning."

I wipe my face, trying to push down the fear rising in my chest. "Did this friend tell you what they were saying?"

"Well, no," Blake says, stammering. "He didn't hear them."

"So you don't know if they were really scheming or not?"

"But isn't it obvious? Look at the way you were tackled. At the very least, the way those guys took you down was dangerous, let alone reckless."

I watch drops run down my window, wondering if I'll ever undo the knot of fear in my stomach.

But I'm going to try.

"If there's no proof that they were directly targeting, then I don't want to talk about it," I say.

Blake groans. "Come on, man," he says. "You're saying you don't believe this was purposeful at all?"

The slur 'faggot' echoes in my head, the word I heard right before the play where I was tackled—where I was tackled and tore my ACL. Blake doesn't know about that, but he doesn't need to. I expected to be called a slur here and there. It had nothing to do with the tackle.

"I don't," I insist.

"Wyatt," he says, almost chiding me. "Come on, man. I'm worried about this. I'm worried about you. It could have been so much worse than it turned out."

"A torn ACL does suck," I say. "It's not like it's nothing."

"Yeah," he says. "But what if, next time, one of these guys finds you after a game? Or worse—they target others, too?"

It's now I realize that my free hand is clutching the comforter so hard my knuckles are going white. Blake has always been the worrier—even back at Miss U. He was always worried, whenever the gay players would get together to fool around, that we would be caught. In reality, though, he was always just afraid of being outed. And I think, now that I'm out, he sees his sexuality being leaked as more possible than ever. So he's trying to push me down and keep me quiet. But that's not going to happen.

"Blake," I say. "You need to relax. I'm fine. Injuries are normal. I'm not being targeted, and I'm definitely not the victim of a hate crime." The word 'faggot' echoes in my head again, and I deliberately push it to the farthest recesses of my mind.

"I don't know man," he says. "Maybe you should take this as a sign. Heal, recover—but don't play again."

I stare at the phone like Blake just started speaking Chinese. "I beg your pardon?"

"I'm serious, man."

"Blake," I say, turning over to sit up. "I'm offended. You know what becoming a legendary tight end means to me. I wanna be the best of the best."

"You already are one of the best. Be satisfied with that. Look out for yourself."

I shake my head. This is the absolute last thing I wanted to have happen.

My whole life, I've been taught that gay people—queer people anywhere—are less than. Specifically, that gay men are bad at sports, math, and anything masculine. But also that we're emotional. We're supposedly a collection of all the bad traits that women are stereotypically told to have, but yet we're not as attractive as straight men because we've fallen from the masculine ideal. But so often, what I've seen is that society engineers us this way. It tells us that we're bad at these things, and then we start believing in these lies, fulfilling the prophecy that they've out for us.

And you know what? I'm writing my own fucking prophecy.

"Blake," I say, trying to keep my voice low even though it's filled to the brim with anger. "I know you're my friend and that you're trying to look out for me, but keep your fucking internalized homophobia to yourself."

"What?" he asks, and it almost sounds like he's crying.

"I will not let your fears about being gay seep into the way that I live my life. I came out, and I absolutely do not regret it. And nothing's going to stop me from recovering as fast as I can and getting back out on the field. I'm gonna show all those gay kids that we are not only just as competent as straight people but that we can also be the best."

Blake sighs, and I know that he's shaking his head in disapproval.

"You've always been the brave one," he admits.

And then there's silence between us, and the fear in my chest turns into aching sadness. Both of us deserve better than this. He should feel free to ask me about my time in Glamour Springs, and I should feel free to ask how the team is doing without me. Instead, we're arguing with each other over the merits of making ourselves invisible.

"I'll support you no matter what," he eventually says.

I feel my chest pain release a little bit. "Thanks, man."

"But just know that I'm still concerned," he says. "And I think you should be more than you are."

I hear that f-word again in my head, and I sigh. "Thanks for your concern, Blake," I say. "But really: there's nothing to worry about."

Eventually, once we've both made it clear what our stances are, we are finally able to catch up about more mundane things, like what off-season events our team as planned in the coming months and how I'm liking Glamour Springs. But the tension from our conversation about my injury lingers between us like a taut rope that neither of us are quite willing to drop.

"You take it easy," he says. "And I wish you a speedy recovery."

"Appreciate it," I say. And then I hang up.

Exhausted, I'm tempted to curl into a ball under my covers and let the rain serenade me to sleep. But then I remember I have something more exciting to do. I need to head out for my physical therapy appointment with Silas.

And you know what? Screw what both my mom and Blake have said. I deserve to be who I am in the NFO, and that means dating who I'd like. So if things go in a positive direction between me and this cowboy Silas, I definitely won't be one to stop it. In fact, I might just be the person facilitating the relationship.

Chapter 8

Silas King

By the time 5PM rolls around and I'm finishing up with my last client, I know I should be excited to see Wyatt Nelson, especially after the steamy interaction we had a couple days ago. That football player was shirtless right in front of me, flaunting himself and schmoozing me with his smooth words. I was charmed, to say the least.

But now I'm getting my doubts about the whole thing. He was so self-aware during our conversation, but I now realize I may have been mistaken in seeing this trait in him.

He said he wanted a playlist of the music I listen to, so I made it and sent it to him last night. He was so insistent about it too, saying that I was interesting, so the music I was listening to had to be interesting as well. Now that was flattering. But I've heard nothing from the man since. During our time together, I even asked him if he would send me a playlist of his own stuff.

Yet he hasn't.

I know Jimmy or Linda or Llewellyn would say I'm being dramatic, but I'm not. This is how it goes with men. They express immediate interest—almost too much interest, like they're love-bombing me. Clearly, sex is on their mind, but it's not something I like to do right away anymore, so I don't immediately give it to them. Then, they do or say or promise something to secure a next time where sex can happen—in this case with Wyatt, it was the playlists. But since they never got the sex with me in the first place, they go off and find it elsewhere, completely abandoning the promise they made me because they got their satisfaction.

So, no. I'm not being dramatic. I've caught a pattern, and I'm no longer falling for it. No matter how charming Wyatt is today, I'm not gonna fall for his games anymore.

Which, I guess, is for the better. I don't need to be catching feelings for a patient. At the end of the day, I need my license. I'm not gonna let a stupid boy get in the way of that.

Once everyone's gone, I sit in the therapist's lounge when I hear the waiting room door open. I hear the sound of crutches coming in, so I know that Wyatt is here.

I put on my cowboy hat and make my way to the waiting room. "Hey, Wyatt," I say kindly, spotting him as I open the door. I may not be falling for him, but I can still be cordial. He is my way to the NFO, after all.

"Hey, Silas," he says, standing up and making his way to me. I hold the door open for him as he makes his way into the lounge. Inside, I have a treatment table set up.

"What sorta physical therapy torture device is this?" he says, nodding his head to the table as he sits down at one of the round lounge tables.

I try not to smirk at his little joke. "Figured we'd some stretches before we get you into the pool," I say. "So you're not as sore afterwards."

"Works for me," he says. "Mind giving me a minute? It takes a lot out of me to walk this far in my crutches."

"Sure," I say, nodding. But now I don't know what to do with my time or the silence. I was sort of hoping to get him in and out.

"So, did you go to Miss U?" he asks me.

"I did," I say, propping my leg up on a chair to stretch. My scrubs tighten around my thighs, and Wyatt's eyes immediately drift downward. I lower my leg quickly, hoping my face isn't turning red.

"Me, too," I say. "But you might have known that. Came all the way from Texas."

I nod and sit down in the chair across from him. "I did," I say. "But I don't actually know when. How old are you?"

"27," he says. "You?"

"28."

"Cool," he says with a smile. "Almost the same age."

To avoid his gaze, I look over to the treatment table. Best to get started now so we end sooner. The less time with him the better.

"You, uh, ready?" I ask.

He sighs. "I think so." He makes his way to his feet. Using his crutches, he walks over to the table. "Should I just lay down on it?"

"Yeah, just get comfortable," I say.

He hands the crutches to me and then lays down. He's wearing a tight henley and shorts. His copper chest hair pokes out from his undone collar buttons, and his shorts have a small inseam, making his thick thighs pop.

"Alright," I say, getting situated by his legs. "I'm gonna help stretch your knees out."

"Have at it," he says, as if I would enjoy touching him. Which, it's not like I dislike touching him. It's fine. But I don't *like* touching him. Fuck. Last time I did this, he got a boner. If that happens again...

Staring at a fixed point on the wall, I raise his leg and bend it toward his head, slowly extending his leg upward and back down several times.

"How's that feel?" I ask.

"Not bad," he says in that rich voice of his. "Oh, hey, I nearly forgot."

I look over at him for the first time, and he's looking down at past his ginger beard, and from here I can see just how thick his pecs are, at least an inch or two raised above his stomach. I wonder what if would feel like to run my hands...

"I listened to some of your playlist."

My stomach jumps, and I look away. "Oh, yeah?" I ask, completely forgetting for a brief moment that I sent him one. And now I'm embarrassed. Surely, he thinks I'm a weirdo just like every other guy who I've shared my music taste with. Now that I'm with him, I almost wish he did just blow me off. Then we

could just go about his sessions, get him healed, and then pretend like we never me
t.

But that can't happen now. We're connecting.

"Dude, I fucking loved it," he says.

I look down at him, almost confused as I extend his leg out and back again. "Seriously?"

He nods, resting his head back and looking at the ceiling. "I didn't even know that they made music like that."

Okay, now my intestines feel like they're coiling around each other, which I know they're obviously not doing, but they might as well be with how bunched up I feel.

I let out a nervous chuckle. "Is that a compliment?"

"Of course it is," he says with more sincerity than Linda or Jimmy could muster, which is saying something. "I specifically liked..." he pauses to think.

Great. Here we go. I don't know why I'm nervous to hear what songs he liked, but I'm trying to resist grimacing as I handle his leg. I feel like a little kid giving his teacher a poem, and now she's reading it to the class. Like I'm being tested and judged at the same time. Why'd I agree to share my music with him?

"Oh my God," he says. "'Seconds' by Alaskan Tapes. My goodness." He wipes his face.

"You liked it?" I ask, not knowing if I'd rather hear his opinion or not. But I ask anyways.

"Oh man," he says, briefly looking down at me than back up at the ceiling, a small smile forming on his face. "It was like—I felt like I was standing at the edge of a dock on a dark night watching the ocean waves. Slightly haunting, but peaceful. Almost cozy."

My chest heats up, and I feel my face go red. Having someone to listen to the music that I feel like represents me more than anything else—the music that I insist listens to me just as much as I listen to it—it feels like Wyatt is staring right into my soul. It feels more intimate than touching, kissing—even having sex. Obviously, Wyatt knows nothing about how dark my mind can get. No one does. But having him praise my music now makes me feel like one day, he could. Like I'm not really as alone as I think I am.

"I think the same," I say, looking down at his feet to hide my blush. And damn, he's got nice feet, too. He's wearing tennis shoes that have to at least be size thirteen, and thick hair pocks above his socks, which makes me think his feet are hairy. I feel embarrassed to admit that I'm into feet. The few times I've hooked up with other guys, they've thought it was weird. But I'm sorry—seeing Wyatt so casually handsome now definitely makes me want to smell him. Which means I desperately want to take Wyatt's shoes off and press my nose against the soles of his feet. I know that's like perverted or whatever. But my dick likes what it likes. Sue me, I guess.

"Any others?" I ask, looking away from his feet as I set his leg down. It's time to massage it.

"Oh, yeah," he says. "Martin Gauffin. His stuff made me feel like—I don't know. You know summer nights where the sun stays out really late?"

"Yeah," I say, now looking him in the eye, finding myself unable to look away from his green eyes.

"It's like that. Where when the sun eventually goes away, the stars shine in the sky, and it's just as bright and happy as if it were noon day. You're with your friends. Maybe it's the Fourth and there are fireworks. Maybe there's burgers and beer or whatever. But what I feel is the joy and carefree vibes of being a kid and enjoying the summer night. Especially 'Sunlight in The Night' and 'Point of You'. Those two slapped."

I let out a chuckle, my chest almost so buoyant that I swear I'm floating in the air. "I love that description," I say, massaging around his knee. "Are there others you liked?"

"Oh, yeah," he says. "A couple others by *Alaskan Tapes*. 'Under the Viaduct', the one with lyrics, was a banger. Not that they need lyrics to be bangers, but I liked that one. Also 'And Yet They Float'. Made me think of being resilient, like floating on water despite what may be dragging us down."

"That's exactly what I think about that one," I say a little too eagerly.

"Cool," he says, smiling up at me.

We stare at each other for a minute as I dig my fingers into his thigh and calf.

"That feels really good," he says, low and deep. Almost sensual.

I bristle slightly at his words. I told myself I wouldn't let this go anywhere, that I wouldn't let myself get close to him. But it feels like magic hearing what Wyatt has to say about the music that I love. It's like I've built this stone fortress that everyone has thought is imposing and ugly and domineering. But Wyatt's just walked inside and praised the architecture. I want—I need to hear more.

"Are there any others you liked?" I ask, not wanting this conversation to end.

"I mean, I like all of them," he says, which disappoints me slightly. I feel like that's a nice way of saying 'I didn't really like any of it, but I don't want to be rude'. But he did say he liked some specifics, so that's good.

He pulls out his phone from his pocket, and my stomach sinks. Great. He's bored with the conversation. Which makes sense. I'm boring. My music taste is boring. There's no way—

"Sorry," he says. "Don't want to be rude." He sets his phone back into his pocket. "I wanted to check the playlist again."

"Oh?" I ask, somewhat hopeful.

"The song that I was thinking of—I thought it was one song, but it was actually two."

I tilt my head. "And that is?"

He picks up his phone quickly, then sets it down again. "'Ships Along the Harbor' and 'Boy in a Water Globe' by *Slow Meadow*."

My chest squeezes so tight that it feels like someone's grabbed my heart and wringed it out like a wet towel.

"It's just—that first song," Wyatt continues. "'Ships Along the Harber'—it gave me the imagery of being tossed about in some storm, like on a ship in the water or something. And the way the song seemingly transitions into the next—'Boy in a Water Globe'—it's like the waves finally capsized my ship." He laughs. "I know this sounds weird, but I'm a visual guy. I see things when I listen to music."

I nod, staring down at his knee as I massage him, feeling tears heat up my eyes.

"And as I listened to 'Boy in a Water Globe', it was like I was washed up on some island. And the rest of the song was me gathering the courage to build a ship on this island and sail away. I don't know, man—these two songs together told a story. One of deep sadness, I think. But of resilience, too. I don't know. That's how they sounded."

A drop of water falls from my eye on his knee, and he flinches.

"What are you—" he stops and raises onto his elbows. "Silas, are you okay?"

And those magic words break the dam.

I step away, grab a nearby chair, and collapse into it. I take off my hat and let myself weep into my hands, not even caring that I'm weeping in front of a virtual stranger. Because that's who Wyatt Nelson is—a virtual stranger.

I remember driving back my parents' ranch in Alabama after my first Christmas break during my undergrad at Miss U. I remember crying in the car, their harsh words echoing in my head. 'Too big for your britches', they said. 'You think you're better than us', they said. 'You'll never make it—you're not meant for that kinda world', they said. And though from that moment on I swore that I would prove them wrong, I felt uprooted, tossed about—or like a ship in stormy waters like Wyatt described. I had never felt so alone, confused, and scared. But I knew from that moment I had no one to turn to. So I kept to myself. And I have ever since.

But then Wyatt goes on to say that that's not the end of the story—that 'Boy in a Water Globe', which I always thought represented a continuation of my sorrow, is actually about triumphing the shipwreck. He says it's about building another ship and getting off the island of isolation, loneliness, and sadness.

Could that be true? Can I recover from the darkness that sits on my mind like a boulder at the bottom of the hill?

"Silas, I—"

I glance up and see Wyatt sitting up, his legs off the table.

"Are you okay?" he asks. "I'm sorry if I—"

"You didn't do anything wrong," I say, shaking my head. I grab a tissue off the table and blow my nose.

He adjusts himself on the table, no doubt having no idea what to say.

Great. I have a gorgeous man take interest in my music, describe his thoughts about it in beautiful, genuine detail, and then I show my appreciation by losing my shit in front of him? He probably thinks I'm crazy.

"It's really great music," he says.

I lower my hands and look up at him, still crying a bit, touched that every new word that comes out of his mouth is somehow kinder and more thoughtful than the last.

"Who are you?" I ask.

He frowns. "Who am I? I'm Wyatt—"

"And where did you come from?" I ask more seriously.

He furrows his brow. "What do you mean?"

I shake my head. "I've showed my music to people before. Maybe no more than a few guys I've tried to get to know. And you know what they think about my music? They think it's boring, or it's weird, or it's emo or whatever."

"I don't think it's weird or emo," he says with a shrug.

"And that's exactly it," I say. "Here you are, somebody I've only seen a few times, and yet you are able to not only appreciate my music but interpret it in a way that touches me all the way down to my soul." I let out a sharp laugh. "You have no idea what these songs mean to me. And it feels like you've just ripped my heart out of my own chest and presented it to me by describing them the way you did. Like you've seen me in ways that no one else has."

I shake my head and let out a heavy sigh. I scratch the back of my neck, and that's when Wyatt starts to slide off the table.

"I'm sorry," I say, quickly standing up. "You paid for this session—well, your mom has. We still need to do some stretches."

Wyatt freezes. "Are you sure?"

I nod and wipe my eyes. "Yeah, I'm sure."

After a brief moment, Wyatt lays back down. For a minute, I swear I see his dick hard, but I'm too emotional to care. Plus, it could be the tears making me see things.

Once he's in position, I grab hold of his leg again and continue the stretches.

"Sorry about that," I say, sniffling. "Only a couple more stretches and then we'll be good for the pool."

"It's no worries, man," he says, facing the ceiling with his hands on his stomach. "We gotta let it out sometimes."

I nod, embarrassed that I essentially just poured my heart out to him, and now we're acting like nothing happened. Typical of me to have found a guy who sees me and then have it fall flat.

"I haven't finished my playlist for you yet," he says. "But if you'd like, I can share one song with you right now. One that reminds me of you."

My heart picks up speed. "Oh?"

He picks up his phone from the table. "Want to hear it? It's an original recording of me."

I perk up, still sniffling a little. "Of you singing opera? That sounds cool."

"Alright," he says, excitement in his voice. "Let me pull it up."

He opens up a YouTube video and sets it down on the table for me to see as I'm finishing up the last of his stretches.

"This is me performing in the opera *La Boheme*," he says, pressing play. "Have you heard of it?"

I shake my head.

"Well, it's a kinda depressing play about poor, sick people falling in love in Paris around 1830," he says. "But the music is to die for. This is me singing 'Che Gelida Manina'."

Instrumental music starts playing, but I stare at Wyatt, confused. "'Che Gelida Manina'? Is that Spanish?" I ask.

"Italian," he says. He reaches out to grab one of my hands, and I freeze. "'What a frozen little hand' is what it means."

I feel saliva thicken in my mouth, but that's when I hear the singing begin. A rich, broad voice emanates from his speakers, and I stare at him with my jaw dropped. "Is this you?"

He nods and lets go of me, unable to hide his smile.

As I massage his leg, I listen and watch as the NFO player before me sings on stage in old clothing and makeup but sounding like an absolute legend. I didn't even know humans could be this loud. But it's not annoying or shrill—it's full, purposeful. Like his voice is pure strength and what's behind it is endurance, hard work, and talent. By the time the song's over, the hairs on my arms are standing up.

"I've got goosebumps, man," I say, still massaging his leg.

"You like it?" he asks with a smug smile, as if there's no possibility that I didn't—which, like, he's right about.

"I don't know how you do that," I say. "How'd you learn to sing like that?"

"Had a voice," he says, turning off his phone. "And then people taught me how to use it."

I chuckle, hardly believing that just earlier I broke down. Somehow, this man's got me laughing and crying tonight, all while I'm massaging *his* body. He must be magical or something. That's the only explanation. Especially with the way he described my music.

"But this song also reminds me of you."

My chest lights up. "Does it now?"

He nods. "I feel like when I first touched you, I reached just how Rodolfo does in the opera. 'Che gelida manina, se la lasci riscaldar'," he says. "'How cold is your hand. Let me warm it into life'."

I raise a brow. "Is that the translation of the song?"

He nods. "The first two lines."

"Why'd that remind you of me?"

He shifts a little bit, and I see something bounce beneath his shorts. I look clear away to his knee. I think I know what that is...

"You seem like a thoughtful guy," he says. "Like there's a lot on your mind. I hope this doesn't sound weird, but I can see it in the way you hold yourself. In your eyes. The way you talk."

I thin my lips. Can Wyatt Nelson read my mind or something? Does he know how sad I am? Could he possibly know about my nightly ritual?

"And it makes me want to get to know you," he says. "Inside and out. The good and the bad."

I look over at him, my eyes squinted. "What are you saying?"

He looks at me with a warm face—not smiling, but not frowning either. He's serious. "Maybe you could give me a chance. You're a cute guy."

Wanting to avoid his gaze, I glance down and finally see what I've been trying to avoid. Which I feel stupid for not considering. The same thing happened last time I massaged him. Underneath his small inseam shorts, he's rock-hard.

"Dating of course," he says, looking up at the ceiling as I stare down at his dick. "We don't have to do anything you don't want."

But as he finishes speaking, his dick twitches, and I jump.

As I've mentioned before, I'm a big fan of space and everything in it. The things that fascinate me the most are black holes. They are cosmic entities that defy the laws of physics as we know them—yet, at their core, they likely contain the truth to all our questions about the universe. But the problem is that once you go to one, you can never get out. The gravity is so strong that not even light can escape. In fact, there's a certain point where if you get too close to one, it's too late. You can't turn back, like a kayaker approaching a waterfall and not having the strength to paddle away.

That's how I feel right now. Wyatt's my black hole, and I'm a lone astronaut teetering on the edge of the abyss. If I let myself fall in, I have a feeling that there's a chance I'll never break myself free of him.

But, if I reach the core of the black hole—if I let myself find love in Wyatt—then maybe I can find the singularity or the truth to all things. In other words, maybe I can find a reason to be truly happy.

I know I can't sleep with a patient, but Joan's been paying me under the table. We're just using the clinic. In other words, I could let myself fall into Wyatt and still have my license if I play my cards right. And maybe a job with the NFO, too.

So I think I'm gonna stop paddling away from the waterfall. I'll let gravity take me.

Chapter 9

Wyatt Nelson

"But what if there is something I want to do?" Silas asks. He places one of his hands right at the bottom of my shorts and starts massaging there. He hasn't massaged here before, and I see him looking at my rock-hard dick, so I know exactly what he's referring to.

"Of course, only if you want to," he says, removing his hand.

That's when I grab his hand and place it right on my shaft.

He stares at his hand like it's been removed from his body, and I flex my dick so that jumps up into his grip. And, to my satisfaction, he keeps it right there.

"Are you sure this is what you want?" he asks. "I know you just came out, and there's probably—"

"Yes," I say softly. "I do want this. But I won't pressure you into it if you can't. I know physical therapists—"

"I want this," he says. He licks his lips, looking at my eyes now. "I'm ready. But that probably means that we're not going to have time for the pool."

I reach out and grab his scrubs to pull him in until he's only inches from my face. I look between his eyes and his lips, and he looks back at me like I'm a wild animal about to tear him apart—fear mixed with pure fascination.

"I'd much rather we stretch each other out," I say. I have no idea what that will look like—if I fuck him or he me or something else entirely, but I can't wait to find out.

He swallows. "Okay," he says. "Why don't we—"

And that's when I pull him in for a kiss. And I swear he tastes like sweet cinnamon or something. Because I want to keep his lips pressed against mine until the day I die. I pull him down onto me as we kiss, and I run my hands through his short, cowboy hair. His tongue dances with mine as he runs one of his hands through my long beard. The other trails town my chest, but I decide to help him out and guide it back to my dick. He squeezes, and my entire body bucks.

He pulls away and smiles down at me mischievously. "That feel good?"

"What do you think?" I pull him back toward me and kiss him again, but then he pulls away.

"What?" I ask. "Do you not want to do this?"

"I do, I do," he says. "But—" he gestures to the windows. "We're in plain sight. I can't be seen kissing a patient."

Fuck. I'd take him back to the cabin, but then my mom would see him, and I definitely don't want that to happen after our conversation today. I'd get another lecture about why being gay and dating in the NFO will ruin my career before I'm even back out on the field.

"We can go back to your place," I say.

He pauses and presses his lips together, his face contorted in worry. He observes me steadfastly, breathing rapidly in and out of his nose, like if he closes his eyes I'll disappear. He wants to fuck, and he wants to fuck right now.

I lean up on my elbows, my dick still rock-solid.

Then he brightens. "I got an idea. Follow me."

He hands me my crutches, and I follow him into what looks like the patient room hallway. He opens the door and guides me into a windowless room with a long, mechanical patient table.

I shut the door behind me and nod. "Come here."

He presses himself against my chest as our lips meet, and I wrap my arms around him.

He feels so perfect here, like he was meant to fit. I meant every word I said to him back there. There's something more to him that I want to get to know. And I don't know. He's clearly upset about something, and I want to be there for him. Just like Rodolfo and Mimi. I want to warm his frozen little hand to life.

With this in mind, I kiss him more passionately, using my whole tongue to kiss him, like there's a taste in the back of his throat I'm trying to reach. He starts moaning desperately, and that's when I grab his neck with both hands. I hold him in place as I pull away, then lick both of his lips with my whole tongue like I'm some feral dog who can't get enough. Because I can't. And I can't decide if I want to please him more or be pleased by him.

He whimpers as I lick his lips one last time, then let him go back to kissing me.

"I want to worship your body," he says in between kisses.

I smile. Looks like he'll be pleasing me.

"I'd like that."

"Here," he says.

He steps away and puts his hand on the lever of the mechanical patient table. He cranks it so the top third is facing up at a steep angle.

"This might be weird," he says.

I put my hand on the back of his neck. "It won't be weird at all," I say. "How do you want me?"

He sighs, relaxing himself. "Well, first..." He gestures for me to take off my shirt.

I put my crutches against the wall and slip off my henley. He gawks at my body.

"And your shorts," he says shyly.

I hop on one foot over to the table and sit down. I first slip off my shoes. Then, hovering over the edge, I easily slip my shorts and underwear off, letting my hard dick finally see light. I swear Silas's face nearly goes white when he sees it.

"You are one of the most beautiful men I've ever seen," he says, his Southern accent stronger than ever.

That makes my dick jump. "Why don't you show me how much you mean it, handsome?"

He gets on his knees just before me at the end of the table. But, to my surprise, he doesn't start with my dick. Instead, he lifts my good leg and puts my foot into his face.

And sniffs.

He situates his nose just between the toes and sole of my foot and takes a big sniff again, letting out a desperate moan with his exhale.

Now, I had a good amount of sex when I was at Miss U. But that sex consisted of blowjobs or the occasional penetration. This, though—I've never done anything like this. Having my foot worshipped? Sniffed? I wanna say this is weird. But I can see by Silas's pained face as he takes my smell in that he's in ecstasy. Which only makes my dick harder. This man likes my smell—not deodorant or cologne I put on—but *my* natural scent.

"You like that, huh?"

He stops. "What? Is it weird?"

I shake my head emphatically. "No, it's—well, it's new for me. But I like it."

He laughs a little nervously. "I don't know—I have this thing. I know it's weird. But when I see a guy who's really hot, the first thing I want to do is—never mind."

"Awh, come on," I say. "Don't leave me hanging."

My foot rests on his shoulder as he sighs. "The first thing I want to do when I see a hot guy is see what he smells like," he says as fast as he can. "I know that sounds weird and perverted."

"It's not."

"You don't think so?"

I smirk at him. "I think that's hot," I say. "Especially when you're doing it to me. Like you're breathing me in like air."

He nods eagerly. "Yeah, it's like—I'm so attracted to you that even the 'worst' parts I enjoy."

"Then keep going."

Less self-consciously this time, he sniffs in between my toes, rubbing his thumbs into my sole. I lean my head back and moan as he takes in another sniff.

Then, he lifts up my other leg. I wince slightly at the pain, but then he gently as ever extends my leg and presses my other foot against his face.

"This one deserves just as much attention, too," he says. He takes a big sniff. "I don't want to leave any part of you un-worshipped."

"I don't think there's anyone else I would trust with this leg," I say.

"Good," he says. Then he rubs his face all over my sweaty sock, and I love the way some of his mustache hairs get caught in the sock and tickle me.

And that's when I want us to be closer.

"I want your clothes off," I say.

He looks up at me, slightly worried, like I'll judge him, but then he nods. He takes off his scrub top and under shirt at the same time. Then he stands up, turns around, and strips off his scrub bottoms. I try to sneak a peek at his huge ass, but he turns around before I can. But I won't complain.

Silas is almost as hairy as I am. He's got firm pecs, a nice belly, and strong line of hair that goes all the way from the bottom of his neck to his waist. He's got a sizable dick with some girth to it and a ton of pubic hair.

"Sorry," he says. "Haven't been naked in front—"

"Shh," I say, taking him all in. "You're a gorgeous man."

"You think so?"

"Yes, Silas," I say, my chest burning. Who or what hurt this man for him to be so unsure of himself? He's objectively one of the hottest men I've ever seen, and he's so present and thoughtful. When he cried earlier and told me all about what that music meant to him, I was at a loss for words because I've never met someone so thoughtful about what they listened to. Or at least vulnerable enough to show me.

Silas is like a vast cathedral, and every piece of stained glass I find is more breathtaking than the last. I want to get to know him—to see every feature he has to offer. And if that means plumbing the depths of his catacombs, I will. I want Silas to be happy and whole. And I wouldn't be lying if I said I want to be the one to make him happy and whole.

"Now I want you to take my socks off," I say.

He obeys immediately. He moves with eager swiftness, and I get a feeling that if I told him to run out in the street naked, he would. Now, I would never do that. But I can't help but smile realizing the power that I have right now.

"Put one in your mouth," I command.

And, as I suspected he would, he puts it in his mouth without pause or protest.

"And the other one," I say calmly.

He stuffs it in, nearly gagging—not from the stench, I know, but from the sheer volume of what's in his mouth. But when he finally gets them both in there, I nod.

"Good. Now, smell my feet and massage them. With my socks in your mouth."

He lifts my good leg up and immediately gets to it. My dick throbs as I watch him desperately smell me in, and I raise one of my hands to stroke it. But I do it lightly. I have a feeling Silas will get me to cum easily. And I want to wait until it's just right to do that.

After a while of this, Silas looks up at me imploringly.

"You can take them out," I say.

He nods and removes the socks, then gently places them on top of the rest of our clothes. "Can I worship other parts of your body?" he asks. "Absolutely," I say. "How do you want me?"

"Scooch back and lean against the steep end of the table," he says.

I do, which allows me to rest my long legs on the rest of the table with my back propped up. That's when Silas crawls onto the table, in between my legs, the lowers himself right in front of my dick. But, just like before, he doesn't start with my dick. Instead, he sticks out his tongue and traces up the line of belly hair that leads from my waist to my belly button. He briefly sniffs it, kisses it, then does something that sends warm chills down my back. He keeps his tongue and traces the lines of my abs, going deadly slow, as if there isn't one patch of skin he doesn't want touching his tongue. Man, when he said worship, he really mea
nt it.

By the time he reaches the underside of my right pec, he seamlessly cradles my nipple in his tongue and swallows it with his mouth.

I lean my head back and moan as he goes back and forth between massaging it and flicking it with his tongue. Just when I think I'm about to lose my mind, he goes to my other pec and does the same thing, except this time he swirls his tongue around it, making desperate slurping sounds.

"Fuck, Silas," he says.

"I love it when you say my name," he says.

"Then I'll say it any time I can," I say. "Fuck, Silas," I say more softly.

He more eagerly sucks on my nipple, and just when I think I'll cum from this alone. He kisses my pec, then down my stomach.

All the way to my dick.

And instead of putting it right in his mouth, he teases me. He buries his nose deep in my dirty blonde crotch and sniffs.

"Damn, Silas," I say. "You're a fucking pervert, aren't you?"

He nods, digging his nose deeper into my pubes. "I am."

I smile. I was worried he wouldn't want me talking dirty to him, but he fucking loves it.

He comes up to take a breath, his face red and groggy like he's just gotten up from a nap. He approaches my dick, and my stomach jumps. With how much pleasure he's given me so far, I don't know if I'll be able to hand him going straight for my dick.

But again, he fucking teases me.

He grabs hold of the base of my dick, keeping it still, then runs his nose along the shaft, breathing me in slowly. And when I say slowly, I mean *slowly*. It takes him about ten seconds to move no more than an inch, and my dick's about eight of those, so he's got a long way to go. But I'm okay with him taking his time. It's like I'm his ecstasy. I didn't even know sex could be this fucking hot.

When he's halfway up my dick, he cradles it with two hands and stops. Then he takes in the deepest breath I've heard him take tonight—which is saying something—and exhales with an almost inhuman moan. The sound makes my dick jump, but he keeps it right in place with his hands and nose, like my penis is his now. And you know what? I'd give it to him. Fuck.

He continues his way up my dick until, finally, he reaches the head. He opens his mouth, and that's when I think it's over. Because I know the second he puts his lips on my dick, I'm cumming.

But, goddamn, he surprises me again.

He spits a healthy glob of spit right on the head. Slowly, like lava pouring from a volcano, the spit comes down on all sides, gradually splitting into tiny rivers. Two roll off the head of my dick and down my veiny shaft. But the other one? It slowly drips from my head all the way to the cushion, reflecting the fluorescents in this patient room. Silas extends his tongue, laps up the falling spit like it's my cum and spits it back out on the top of my dick just to watch it fall again.

"Christ almighty," I say. "Silas..."

He looks up at me, such a genuine gleam in his eyes.

But before I can think of anything else to say, he presses his nose to the other side of my shaft again and, just as slowly as before, breathes me in as he makes his way toward the base.

"Silas, I—"

But he doesn't even look up. He slowly makes his way toward my crotch. As he lowers down, I finally get a good look at his ass. And it's huge. And hairy. And every time he moves his body, the whole thing shakes.

I hear him breathe me in one more time, desperately so, and I know I can't hold back what I want any longer. I gotta say it.

"I want to fuck you," I finally say.

He removes his face from my crotch and looks up at me with a raised brow, my dick still dripping his spit.

"I know it's soon and not the most ideal place, but—"

"I want you to fuck me, too," he says.

And it feels like there are fireworks in my chest.

"Do you have lube?" I ask. But I feel like I already know the answer. I doubt it.

He furrows his brow for a second, then he perks up. "I got an idea," he says. "I'll be right back."

And that's when he stands up and rushes out of the room, leaving me naked with spit and precum dripping from my dick.

And for a moment, I'm lucid.

What the hell am I doing?

Sure, I'm about to fuck a handsome cowboy—one that I've been crushing on since I met him. Hell, since my mom made me privy to his existence.

But is he someone I'm willing to commit to?I'm not the kinda guy just to fuck and run away. I learned that when I was in college. I prefer the long-term. That's sort of why I wanted to come out. I was tired of doing intimate things in secret where they would inevitably wither away.

But can I be good for Silas? I know how risky it can be for a physical therapist to do anything with their patients. Yet this isn't the only thing giving me pause.

I hear the word 'faggot' echo in my mind again. And then I think of what Blake and my mom said.

And for a second, I think they may be right. Not only is it risky for my career to be openly gay in the NFO, but it also might be dangerous. There's a possibility that Blake is right—that I was the target of some hate crime by those Sparrows players. Which means I'm not exactly safe, especially if I go against his warning by getting well and returning to the field.

Would it be irresponsible to drag Silas into this world? Especially when it's clear he's got his own personal issues?

But Silas quickly walks back in and closes the door, so I have no time to think about the answer.

"Hope you're okay with coconut oil," he says, holding up a jar of it. "There was some in the break room."

I chuckle and shrug. "That could work."

His shoulders deflate. "Do you still want to do this?"

I take a moment to take him all in. He's standing at an angle, letting me see how big his ass really is. It's like he works out every day but the only thing he works on is his ass. Christ. And he's so hairy with the perfect percentage of beef. He's the guy I dreamed about dating in college.

But it's not just his looks. The way he's looking at me—he genuinely likes me. And the man fascinates me. He likes some of the most interesting music I've ever heard, and the way he touches and holds my body. There's an emotional intelligence that I should be jealous to have for myself. And most importantly, there's hurt there—hurt that I could help heal if he I let myself get to know him—if I let myself fall into him.

Screw what Blake and my mom have said. I was not the victim of a hate crime. At the very worst, I was called a slur, and I happened to be injured. That's all. Not only am I safe, but Silas should be safe, too. If he chooses to let himself fall into me, too.

"I absolutely do," I say, sitting up. "Come here and kiss me."

Silas crawls onto the table in between my spread legs and locks lips with mine. Somehow, he tastes sweeter than before.

He pulls away. "How do you want me?"

I put his hand behind his neck and pull him into me, greedy for his lips.

"I want you," I say, briefly taking a breath. "To have your ass face me. Put your legs on either side of the table. And I want to fuck you exactly how I'm sitting now."

He nods. He kisses me one more time, and with a swiftness that surprises me, he gets into position. And I swear I could cum from the sight of him alone. With his legs spread like this, it opens up his cheeks, and I can see just how hairy his hole is. I'm tempted to stick my face in there and get to know his smell, too, but I can't delay this any longer. I need to be inside Silas.

"God, you're fucking perfect," I say. "Just get a little closer."

He slowly inches back until the wet head of my dick presses against his hairy hole, and both of us nearly jump out of his skin.

"Fuck," he says. "That feels—I want that bad, Wyatt."

"I know," I say. "But I want you more."

He rolls the jar of coconut oil under his legs to me, and I can't help but laugh to myself. Here I am, using coconut oil to fuck my hot cowboy physical therapist in one of his patient rooms.

"What?" he asks. "Am I not clean or something?"

I stare at his pink, hairy hole. "Oh, your ass couldn't be more pristine."

He lowers his head, and even without seeing his face I can tell he's blushing. But then he also arches his body, flexing his back and triceps, then sticks his ass out even further back. If adrenaline wasn't pumping through me, I swear I'd pass out at the sight.

"I'm just laughing at the situation is all," I say. "Feels really junior high to fuck in the first private place we can find."

"Next time we can go to my place," he says. "I mean, of course if there is a next time."

I take some of the coconut oil and lather my dick, then I apply some to his hole, gently pushing my oil coated finger inside him. God, he's just the perfect amount of tight—the kind that will let me in but hold on for dear life.

He looks back at me. "Sorry if I made it weird."

I wrap my hand around him and press it against his chest. Then I push him upward until our bodies are spooning perpendicular to the bench. I kiss his neck, then his ear.

"Let's not worry about anything but the moment," I say. Truth is, I do want to see him again. But I just want to focus on the beautiful naked man in front of me. I want to give him as much pleasure as possible.

He pauses for a beat, then nods as I kiss the back of his neck. "Alright."

"Hey," I say, moving my hand up to the base of his neck. If I squeezed a little bit, I could choke him.

He turns his head to me. I see doubt on his face, so I want to reassure him.

"I like you, okay?" I say. "You're cool. You're handsome. You're sweet. I'm not blowing you off. Let's just both get lost in the moment, okay?"

Without pausing this time, he nods, and I feel reassured that he's relieved. I start to lower my hand from his neck, but he reaches up and stops me.

"Keep it there," he says. "Your strong hands—I liked it when you grab my neck. I want you to keep it there."

I increase the pressure of my grip around his neck. "Like this?"

He nods solemnly, and I know I've just found one of his buttons.

He lowers back down slowly, keeping his back arched, while my throbbing, coconut-oil-covered dick messes up the perfectly black hair that guards his hole. But now I have both hands around his neck, pressing lightly.

"This good?" I ask.

"Harder," he says.

I press my fingers into the sides of his neck. In college, I did this a couple times with another guy, and that's where I learned that you gotta put pressure on the sides of the neck, where the blood flows, rather than on the windpipe, unless the guy really wants to go hard.

"How's that?"

He lifts his hand up to give me a thumbs up.

"I'm gonna put it in now," I say, and he responds by pressing his ass into my dick. Man, I can't believe how horny this man is. And to think I almost didn't let this happen.

Gently, but steadily, I insert the head of my dick inside him—the head that he worshipped in a way I'd never seen before. Then the shaft of my dick that he so tenderly and painstakingly smelled. Fuck, Silas isn't just a handsome cowboy. He's a pervert. And I fucking love it.

Soon, I'm inside him completely, and my dick twitches from how good his hole feels. I was right. He's the perfect amount of tightness.

But Silas doesn't even so much as flinch. I press my fingers into his neck slightly harder, and all that does is make him press into me.

"How's that feel?" I ask.

"Harder," he says, his voice gruff. "I want it all hard. Choking. Fucking. I want you to bruise my insides. I want you to rearrange my guts. If you think you're going hard, you're not. Go harder."

His words make my stomach flutter. "You sure?"

"I'm positive," he says in the most serious voice I've heard from him, his hairy back taut and sweaty, his thighs flexing from keeping him upright on the table.

"Alright," I say, hoping I can live up to what he wants. "You say something if it's too much, you hear me?"

He nods. "Fucking go for it."

And I do. I pull my entire dick out, then slam it back inside. He whimpers slightly, but that's the only reaction I get. He doesn't want me to stop, so I'll keep going. I slam inside him again, my fingers wrapped tightly around his neck. And as I get into a rhythm, my dick lit up with more pleasure each time I slam inside him, a wicked grin forms on my face.

I could get used to this. A hot, slutty man who just wants me to use and abuse him? But who's actually really sweet and thoughtful? That sounds like heaven.

Using his neck as a handle, I hold on tight as I start fucking him as fast as I can. Sweat drips from my body to his and onto the table, but that doesn't matter. Because it's not enough. I need to go faster. Harder.

"Yeah," he says, low and deep. "Just like that. Fuck me like the slut I am."

Somehow, I pick up speed, going at a pace I don't know how I'm sustaining but I somehow do. I'm clapping his cheeks so hard and fast it sounds like an applause after one of my vocal performances back at Miss U.

Silas moans and lowers himself to his elbows, which makes me lose hold of his neck. But I don't let up on my speed. Instead, I grab the glorious fat around his waist as my handles. And that just gives me more force to rail him.

"Fucking slap me," Silas says. "Slap my ass."

I release one of my hands and bring it down, letting out a thunderous clap. It leaves a red mark against his pale, hairy ass.

"Harder," he says.

I lift the same hand higher and bring it down with even more force. This one sounds like it hurts, but I'm reassured when Silas moans 'yes', his head buried into the table.

"Keep slapping me," he says. "Keep fucking me."

Gripping his love handles hard enough to leave a mark, I occasionally let go to slap him hard. But I do so unexpectedly. Because every time it comes as a surprise to him, he either whimpers or moans, and I love hearing him so desperate for me.

Yet part of me feels slightly bad. Earlier, Silas just broke down in front of me. And sure we talked about it for a minute, but after he just dismissed it like it didn't happen. And I wish we could have talked about it. Because it looked like he was hurting, and I wanted to help.

But now we're fucking, and I'm slapping his ass hard. He likes it, but I only think this can stay as good as it feels now if it's not the only thing we do. I want to get to know him, too.

And suddenly, this position feels too impersonal. Sure, Silas has a sexy back and killer ass, but I don't want him to be just a body. I want him to be him.

"I wanna fuck you on your back," I say, slowly pulling out.

For some reason, I expect Silas to protest, wanting to stay in this more impersonal position. But without a word, he flips over, revealing his sweat-stained torso, and red, mustached face. His short hair is clamped down with moisture, and the sweat of his torso forms small little rivulets that move the hair along with it, like seaweed moving with the flow of a current along the ocean floor.

And the sight just makes me want to go swimming in him.

We don't even take a pause. Holding one of his legs in the air, I use my other hand to guide myself smoothly inside him. Then, I grab hold of his other ankle, and I slam him as hard as I can.

"Oh," Silas says, closing his eyes in ecstasy. "Wyatt, you feel so good."

I put his legs under my arms and behind my back, and he hugs them behind me. I lean over him. I'm the perfect height over him to where I can bend over and kiss him on the lips without a struggle, and that's what I do.

"Please look at me when I fuck you," I say, pulling away from his lips.

He opens his eyes immediately and looks into mine, our faces inches apart. He searches between them like he'll find buried treasure, and that only makes me fuck him harder.

But it doesn't feel deep enough.

I sit up and untangle his legs from behind me. I prop them up on my shoulders, then bend down over him again. I'm worried his legs won't be able to stretch this far, but pretty soon, I'm face to face with him again, running hands through his short hair.

"Goddamn, you're flexible," I say. "Fuck."

He smirks at me. "I take my stretches seriously," he says. "And you should too." He nods in the direction of my injured leg.

I laugh. "Don't worry. My leg's fine." I thrust into him so hard it takes his breath away. "But what we need to worry about is my third one."

"It's just as big as your other legs," he says, sighing through pursed lips. "Jesus."

I keep fucking him this way, my fingers buried into his shoulders, and it feels like heaven. That's when Silas moves my hands to his neck.

"Squeeze," he says. "Hard."

I wrap both hands around the sides of his neck and squeeze as hard and thoughtfully as I can. When I think I'm doing it too hard, he nods, communicating to me my grip is just right.

To help my balance, I sit up, still gripping and thrusting into him hard.

"Wyatt," he breathes out. "Put your weight on my neck. And keep fucking me."

I slow down for a minute. "You sure, Silas? I don't want to hurt you."

"You won't hurt me," he says. "Please."

So I accept his request. I lean over and press my weight into his neck, this time putting a little pressure on his windpipe.

"Oh," he says, reaching down to stroke his dick. "Like this. Keep fucking me and holding me like this."

And with how tight his face is with pleasure, I can't help but obey. I use all my strength—just like what I do in the last minute of any football game—and fuck him like crazy. I thrust into him at the fastest rate yet, and I have my entire upper body pressing into his neck.

"Fuck," he groans. "I'm gonna—"

His white-hot load shoots all the way to my wrists. I slow my pace and watch, mesmerized by the pleasure of his climax.

"Please, don't stop," he says. "Cum inside me. Please."

Seeing his pleasure, paired with hearing his desperation, it doesn't take me long. His legs still over my shoulders, I lean over into a half-plank position, my legs hanging off the table, and I go so fast that I'm afraid I'll knock both of us off. But seeing Silas so happy post-orgasm, his face flush with a smile, and his cum mixed with his sweaty torso hair, I cum before that can happen. I moan and thrust deep inside him, so entranced by my climax that I'm tempted to have another go right after this.

But as I come down, my body convulsing, Silas running his hands along my chest, I know that I have very little energy left in me. I'm sleeping well tonight.

I collapse onto the sweet, hot cowboy and find myself running tiny kisses all along his chest, neck and face. Then, finally, I rest my head against his shoulder, ready for sleep.

"Let's do this again?" Silas asks.

But just as I register his words, my eyelids grow heavy, and I fall asleep on his shoulder on the treatment table in the physical therapy clinic.

Chapter 10

Silas King

I HATE EMOTIONS. THEY'RE confusing. These past forty-eight hours, I don't know if I've been angry, scared, excited, bored, or happy. But once I park in the downtown gravel lot and make my way to Jimmy's diner on this cold and cloudy February day, I start to think I'm feeling some insidious combination of each o ne.

And it's all because of Wyatt Nelson.

When we were having the most explosively amazing sex of my life, I tried to get some reassurance from him that this wasn't going to be the only time—that we wouldn't just have sex and then go back to being strangers like has happened to me so often before.

And I never got it.

When I asked if there would be a next time—twice—he blew me off both times. The first time he just said that we should focus on the moment, and I was convinced enough. The second time? The sweaty lug fell asleep right on top of me. I had to wake him up, get him dressed, and help him all the way to his car so he wouldn't hurt his knee further, leaving me to clean up the mess we made in that patient room. I had to spray Febreze and light a candle to get rid of the sweaty stench, and even then it still lingered. Luckily it was gone when I checked the clinic this morning.

And since then? He's just said that he had a great time with me. I said I did, too, but I stopped myself from asking if we could see each other for a third time.

I think he made it clear by blowing me off twice that this was a one-and-done thing.

As I walk into the diner, I spot the buddies I'm meeting. Michael and Kyle are here to watch the Championship Game with Tanner and Jimmy, and I'll be joining them, too. I try to shake all the loose emotions from my body, but it's no use. I feel uneasy. Any moment of free time today, I've listened to music that usually always subdues me, but I'm hardly consoled. All I can think about is Wyatt squeezing my neck and shoving his fat dick into my—

"Silas!" Jimmy says, waving to me. I nod and walk over to them.

Michael slides out of the booth and gives me a warm hug, followed by Kyle.

"Good to see both of you," I say, adjusting my cowboy hat.

"Likewise," Michael says, patting my elbow.

"How's your residency?" Kyle asks as I shimmy on next to Jimmy across from them.

I sigh. "Well, I would say it pays the bills, but even then I'd be lying."

He frowns. "I know the NFO really prioritizes those with residencies," he says. "But I know that's not very helpful. Wish I could do more. If I was still with the Tigers, I could get you a position easily."

"Yeah, it's a shame," Tanner, Jimmy's fiancé, says, poking his head in front of Jimmy. "I know that the Seals were looking for a couple just as I retired. If only I coulda gotten them to hire you then."

"Hey, I appreciate it," I say, uncomfortable with all the attention. "But I'll figure something out. I can always help out Martha and Llewellyn again if things go South, so no need to worry."

"We'll keep our eyes peeled," Kyle says.

"Appreciate it."

Michael, Tanner, and Jimmy start talking about the Championship game—Vanguards vs. Sparrows—and I catch Michael's eye from across the table.

"How goes it, Mr. Author?" I ask.

He smiles and takes a sip of his water. "Have a contract for a fantasy trilogy," he says. "And that's been a struggle."

"A trilogy, huh?" I ask, folding my arms. "That's cool that they're paying you to write three books instead of one."

"Yeah," he says with a raise of his brow. "You would think. But a trilogy has to be perfectly planned. When you write a novel, there's always a certain structure that you gotta follow—you know, important things happen at the ten percent, fifty percent, eighty percent mark, and so on."

"Sure," I say, fiddling with my straw paper as if I understand all that Michael's saying. I enjoy reading, but writing is just beyond me.

"But with a trilogy, you don't just plan those moments for the book. You plan them for the whole series, too. So you have to make sure everything aligns. Lots of planning and work."

"Sheesh," I say. "Well, I've read your stuff, and I'd say if anyone can do it, you can."

"Awh," Michael says, flattered. "Thank you."

"I mean it," I say. "You'll figure it out."

After Lilah, one of Jimmy's managers, takes our order, Michael gets to asking me about my residency, and I deflate slightly. But there's something familiar and comfortable about that. For the past two days, I've been on edge—feeling all these emotions, like I said. And I'm not used to it.

But sadness? That I'm used to. And telling Michael all about egotistical football players that I have to deal with, paired with the uncertainty of what job I'll hold afterwards, helps me return to my melancholy like putting on an old shirt. It's not like I *like* feeling sad, but when that's all I've felt for the past couple years? It's safe. Familiar.

And it's the exact opposite of how Wyatt Nelson makes me feel.

"Well, well, well," a strong voice almost sings out. A Southern voice. One from Texas.

My stomach curdles as I turn to face the man of the hour himself.

"Wyatt Nelson," Kyle says, standing up. He leans over Michael and the table to hug him.

"No time no see, man," Tanner says, reaching out to shake his head.

"Tell me about it," Wyatt says, shaking his hand back. He's without his crutches, wearing a brace only. I told him he didn't need to use crutches as long as he did, but he wanted to be safe. Guess he finally took my advice.

What am I talking about? Wyatt wants nothing to do with me.

"Wyatt, this is my fiancé, Michael," Kyle says, sitting down.

"Nice to meet you," Michael says.

"We're getting married later this year," Kyle continues.

"Right on right on," Wyatt says, folding his arms. "I still remember watching that half-time show where he apologized to you, Michael. That was really something."

Michael blushes and puts his hand on Kyle's knee. "It really was."

"Sit down!" Kyle implores. "I invited you to watch the Championship Game *and* have dinner with us."

Wyatt smiles. "Alright, you got me." And Wyatt sits, taking his place next to Michael.

Right across from me.

For a moment, we lock eyes as his chin rests on his fist.

And then he does the unthinkable.

He winks at me.

My stomach turns over itself as Tanner introduces him to Jimmy, his fiancé. And Wyatt greets him, as if his wink alone didn't just shoot me out of my accustomed sadness right into the storm of feelings I don't know how to handle. It was easier to think that Wyatt just wasn't interested in me. But after this wink? I can't pretend that he doesn't.

"And have you met Silas?" Kyle asks him.

Wyatt meets my eyes again, and he thankfully doesn't wink this time. But he does look at me with this smolder that could make the icy moons around Saturn melt. He adjusts his legs underneath the table, and suddenly, his good leg is pressed to the side of one of mine, and I swear I can feel the heat of his leg through my jeans.

"I have," he says, still looking at me. "He's helping me recover."

"No way," Jimmy says, squeezing my arm. "You didn't tell us you were helping out an NFO player."

I huff air out of my nose as Lilah takes Wyatt's order. "We've only been going for about a week," I say. "It's no big deal."

"It is a big deal if you want to work in the NFO," Kyle says. "Hell, he could get you set up right now if he wanted."

My stomach lurches as Wyatt looks over at me, his brows scrunched like he's seeing me as a completely new person.

"I didn't know you wanted to work in the NFO," he says, his leg pressing even harder into me—just like how he was balls deep in me two nights ago.

I sigh, trying to hide my blush, but my face burns under the gazes of every man at this table.

"I was gonna get around to asking you about how that could happen," I say, looking down at the table. "But I didn't want to bring it up right away."

Wyatt's leg weighs heavier against mine, and I move it so I don't have to feel him against me. Thankfully, he doesn't try to follow.

"Could it happen?" Kyle asks Wyatt.

"Oh, yeah," Wyatt says as if it's nothing, as if I haven't dreamed of working in the NFO since I was in middle school. Yeah, he and I could never work. Wyatt's probably had everything he's wanted at the tips of his fingertips, while I've had to scrape and bleed just to get by. We're nothing alike. Plus, if he does get me this position in the NFO, it would surely be a conflict of interest if we were together. Even if being gay in the NFO is supposedly okay.

"You're in your residency, right?" Wyatt asks.

I nod, still playing with my straw wrapper.

"Well, since you don't have a ton of industry experience, it might be a stretch, but you are a resident for one of the best college football teams in the country," Wyatt says. "I'm sure I could easily convince them to hire you on probation or something."

My heart picks up speed, and I try to calm it. "Really?" I ask.

"Yeah," he says, giving me that smolder again. "Easy."

I look away and adjust my legs, this time running right into his. I try to move it them, but now his injured leg is sandwiching them in. And I don't want to put any stress on that. So I keep my legs where they are—not because I like touching Wyatt like this, but because I have no choice.

Our food arrives, and everyone, including Michael, gets to talking about the game this afternoon, which gives me the quiet and solace I so desperately want right now. Occasionally, Wyatt's leg bumps against mine, and I have to resist glaring at him. I don't want to be rude, but even more importantly, I don't want others knowing that Wyatt and I slept together. And for some reason, I feel like being a dick to him will be a dead giveaway.

But as we eat, I hear the echoes of one of my favorite Eluvium songs in my head—"Don't Get Any Closer". It's a steady 6:8 rhythm, reminding me of a slow march. The title represents exactly how I feel about Wyatt right now. I don't want him any closer. And it isn't just because I don't want to compromise my career as a PT.

But it's also because I don't like the way this feels.

The past two nights, when I've opened the box underneath my nightstand, I don't think I've ever written such confident x's next to the date before.

And, bizarrely enough, I hate that. I hate it so much.

Because, back in college, when darkness started visiting me regularly, when I slowly began to realize that loneliness would be my closest companion and shame my most frequent visitor, suicide became a privilege. An anchor keeping me steady in the storm that Wyatt described so well. After all, if life became too unbearable, how wonderfully gentle is it to know that I could guarantee its end? That I could press 'Pause' and then 'Quit' in this game called life? Suicide, in a way, has been my one and only refuge.

And Wyatt has taken this away from me.

Because, for what feels like the first time in my life, suicide isn't on my mind. Instead, I'm mentally replaying Wyatt fucking me deep and hard. I'm replaying the memories of him describing his thoughts about my music. I'm replaying him singing that Italian opera song.

In short: instead of the dark wraith in my head, I see him.

And I know this isn't healthy. I know that one person shouldn't have such emotional sway over me. Hell, this is partly why I've avoided boys, dates, and hookups for so long. I knew what effect they could have on me if they went well.

But there's a teeny, tiny part of me that tells me that this is good. That this is just what I've needed. Because I think this teeny, tiny part of me not only wants to stay alive. It also wants me to learn how to live in a way where suicide doesn't have to be my anchor.

"Hey man," Jimmy says, nudging my arm. "You good?"

I shake myself from my thoughts and look over to him. "Yeah, why?"

"You got that spacy look," he says.

"I'm good," I lie. "I promise."

"You know you can talk to me."

"I know," I say, picking up one of my fries.

Jimmy looks in my direction for a little longer, lingering on the conversation, then nods and lets me be.

I wish I could tell him everything. I really do. But I wouldn't even know what words to use. Plus, he and all the others would think I'm crazy. It's best to keep this to myself.

We finish up eating, and I try my best to keep myself looking content. But I don't think it's working. Because not only does Michael eye me during our meal, asking silently if I'm okay, but Wyatt even notices my funk. He kicks me once, asking 'you good?' with a subtle gesture. I just give him a thumbs up.

"Well," Kyle says, leaning back into the corner of the booth. He puts his arm around Michael, and they snuggle into each other. "We ready to go watch the game?"

Tanner wipes his mouth with a napkin. "I think we're ready." He turns to Jimmy. "Assuming the cabin's in order?"

"It's all clean," Jimmy says. "And I got us a bunch of snacks, too."

Kyle pats his belly. "I love Championship Game Sunday even more now that I'm retired," he says. "It's like a holiday."

"Amen," Tanner says.

After Lilah takes our payment, Wyatt and I shimmy out of the booth, and the others follow. Jimmy and Kyle are arguing about who's best set up to win, with Tanner and Michael following just behind. I think they're talking about video games if I'm hearing them correctly.

And then there's me. All I have on my mind is the repeating 6:8 pattern from "Don't Get Any Closer". And it's fitting. Because I feel myself drifting farther and farther away from my friends. Maybe it's best I just be alone tonight. Maybe it's best that I don't stay and watch the Championship Game. Especially if Wyatt's gonna be there.

"Alright," Jimmy says, taking his car keys from Tanner. "Assuming I'll see y'all back at our place?"

"We'll be there," Michael says, he and Kyle walking to their car.

"See you soon," Wyatt says.

But I just stand there like an indecisive idiot.

"Silas," Jimmy says, leaning on his car door. "You're still coming, right?"

Above, the clouds have darkened, threatening rain. Fitting for my mood. But at least it's comfortable and safe. Sadness, as overwhelming and obviously depressing as it is, is what I know best. And to get Wyatt off my mind, it might be best to stew in it.

"Come on, man," Wyatt says, stepping toward me. "Join us. I can talk to you about getting a job with the Pioneers."

My stomach lifts, and I'm overwhelmed by another emotion besides sadness: excitement. I look around at my friends, and they all stare back, waiting on my answer.

And these *are* my friends. I know these guys, as well as Martha, Llewellyn, and Linda genuinely care about me. I should at least spend some time with them, even if my heart's not in it.

And there's Wyatt. I don't want to hang out with him because he's cute or anything. He just said himself that he could probably get me a job in the NFO with the Pioneers.

"Alright," I say, starting toward my car. "I'll see you there."

Jimmy and Kyle cheer as I walk away, and I'm not looking back, but I swear I can feel Wyatt's gaze burning into the back of my head. Or my ass. Either way, I wouldn't be disappointed.

By the time we all make it to Jimmy and Tanner's place, it's pouring. We all hurry inside, and Jimmy turns on the lights as we take off our shoes. I've seen their home a couple times, but I love it every time I'm here. I swear it's my favorite cabin in Glamour Springs.

The front door leads into a big, wooden hallway constructed of dark logs. There's a doorway to our left that has stairs leading up to the second floor where the master bedroom and bathroom are located. On the right we have another entryway into the massive kitchen. Jimmy and Tanner go in there now, likely to grab all the snacks.

The rest of us walk into the main area, and it always takes my breath away. The far wall is covered in windows taller than Wyatt that face out onto the lake, which is a sight to see with the pouring rain. There's a chimney right in the middle just turning on, and before that sits one giant U-shaped couch covered in comfortable pillows and blankets. I'm glad I came here. This will be cozy as hell.

Wyatt nudges me. "This is better than my cabin, huh," he says.

I laugh and nod, rubbing where he touched me. We're close enough to where I can smell him, and there's hints of how he smelled a couple nights ago—the night were I fucking rubbed my nose all over his body. Christ, I was a fucking pig. And I did all that for him just to basically ghost me. Fuck. Maybe I don't want the job with the Pioneers after all. That would mean I would have to see Wyatt Nelson all the time.

Okay, no, I do need that job. But I'm still embarrassed.

"Alright," Jimmy says, walking out with a tray of popcorn, chocolates, cheeseballs, chicken nuggets, and a host of other things. He sets it down on the ottoman inside the U of the couch. "Let's get this started."

Tanner turns on the TV just as the Vanguards and Sparrows are warming up. It's snowing over in Kansas where they're playing. Above, the rain patters against the roof, and I decide I just might take a nap while the game's on. I love football, but I enjoy cozy cabin time in the rain a little bit more.

We all take our seats. Kyle and Michael sit together on one leg of the couch, while Jimmy and Tanner take the other, leaving the middle for me and Wyatt to sit together. He gets there first, and to my chagrin, sits right in the little, not giving me the room to spread out and lay down. Flustered, I sit by the armrest next to Jimmy as far away from him as I can.

Soon, kickoff begins, and Jimmy and Kyle are already losing their shit. Michael just laughs and occasionally reads the book he brought, while Tanner's playing on his Nintendo Switch and looking up only when Kyle and Jimmy react to something.

Wyatt, on the other hand, is a perfect balance of everyone in the room. He's attentive—sitting on the edge of the couch with his legs spread, watching the TV intently, and only cheering when something monumental happens. He glances at me, likely sensing that I'm looking at him, and I immediately turn to the TV.

He leans back into the couch, and now I can't resist looking at him. The angle he's sitting at is the exact same as the other night when I worshipped his whole body. I can see how his huge pecs protrude from his chest, and his bearded, scraggly face looks more handsome from the side. Part of me wishes I could just strip my clothes and straddle him right now.

Wyatt removes the brace on his left knee and starts doing some stretches. He winces as he extends his leg all the way out and back in a rapid manner, almost as if he's trying to loosen it or get it to pop.

"Woah there," I say, scooching closer to him, afraid he'll hurt himself. He's my patient, after all. "Can I help you with that?"

He turns to me, and there's a slight tug upward on his lips. "Be my guest."

I close the distance between us. I reach out to grab his leg, but it's hard to help him stretch from the side.

"Here," I say, still holding his leg. "Turn to the side and rest your legs on me."

He shifts and rests his thighs on my lap, and the movement wafts the smell of his feet up to my nose. For a second, I freeze, intoxicated. He smells just like he did two nights ago. And now his thick, hairy thighs are resting right on mine. What the fuck was I thinking trying to help him stretch right here and right n ow?

I sigh and start working through some stretches for him. I'm here, so I might as well help.

"Mmm," he says. "That feels good."

I bite my lip and try to hold my breath. Because the more I breathe, the more I take his scent in. And it's driving me wild.

Feeling my crotch stir, I slide down so his legs are resting on my lower stomach rather than my thighs. While I'm helping Wyatt stretch, the rain intensifies above, which acts as a sedative for me. Pretty soon, I find my eyelids growing heavy. Half-asleep, I shift my legs up onto the couch. Without a thought, I close my eyes, scooch up, and rest my head on something soft and warm.

I wake up some time later to the sound of Jimmy's laugh. My head shoots up, and he looks at me with a forced frown.

"Sorry to wake you," he says.

"It's okay," I say, yawning. I lower my head, and something hairy tickles my nose. I take a deep breath, and I smell something familiar—something I smelled two nights ago when Wyatt fucked me in a patient room.

Completely alert, I lift my head again, and it feels like a cement block has fallen in my stomach. Wyatt stares up at me, a stupid grin on his face. Looking down, I see that I fell asleep on his bare belly. There's a shape the size of my face where his belly hair is flattened. And that scent—I smelled it because my face was only inches away from his crotch.

"Sorry," I say, sitting up. "I didn't realize that was—"

"It's all good," Wyatt says, sitting up.

Everyone in the room eyes us for just a moment, and I know what they're all thinking—that I'm no longer about to be the single person in the friend group. But no, that's not happening. Wyatt and I fucked, but it's clear he just wanted a one-time thing. And I just made a huge mistake letting myself fall asleep on him. I don't want him thinking I'm into him at all. Especially if he's about to help me get a job.

I gently move his legs off me just as the half-time show begins. It's Beyonce performing this year.

"I'm gonna go get some water," I say. I quickly pass through Kyle and Michael's line of sight and rush into the kitchen. In there, I wipe my eyes and fill a glass of water. I watch Beyonce's performance as I take a sip.

Part of me wants to leave right now. I know Jimmy and Michael and the others are my friends, but I don't want to be around Wyatt anymore. It's confusing—all these feelings he's bringing up in me. And I don't want him thinking I'm into him when he clearly has no interest in me anymore.

I turn around to pour the rest of my water in the sink, and that's when I hear footsteps into the kitchen.

"I'm good," I say, anticipating it's Jimmy. "I just wanted something to dri—"

But I can't finish my sentence. Because when I turn around, it's the last man I want to talk to."I believe you," Wyatt says, approaching me. It feels like my heart stops and starts again as he passes me. He grabs a glass and starts filling it up.

"So it's true you want to work in the NFO?" he asks.

There's a hot pain in my sternum. I think it's anger. Because it's been forty-eight hours since Wyatt not only gave me the best sex of my life but also replaced my sadness with a whole host of confusing emotions. Yet all he's managed to say is that he's had a good time. And now he wants to talk about something else? This guy's nothing more than a fuckboy.

"I do," I say, leaning against the counter and crossing my arms. I know I could go out and join the others, but the curious part of me—the stronger part—wants to stay here and hear how Wyatt can help me get a job in the NFO.

"I could easily get you an interview with our head PT," he says, then takes a sip of water. He's leaning nonchalantly against the sink across from me.

With the way he's talking, it feels like he's asking me out. So I'm tempted to say 'no'. But I would be an idiot to turn this down.

"Would you really do that?" I ask.

"Like I said, it would be easy," he says, pouring out the rest of his water. He barely took a sip, so he clearly didn't just come in here for a drink.

"Wouldn't be a guarantee," he continues. "But I'm pretty sure I could get you on probation. Six months or so. Prove yourself with the team and then we might keep you on for good."

Butterflies flutter in my stomach.

This would mean everything. It would mean a higher salary, so I could actually start paying back my student loans. It would mean moving to a new place—Salt Lake City, which would be pretty cool. And most importantly, it would mean that I finally got the big boy job my parents said I was never good enough to get.

"Could you put in a word for me?" I ask.

He frowns for a minute, then nods. "I can."

In the other room, I hear my friends comment on Beyonce's performance. I don't want them to wonder what the two of us are doing in here alone. We need to wrap this up.

"Well thanks," I say. "Let me know what I need to do for the process." And then I turn and walk to get the hell out of that kitchen, not wanting to be alone with Wyatt for a moment longer.

"Silas," he says, rich and deep.

I pause at the kitchen door.

"I want to talk to you," he says.

If Wyatt had the ability to see into the dimension where emotions reside, he would see the blue and black little ball in my stomach explode into purples and reds and oranges and greens and yellows. Hell, he'd probably see colors that fall outside of the visible spectrum. In short, he'd see all the emotions he stirs within me. But most of all, he'd see a bright red ball glowing in my chest. Because, more than anything, I'm angry that he has this effect on me.

I turn around and take my place back at the counter across from him, my arms crossed. I reach up to adjust my hat, but I realize I left it on the couch after I fell asleep on his hairy body. Wyatt just stares at me like I'm the cutest thing in the world and that it was inevitable for us to find each other alone.

"I finished my playlist for you."

My stomach bunches up. "You remembered?"

He chuckles, then crosses his arms, making both them and his chest bunch up and flex. "Of course. Just took me a minute to get it together."

I shift on my feet. Part of how I calculated Wyatt to be the asshole he is—the asshole I want him to be—was with his failure to provide me a playlist. As I mentioned, he gave me that promise as a way to secure seeing me again—as a way to get us to fuck. And now that we have, it wouldn't make sense for him to finish the playlist based on my calculation that he's an asshole.

But he finished the playlist.

So my calculations are wrong.

I don't think he's trying to have a one-and-done hookup.

"Well," I say. "Does it have that Italian song that you showed?" *The one where you sound like a goddamn angel?*

"I have a playlist on Spotify for just some general classical art songs and arias that I think you'll like," he says. "And then one on YouTube where I have recordings of me singing."

My stomach twists over itself. I hate to admit it, but I'm excited to hear Wyatt's huge voice again.

He stares at me with his huge arms still crossed, as if expecting me to say something.

"Can't wait to hear it," I say. "You should send it over."

Over in the other room, the half-time show ends, which means the game's about to start back up. I would expect Wyatt to rush in there to watch it. He's still in the NFO after all, and the Pioneers have been doing pretty well lately. They have a shot at making it to the end. So why is he not going in there to watch how the best teams are playing?

"I didn't just come in here because I wanted to talk about getting you into the NFO," he says. "Though I am happy to do that."

There's another sharp pain in my sternum. I reach up to rub it. "And that is?"

He pushes himself off the counter and stands right in front of me. He grabs both of my hands, which feel tiny compared to his, and holds them up between us. Both his thumbs run over my knuckles, which is more soothing than I would expect. And 'soothing' is exactly what I need considering how fast my heart is racing.

I look up at him, and he's staring down at me intently. Like he's choosing to be here, touching me like this. Like he wouldn't rather be anywhere else. Like I'm everything to him.

"I had a really good time the other night," he says.

I scoff and look away. "Yeah, it was good, I guess."

He gently squeezes my hands. "You didn't think so?"

I look back at him, and there's genuine hurt in his eyes.

"No, I—" I shake my head. Of course the hottest man ever is trying to be intimate and I'm somehow fucking it up.

"I loved it," I say, with a little too much enthusiasm. "It was great," I say, toning it down. "I just—"

His brow furrows. "What?"

I sigh. "I just thought that—since—you know." I trill my lips. "When I didn't hear back from you, I thought that that was all you wanted—just a one-night stand or whatever." I wince, equally afraid that I'm still exactly right or that he'll be upset I'm judging him for being a fuckboy.

He places his hands on the sides of my arms, and I get a feeling that it's neither.

"Look at me," he says.

And I obey.

"I thought the same thing about you," he says. "That you weren't interested after the sex either."

I recoil, almost grimacing. "Are you serious?"

He nods. "I didn't hear from you either."

"But," I say. "I tried—" I recall our conversation. "I asked about a next time, and you just said not to worry."

He lets go and steps back. He wipes his face, laughing. "Yeah, because I had my mind too focused on fucking you right."

I shake my head. "But then, after it was all done, I asked if you wanted to do it again, and you—"

"If I remember correctly," he says, leaning against the counter again. "I fell asleep on you."

I nod. "So you were asleep."

As I'm looking away and scratching my arm, embarrassed, Wyatt closes the distance between us. He places his hands around the base of my neck, softly this time, and gently presses a kiss against his forehead, and I swear this act alone generates enough electricity in me to power the entire town of Glamour Springs.

"Seems like we both misunderstood," he says softly as our eyes meet.

I let out a nervous laugh. "I guess we did." Which makes no sense. It seemed so certain to me that Wyatt wasn't interested in me based on the evidence that I had. After I didn't hear much from him over these last couple days, that was the nail in the coffin.

But Wyatt's right. I didn't reach out either, so he was making similar conclusions about me. Yet he was the one brave enough to confront me about it. And I just planned on icing him out.

I sigh and start rubbing my head.

"What's wrong?" he asks.

"I'm sorry," I say. "I'm just—it's been a while since I've been in any sort of relationship."

He just stares at me, listening.

"Not that we have a relationship. Fuck, I'm sorry," I say, rubbing the bridge of my nose.

He grabs the sides of my arms again and plants another kiss on my forehead, and this time he lets it linger. Then, he plants another kiss between my eyebrows, the bridge of my nose, the tip of my nose. And just when I'm expecting to meet his lips, he pulls away.

"I like you, Silas," he says. "And I want to keep getting to know you."

"What?" I ask, almost laughing, my body still electrified from his kisses. "You want to date me or something?"

He shrugs. "Actually, yeah."

It feels like there's a storm inside me, all these emotions that Wyatt elicits the cause. I'm excited for what a relationship with Wyatt could be, but I'm also afraid of all that could happen. I'm angry that his charm alone makes my sadness go away, but I feel so happy around him. When you've felt sadness most of your life, everything else feels alien. Right now, I only get stirred up when I think about or am around Wyatt. Yet if I were to date him, these emotions would be ever present. I would be living permanently in this storm.

"Listen," he says, putting his hands on my shoulders. "We could take it slow. Just dates and stuff. I'll be in Glamour Springs for a while, and I could find another therapist so there's no conflict of interest. But most importantly, I want to reassure you that I won't be like Kyle or Tanner."

I furrow my brow. "What do you mean?"

He looks over to the living room, gesturing to them, even though all we can see is the TV. Then he looks back at me, probably content that they can't hear.

"I came out," he says. "I know who I am. I know what I want. So with me, you won't have to worry about any internalized homophobic bullshit. You'll have me and all of me."

The pain in my sternum returns, and it's hotter than ever.

I hate to admit it, but that's part of the problem. What was nice about Wyatt blowing off my requests to see him again was that this was a sufficient excuse to let him go. Similarly, if he was still in the closet, that would be the easiest excuse ever to push him away.

But there's no discernible reason to keep Wyatt at arm's length. Especially with how much I already genuinely like him. There is my job, but yeah—he could easily find another therapist.

The haunting 6:8 melody of "Don't Get Any Closer" increases in volume in my head. A huge part of me wants to push Wyatt off me. It wants to go home, curl under my blanket with my cat Chesire nearby, and sleep all this away. It wants to peddle off Wyatt as a client to someone else and find some other way to fulfill my dream of working in the NFO. It wants to go back to what I'm used to: sadness.

And an even bigger part of me is screaming that this is unhealthy. The emotional sway this man has over me is diabolical. And if I jump into a relationship with him, I just know that my mood would depend on him so heavily. If I perceived anything as a rejection, I know I would crash. I just know I would. Similarly, if anything was ever good, I'd be over the moon. Hell, not just over the moon—I'd be in outer space. And the come down from this euphoria, I already know, would be terrifying.

But then there's a tiny part of me that says something completely different—a part that, though small, shines brighter than all the rest. It tells me that I've lived my life long enough under the shroud of depression and loneliness. And that maybe, just maybe, Wyatt may be the person who helps me feel different—no matter how fleeting the relationship could be. I feel like I'd be a fool to give up the only person who makes me feel happy. And though I hear the voices of my parents loudly telling me otherwise, don't I deserve something good? For once?

"But if we do this," he says. "I can't help you get a job in the NFO."

It feels like someone is squeezing my heart in their fist. "What? Why?"

He folds his arms and steps back to lean against the counter. "I'm sure you never dated a patient."

My eyes widen as I realize the predicament. "I haven't."

He rubs the bridge of his nose. "The Pioneers would never hire you if they knew we were dating. And they'd fire you and punish me if they found out later on. I don't have any strong connections with other teams, so that's not an option, either."

Suddenly, it becomes difficult to breathe.

Of course this is the situation. I'm presented with two things I've always wanted: to be happy and to get my dream job. Yet I can't have both. The universe is fucking laughing at me right now.

"But if we ended things between us now, I could easily recommend you the Pioneers. You'd be interviewed. Hired. And no one would know about our past."

"But then we couldn't date," I say.

He nods, his lips thinned. "Correct."

I chew on my lips, my arms tightly folded.

I can choose between a man who sees me so vividly—who described the emotional connection to my music better than I could. Who fucked me into the next dimension. Who would help me advance my career—even if it meant we couldn't be together.

Or I can choose to finally be the successful man I always dreamed of being. I'd finally be able to prove my parents wrong.

"The choice is yours," he says, pulling on his red beard. "You have a lot more to gain than just a relationship."

I nod as "Don't Get Any Closer" gets louder in my head. Maybe this predicament is a good thing. Maybe the universe is looking out for me by making it impossible for me to have both things at once. Because if I date Wyatt, I'll be happy, but I'll probably go insane, too. But if I choose my career, I'll have money, stability, and cachet. Which, I think, would make me happier in the long run.

"I think," I say, wincing. "I wanna shoot for being a PT for the Tigers."

He nods, biting his lip. "I get it. I'm happy to help."

"I'm sorry," I say.

He shrugs. "Not your fault," he says. "Just the way it is. Funny how it's not even a homophobic thing holding us apart. It's just organizational logistics."

"Yeah," I say with a dry laugh. "Funny."

"But you still wanna help me recover while I'm here?"

"Of course."

He gives me a lukewarm, mouthless smile. "Thanks." He pushes himself off the sink and pats me on the shoulder as he makes his way out of the kitchen. "I'll text you the details about the Pioneers."

But then he stops at the door and pauses, and my heart picks up speed.

"Do you still want my playlist?" he asks.

I shift on my feet. I know that's probably not a good idea, but having it would be like a memento of him, a help to not forget what we could have been. I think I at least want that.

"Yes," I say.

He pats the doorframe. "I'll get it to you tonight," he says. Then he's gone.

And I feel my entire body deflate.

All the colors in my body that Wyatt brought out before—purple, green, orange, red, yellow—are slowly shifting back to black and blue in the pit of my stomach. Which is good, I guess. It's what I'm used to.

Yet I can't help but hear that tiny, bright part of me yelling that I just made the wrong decision.

Chapter 11

Wyatt Nelson

"WHAT ARE YOU ORDERING?" my mom asks.

We sit in Jimmy's diner just as the morning sun begins to shine. It's early March, and the weather's already starting to warm up here in Glamour Springs.

"Pancake's look good," I say. "Jimmy says that's what his place is known for."

My mom sucks on her lips. "You sure? How are your exercises with Silas going?"

My stomach clenches.

Silas.

The one who got away.

We didn't just have the best sex ever. I felt connected to the man. He shared his music with me. He opened up with me about how much it means to him. I saw the hurt in his eyes.

And we almost got together.

But he's wanted to work in the NFO for a while. I told him I could get him on staff as a physical therapist and athletic trainer, but if I did, we'd have to keep it professional. No sharing music. No sex. No dating.

And that's what he chose.

I almost wish I didn't tell him I could get him a job. That way, I could have dated him while I was living here in Glamour Springs. That way, I'd not only have been an out football player at the top of his career but also one with a partner—a gay football player brave enough to be who he is. I'd have shown the world that we gays are just as good as any straight player.

"Wyatt?" she asks. "You there?"

When I come to, I find myself staring at the window at the wet grass.

"Yeah," I say flatly. "Exercises are good."

Ever since he asked me to talk to Pioneer's staff about getting him hired, he and I have continued to meet, but we've kept it boring and professional. We meet at his clinic—during his office hours now—and he helps me with my exercises. We talk cordially. Then I leave. Meanwhile, I've given the Pioneers' head PT my recommendation for Silas. They said they'd reach out to him and see if he's a good fit. But now that Silas and I aren't talking personally, I don't know how it's going. And part of me is selfishly hoping that he doesn't get hired. Because that will give us another chance.

My new friend Jimmy comes and takes our order. After he leaves, I get an idea. He's close to Silas. Maybe he knows if he's been hired yet.

"So you decided on the pancakes," Mom says.

I take a long sip of my water, taking my time to prolong talking to her.

"Is there a problem?" I ask.

She sighs. "You need to be eating well. You need to be ready for the season to start."

"Mom," I say, rubbing my brow. "I care about my performance just as much as you do. But I can afford to relax every now and then. Especially when it's off season and I'm recovering."

"I'm just saying," she says. "Every little thing counts."

I fold my arms and rest my head back against the booth. I agreed to breakfast with my mom not just because she's asked me to but also for what she told me before I came out here to stay with her. She apologized for the way she treated me when I was younger and said that she wanted to be a better mother. The entire time I've been here, I've been hoping to see some of these efforts. But she's continuing to be the same kinda woman I grew up with: controlling and invasive.

Jimmy comes with our food—an egg-white spinach omelet for mom and pancakes with a side of sausage for me. As he sets the plate in front of me, my mom grimaces, and anger starts to heat up in my chest. I didn't come here to be continually judged by my mom. I came here because I thought things would get better. If she's gonna keep making me feel bad for taking care of myself in the way that I feel is best, then I may just leave. I don't need to be here, after all. Especially now that Silas and I can't be a thing.

"As you know," Mom says, cutting up her omelet. "There's a new gym that opened up in Glamour Springs."

I give her a microscopic nod and stick a piece of sausage in my mouth. Glamour Springs has apparently been growing pretty rapidly, so it makes sense for commercial gyms to open up shop here.

"I figured I'd go there with Linda and some of my new girlfriends," she says. "But I also got the family plan so you could go."

I stop cutting my pancakes and glare up at her. "Mom, I can't workout at a commercial gym."

She swats her hand at me like my concern is nothing.

"It's a nice gym. It has a ton of weights, a sled, ropes, even tires—you know, all the things you'd have in an NFO gym."

I pour a hefty amount of syrup on my pancakes. I see what she's doing here.

"Mom, I work out at the physical therapist's clinic, mostly with Silas," I say.

She half-scoffs. "Well I'm sure they don't have all the equipment that the gym has."

I half-scowl in return. "They surely don't have the equipment or trainer I need to make sure I won't injure myself further." I shake my head. "And even if I could get a good workout in a commercial gym, I'd be recognized immediately. Hell, even while we've been here, I've been getting some looks. I'm not just a good tight end. I'm the biggest out player right now. The ESB is constantly talking about me. I'd surely be recognized."

She rolls her eyes.

"What?" I ask. "Is this some joke to you?"

She takes a sip of her water and dabs her face with her napkin. "I'm not saying it's a joke," she says. "I just think you're letting other things get in the way of your playing."

I sigh through my pursed lips, feeling my heartrate increase. It's not even 9AM, and yet Mom wants to start with me.

"Mom, being gay is who I am. It's not getting in the way of my playing. It *is* my playing. Being straight has never affected a man's performance. Why should it stop mine?"

"I know, I know," she says, almost condescendingly—like being gay is a phase that I'll soon pass through and not care about.

"Mom," I say, my chest burning with anger now.

"Look, honey," she says. "Just eat your pancakes."

I thin my lips as she continues eating. Now, because she told me to, I don't even want to touch them. I finish off the rest of my sausage quickly and glare out the window, trying to calm my racing heart.

Why do I do this with her? Clearly, she's not willing to see from my perspective. It's pointless to try and reason with her. And if she's going to continue harassing me about my playing and my sexuality, then I don't see a reason to even be around her.

After we pay Jimmy, we both slide out of the booth. But I'm not ready to leave just yet.

"I'll meet you in the car," I say as we walk toward the door. "Wanna talk to Jimmy about something."

She gives me a quizzical look.

"It's, uh—" I pull on my beard and think. "His fiancé Tanner had some advice for me about recovering from my injury," I say.

She nods and opens the diner door. "I'll be in the car."

When she leaves, there's a noticeable weight that's lifted off my shoulders. It makes me realize how on edge I've been living with my parents—well, my mom. My dad is so absent, both literally and metaphorically, that I hardly notice him around. But she's enough of a helicopter parent, even when I'm twenty-eight, to compensate.

Jimmy's wiping down one of the booths, wearing an apron that says 'Kiss the Hot Chef'. I smirk at him as I approach.

"Nice apron," I say.

He stops what he's doing to look down at it and laugh. "Thanks," he says. "Wore it a lot when I was working for Tanner."

"Musta been wild," I say. "For him to hook up with his personal chef."

He wipes his thick, sweaty brows and puts his hand on his hips. "Oh, it was a wild ride for sure," he says. "What's going on? You like your food?"

I nod. "Pancakes were fantastic," I say, even though I didn't eat a lot of them. Mom made me lose my appetite.

"But, uh, I was wondering…" I step closer, not wanting to be overheard. Not like it matters. But I have noticed some people staring, and I would at least like a private conversation. Especially since it's about Silas.

"Silas," I say. "Has he—has he made any decision about whether he's working for the Pioneer's or not?"

Jimmy's brow forms a V as he frowns. "You haven't heard?"

My stomach sinks. "Heard what?"

He shrugs. "Woulda thought that since you recommended him he'd be keeping you in the loop."

I reflect on the stilted, cold, and distant conversations we have during our appointments. We talk about the weather, how my knee is feeling, and how his day was. We don't go any further than that. We don't say it, but I think we both know what would happen if we let ourselves fall into the other again.

"He, uh—" I scratch the back of my head. "He likes to keep things private."

Jimmy nods, his eyes busy, like there's something on his mind. "That he does."

"So what's this thing I don't know about?" I ask.

"Silas had an interview with Brigham, the head PT," he says. "Silas hasn't received the confirmation, but he says things are looking pretty good. He thinks they'll hire him."

My stomach curdles, and I have to stick my hand out to the booth to keep myself standing. "Oh really?"

"Yeah," Jimmy says. "He's real happy about it."

"That's great," I lie. Which sucks. I should be happy for him. That's what he wants. But, assuming Brigham really does hire Silas for this next season, that means two horrible things: one, Silas and I will be in close proximity; and two, Silas and I, under no circumstances, can date.

"Yeah," he says. He pats me on the shoulder. "Talk to him about it. I know he can be kinda a quiet guy, but working in the NFO means a lot to him. And since you helped him get the job, I'm sure he'd want to share with you what's going on."

There's a tightening in my chest, and I reach my free hand up to rub it.

I think of all the conversations Silas and I had that first week we knew each other, before we hand to tone it down between us. Those conversations were raw, vulnerable, and true. He didn't seem quiet at all. Maybe misunderstood at times, sure. But I didn't misunderstand him. He made perfect sense to me. And I wanted to get the chance to understand him more.

But now that can never happen.

"Well, I'm seeing him in a little bit for a session," I say. "Maybe I'll ask him them."

He taps me on the shoulder. "You should," he says, then starts making his way to the kitchen. "I gotta get going, but great talking."

"Thanks," I say. "See ya around."

I make my way out to the car. These days, I'm not using crutches or a brace, but I'm extra careful with how I walk, especially on tricky surfaces like gravel. I watch each of my steps, making sure that I keep my leg vertical with my body and that each of my steps are thoughtful and balanced. Occasionally, there's a twitch of soreness in my knee, making me limp a little, but Silas says that's normal.

When I make it to the car, I open the door and sit down in the passenger seat with a sigh, hoping to just relax after hearing the bad news. Well, good news for Silas but bad for me. As long as my mom stays quiet in this car ride, I think I'll be able to get some peace.

My mom puts the car into drive, and we head home.

"I saw you limping," she eventually says.

I sigh and rub my eyes. Guess this won't be a peaceful ride after all.

"Yeah," I say. "That's pretty normal for post-ACL surgery. I'm basically learning how to walk again."

"But it's been two months since you started treatment," she says. "Shouldn't you at least be walking normal now?"

I sigh. What is it with my mom and being 'normal'? Being gay clearly isn't normal. And now recovering just as I should isn't normal either? I have to be fully healed from getting my knee obliterated in less than three months?

"Mom," I say, still rubbing my eyes. "I can't do this right now. I can't."

"It's just," she continues as if she didn't hear me. "Maybe we need to find you another therapist who can help you recover faster."

I drop my hands and glare at her. "What?"

She shrugs as she turns onto our road. "Silas is only a resident. I think we need someone with a little more experience."

"Mom, no," I say, turning my entire body to her, my chest tightening. "I like Silas."

"And this is another reason to find another," she says. "He's distracting you. You need to focus completely on recovery and getting back out onto the field. Having some therapist you're crushing on gets in the way of that."

I sit back in my seat and stare out at the moving road, my eyes beginning to water. This can't be happening. Sure, my conversations with Silas are stilted and cold. But we're still having them, and I'd rather have that than nothing. And now my mom is threatening to even take that away from me. This is just like high school when I told her I wanted to spend more time focusing on my voice. She didn't even have a conversation with me about it. She just said it wasn't happening and practically made my decision for me.

I clench my fists, feeling my breath quicken.

As a kid, I watched my dad praise my oldest sister for following in his footsteps. I watched my other two siblings become so successful, as well as emotionally and financially independent, that they left the house at eighteen without looking back once. As I grew up, I wanted to possess the confidence, skill, and intelligence that all my siblings had. Mom saw my talent as a football player, so she pushed me in that direction. And I complied. But I also developed a growing skill and interest in singing. I loved performing. I loved the way I felt when I hit the notes in just the right way. Yet because my mom only really cared about football, that was where my received my support. That was where I was nurtured. Consequently, the only way I saw myself being as successful as my siblings was through football. And being a gay football only makes this achievement more notable. So when I sang, I was alone—unsupported. But when I was playing football, I had my mother's support—the only one in my family who was really by my side. And because of this, I've learned to bow before my mother and take her advice whenever she gives it. After all, she's been the only one there for me.

But I don't want to blindly obey her anymore, especially if that means I can no longer work with Silas. I want to live my own life. And I think the only way for me to do that is to get the hell out of her house. No matter how painful that will be.

"Mom," I say, my voice shaky. "I can't do this anymore."

She whips her head to me as she drives, then quickly turns back to the road. "What do you mean? You're quitting football?"

"No," I say. "I can't stay here."

"Here?" she asks, shaking her head with a scoff. "What do you mean?"

I sigh. "It's time for me to go back to Salt Lake."

Her brow furrows tightly. "Are you serious?"

I nod. "I need space to recover on my own," I say, not just referring to my physical recovery.

"But—" she winces. "I thought we were connecting. You don't want to stay longer?"

"Mom," I say, somehow managing to keep it together. "I just need to do this, okay?"

She sighs and presses her fingers against her chest. The gesture makes me wonder if she's as pained there as I am.

"Okay," she says.

The second we get home, I hop on my computer and buy a flight home that night. Not wanting my mom to drive me, I text Kyle and ask him if he could give me a ride. He agrees. Then I start packing.

There's a knock on my door. I'm afraid my mom will just open it right away, but to my surprise, she just speaks up.

"Wyatt," she says. "Can I come in?"

I sigh and sit down on my bed. "Sure."

She gently opens the door and walks in, her head hung low. She stands there with the door half-open, her hand on the doorknob.

"Was it something I said?" she asks.

I'm tempted to scowl at her. She has to know that her controlling behavior is driving me crazy, especially if just months ago she expressed remorse on the phone.

But truthfully, at the end of the day, I love my mom. Even though she was pushing me as a child, she was the only one pushing me—the only one there. And that has to count for something. Yet I can't stay here and let things get any worse.

"I don't want to talk about it," I say, grabbing my suitcase and throwing some clothes inside. "I'm leaving tonight."

She leans against the open door. "Can I drive you?"

"I got it taken care of."

She stands there, and I know she wants to say something—apologize again maybe? But I don't think an apology will cut it right now. If my mom wants my trust, she needs to actually change.

"Will you let me know when you land?" she asks.

I think about calling her, and I frown.

"I'll text you," I say.

"Alright," she says, opening the door for her to leave. "And Wyatt?"

I stop packing, my suitcase overflowing with the clothes that I'm haphazardly throwing in there.

"I love you, okay?"

I sigh. "I love you, too."

And when she shuts the door behind her, I finally let my tears flow.

I know my mom's just trying to help, but it's not working. I just wish that I could cut out the controlling parts of her and get the thoughtful parts. She makes breakfast for me? It isn't just food she thinks I need to be eating. She invites me to live with her? It's to actually get to know me and not control my recovery. She takes me out to breakfast? She doesn't comment on what I eat.

But that's clearly not realistic. That isn't her.

Once I'm all finished packing, I text Blake that I'm headed back tonight and hobble my way to my front door. In the foyer, my mom and dad are waiting.

"It was good to have you here," my dad says, reaching out to hug me.

I awkwardly hug him back, stiffening in his lukewarm embrace. I can't remember the last time I've hugged my dad, but I'm sure it was as immemorable as this.

Then my mom hugs me, and it's much more tender—so much more tender that I almost rethink my decision to leave.

Almost.

"Call me when you get in," she says, letting me go.

"I'll text you," I remind her.

She nods, and then I walk out the door.

Before I head to Kyle's, I drive my rental car to the physical therapy clinic. There is one person I want to say goodbye to. Even if our relationship is pretty much nonexistent at this point.

I head to the clinic around noon. When I walk into the waiting room, I head to the front desk and ask if Silas is available.

"Sure," the secretary says. "But he's actually at lunch right now. I can leave a message though."

I shift on my feet, putting more weight on my injured leg. "Can you tell him that Wyatt's here and that he needs to talk to him?"

She pauses for a moment, then nods. "One minute."

I rest my elbow on the counter and look around the room. There's a beefy undergrad sitting near the entrance—probably a football player—and another attractive young man. For a brief moment—almost like seeing a shooting star—I watch the two of them lock eyes. There's charge there—an intimate electricity. And, just as quickly as it happened, they look away. Immediately, the thought appears in my head: those two are fucking.

I remember being a closeted gay kid here at Miss U. It was fun, in some ways. I knew I was gay in high school, but I kept it on the DL besides telling my mom. When I got to Miss U, I discovered I wasn't the only one. But that wasn't an exclusively good thing. On the Miss U football team, there were several others who were gay and were regularly fucking each other. Kyle and Tanner were just leaving when I joined. I hoped I could find others there who were ready to be themselves. But that's not what I got. Instead, we'd fuck each other in secret, and then we'd go on with our lives. There was no emotional intimacy, no thirst for connection beyond a penis inside an asshole. Every time I tried to pursue more with a guy, they'd blow me off.

Today, I'm happy for those who've found love: Kyle, Tanner. I've even heard Dominic from the St. Louis Steamers is dating a man now. But I'm still bitter that when I first came out—when I needed the most love and care—I was only met with sex and indifference. This is partly why I still care about my mom so much, despite her tendency to control. At least I know her love is authentic.

Which is why this whole situation with Silas blows beyond belief. I finally meet a guy who has the emotional depth I've been craving in a partner my whole life. And now I can't date him. Even worse, we'll likely become coworkers.

The door next to the desk opens, and out walks Silas. Of course, he's wearing his tan cowboy hat, and his blue scrubs just bring out his dark mustache and brown eyes.

"Wyatt," he says. He glances at the clock. "Our appointment isn't for a few—"

"I know," I say, my voice heavy. "You got a minute?"

"Sure," he says, putting his hands in his pockets. "Outside?"

I nod.

The two of us step outside. It's one of those spring days where it's chilly in the morning but hot during the day, and we're just transitioning to the heat. I wince and make my hand a visor above my eyes.

"Here," Silas says. He leads us to a bench under a low tree. There, we're shaded, so it's slightly cooler.

"Thanks," I say, sitting down and adjusting my leg.

"'Course," he says. "What's going on?"

I fold my arms and lean back into the bench. "I hear the interview process with the Pioneers is going well," I say.

Silas leans against the metal railing, facing me. "You heard?"

"I asked Jimmy about you," I say, glancing at him. He's got his legs crossed, and I have his full attention. God, I love how present he is. Even when we're keeping each other at a distance.

"That's cool," he says. "Yeah. I'm pretty much waiting to hear back."

"I'd be surprised if they didn't take you," I say. "You really know your stuff."

"Thanks again for talking to them for me," he says. "It, uh, really means a lot. I've been waiting for this for a long time."

"It's my pleasure," I say, smiling with my lips only at him. I wish my smile could be more genuine, but I just don't feel good about this at all.

"Is everything okay?" he asks. "With your knee, I mean. Is that why you came?"

I sigh. I've hated having to stick strictly professional with him, keeping the focus just on my recovery. But if he really works for the team this next season, I'll be healed by the time he's onboarded. So we won't have to interact like we are now. We won't have to interact at all.

"They're fine," I say. "I actually came to tell you that I'm leaving."

He raises his hand to cover his heart, like he's saying the pledge of allegiance. "Leaving? Where?"

I bend my good knee, then my bad knee carefully. I rest my elbows on my thighs. "I'm headed home. I'm gonna finish my recovery there."

Silas slides on the bench so he's facing forward just like me. "Oh."

"Yeah."

There's a long pause between us. We watch as two more students walk into the clinic while one walks out.

"Were you dissatisfied with the treatment you were receiving?" he asks.

"Not at all," I say, shaking my head. "You were phenomenal." Which I mean in so many more ways than one. "I just—just some issues with my folks. I need to be on my own again."

He nods without missing a beat. "I understand. You gotta do what you gotta do."

I turn my head to him, and he still looks at me like I'm the only person who could ever exist in the world.

"Alright," he says. "Well, hopefully I see you out there."

My lips curl upward as I reach out to pat him on the knee. "That would be grand."

We sit there for a beat longer, both of us stewing in all the words unsaid. I'm still just fucking pissed that what's stopping us isn't some homophobic institutional bullshit. It's literally PT ethical guidelines. We could be straight and have the exact same thing happen. I hoped that coming out would make life easier. But it's still just as hard.

"Well," I say, patting my knees and standing up. I extend my hand, he grabs it, and I help him up. Once he's standing, I can't tell who's quicker to let go.

"I'll see you soon," he says. "Hopefully."

"Yeah," I say. "Hopefully." Even though it would be much more merciful for both of us to never see the other again. Having him this close, without the ability to call him mine, is torture.

I wave him goodbye, then we both go our separate ways. When I get in the car, I look at the campus that set the trajectory for my life. One of my favorite art songs comes to my head. "Into My Heart an Air That Kills", it begins. It's about a man coming back to the town he grew up in, seeing how much it's changed. I can lament that, sure, but I'm also lamenting how things stay exactly the same.

In college, I thought that love would be easy once I was older and out. But it's not. It's as painful as it was, just for different reasons. And back then, I thought I'd be able to distance myself from my mother's controlling nature. Yet I still find myself pushed by her words.

I sigh and start my car, ready to drop off my rental and head to the Memphis airport with Kyle. Hopefully, once I recover, I can get back on the road to becoming the best tight end the NFO has ever seen. At least then, one thing will change: I'll have proved my point that I'm just as good as any straight man.

Chapter 12

Silas King

"WATCH OUT!" JIMMY YELLS.

From one end of the deck, he sprints toward Glamour Springs Lake as fast he can. Then he cannonballs into the water, splashing it everywhere. It almost reaches me sitting in a lawn chair several feet away from the edge.

"Nine," Martha says from the water.

"Ugh, three," Llewellyn says on the edge of the dock, wiping off her sunglasses.

Tanner sneaks up behind Jimmy in the water and wraps his arms around him. They wrestle for a bit, and I can't help but laugh. I may be as sad as ever, but Jimmy and Tanner always know how to make me smile.

"Are you gonna join us?" Martha asks.

"Maybe in a bit," I say. "Just resting now."

I lay my head back in the lawn chair. It's a hot day in late May. Summer finally feels like it's here to stay, and I'm hanging out at the lake with my friends. And sadness, like it always has, covers me like a cloak.

It's been over two months since Wyatt up and left. Looking back, it feels like he left just as quickly as he came. And it hurts just that way, too. It's the equivalent of someone breaking into my home, startling the hell out of me, but then giving me a thousand dollars, listening to all my music and loving it, giving me the best sex of my life, and then leaving without a trace. Of course, this is an unfair analogy—Wyatt and I both decided not to pursue each other so he could help me get a physical therapy job with the Pioneers. Which is only evidence of what a wonderful man he is. And since he's left, there hasn't been one day where I haven't listened to the playlist he made for me. It makes me feel like he's still here.

Nearby, I hear Llewellyn sigh. She stands up and makes her way to the chair next to me. She lays down and puts her now foggy sunglasses over her eyes.

"We need a rule around the lake that says that people just trying to relax deserve not to be bothered," she says.

I chuckle as I hear Martha, Jimmy, and Tanner playing some game. Marco Polo maybe?

"I don't know," I say. "It's kinda nice to be around it. Less lonely."

She huffs out a short laugh. "I think I prefer lonely at this point." I glance at her, and I can see a small smile on her face.

"How's life treating you, Llew?" I ask.

"The same," she says. "Book store's doing well, even without you."

"Bummer," I say. "And to think I was really needed."

"Well, we have taken a hit in terms of gay men visitors," she says. "Apparently a certain hot gay cowboy attracted a lot of them."

This time I let out a short laugh. "Sure."

We both sit in silence for a bit, soaking up the sun. Sometimes, Llewellyn is the perfect person to be around. She lets me be self-deprecating.

"How's Mom?" I ask.

"Did I not tell you?" she asks, turning to me. "She let that toxic guy go."I glance at her, my brow raised. "No way? Good for her."

"I know," she says. "Maybe she'll finally work on herself."

There's a sinking feeling in my chest. I'm alone without Wyatt, but it feels like there's nothing in myself to work on. Like I'm a husk the self I was with him in my life.

"Have you heard back from Brigham?" she asks, referring to the head PT for the Salt Lake Pioneers.

I suck on my lip. "Still nothing."

"Still?" she asks. "It's been months."

"Yeah, tell me about it," I say. "It's all starting to feel like a distant dream."

I remember back in Jimmy's cabin kitchen where Wyatt found me during the Championship game half-time show. He said that he wanted to get to know me better—to date. But he also said he could help me get a job with the Salt Lake Pioneers as a PT. Yet if I wanted that, we couldn't date. The choices were mutually exclusive. Knowing it was the safer choice—and what I've wanted my whole life—I made the decision to pursue a job with the Pioneers. But I feel like an idiot. Because now I haven't heard back about the job in months, and I don't have Wyatt either. Back in that kitchen, I thought I could have both. But now I have neither. I've only held out hope this long on the off chance that I get a call back.

"You'll find something else," she says. "If you got one opportunity, another will come."

I trill my lips. "I hope you're right," I say. But I doubt she is. I just finished my first year of PT residency, and I don't have any job prospects that I like. So I'm debating doing another year or cutting my losses and just taking something that's not in my specialty. If I choose that, I get to start paying down my loans. Yay.

We lay there for a little longer, but thinking about my job prospects, paired with how I just may have lost two great opportunities, has me itching to be alone.

I force out a yawn. "I'm gonna go lay down inside."

"Alright," she says. "We'll be in soon for dinner."

I wave to the others, but they don't see me. I make my way onto Jimmy's porch and into his living room. His house is nice and cold, and I'm ready to curl into a ball under a nice blanket. The sun's tuckered me out, and sleep sounds real nice right now.

I pick up my phone, hoping that while I was gone I received a text from a special someone, which I've been hoping for a lot lately.

There are no texts, but there is a missed call and message. Could he have called me? That would be weird. I click to see who the message is from. It's an 801 number, which makes my stomach curl over itself. 801 is Utah. Utah is where Wyatt is right now.

Without even listening to the message, I immediately call the number back. Maybe Wyatt got a new number and was trying to reach me. Ever since he left, my emotions have flatlined back down to primarily sadness, which is what I'm used to. But I'd be lying if I said I haven't missed the crazy emotions he made me feel.

"Hello?" a voice answers, one I hardly recognize. It's definitely not Wyatt's rich, tenor voice.

"Hi," I say. "This is Silas. I'm calling you back?"

"Oh, Silas," he says, more relaxed. "I'm Brigham, head PT over with the Pioneers."

My stomach clenches. "Oh, my God. How are you? It's been—" I glance at my phone to check the date. "A while." More than two months.

"It has," he says. "I'm sorry we haven't gotten back to you. We've had some mix-ups with staff this summer."

"That's okay," I say, my heart racing.

"I was actually calling to tell you some good news."

"Oh, I—thank you. What is it?"

He goes on to explain that they are in need of one new therapist, and they think I'd be a perfect fit due to my experience working with the Miss U football team. I'd be with them through this next season, and if things work out they'll keep me on for good. When he describes to me the pay and benefits, I nearly collapse into the couch. I might actually pay off my loans before I die.

"Now," he says. "We'd want you here by the beginning of July. That's when we'll start practices. I know it's a bit short notice, and I'm sorry about that."

"That's no worries," I say. "I'll be able to find a place to live."

"Great," he says. "Of course, I'll send over some emails with some paperwork you need to fill out. But welcome to the team. Any questions for me?"

I do have a bunch of questions, but they're not about my position. I wanna know how Wyatt is doing. How's his knee feeling? Is he projected to start this season despite the injury? Does he still think about me like I do him?

"I think I'm good for now," I say.

"Wonderful," Brigham says. "Looking forward to have you as part of the team."

The very same team that Wyatt Nelson plays on. "Me too."

* * *

The next weeks pass by in a dizzying blur. I help Martha and Llewellyn find someone else to rent out their basement, which was easy considering how cheap they keep their rent. I was able to secure a nice apartment in downtown Salt Lake. And, while doing all this, I've picked up shifts at the clinic for all our summer athletes, padding my wallet and thus making the move a little less stressful. And now that I'm flying out tomorrow, my moving truck already gone, I decided to throw a little small party in my basement.

I have over my closest friends in Glamour Springs: Jimmy, Tanner, Martha, Llewellyn, Linda, Michael, Kyle, Marissa, and Lilah. Linda's baked me a cake, while Jimmy made us some of his famous sliders. As we all talk and laugh, I think I may actually feel happy. It's amazing what a little bit of hope in the future can do for you. I'm finally getting what I've wanted: a job in the NFO. And I'd be lying if I said I wasn't excited to see Wyatt again—to live in the same city and work on the same team. Even if we can't be anything beyond professional. It'll just be good to see him.

Just before the night's over, Linda has everyone go around the room and say their favorite thing about me. I blush when she suggests it, thinking people are just gonna stay something stupid or silly—it's not like there's that much to like about me.

But I'm blown away by how tender it is.

Kyle starts, and he remarks that when he first saw me, I inspired him to be his authentic self—that I eventually helped him realize that he could come out as a gay man. Michael says that I made one of the best—and worst—Thanksgivings of his life better because of our conversation about books. Lilah says she loves that I stick to my fashionable roots, while Marissa says I'm the kindest man in the South, much the annoyance of every other man in the room. Linda tells me that she thinks of me as a son of her own, one who is more pensive, thoughtful, and kind than any man she's ever known. Kyle doesn't even protest at that. Martha says I'm the best coworker she's ever had, earning her a scoff from her wife. Llewellyn says she doesn't have a better banter buddy. Tanner's grateful that Jimmy had such a levelheaded friend to keep him in check before they met, which only makes me laugh. No one could keep Jimmy in check if they tried. And finally, Jimmy puts his hand on my shoulder and thanks me for being the best friend he's had.

"To the man who's been there for me since Joe," he says. "And will be there until the end of our days."

We all toast to that, and there's a ball of guilt that forms in my stomach.

I've heard the argument before that suicide is selfish—that taking away my life would bring untold sadness to those around me. But the thing is I know that. I'm aware of what a devastating effect my unexpected departure would leave on the world. In fact, thinking about Jimmy or Llewellyn or Linda or Martha is usually what has stopped me in the past. But isn't it also selfish for that to be my only reason to live? Not selfish for me, but selfish for them?

Ursula Le Guin has a compelling short story about just this. In this story, there's a city called Omelas that's a veritable utopia. There is no inequality, and everyone's happy—except for a single child. This child is in perpetual filth in misery. And they are kept in this misery so that everyone else may live in paradise.

What difference is there between me and this child if I keep myself in perpetual misery so that those around me can stay happy?

My friends have kept me sustained long enough. But I don't know how much longer I can go just riding on guilt for hurting them alone. I'm excited by new job prospect—and the fact that I'll see Wyatt again. Yet I doubt these will last me long either, especially since Wyatt and I have to keep a professional wall between us.

After we wrap up the party, Jimmy lingers behind to help me get the rest of my things packed into my car. I'm driving out to Salt Lake City tomorrow morning.

While he's in the kitchen, I walk into my room and scratch behind Cheshire's. He's sitting as a contented little loaf on my bed. I'm impressed with his stoicism throughout this entire moving process. His world is turning upside down, and he isn't batting an eye. But when I get into bed after he's already settled, he gives me the nastiest side eye. Guess that's cats for you.

Hearing Jimmy still packing in the kitchen, I kneel next to my bed and pull out the box underneath my nightstand. I gingerly open it and assess its contents. I put an x in my journal for today since I obviously won't make any big decisions before my move. It's almost completely filled, so I'll have to buy another one soon. But the pills and liquor are still potent. I won't obviously do it tonight, but I'm wondering when there will come a time Utah when I need to whip these out.

Part of me is so excited to see potentially Wyatt again. But there's also a lot of dread. Wyatt's the only one who's gotten me excited enough about life to not want to end it. And I know how fucking stupid and codependent that sounds. But I would be lying if I said I didn't enjoy that. And I'd be lying if I said I didn't hate it, too. Nevertheless, I *do* want to see him again. Even if we still have to stay professional.

"Whatcha looking at?" Jimmy asks in my doorway.

I toss a bottle of pills into the box and shut it so quickly it startles Cheshire. "Fuck, you scared me."

"Sorry," he says, stepping inside. "Is that like a memory box or something?"

I think about the journal I write in everyday as I put inside my nearby backpack. "You could say that," I say, feeling my forehead begin to sweat. Jimmy's suspicious gaze lingers on me for a beat longer than I feel comfortable, but then he relaxes. He comes over and strokes the back of Cheshire's head. I can hear him purring from here.

"Got all kitchen stuff packed away," he says, still stroking him. "You should be all good to go."

"Thanks again so much for your help," I say, tucking my backpack away between my bed and nightstand. I don't want Jimmy searching through it. "It really means a lot."

He sits down on the edge of my bed. "My pleasure. This is kinda crazy. You're leaving us for good."

I let out a short laugh. "Maybe not for good," I say. *Not yet at least.* "Depends on how I perform this season."

"I know you'll do well," he says. "I'd be surprised if they didn't hire you on for good."

I think about the sex Wyatt and I had back in the clinic. I'm surprised we both had the balls to do that and how we somehow got away with it. If we did anything a fraction as intense as that out in Salt Lake City with how serious NFO teams can be, I could kiss my career as a physical therapist goodbye.

"I think luck's on my side, but time will tell," I say with a sigh, sitting down on my bed as well.

Jimmy pats my shoulder. "Luck's got nothing to do with it. You're a good therapist. You're easy to get along with. You'll be just fine."

He removes his hand, and my shoulder feels warm where he touched. If and when I ever leave this earth, I'll miss Jimmy the most. Almost more than I do Wyatt. He's been more constant than anyone.

"Thanks, man," I say.

After we double-check that everything's in order, I walk Jimmy to the door.

"You're still coming for the wedding, right?"

I scoff. "Duh." Kyle and Michael are getting married around Thanksgiving this year, but I'm not sure I'll live that long. Jimmy can't know that, though.

We hug, and then he salutes me as he pulls away.

"See you then," he says. "Drive safe, my friend."

"I'll see you soon," I say as I watch him walk to his car.

And my chest tightens as I realize this could be the last time he sees me.

Chapter 13

Wyatt Nelson

As I PULL INTO the Pioneers stadium in downtown Salt Lake, my stomach is jumping with anticipation. It's early July, and it's our first official practice. I'm still recovering from my ACL surgery back in December, but I'm right on track. In fact, Brigham, the head PT for the Pioneers, has said that I'm actually ahead of the curve. He said that Silas—the handsome cowboy PT who worked on me back in Glamour Springs—did an excellent job helping me heal.

Silas. The man I felt more connected to than anyone else.

And the same man I had to let go.

When he told me he wanted help getting a PT job with the Pioneers, I decided to help him. But that meant that nothing between us could develop. From that moment on, we had to keep it professional so his hire wouldn't be seen as a conflict of interest.

Yet I haven't heard if he was actually hired. Our team of physical therapists and athletic trainers has had a big mix up during the off-season, but Brigham hasn't mentioned anything to me about Silas. Not that he needed to, of course—because, according to him, Silas is just the physical therapist who helped me recover while I was away. Nothing more.

Once I park, I make my way down to the locker rooms. There, I find a good number of my team already getting booted up. I sit down on the bench right next to our quarterback, and my good buddy, Blake.

"So you're practicing?" he asks, his brow tightly furrowed.

"Not with you all," I say, changing into some gym clothes. "I'm gonna go do some exercises with Brigham."

His jaw tightens as he leans down to tie his cleats, and I just roll my eyes.

Ever since I moved back to Salt Lake, Wyatt has been trying to get me to see that I'm actually in danger now. He says I'm the biggest out and active player in the NFO right now, and that puts a target on my back. He insists that the tackle that led me to tearing my ACL was purposeful—that it was a hate crime. And when I came back, he even went as far as to say I should retire early.

But that's the last thing I'll do.

I spent my entire life living in the closet, afraid to be who I was and limiting myself from authentic connection with others. And now that I'm out, I'm supposed to still live in fear? I'm still supposed to tone myself down so others can be comfortable? Truthfully, I don't even care if it was a hate crime. I still haven't mentioned to anyone the slur I heard before I was tackled. Because it ultimately doesn't matter. This season, I'm gonna go out and be the best tight end the NFO has ever seen. And I'm gonna be gay doing it. Nothing will stop m e.

"You still thinking about playing this season?" he asks me quietly.

I scoff at full volume, which causes him to cower and look around in fear for anyone who may have heard his question.

"I am," I say firmly.

He sighs. "You know—"

"Yes, I know," I say with a sigh. "You have gone to great lengths to tell me. I hear you. And I don't care."

"Alright," he says with the shake of his head. "Like I said, I support you—"

"Then fucking support me," I hiss quietly. "I'm playing this season. That's not up for debate. Support me here."

He nods, properly chastised. "Okay. I will."

"Thank you," I say, mildly relieved. I thought that coming out was going to make my life easier. But it's just been infinitely more complicated. Because not only has there been a ton of media coverage on my sexuality, rather than my playing, my relationship with one of my best friends who's also gay—Blake—has been compromised, too. Now all of our conversations are about my sexuality, rather than my recovery or my playing. Or the fact that I met the most special man in Glamour Springs and now can't have him because of stupid professional logistics. And that this man was the only one in my adult life who has made me feel like I can be 100% myself. No conditions. Just me.

And now I'll probably never see him again.

Once Blake is all booted, he gives me a supportive pat on the shoulder and makes his way out onto the field. I head out of the locker room and down to the hallway to our in-stadium gym where all of our therapists reside.

I walk into the warehouse style room with bright fluorescent lights, a black ceiling, and wide spinning fans. I walk across a patch of turf to the PT office, passing all of our different equipment along the way. When I make it to the office, I find Brigham at his desk working on his laptop. He's a middle-aged ex-Mormon man with seven children. He studied exercise science at BYU, which is apparently like the most popular major there, and went off to become a physical therapist. When Salt Lake City got an NFO team, he jumped at the opportunity to become one of the first PTs involved.

"Hey, Wyatt," he says, looking up from his computer. He's a wiry guy, wearing a brown polo, our team's main color.

"Hey there," I say. "Excited for the first practice?"

He smiles, looking back down at his computer. "You betcha. Just sending off the last email..." He clicks his keyboard, then closes his computer. He stands up and shakes my hand.

"What are we doing today?" I ask.

"Actually," Brigham says, looking at his watch. "We have a new PT on staff, and I was hoping for him to work with you today. Just to get him acclimated."

My stomach jumps. A new PT. Could that mean...?

He looks out of the office down the hallway toward the PT's breakroom. "He must still be getting ready," he says. He turns to me. "Sorry to do this to you, but I figured it'd be best for me to be out on the field to watch for any players hurting themselves going back to a full practice."

"Sure," I say, nodding.

"Thanks for understanding," he says in that overly polite way a lot Utahns here talk. "He should be—ah, here he is."

I turn around just as someone walks into the office, and I get so weak in the knees that I'm afraid I'll fall and re-tear my ACL.

Silas King stands in the doorway to the PT office. He's wearing his same cowboy hat, but instead of scrubs, he's wearing the same brown polo that Brigham has on, which only makes his brown eyes and mustache more pronounced. In the months we've been separated, he almost seems to have gotten more muscular. His arms crossed in front of him, I see more bulges in his biceps and triceps.

He's staring at me with wide eyes, the same way I'm probably looking at him.

Brigham looks between us, then nods. "Right, of course," he says, tapping his palm against his forehead. "You two know each other. You recommended Silas to me. I need another Diet Coke."

Silas is looking at me like he's about to be tackled. I decide to ease the tension. I step forward and shake his hand.

"Good to see you again, Silas," I say.

He extends his hand, and when it touches mine, I swear I get that same electricity I felt when he handed me that towel after our first session in the pool. Suddenly, "Che Gelida Manina" starts blaring in my head. My Mimi.

"Hey, Wyatt," he says, trying to keep his voice flat. It's been months since we've seen each other, and even last time we spoke we were just on a professional basis. But I can hear the emotion there, and I can see it in the way his eyes hang on me.

"This is perfect," he says. "Silas has already worked with you before, so you already know each other well."

I remember being balls-deep in his ass on that patient table in that bright room back at his clinic. I know him well, alright.

"I gotta run to practice," he says, picking up a tablet. "But I can leave you two to get settled. Silas," he says, turning to my old cowboy friend. "You have everything you need?"

He glances down at his tablet, then nods at Brigham.

"Perfect," Brigham says. "I'll be back soon to check how things are going." And then he jogs out of the office, leaving me alone with the man I was afraid I'd never see again—the man I feel more connected to than anyone else.

The man I have to keep at arm's length.

"How's—" Silas clears his throat. "How's your recovery been?"

I bite my lip and nod my head slowly, wondering how the hell I'm going to get through today, let alone the rest of the season with Silas this close to me. Hell, the season hasn't even begun, and I'll probably see him at least on a weekly basis. Fuck.

"It's been good," I say. "Been working a lot with Brigham."

"Yeah, he mentioned he was working with you," Silas says. "I just—I've just been overwhelmed with onboarding that I didn't look at my schedule. I didn't know we'd be working together today."

"Is that problem?" I ask, trying to keep my voice as level as possible.

"No, no," he says, shaking his head. "It's fine. I'm happy to work with you."

I blow hot air out of my nose. I don't think he really means that, which hurts, but I'm not thrilled about this either. I mean, I should be—I get to see Silas again. But it's like watching him behind a thick, glass wall. I can see him, take him in—but that's where it ends.

"Should we get started?" I ask.

"Of course," Silas says, stepping aside and gesturing for me to leave the office.

I make my way out into the gym area and point to the turf. "Start here?" I ask. "This is what I've been doing with Brigham."

"Yep," he says, his voice short.

He gets me started with some lunges. As I lunge away from Silas, I try to think how I'm going to make this work. I guess I gotta do what I did back in Glamour Springs when we were keeping it professional—talk about the workouts, my recovery, and nothing else. Nothing personal.

But so much has changed since then.

Even back in Salt Lake with my best friend and team, I've been feeling isolated as ever. My relationship with Blake has fundamentally changed now that he sees me as a threat to his safety. And it's not like I can be out practicing with my team right now. I have to be getting my knee back to 100%.

So having Silas back is like being handed a water bottle with a lock on it after walking through the desert: I'm tempted with what I need yet can't access it.

When I turn around, Silas's head whips away like he's afraid to be seen looking at me. Once I make my way back to him, he's looking down at his tablet, his shoulder tense and jaw locked. Great. If Brigham's going to have Silas work with me regularly, this is going to be a long season.

After we finish the lunges, we done some other exercises that Brigham's been having me do: squats, jumping lunges, side-to-side lunges. We get some weights out and repeat the exercises with more resistance. Pretty soon, Silas has me sweating—from the workout, of course—and I'm feeling a little bit better. We only talk about proper form and how I'm feeling, nothing more or less. This might be more manageable than I thought.

Until it's time to cool down.

I finish with some light lunges. Once I'm done, Silas points to a nearby patient table, and my stomach jumps to my throat.

"Let's, uh, finish you with some stretches," he says.

I take a deep breath and wipe sweat from my forehead. "Alright."

We both make our way over there. When he sees me walking a little faster, he awkwardly stops and gestures for me to go ahead. Fuck. More than anything, I hate seeing how uncomfortable Silas is. I can't imagine what he's feeling. I remember when he opened up to me about the music he shared with me and how much it meant to him. I loved seeing how raw and vulnerable he was. I don't think I've ever been that open with someone, maybe besides my mom. But with my mom, there's always been conditions and strings attached to opening myself up. With Silas, I could just be.

And now we're nothing more than colleagues.

"How do you want me?" I ask. And then I recall how I asked the same thing last time we had sex on a patient table that eerily resembles this one. Fucking perfect.

"On your back," he says quickly. I take off my shoes and lay flat on the table.

"Alright," he says. "I'm just gonna stretch your leg a little bit, and then we should be good for the day."

"You really got me going," I say, wiping my forehead again. "With the workout, of course. It was good. And my knee's feeling great."

"Great," Silas says with a genuine smile, making my chest all tight. He bends my knee, stretches my leg back to my face, and holds it there. He gently rubs the muscles around my knee, gradually closing in to my knee cap. It hurts a bit at first, but then it relaxes me. I get the visual in my head of my sore muscles being tenderly massaged back to health.

And that's when blood starts to rush to my groin. Fuck. Doesn't Silas remember that massaging me like this gives me a fucking boner? This happened the first time we met. And the night we had sex.

I use my other leg and to squeeze my dick uncomfortably. We are not having a repeat of what happened the first time, especially when we have to keep this professional.

"You good?" he asks.

"Yeah," I lie. "Just getting comfortable."

He extends my leg, then stretches it back, going back and forth.

"You ready for the season to start?" he asks.

My stomach jumps a bit as I think about finally getting back out on the field. "Oh yeah," I say. "Being counted out because of this injury sucks. I'm also trying to improve as a tight end, so I'll be happy finally be back on that grind."

He looks at me with his brow furrowed, his hands on my leg. "Improve as a tight end? You're already pretty legendary. What do you mean?"

My heart picks up speed. The last time he and I spoke about something that wasn't related to my injury or something trivial was when I said goodbye to him. And I don't think I've ever talked to him about my football aspirations.

"Yeah, well I'm a pretty good blocker," I say. "Usually no one gets past me. But most tight ends who get memorialized—whose legacies last longer than their careers—are the ones who are good at receiving. So I've really been working on my ability to catch a ball and run with it."

"Cool," Silas says, straightening my leg and stretching it to work my hamstrings. "I didn't know this about you."

My chest warms. There's a bubbly eagerness to his voice. He wants to know more.

"So you want to be memorialized?" he asks. "Why? I mean, sure, that would be cool, but this sounds like a specific goal you have. And usually specific goals have a reason."

Man, talking with Silas is like slipping on an old shoe: easy and comfortable.

"Growing up, I knew I was gay pretty young. But I kept myself in the closet for a while. I thought I'd be able to find a tribe at Miss U. I did find other gay men, but none of them were really ready to be out like I was. But I got swept up in the fear of it. Kept myself hidden until I came out last year."

"What made you come out when you did?" Silas asks.

"I was tired of living so inauthentically," I say. I sigh. "I feel like I've been fake my whole life. Growing up, I chose football over music because it's what mom wanted me to do. I also felt pressure from my siblings to do something great, so that didn't help. And the entire time, I kept my sexuality hidden. So last year, I decided I had enough. I was gonna be my true self."

"Wow," Silas says. He sets me leg down, leans against the table, and just looks at me. "That's honestly pretty impressive."

I raise a brow. "You think so?"

He nods. "There are so many people who just choose to keep quiet about who they are. They think it's easier that way. But you chose authenticity over safety, which I think is pretty cool."

I smile, feeling my entire body warm from his compliment. "Glad you think so."

He gets back to stretching me, which is good because I don't know if we could stand just looking at each other any longer. We're both quiet, but it doesn't feel uncomfortable.

This is the Silas that I've missed. The one who sees me as I am—not like my mom or Blake does. No conditions. No strings attached. Except, of course, for the fact that it's not okay for us to be romantically involved.

"I've, uh," Silas says. He clears his throat. "I've been listening to the playlist you sent me."

"No way," I say, getting up on my elbows. "What do you think?"

"Oh man," he says, stretching my leg far up in the air. "I've really been missing out not listening to classical voice stuff. It's—wow."

It feels like a fire's burning in my chest. I want to hear more. Like him, music means a lot to me too. And to have someone like Silas acknowledge that...

"There was that collection of songs in there," he says. "Roderick Williams sings them. It was the..."

"Songs of Travel by Ralph Vaughan Williams," I say. "Probably my favorite collection of English art song."

He nods. "Yeah, that. Oh my God. Wyatt, that was beautiful. I loved 'Youth and Love'."

"That one's my favorite on the cycle," I say immediately.

"So powerful and... moving. There are so many songs about falling in love at a young age, so it was cool to hear one in such a different medium than I'm used to hearing."

Silas sets my leg down, and I find myself sitting entirely, swinging my legs off the table.

"Were there others?" I ask.

"'The Infinite Shining Heavens'," he says. "That one touched me the most."

I nod. That makes the most sense. That one's the most dark and brooding. The most thoughtful, too. And knowing what kind of music Silas likes, I can't see why he'd like any other song better.

"To me, it was about someone searching for truth, and after a long, weary journey, he finally finds it. And this reward makes the long journey worth it," he says.

"I think the same," I say, fully energized by his interest in my music. After I gave it to him, we had to keep it professional, so I never really thought he'd listen. And I'm so happy that he has. Because this is opening him up to a whole new part of me that no one has ever really wanted to see.

"Oh," he says, leaning against the table, putting his hand on his chest. "And the German."

"Which ones did you like?"

"Okay, I actually found one that I recognized," he says.

"You did?"

He nods. "It was the song you sang when I first met you—the one you sang right before your mom introduced me to you."

I cover my face with my hands, embarrassed, then drop them. "Oh man! The day I learned those walls were thin. It was 'Die Forelle' by Schubert, right?"

He points at me. "That's the one! The jovial, bouncy one—the one that sounds like a kangaroo hopping or a fish jumping out of water."

"That's literally what the song is about!" I say. "Well, the fish part."

"Really?" Silas asks, a wide smile forming on his face.

"Yes, well—it has a deeper meaning about men seducing women. But the poem is about a fish. The song literally means 'The Trout'."

"Wow," Silas says. "I should have looked up the translation to that one, too."

"You looked up translations to the songs?" I ask, fascinated. The only other person I'm still close with interested in music is Blake. Like me, he was a singer in college. He sang and played piano in the jazz program. But even if I got him to somehow listen to my music, he wouldn't care enough to look up the translation. Yet Silas did it unprompted.

"Just one," he says. "But that's because the title interested me."

"And that was...?"

"'An Die Musik'," he says.

And it feels like my heart skips a beat.

"'To Music'," he says. "When I saw the word 'Musik', I thought it must have been music. So I was curious to see its direct translation. And what I found blew me away."

I scooch closer to him, my leg almost touching his hip. "Tell me."

"The poem," he starts. "It's a tribute to music. Franz von Schober, the au-thor, describes music as something that transports him to another world—how harmony lifts the sorrows off his shoulders. I nearly cried when I read that because that's just how I feel about music."

And I feel like I'm about to cry right now.

"'Music opens up the heavens'," the poem says. "And it's true. Music for me—" he pauses and sucks on his lips. "I can say it's made my life so, so much better."

My heart races as I listen to Silas describe my music passionately. I want to reach out and hold his hand. I want to turn him to me and kiss him below his handsome mustache.

"The last line," he says. "I loved it. It was..." He shakes his head, unable to remember.

But I do.

"'Du holde kunst'," I say. "'ich danke dir."

"Yes, that's it!" he exclaims, turning fully to me. "What does it mean again?"

"'Blessed art'," I say. "Or in this case, music—'I thank you'."

"Yeah," he says, nodding. "Powerful stuff man."

I nod, biting down my quivering lip.

I remember sitting in a practice room in Miss U's music building. God, that basement was dingy. But I'll admit I loved going in there. Every time I walked into a practice room, it was like a time machine. Hours later, I would emerge, and I felt like a new person, not unlike Moses or that character Zarathustra going up a mountain and coming down enlightened. Like the poem says, it was like music opened me up the heavens to me. I got to see different versions of myself. I loved the way the notes sounded coming out of my mouth. I loved *creating* music.

But there was one day in the practice rooms that was particularly dark. I had just spoken to my mom. My football career was getting more serious—I was being scouted out for the NFO. Now, I loved football. And I still do. But I loved singing, too. Yet my mom had just drilled into me that I needed to start pouring all my energy into the sport. Singing was taking up too much of my schedule. It was time to get serious.

So that session in the practice room, I gave it my all. I sang everything I could think of until my voice got hoarse. Of course, I ended with the very song that Silas is talking about right now—'An Die Musik'. Because I knew that after that, it was never going to be the same.

And it wasn't. Football took up a majority of my time. I hardly had any room for my studies, let alone music.

I did all this because I thought it was what I was supposed to do. At the time, my siblings were seeing remarkable success with their careers. I knew I could never achieve anything similar with my singing, even though I was pretty good. So football it was.

But at the time, it felt like I was giving up a key part of myself. Because, in a way, I was. I know my mom loved and still loves me, but she never cared for my singing. And neither did anyone else, really. It was my football skills that interested everyone.

Until now when my handsome cowboy PT is telling me how much he loves my music. 'Du holde Kunst, ich danke dir'. Thank you, music, for bringing me close to Silas again.

"Wyatt," Silas says. "You good?"

I look up at him, and his eyes shine. I could close the distance between us. I could pull him in and kiss right now and—

"How'd the session go?"

Silas and I turn to the source of the voice. Brigham walks into the gym, followed by several other personal trainers. Silas steps away from me, and I slide away from him.

"Great," I say. "It's nice to be back with Silas again."

I sneak a glance at the most interesting man in the world. He meets my gaze for just a second, and then he looks away. And I swear in that moment he shakes his head, almost as if he's saying 'no'—telling me that we can't be doing this. All the excitement in my chest from talking about music earlier morphs into anger, and I bite my lip to contain myself. Come on. The universe gives me one person who understands, and I can't have him? Brigham joins us as the rest of the PTs go about their business, some in the office and some with other players.

Suddenly, I'm so grateful for the alone time I got with Silas. Because now it feels like I'll never have it again.

"So I'm thinking," Brigham says to the both of us. "Before the season starts…"

And as Brigham explains his plans for my recovery so I can play when the season begins, I try to sneak a couple glances at Silas, begging for him to recognize the beauty of the conversation that we just had.

But he doesn't even look my way.

Furious, I try to focus on what Brigham's saying, but all I can think about are Silas's thoughtful words about my music. I know it's risky for him to have any sort of personal conversation with me. Hell, it is for me, too. Things could get intense fast, putting us both in hot water with the PT ethics board.

But I can't just abandon what we have. Not when I already feel so connected to Silas.

So I'm gonna try. I'm gonna try to find a way for us to connect. I don't want to compromise his position as a physical therapist, but I just want to be closer to him in a way that won't be unprofessional. And, judging by the way Silas looked at me during this conversation, I know he wants it, too.

Chapter 14

Silas King

As I MAKE MY way into the Pioneers Stadium, I take a deep breath. It's early September, and this is the last practice before the football season officially begins.

I get to the PT quarters and set my stuff inside my locker. I pick up my tablet and check my schedule for one thing in particular. I breathe a sigh of relief. It's not happening today.

For the past couple months, Brigham and I have been switching off working with Wyatt. Ever since my first session with Wyatt—when I made the mistake of sharing that I had been listening to his music—I've tried my best to give all these sessions to Brigham. But even then, some of them have fallen to me, and I've had to do my best to feign disinterest and stay professional. But it's taken everything in me to not talk more about his music or mine, the thing that connects us most. I was an idiot to bring it up in the first place. I just missed him so much. I wanted to talk about something personal.

And I deeply regret it.

Now, he's deliberately trying to break our professional boundary. He'll constantly bring up music, or he'll ask me about Glamour Springs, or about my time at Miss U. These things may sound innocuous, but with us, they're just slippery slopes to something more intimate. And seeing as I don't want to lose my job or credentials, I won't let that happen. But I'm getting worn down. Desperately, I just want to let myself fall into Wyatt. I wish I had the chance to do so without any consequences.

Nevertheless, I'm relieved that Wyatt isn't on my schedule today. In fact, I think he's practicing on the field with the others. I don't need to worry about resisting him, thank God.

Seeing as I don't have any specific appointments on my schedule, I decide to head onto the field with Brigham to see how the team is going. When I walk out and see the entire Pioneers team lined up, I have to pinch myself. I still can't believe I got my dream job of working as a PT for the NFO. And it's all thanks to Wyatt.

From the sidelines, I watch the center snap the ball to the quarterback—Wyatt's friend, Blake. Blake spots Wyatt and throws it to him. In a stunning show of just what physical therapy can do, Wyatt jumps, grabs the ball, and lands safely. Just as he breaks away, the coach blows the whistle.

"He's really looking good," Brigham says over his shoulder to me.

I watch as all the players jog to the sidelines for a water break. And Brigham's right. Wyatt's ass and legs look fantastic in uniform. When we first fucked, I never even touched his ass. I wonder if next time—

Okay, I can't be thinking about him this way. He's my patient. There will not be a 'next time'. And if it was even made known that this man and I slept together before he got me this job, I doubt I'd be able to keep it.

But if I lost the job, then we'd be able to date freely...

No. I've been working my whole life to work in the NFO. I finally have a big boy job. And to finally stick it to my parents, I just need to secure it by the end of the season. Then I'll have officially made it out of small-town Alabama.

Yet, just as I predicted, life here in Salt Lake isn't much better than back home. Most players, besides Wyatt, are just worse versions of the Miss U football players. They're more entitled and egotistical. I also don't know many people here, and I miss my friends. I knew that I wouldn't be cured of my sadness here, but I was at least hoping to feel a little better. Guess life can even spare me that mercy.

But I'm still putting x's next to the date in my journal every night. I don't want to end my life, yet I have no idea why.

Pretty soon, practice is over. Brigham has me and the rest of the PTs come into the gym to work with some players experiencing some soreness and range of motion issues. And of course, even though he's practically healed at this point, Wyatt comes in, too.

"Could you work with him?" Brigham says, stepping away from one of our linemen who's having an issue with his ankle. He nods to Wyatt who's standing by one of the treatment tables.

I take a deep breath. "Sure, yeah, I can do that."

"Thanks. He should be good at this point," Brigham says. "But just make sure he's okay."

"On it."

Reluctantly, I make my way over to Brigham. There are people around, but no one is close enough to eavesdrop on what we may say to each other. Not that we're planning on saying anything that needs to stay private.

"How was I out there?" he asks, leaning against the treatment table.

I hold my tablet tightly against my chest. This is okay to talk about. It's his recovery.

"Honestly doesn't even look like you've been injured," I say. "How are you feeling?"

"Honestly like I haven't been injured," he says, smirking at me. "I appreciate your hard work with me. And Brigham, of course."

"Yeah, Brigham's a nice guy." And he is. A couple weeks back, Brigham took me out to lunch after practice, and I got to know him better. Turns out he's not Mormon like I thought he was, though he did grow up in the religion. He left the church about a decade back when all their kids were still little. And now their sixteen-year-old daughter, Belle, has come out as trans. Apparently, being LGBTQ+ in Utah isn't very fun, and what's even worse is the suicide rate for this group is high. When he told me that, a pit formed in my stomach. I couldn't help but wonder how my life would have turned out—or if it would have ended—if I was born and raised here.

"So," Wyatt says, running his hand along the treatment table.

"So," I respond, breaking from my stupor. "Since you're feeling well, maybe you can just do some stretches and call it a day."

"I'm all for that," Wyatt says. "But I was also wondering if I could ask you a favor."

My chest clenches. "A favor?"

He tilts his head back and forth. "Maybe less a favor and more an ask."

"Okay," I say, shifting on my feet, lowering my tablet to my side. "What?"

"You busy tonight?"

I furrow my brow, and my heart starts to race. "I was planning on hanging out with my cat and watching a movie. Wanted to relax before the first game of the season this Saturday. Why?"

"Well," Wyatt says, putting his foot on the bottom shelf of the treatment table, which shows off his thick thigh to me. But I use all my strength to keep my eyes on his.

"I wanted to do a little fun before the season starts, and now that I'm fully healed, I may be able to do it."

I swallow. *Something fun.*

"And that is?" I ask.

"I want to go on a night hike," he says. "And I want you to come with me."

My stomach clenches and tumbles over, and I'm worried it'll pour out of me just like I feared it would during my first session with Wyatt in the pool.

"A night hike? Are you sure that's a good idea with your knee?"

"You, Brigham, and my physician have all said that I'm virtually healed by now," he says. "I'm cleared to play. I have head lanterns and hiking poles for the both of us. There's a beautiful trail just outside Salt Lake City that I really like."

And suddenly, it hits me.

I know why I've been putting x's next to the date since I've been in Utah.

I've been hoping for this—for Wyatt. For us to have another chance.

And now I have it.

"Just the two of us?" I ask.

He nods. "But I know what you're thinking—we agreed we'd stay professional. And we will. It would just be nice to have a hiking buddy."

I lean against the treatment table and fold my arms as I watch Brigham work with a lineman on a bicycle machine.

This entire time I've lived in Utah, I've held out hope for me and Wyatt to be an item again. And this realization sickens me. Because I don't know what would be worse: pushing him away or finally holding him close.

Wyatt ignites within me a score of emotions that, at best, distress me. But one of these emotions—the strongest, I'd argue—is happiness. Besides with him, I can't remember the last time I've felt true happiness.

And this is really, really bad. It's not good to depend on someone like this—especially if there are institutional barriers preventing us from being any more than friendly acquaintances. But wouldn't I be a fool to let someone like this go? The only one to break me from my funk and help me feel like it's worth it to live? No wonder I've been writing x's next to the date since I've been here. It's like my body knows Wyatt is out there, and it's banking on our reunion for its survival.

"Oh, and look—you're gonna like this." He pulls out his phone, opens Spotify, and puts it in my hands. There's a picture split right down the middle with two different locations: the left, the Glamour Springs Lake; the right, Salt Lake City. Next to it, it says "The Silas and Wyatt Playlist". Scrolling down, I see a mixture of all the songs in the playlist I sent to him and all of the songs in the playlist he sent to me.

"Is this—" I scroll up and down again, then look at him. "You combined our playlists?"

He shrugs. "I always like to listen to music when I hike. And since you and I love each other's music, I figured we could listen to it together as we hike. We don't have to talk or do anything else if you don't want. I just think it'd be nice to spend time together. Even if it's at a distance."

I stare down at the playlist at a loss for words. Wyatt didn't just include music that I sent him—he included other ambient songs that I love but have never mentioned, which means he's listened to my favorite type of music without my request.

Heat swells in my chest, threatening to break past the barrier I created to keep my emotions at bay, the same barrier I use to keep it professional between me and Wyatt.

Wyatt sighs. "I understand if you don't want to," he says, putting his phone away. "I'm sorry—"

"I'll go," I almost blurt out.

Wyatt looks at me with a furrowed brow. "Are you sure?"

I nod quickly, afraid that if I'm not fast enough I'll rescind my answer. I don't know what's possessed me to agree to this, but I know in my bones it's what I need. I'm tired of feeling sadness and only sadness. I want to live again. I need Wyatt.

I need him.

He smiles, making my stomach jump, so I look away, and then he pats me on the shoulder. "Send me your location," he says. "I'll pick you up just before sundown."

* * *

After Wyatt picks me up, we ride in his Jeep Wrangler eastward into the Wasatch mountains.

And there's so much I want to say, to ask.

Has he liked living in Salt Lake? Does he miss Texas? Or Glamour Springs? Is he close with his family? He didn't really like he had a great relationship with his mom.

But all of that feels too personal.

As I was waiting for him to pick me up, I almost cancelled the whole thing. But I knew I needed this, so I made a promise to myself: I'd let myself spend this time with Wyatt, but I would still keep the professional barrier up. I reasoned that spending this time with him will give me the emotional boost I need and inoculate me to his charm. So I'll keep the questions tame.

"You're improving your catching skills," I say. "So what does that entail?"

He shifts in his seat, replacing the right hand on the steering wheel with his left. "It's actually a lot of cooperation with the quarterback, which makes me pretty lucky," I say. "Blake and I have been good buddies since college, so we know how to communicate with each other."

"Blake Farmer," I say, nodding. "So you guys are close?"

I glance over, and I can see him smiling, as if he's reliving memories with Blake. Fuck. This is probably too personal. But look how I made him smile.

"I mentioned a while back that he's a musician, too," he says. "That's how we initially bonded. It seemed that no one else on the Miss U football team gave a rat's ass about music. And then we started hanging out—it was never anything romantic or anything. Blake's straight, after all." He coughs, which makes me think he isn't telling the complete truth, but I won't pry there. "But kinda like you and me, that's how Blake and I bonded, too."

"Huh," I say, feeling the heat from earlier swelling even bigger in my chest.

I don't know what it is. Being around Wyatt makes me want to break out and talk freely—to be who I am, which is weird. Back home, I have great friends—Jimmy, Llewellyn, Linda, and all the others. But there's something different about Wyatt—where, if I let myself get close to him, there wouldn't be a limit to our intimacy. Just like how a black hole approaches infinite gravity. If I let myself get close to Wyatt, I don't think there would be a limit to how close we could get emotionally.

And I think I like that.

"Now tell me," he says, putting his hand on the center console, but part of me feels like he wanted to put it on my knee. And this same part of me feels like I would have let him.

"If you had no moral compass—meaning you had no morals at all—what profession would you choose to get as rich as possible?"

I look at him and laugh. "What kinda question is that?"He shrugs nonchalantly. "Just a get-to-know-you question. I know we said we'd keep it professional, but I'm just throwing it out there."

I chew on my lips as we drive into the mountains, the sun finally disappearing beneath the horizon.

I keep fucking telling myself that we won't go beyond our professional boundaries, but you know what? I'm fucking sick of that. For the first time in my life, there's a beautiful man right next to me who's willing to get to know me for who I am. And I have to push him away just because my job says that I can't date my patients?

You know what? Fuck that. I want to feel the riotous emotions inside me full force. I'm letting them go, and I'm letting myself fall into Wyatt. For real this time. And I have a feeling that Wyatt is letting himself do the same.

And it's not like this is harmful. We're not having sex or anything. This is normal. Nothing bad will happen.

"I think I'd go be one of those finance bros in New York," I say. "Like a finance investor bro."

He laughs and flashes a grin at me, which makes my stomach jumble all over itself. Good. That's what I'm doing this for. To feel and bring myself closer to Wyatt.

"I cannot imagine cowboy Silas working as a douchey finance bro," he says.

"What?" I say, feigning offense. "I got some hustle in me."

He laughs. "Yeah right."

"And you?" I ask.

"Oh, easy," he says, his right hand lazily steering us up and through the mountains while his other props his head up against the car door. "I'd use my platform as the biggest gay-and-out NFO player and do porn."

I look at him with wide eyes, feeling a stirring down below. "You'd do what?"

"Not that porn is morally wrong or anything," he says. "I just think this would be reprehensible to some people, but I don't care. I know I'm hot, and I know there are a lot of women—and men—out there who's biggest dream is fuck an NFO player."

He winks at me, and I swear I melt into the seat. It's one thing to be hot. It's a completely different thing to know you're hot and flaunt, and that just makes Wyatt Nelson so, so much hotter. Fuck, I feel my heart racing from the anxiety of it all—to letting myself be vulnerable with someone.

But I'm gonna keep going.

By the time we reach what Wyatt calls 'Little Mountain Summit', he and I have discussed what type of Ted Talk he would give—me on the mysteries of space and him on the ways different musical keys affect our mood. I also bring up a second topic: what type of colors we could see if our eyes let us detect wavelengths beyond the visible spectrum. I said I would want to see how different planets and celestial bodies sound, while he says he'd love to see emotions. And you know what, after he said that, I think I'd like to do the same. Especially with all that I'm feeling right now.

"Here," Wyatt says as we stand in front of his trunk. He hands me one wireless earbud and puts the other in his ear. He hands me a head lantern and some hiking poles, then gets his own.

"You ready?" he asks, situating his headlamp. It's fully nighttime now.

"Sounds gorgeous," I say, putting my cowboy hat back on now that my headlamp's in place. "Let's go."

Just when we step onto the summit, Wyatt starts the playlist, and the first song is sung by a woman with a gorgeously robust voice, and I think she's singing some Italian.

"Renee Fleming," he says. "'O mio babbino caro'."

As we make our way up the trail, it's like the music is our soundtrack. And it never gets old. When this Italian beauty is over, it transitions to one of my songs, "Agony" by Martin Klem.

And a pit forms in my stomach.

My entire life, I've let myself stew in agony, almost as if I've deserved it. I know that's technically not true, but it's all I've known. Ever since I practically ran away from home, I've never really felt like I had one, even Glamour Springs. Sure, I have what I would call my new family there, and it is 'home' in a way, but I've still felt untethered. Incomplete. And I think that this, in a way, has been what's fueled my sadness. I've just felt so fundamentally disconnected from anything meaningful—relationships, careers, personal achievements—for s o long.

But I don't feel this way around Wyatt.

It feels like, for the first time, somebody's peeled off the mask I've worn my whole life—this somebody obviously being Wyatt. And he likes what he sees underneath.

Every now and then, we stop to look up at the starry sky. While we walk, I'm worried Wyatt will re-injure himself, but he's doing better than me. I have to remind myself that he's a professional athlete. Getting sweaty is what he does for a living.

Fuck. I have to shake my head to get the image of sweaty Wyatt out of my head. I may let myself connect with Wyatt, but sex would be too far. Then we'd both really be done for. I know I would lose everything—my job, my license. And I'm sure Wyatt, with as much attention as he's receiving for his coming out, would get far worse press about sleeping with his physical therapist.

Soon, I start to feel the strain on my legs, and I'm sweating like crazy. But then right after one of Wyatt's favorite Wagner arias, we get "Zenith" by *Sun Rain*, which by its very title encourages me to continue on to the very top.

We soon reach a fork in the road, and Wyatt guides us to the right.

"How you doing?" he asks.

"Good," I say, out of breath, definitely not sounding good.

"You sure?" he asks, turning and waiting for me to catch up. When I make it to him, I expect him to continue on, but he remains still, giving me a chance to catch my breath.

"How much farther?" I ask, a German art song now playing in my ear.

"Little over halfway," he says.

"Alright," I say, taking a deep breath.

He pats me on the shoulder, sweat staining just under the pecs of his hiking shirt. My headlamp shines light on the sweat dripping from the long ginger beard he decided to keep. And he's gotten more muscular since the last time I've seen him. God, he's such a specimen.

But he isn't just physically beautiful. Through his actions, he shows that he genuinely cares about me. He discovers I want a job in the NFO, so he helps me get it. He listens to my music. He creates a fucking playlist with both of our favorite music, then takes me on this gorgeous hike. I didn't think that they made men like this. And he's in the fucking NFO for fuck's sake!

Just when I think I'm not going to make it, Wyatt reassures me that we're only a couple minutes from the summit.

And then one of my favorite songs comes on, and I become laser focused.

Riceboy Sleeps by *Jónsi* and *Alex Somers* is regarded as one of the most seminal albums in all of post-rock, and there's no doubt as to why. It's contemplative, peaceful, and thought-provoking. And there couldn't be a better time for "Indian Summer", one of my favorite songs on the album, to play.

The first half of the song reminds me of drudgery, not unlike what we've been doing this entire time. Hard work. It reminds me how sometimes, when we get caught up in something that requires a ton of work, we lose sight of why we started the project or the journey in the first place. When I agreed to hike with Wyatt, I imagined what the end of the hike would be like—the vista, a good view of the stars. But I didn't imagine what a slog the hike would be. What also doesn't help is that I'm still not really accustomed to this altitude. The air is thin in the mountains, man.

"Aaaaaand we're here," Wyatt says.

When I take my place right next to him, my breath is taken away from me.

The sun has just dipped below the horizon, creating a thin, orange line pushing against the indigo sky. Just above us, the stars are beginning to shine, and I don't think I've ever seen so many in my life.

Wyatt pauses the song just before it shifts into the second part, but I don't complain.

"How do you like it?"

I stare up at the constellations, and just as I'm gazing into Jupiter's bright light, I see a shooting star.

I grab his shoulder. "Did you see that?" I ask, pointing. "A shooting star!"

"No way!" Wyatt says, looking up into the sky with me. But his gaze soon drifts back to me, like I'm the only thing that could impress him.

"Wow," I say, my neck starting to hurt from craning it so high. But I don't care. This is so worth it.

"Here," he says, putting his hand on my sweaty back. "Before you hurt your neck."

He guides us to a patch of grass. He sets down his hiking poles, and I do the same. Then he sits down.

"Lay in the grass with me," he says, gesturing to me.

I hesitate briefly. Everything we're doing is beyond professional now, but as long as we don't do anything physical, we'll be okay. And I don't think I need sex. Just feeling this connected to him is perfect.

I take off my cowboy hat and lay down next to him, giving us about a foot of space. I rest the hat on my sweaty belly.

"Oh, wow," I say, able to see many more stars now without pain in my neck. "This is—holy shit, Wyatt."

He turns and smiles at me. "Glad I took you out, huh?"

"Oh yeah."

I gaze into the constellations, and it seems like the longer I stare, the more I see. Ursa major, then minor. The big dipper, then Cassiopeia. And once the sun goes fully down, it's like every star in existence comes out. Like they're here to dance for us.

Wyatt grabs my shoulder. "There, a shooting star!" I look in the direction that he's pointing, but I'm too late to see anything. I laugh.

"I think we'll just have to take each other's word for it," I say.

He chuckles with me, laying his hand out halfway between us.

"What'd you wish for when you saw yours?" he asks.

I pause and think. I didn't wish for anything, but now that I think about it, I feel pretty contented.

Except for one little thing.

I'm glad I risked everything to come out here with Wyatt tonight. And I'm glad we've gotten to talk as more than just colleagues. But if I'm being honest, I wish we could go further. I wish that, tonight, we could connect in the way that only lovers do.

"Nothing," I lie. "I'm pretty content with the way things are."

He smiles at me, then looks at the sky.

"You?" I ask.

"For this night not to end," he says.

"That would be nice."

"And for you to stay by my side."

The feelings inside my body go haywire. But instead of shoving them down, I ride them.

I turn my head to him, smirking. "Good thing the night's just started."He smirks back, and we keep our eyes on each other for a moment or a minute, I can't tell. But we both eventually look back up the stars.

"So I gotta ask," Wyatt says. "Why do you wear the cowboy hat all the time?"

I find myself scratching its leather with my thumb.

"Not that it's weird or anything," he says, adjusting himself in the grass. "It's just—I hardly ever see you without it, so it seems like a deliberate decision. And I'm just curious why you made that deliberate decision."

My chest warms. "I don't think anyone has ever asked me so directly," I say. I take a deep breath. I feel like answering this is as personal as I can be—even more than sex in some ways. But the last thing I want to do is not answer him.

"I grew up on a ranch," I say. "Horses, cattle, chicken—whole nine yards. With my family, I always felt like I was the odd one out. My brothers liked to work on the ranch along with my parents, but I itched for something new—something beyond small-town Alabama. So when I went off to college, I abandoned everything about the ranch lifestyle. I wanted to erase my past and start over. To be a new person that had nothing to do with where I grew up. I got rid of everything that reminded me of home, including my clothing."

"Damn," Wyatt says. "That's... kinda intense. Scary."

I nod. When I've told this story to the few others in my life, they applaud me for being individualistic or whatever, but Wyatt's right. It was terrifying to try and rebuild myself from the ground up.

"When I went back to visit my folks after my first semester, I thought they'd be proud of me for stretching myself. But they were the opposite. They were angry. My dad said I thought I was better than all of them. My mama said that it's rude to forget my roots. And my brothers just made fun of me, calling me a sissy and a liberal and a queer." I laugh. "Even though most of those things are true.

"And so when I went back to school, I decided I would never come home again, but even that wasn't enough. Something was missing. After some long weeks of thinking, I knew what I had to do."

"And what's that?" Wyatt asks, turning his head to me.

I turn on my side to face him, gently moving the hat to the ground between us and propping myself on my elbow. "I didn't want to be close-minded like my parents, and I felt that completely cutting them off would be no different than what they were doing to me. So one long weekend, I drove back to the ranch. I left a note in their mailbox, saying that if they ever wanted to hear where I was coming from, I'd be willing to talk. And I left them my contact info. After that, I went to a our small 'downtown' and bought an authentic cowboy hat along with a bunch of clothes. From that point on, I've worn the hat proudly as a symbol that I'm open-minded."

I sigh when I finish, not really feeling like I told the whole story. And judging by Wyatt's face, I think he thinks the same. He's waiting for me to say more.

"It's just hard," I say, feeling sadness break through all the other emotions that Wyatt's making me feel. "Because after all these years, they still haven't called. It's like they're glad that I'm gone. And I think I'm afraid that they never will reach out, and I'll never talk to my family of origin again."

Without my consent, some tears leak out of my eyes, but I keep it mostly under control.

"I'm sorry, Silas."

I wipe my eyes. "I'm not sad about it," I say, shaking my head, my voice shaky. "I'm just—" I sigh. "Fuck it. I'm sad. I'm angry. But the worst part is that there's nothing I can do. Nothing in the world will make them call me. I'm just fucking powerless."

Not wanting Wyatt to see me like this, I lay on my back again and place my hat back on my stomach. I don't bother to hide the rest of my tears. They clear the dried sweat from my face as they flow.

"You know," Wyatt says, adjusting himself. I can't see all of him, but I think he's just moved closer to me.

"I think this story just shows what a beautiful person you are."

I let out a sharp laugh. "Sure," I say, wiping my eyes. "I really mean it," he says.

Right. I'm not with Llewellyn. I can't make self-deprecating comments.

He turns to me and props himself on his elbow, just like I did earlier. "Think about it," he says. "You were the who took the risk to leave your hometown. You were the one who took on the greater risk of going back and trying to connect with your family. And then it was the greatest risk of all to put the ball in your family's court to contact you. I don't know, Silas, but that feels like love to me. Unconditional love on your part." I turn to him and put my hands underneath my cheek. "You think so?" He reaches out and wipes a loose tear with his thumb. It lingers on my face, and slowly he strokes the edge of my mustache before he pulls away. And more than anything, I wished that he would have just shoved that thumb in my mouth. That and a lot more.

No. Sex is too far.

"Music," I say, pushing myself away from him. "Let's, uh, listen to some music before we go down to the summit."

Wyatt adjusts his shorts as if he's got a boner or something. Fuck. I'm definitely not looking down there.

"Sure," he says, pulling out his phone. "Let me just press play."

While looking up at the stars, I reflect on all that Wyatt said. And that's when the "Indian Summer" resumes.

We reach the midpoint where the music changes entirely. There's a drone note that gradually increases in volume until it's nearly deafening, and it reminds me of a sunrise after a long night or reaching the summit after a long journey like Wyatt and I just have.

And it reflects how I feel right now.

Ever since I left the note with my family, it's felt like a long, monotonous, and tough journey with little payoff. There have been times when I've forgotten about them, but during lonely moments, especially on holidays or boring weekends, I have found myself missing my family deeply, their flaws and all. If I were to liken these experiences to the hike, these have been the moments where my legs get tired and I want to give up—or, literally, when I want my life to end. Because, this entire time, I haven't been able to help but feel like if I could have just been someone else—less gay, more masculine, more interested in staying on the ranch—then maybe they would have reached out to me. Maybe they would have loved me enough to ask me to stay.

But Wyatt's introduced a whole new perspective. Maybe it's not me who's at fault. Maybe, like he said, this whole journey has shown what an amazing person I am.

That's when my heart picks up speed. More than anything, I want to reach out, grab hold of Wyatt and pull him so close that I can never lose him. Because he, before anyone else—before Jimmy, Linda, Llewellyn, Kyle, Michael, or even myself—could see this amount of good in me.

"Wyatt," I say, turning my head to him just as "Indian Summer" quietly fades into another song I can't recognize.

And I'm more than relieved to see he already has his head turned to me. I'm ecstatic.

"What?" he asks, a warm, sleepy smile on his face.

I reach out and grab his hand. I hold it between us and assess it. He has thick calluses around the bases of his fingers as well as just beneath the first crease of his fingers, probably from deadlifting. I slide my fingers between his, and he grips me back tightly, probably just like he holds onto a football.

And my neck while he's fucking me.

"What's on your mind, Silas?" he asks.

I let out some shallow breaths, vacillating over whether or not I really want to say this. Because if we do what I'm about to say, then there's no going back. We could just pretend this didn't happen, and we could go back to being professional. We could both keep our jobs and reputations, and nobody would know a thing.

But that is not what I want.

And seeing the way that Wyatt's looking at me, I don't think it's what he wants, either.

"Silas," he says. "If you want to head back now, we can st—"

"Will you come home with me?" I ask.

He moves our hands from between us, letting us both see the other clearly.

I swallow what feels like sand in my throat. Maybe he didn't hear me. I'll ask again.

"Will you—"

"Yes," he says, low and strong. "Yes, I will come home with you."

I lay there, astounded that this might actually be happening. I maybe have a few seconds to stop this before it goes past the point of no return.

But I let those pass. Happily.

"Okay," I say. "Great."

"Well," he says, squeezing my hand. "Should we head there now?"

I look back at the stars one last time, thanking them that my wish is actually coming true.

"Yeah," I say, squeezing his hand back. "Let's go."

Chapter 15

Silas King

I SWEAR, OUR HIKE down the trail feels like it passes in a quarter of the time it took us to ascend. I get worried that Wyatt will hurt himself again, especially when he accidentally sticks his hiking pole in a hole, causing him to stumble. But after he reassures me he's fine—and I double check his left leg to be sure—we finally make it back to the car. We both get inside without a word, and the next stop is my apartment. Once we're back out on the main road, I have to remind myself to breathe.

I'm about to have sex with Wyatt Nelson.

"So," Wyatt says, tapping on his steering wheel. "See anyone while I'm gone?"

I shake my head. "Can I be honest?"

He looks at me briefly, then back at the road, his shoulders tense. "Of course." He's nervous for some reason.

"I haven't even wanted to see anyone else," I say. "You've been the only one on my mind."

I glance over to see his shoulders relax, as if I told him exactly what he wanted to hear.

"Cool," he says.

"What about you?"

"I've been too busy recovering," he says. "But you've been the only man on my mind, too. And can I tell you why?"

A pit forms in my stomach, and all the emotions that Wyatt makes me feel pool in: fear that we'll be caught, anger that I've waited this long to say what I've wanted, excitement to finally have him inside me again, and so many more I don't know how to describe.

"Tell me," I say, tightly gripping handle above the passenger window.

"Ever since I met you," he says, shaking his head and grinning out at the road. "I just felt this special connection to you. You were so—I don't know. I felt like you saw me. Like you could understand me more than anyone else. My entire life, I've been known as a guy good at football, which is true, but I'm more than that. I love to sing. I'm gay, for fuck's sake. And I fucking love music. And I feel like you see all of these parts equally in a way that no one else does."

It feels like someone has inserted hundreds of little helium balloons in my torso because I swear I'm floating out of my seat. Wyatt's gravity is pulling me in strong. There's no stopping this now.

"Well, you are a really cool guy," I say, trying to sound nonchalant, even though my heart is racing faster than a fucking horse. "It's just natural for me to see you that way."

"And that just makes it natural and easy to like you back," he says. "You're like a comfortable pair of pajamas. Cozy, reliable, and safe."

"That's how you feel with me, too," I say, thinking back to the way his reassurance about my family made me feel. Though it feels too histrionic for me to say it all here right now. I don't want to come off as obsessive.

"Good," he says, a satisfied smile on his face.

Sooner than I would expect, we make it back to my apartment.

"Now," I say as we get out of the car. "My apartment probably isn't as nice as yours, so don't judge me."

He lets out a chuckle, sending warm chills down my spine. "You don't have to worry about that."

Once we make it to my apartment, I set down my keys and Cheshire comes prancing to the door, meowing like crazy.

"Oh my God—he is so cute," Wyatt says, pointing at my fluffy black cat. He squats down to pet him, and Cheshire rubs himself on Wyatt's thick legs, chirruping and purring louder than Wyatt's Jeep Wrangler.

"He's the apple of my eye," I say. "Can I get you anything?"

"No," he says, still petting Cheshire. "I'm good."

And then I freeze up. I invited him back here, but it's been ages since I've been in this sort of situation with a man, let alone one I adore more than my body can take. Literally. My emotions are jumbled mess right now, threating to come out of my mouth or eyes.

Wyatt stands and pulls me close to him before I can panic further. "You're all I need," he says. And then he plants a warm, deep kiss on my lips. I want to hold on, but he pulls away before I can stop him.

"Now, when you said you wanted me over," he says. "Did that mean..."

I think about us fucking on the treatment table back the Miss U PT clinic.

"Yes," I say, nodding. "I was thinking bedroom stuff. If you're okay..."

"More than okay," he says. "That sounds perfect."

"Okay," I say, finally slipping off my hiking boots. Wyatt's still in his dusty attire.

"I should get myself cleaned up," I say. "And cleaned out."

He nods. "I can too," he says, looking down at his outfit, barely dried from how much he sweat. "Or..."

I raise a brow. "What?"

"From what I remember," he says, stepping closer—close enough to where I can smell him. "You liked how funky I smelled."

I recall shoving his feet in my face and burying my nose deep in my crotch. Oh, fuck—and the way the smell lingered in my nostrils as he fucked me so hard I could barely walk right. That night, I didn't even feel ashamed about the freaky things I liked. I just let myself enjoy them. Because, I don't know—Wyatt made me feel comfortable fulfilling these desires. And here he is again, inviting me to fulfill the same desires. No judgment. Just seeing me for who I am and liking me all the same.

"I did," I say, my head low, embarrassed to say it out loud.

Wyatt puts his finger underneath his chin and raises my face to meet his gaze. "That was so hot watching you worship me like that," he says. "I want you to do it again. But this time, now that I'm healed, I got some things up my sleeve to return the favor."

My skin gets warm, and I know I'm flushing. I nod quickly.

He kisses me on the forehead, and I get a nice whiff of him—sweaty, earthy, raw.

And he's mine.

His kiss lingers, sending chills down my spine. When he pulls away and looks at me, he takes me in like I'm the greatest treasure anyone could possess.

"I should get cleaned up," he says. "Before we get too busy. You can wait here on the couch."

Cheshire runs between our legs, and Wyatt nods.

"I'll be here." He steps back and sits on the couch. Cheshire jumps into his lap, and I can't help but smile. Seeing these two together tickles something deep within me. It's like they were meant to be.

"I'll be back," I say. I make my way to bedroom, grab some clothes to change into. Then, I enter my master bathroom, shut the door, and look myself right in the mirror.

"I can't believe I'm doing this," I whisper to myself.

My entire life, I've strived to have the job that I do. And I'm about to throw it all away. To sleep with a patient? There's a power imbalance. There's something inherently wrong with this.

But it doesn't feel inherently wrong. Everything about Wyatt feels inherently right.

Fuck it. Earlier, I said I was going to let myself fall into him. So that's exactly what I'm going to do.

In what feels like record time, I douche and shower, but I keep a little stink on me. I don't know. I like it on Wyatt a lot—maybe he does on me, too. Besides, I think it's hotter to wear my natural scent rather than soaps or artificial scents. Just feels more raw and hot that way.

When I'm all done, I get dressed, take a deep breath, and walk out to meet Wyatt. He's sitting with his hairy legs spread, his boots untied by still on, as he strokes Cheshire in his lap. As I approach him, a smile gradually forms on his lips, and when I'm finally standing just before him, his grin is practically as wide as his shoulders. Sweat from the hike earlier lingers on him, and his ginger beard is disheveled. I just want to run my ringers through it and straighten it all out.

Without a word, he gently removes Cheshire from his lap and raises to his feet. He places his hands on my upper arms and places a sobering kiss right where my third eye would be. Warm shivers ripple out from the point to every part of my body, and it takes all my strength not to convulse under his touch.

And that's when I get scared. *This* is truly the point of no return.

"Are you sure about this?" I ask as he pulls away, as if this was his whole idea.

"Can I be honest again?" he asks, his hands stroking my bare arms. I'm wearing a tank top and loose gym shorts, but Wyatt's looking at me like I'm wearing a three-piece suit.

"I've waited my whole life to find something like we have," he says. "I don't think I've ever felt like I've known someone better. It's like I knew you before this life or something, I swear. And this is what I wanted—exactly what I wanted when I came out. I wanted to find a genuine connection like this.

"And when it became clear that we couldn't pursue each other because it was a conflict of interest, I was furious. Because here I am, waiting my whole life to finally come out and find someone that likes the true me, yet I can't have him. All because of some institutional bullshit."

He rests his forehead against mine, his lips less than an inch away.

"I'm tired of it," he says, his rich voice vibrating my entire body. "But if you tell me to get lost—that you want to keep this relationship professional—I won't protest at all. In fact, I'll leave without question and never try to push this again. No playlists, no hikes, no flirting—no nothing. But given how much I've wanted this, I'm willing to risk it all. For you. Just the say the words and I'll let myself fall into you Silas. And I'll be fucking yours."

His words make the emotions slosh and froth within me, like putting a fizzy drink inside a blender already filled with fruits and juices. I can hardly contain myself with how seen I feel by him, how much I want to date this man and see where it goes. I've never known someone like this—someone that makes me want to live and give it all up.

So I'm not willing to let him go, either.

"Stay here, Wyatt," I say, putting my arms around his neck. "And make love with me."

And that's when we fall into each other, two black holes finally colliding and sending ripples across time and space.

He wraps his arms around my lower back and practically lifts me into his mouth. One of my hands holds his shoulder as the other runs through his short, buzzed brown hair. On anyone else, this hair would just be boring. But on him, I love the way the short hairs tickle my palm and resists my hand as I press down. It's like every inch of Wyatt deserves exploration, like he's vaster than deep space itself.

As my tongue fights his to be inside his mouth, I catch hold of his thick beard hairs, yearning to press myself deep into him so I can feel the beard pressed so tightly against my face that I think it's my own.

"God, I can't get enough of you," Wyatt growls.

That's when he grips my ass and lifts me into the air. Not knowing what else to do, I wrap my legs around Silas's back, propping my ankles up on the shelf of Wyatt's ass. Oh, I want to get in there tonight. If he'll let me.

I hook my arms under Wyatt's and grip the tops of his shoulders like my life depends on it. But it's not like I need to. It's because I want to. Wyatt's huge arms are flexing hard, but he's got a solid grip on me, and I doubt he'd let me fall. Which is impressive. Because I'm somewhere between 240 and 250, but he's handling me like I'm light as a football.

As if he already lives here, he guides us both to my bedroom with ease. He walks me over to the bed and slowly leans over. Reluctantly, because I can't handle being farther away from him, I slowly untangle my limbs from his body, letting myself fall from the bed. But once I land, Wyatt doesn't pull away in the slightest. He crawls onto the bed, pushing me toward the headboard and inserting himself between my legs. He runs his hands through my hair as our lips touch again.

"I swear," he says, breaking hold of my lips to kiss along my cheek, my ear, my neck. He sucks on my collar bone, making me moan. He raises himself to my ear. "I wanna fuck you so hard and long that we won't be able to tell where my skin ends and your skin starts. I wanna be fucking welded as one."

He presses his throbbing dick, through both our clothes, against my hole, making my whole body buck.

"Then let's get our fucking clothes off," I say.

He leans up to slip shirt off seamlessly, and then he helps prop me up as I slip mine off. Just as I remove my pants and underwear, Wyatt jumps off the bed to remove his shorts, and I gasp when I see what he's wearing underneath.

"What?" he asks, startled. He puts a hand on my leg. "Are you okay?"

I look at the mesh fabric that covers his balls, but his dick his too big and erect to contain. It hangs mischievously from the pouch, like an overgrown eggplant, and the waistband of his underwear greedily hugs the hairy waist of this huge man. God, I wish I was his underwear, holding his junk so intimately at all times of the day.

"Turn around," I say, my hand covering my mouth.

He slowly does a 180, gradually revealing to what a perfect butt he has. Thick brown hair fans out from the crack, both on the cheeks and out the top. He adjusts his legs, making his cheeks squeeze into each other, and I nearly faint. Straps dig into the crease just below his ass cheeks, and there's a wide band above it, together framing his perfect butt just for me.

"A jock strap?" I ask, breathless, as Wyatt turns to face me. "You wore a jock strap?"

He shrugs, bracketing his hips with his arms, showing off how wide his frame really is. "Most guys wear compression shorts nowadays, but I still wear the jock every now and then." He smirks. "Especially if I'm meeting up with a hot cowboy."

"You jerk," I say, a wide smile forming on my face. "You planned this. You knew this was going to happen. You wore the jockstrap knowing I would see it."

He chuckles. "Let's just say I'm a gambler, but I know how to play my cards right."

I sigh and roll my eyes. "That you did."

And without needing to say more, he takes his place on top of me, and my lips are more than happy to touch his again.

"Since you like it so much, you want me to keep it on when I fuck you?"

I'm about to nod, but then I stop myself.

I don't want to jump straight to fucking, even as eager as I am to get off with Wyatt. I want to worship him, too—the same way I did the first time so many months ago. That made the penetration when we finally got to it so much hotter.

"Yes. But I need to worship you again," I say. "Before you fuck me."

"Right," he says, kissing me on the forehead, which, even now with us naked and him laying on top of me, still sends warm shivers throughout my entire body. "And I need to return the favor."

Even stronger chills threaten to lock my entire body up, making me a ragdoll in my man's arms. Because that's who Wyatt is—my man. I just know that after this there won't be any abandonment. We'll be steady. I'll be his, and he'll be mine.

"You want my feet again?" he asks.

I picture his huge hairy feet and how fucking manly they must smell after that hike, but when I see it in my head, I know exactly what I want.

"Your ass," I say brutely. "On my face."

"My ass," he says, mimicking my voice, sounding like a cave man. "On your face. Got it."

I laugh, slightly embarrassed. "Sorry."

He shakes his head. "That was—you don't need to be sorry. Was that mean?"

Now I shake my head. "Not at all. That was funny."

He smirks. "Good. I don't want to hurt you."

"You didn't," I say, reassuring him. And I doubt he ever could.

He nods, then holds his body into mine and lifts my arm above my head. He presses his nose into my pit and breathes deeply. I'm glad I kept some of my stink.

"So good," he says, exhaling. He takes some more time breathing me in, and I start to stroke myself, loving having him all on me like this.

"Alright," he says, giving my armpit one last little kiss. "My ass on your face?"

I nod eagerly.

He props a pillow under my head, then turns toward the foot of the bed. It feels like my entire body melts as he slowly backs his hairy, beautiful ass onto my face. He opens his cheeks for me to fit in better, I stick my face inside, and then he gently sits himself down.

And oh. My. God.

"Fuck," I say, breathing him in. "You're so perfect."

He chuckles. "Eat up, little pig."

Him calling me that turns me into one. I ravenously stick my tongue in his hole, pulsing it as fast as I can, getting a nose and mouth full of hair as I do so. As I worship his hole, I can't tell if I want to smell or lick him more. So I do both, sometimes stopping just to smell, other times licking him as aggressively as I can. I swear I could fucking live in here. He smells like a man, and he tastes even better.

I squeeze both of his ass cheeks, and I love how firm they are under my grip. "They don't call you a tight end for nothing. Fuck."

He lets out a loud laugh. "Glad you're enjoying it, but I told you you're getting some attention too."

That's when he grabs my legs and pulls them toward him. He hooks my ankles underneath his arms and props them against his shoulder blades, like I'm a fucking backpack. Suddenly, I feel something warm and wet plop against my hole, then something firm and forceful.

"Fuck," I say, muffled by Wyatt's ass cheeks as he inserts a finger lubed with his own spit inside me. "That feels—oh my god."

"Told you I had something to give you in return," he says, and I can practically hear the smirk on his face. He drops another wad of spit right onto my hole, and just when I think he's going to insert himself, he smacks my ass like a fucking drum.

I moan plaintively, and he just chuckles.

"I didn't tell you to fucking stop, Silas," he says, massaging my hole with his thumb.

"Yes, sir," I say. And I get to worshipping his hole.

Occasionally, he'll move his ass around, like a dog scratching its back against an itching post—except he's the dog and my tongue is the itching post. With my arms around his thighs, I try to press his ass harder onto me so I can get deeper into him.

When I come up for air, I look up the pristine wall of his back. Hair snakes from his ass crack up his spine and fans out like angel wings onto the rest of his back. It's hairiest around his shoulder blades, and I remove my hands from Wyatt's hairy thighs to run my hands through this lush forest. Each time Wyatt spanks me, each hit harder than the one before, I grip his hairy lats and stick my tongue even deeper inside him to keep myself still.

"Man, you are a little whore, aren't you?"

"Fuck yeah, I am," I say, coming up for breath.

"You really love the smell of my sweaty ass, don't you? Fucking pervert?"

My dick twitches against his belly at his words. "Yeah," I say desperately, giving his hole an aggressive lick.

"Good boy," he says, slapping my ass harder than he ever has before. I know his slaps are gonna leave a mark. Good. I want his fucking handprint tattooed on my ass. I'm his fucking property.

"Keep eating my hole, perv," he says, aggressively massaging my ass cheeks, slapping them occasionally. "I'm not done with you yet."

He drops more spit onto my hole and fingers it hard as I get lost in his. To think that this is how he smelled and tasted as he guided me up that summit. As we listened to our music together. As he reassured me that I'm not to blame for my family never reaching out to me.

God, this makes me want him more. I want to fucking bottle up his earthy, masculine, sweaty scent and spray it on my face as a form of discipline. Every time I misbehave or do something Wyatt doesn't want, I want to smell him and remind myself that he fucking owns me. Because he does. He's sitting on me like I'm his throne, the cushion my face and tongue and my legs his armrests. And I wouldn't have it any other way. I want to use his hairy, musky ass as a pillow, arousing myself every time I wake up to his smell. And after I get off with his ass on me, he uses my hole like it's all I'm good for. I want him to breed me, then breed me, and breed me again. Then breed me one last time for good measure.

"Alright," he says, retracting his finger from my hole. Usually, I need lube for any sort of foreign object going inside me. Spit isn't enough.

But not with Wyatt.

I don't know what it is about his spit or his touch, but him going inside me feels like the perfect amount of pain and pleasure. In fact, I'm glad he's just using his spit. I may not even object to him sticking it raw inside me. Maybe one day.

"I think it's time," he says.

"Yes, sir," I say as he slides off me. I itch my mustache wafting up the smell of his ass into my nose. God, I never want to wash my face again. I want his smell on me forever.

"You got lube?" he asks. I nod and reach over to my nightstand drawer to pull it out. Even though I want to try it, I'm not ready for no-lube sex.

He starts applying it to himself as he looks down at me. God, I fucking swear he looks like a pornstar stroking himself this way, smirking down at me. I could take a picture like this and make millions. After all, that's what he said he'd do if he could.

"You ready?" he asks, fingering my hole with some lube.

"Please," I say softly.

He starts fucking me, and, naturally, his hands find their way to the base of my neck again. I give him a reassuring nod.

He clamps his hands down on the sides of my neck, and already my head starts to feel light. As he pounds into me, each thrust feels a little sharper, a little stronger. And I'm in heaven for it.

"Fuck," Wyatt says, his huge, hairy arms flexing as he holds me down. "You make me feel so good. I'm already so close"

I run my hands up and down his arms as he fucks me harder.

"I wanna try something else," he says, slowing down. "Something I've wanted to do for a while, if you'll let me."

I nod as he lets go of my neck and slowly pulls out.

"I know this may be weird, but hear me out. May I...?"

"You can do whatever you want to me," I say honestly.

He smirks and grabs under my legs. He pushes them back until they're just over my head. "Hold them here," he says. And I obey by wrapping my arms around the undersides of my knees, presenting my raw hole to him.

And he does what I'd least expect. He stands up, turns around, and squats down over my ass with his dick pointed downward. That's when he sticks it inside, and I can't help but let out a moan. I've never a dick inside me from this position, and it feels... amazing. I feel all sorts of pressure in different parts of my ass, and it gets my dick rock-hard.

That's when he leans forward into push-up position, sort of like how he fucked me the first time, just turned the opposite direction. Then, he sets one leg down and straightens it back toward my head. When he moves the other, he's in a plank position, his legs supporting him on either side of me and pressing down against my legs, his arms propping the top half of his body up. And, of course, his dick is like a metal rod inside me.

He lifts up slightly, then thrusts into me, and we both moan.

"I fucking—God, I love this position," he says, thrusting into me again. "It's just so underrated. And it feels so good."

"Fuck yeah it does."

"I don't think I'll last long this way," he says. "Can I cum inside you?"

"Please," I say, rubbing the backs of his hairy, sweaty legs.

And he doesn't hold back.

He lifts himself to the perfect height where his dick doesn't slip out, then uses all of his weight to crash down into me. I let out a gasp each time he does because I don't think anyone has been in me like this until now. And each time he thrusts, his perfect hairy ass, which sat on my face just like a seat, flexes each time he thrusts inside me. I also love the way an ass looks mid-thrust, and now I get to watch the one on the man tearing my hole apart. My life couldn't get any better.

Wyatt's ass clenches even harder, and he warns me that he's about to cum. He then thrusts so hard into me that he takes my breath away. He groans and convulses as he spills his side inside me. I reach up and fondle his ass, believing that yes, indeed, my life can't get any better.

To see a beautiful man so into me—into me enough to fucking get into the plank position and cum inside my hairy, beefy body—is the best antidepressant I could have. I know it's not a good idea to have my life depend on people like this, but come the fuck on. I've been sad for years, and now I finally have something to be happy for? I deserve this. I so fucking deserve this.

"Fuck," Wyatt says, his body convulsing one last time as I squeeze my hole around his thick dick. There is not one drop of him that I want to lose. Thank God gravity's on my side with this one.

"Please," I say. "Wyatt, stay inside me. I need to cum with you inside me."

"Then let's do this."

He pulls out of me, but before I can protest, he turns around, his body drenched in sweat from the workout of his orgasm, then puts himself between my legs again. He inserts himself aside me again, no softer than before, and gently thrusts inside me, his face stoic, calm, and kind.

"I'm gonna stay in you 'til you cum," he says, his voice hoarse from his orgasm. "There anything else you want me to do?"

"Choke me?" I ask, loving more than anything the way his grip feels around my neck.

Thrusting at a perfectly slow and steady pace, he reaches over and puts his hands around my neck, applying just enough of his weight like last time for the ideal amount of pressure. I feel my head get light, enhancing the pleasure of his thrusts two-fold. I start stroking myself, sure I can get myself to cum in less than thirty seconds.

"Oh, and one more thing," he says. He gets one leg up, now kneeling, and the movement doesn't even stop his gradual thrusting or grip around my neck.

Then he does the unimaginable.

With a balance that only a freshly recovered NFO tight end could have, Wyatt reaches his foot over my entire body and rests the crook of his toes just on my nose. I take in a shallow-choked breath, and my dick twitches upon smelling his glorious, manly scent. I'm past the point of no-return.

"Oh my God," I say. "You smell—"

"Breathe me in," he says, stroking me, choking me, and pressing down on my face with his foot. But I can still see him just above his toes. He's looking down at me like I'm the most important person to walk the earth. And right now—after everything he's told me tonight—I think that's true.

I stroke myself, watching his handsome, bearded, rugged face as I do, breathing in his musk as rapidly as I can.

"My little pervert," he says, a smirk forming on his face. "If you don't cum for me quick, I might think I wasn't good enough for you."

And for whatever reason, that sends me over the edge. I moan—and practically wail—as I shoot cum onto my hairy belly, using my free hand to press Wyatt's foot harder onto my nose, afraid that if I'm not smelling him he'll disappear.

Gradually, fatigue overwhelms me, and I let go of him and my dick. When Wyatt pulls out, I panic and look around for him. He slides into the bed and wraps his arms around me, then pulls the covers over both of us.

I turn away from him and hold his arms greedily against my chest. I nuzzle back into him as hard as I can.

Wyatt kisses the back of my neck. "How are you feeling?"

"I never said this before," I say, feeling my heartrate increase. But I feel like if I don't say this now Wyatt will disappear overnight or in some other way that I can't control. And I can't have that. I need him with me, now more than ever.

"Tell me," Wyatt says, squeezing me hard.

"I've been sad for so much of my life," I say. "Especially since I walked away from my family." I'm tempted to tell him about the suicidal ideation, but I hold it back. That's too much. And the last thing I want is for him to run away.

"But you—" I say, feeling my voice wobble. I squeeze his arms tighter, and he, in turn, holds me tighter, too.

"You make me feel so many things. But most importantly, you make me feel happy. For so long, I've tried to connect with other men. But then they'll listen to my music or they'll get to know me or they'll fuck me and decide they've had enough." I feel tears wet my cheeks. "And I really like you. So I don't want that to happen between us."

Somehow, he hugs me tighter, planting the deepest kiss tonight against the back of my neck, almost as if he's inserting his love like a flash drive into my spinal chord—into the very structure of my body.

He moves his mouth to my ear, his beard tickling my warm skin as he does.

"I'm not going anywhere," he says. "I know who I am. I know what I want. And I want you, Silas."

I raise his thumb to my mouth and kiss it. "Thank you," I say.

Before we drift off, I let out my little fantasy of waking up against his ass cheeks. So he decides we turn it into a reality.

In the middle of the night, his dick stirs against my ass, waking me up. And that's when he slides to the top corner of the bed, rolls onto his belly, and gives his ass to me.

So I go to town.

And holy shit—his ass smells and tastes the best it ever has. Before I even get enough, he then flips me onto my belly, gets on top, and fucks me senseless. To make sure I'm satisfied, we repeat it one more time that night, then once in the morning for good measure. At this point, I realize I forgot to write in my journal, but it doesn't matter. Because I'm sure as hell not ending my life now.

When we're all done, both of us drifting into deep sleep just as the morning comes up, I realize I've fallen in love—in love with the person who is helping me see that life is worth living.

And just as I let sleep take me on, I say a prayer that I'll never lose him. Because if I do, then it won't be so easy to put an x next to the date anymore.

Chapter 16

Wyatt Nelson

IT'S A CHILLY OCTOBER day in Denver's stadium. We're tied 21 – 21 against the Steeds, and time's almost up. But if I catch the ball and score a touchdown, we'll not only win, but I'll further my reputation as not only a good blocking tight end, but a good catching one, too. Just one more season of this gameplay and I'll likely be memorialized—and not just as the best tight end of the century, but one who is gay as well.

We jog to our positions after a down, and I nod to Blake along the way. He gives me a slight nod back.

These past two months have been a test of our friendship. He still thinks that it's risky for me to play at all this season. He insists that my torn ACL last December was due to a hate crime, and he thinks I'm in danger of something worse happening. But we've both played plenty of games this season, and the only thing of note is that I've been catching passes like a beast. Yet he's still worried. And I'm tired of it. I just wish that he would worry about his own internalized homophobia rather than my coming out. I'm fine, and I'm definitely not in danger. At the very least, though, he's been working with me to help improve my catching.

I get into position, and then I hear it.

Faggot.

The same slur I was called just before I was injured.

Even through all the sound in the stadium—the shouting, the wind, the occasional blast of music—I somehow hear the word loud and clear, and my blood runs cold.

I remember the day vividly—a cold day in Salt Lake. I remember the way the turf burned against my skin as I laid there in agony after I been tackled at the same time by two different Sparrows players. The word 'faggot' echoed in my ears, uttered just before the play began.

Just like I hear now.

Our center snaps the ball to Blake. But the Steed's linebacker and defensive end don't go for him.

They target me instead.

As I rush forward, I try to tell myself that this is just because they anticipate our movement—that they know I've been stellar at catching passes this season, and they're just waiting to block the pass or tackle me.

But even from here, I see the fury in their eyes—fury that isn't just because we're on opposing teams.

It's personal.

I manage to dart past the linebacker, running as fast as I can. I swear, I can feel phantom pain in my knee as I recall how harrowing that tackle was almost a year ago, like my body is anticipating it.

"No," I grunt through my mouth guard. "Not again."

I charge forward, and like my life depends on it, I push the defensive end out of the way. He tries to grab for my leg—which he shouldn't because I don't have the ball—but I manage to pull it away more out of fear for my safety rather than just pure gameplay. Once I'm where Blake and I have agreed upon, I turn to see him throw the ball my way.

Several other players close in on me as I run, I begin to fear for my life. Are all these guys with the Sparrows? Or are the Sparrows part of something bigger? Is Blake right? Is there some larger conspiracy out to get me?

Not wanting to find out, I push myself as hard as I can—too hard, it feels like. There's a slight pain in my left knee. But I don't stop. Because if I do, my injury might be far worse than a torn ACL.

Seeing the ball headed straight for me, I leap into the air and catch it with both hands. When I land, I keep up my speed, not even daring to let the others catch up to me. When I score the touchdown, the game is all but over. My team congratulates me, and Blake does too. In fact, as he hugs me, it almost feels like we haven't been fighting about my safety the past year—that he finally agrees that there's nothing to worry about. Funny how the tables turn.

Once we're in the locker room, reporters storm our team, but I manage to corner Blake before they reach us.

"That was fucking sick, man," he says. "We fucking crushed that."

"Blake, listen," I say, putting my hand on my shoulder and looking around to make sure we're not being overheard. I know since we were the stars of the game, reporters will swarm us any minute, but I gotta get this out. Especially since I've still got chills that are my making the many hairs on my body stand on e nd.

'Faggot', I heard so clearly.

And to think I've been safe this whole time. I think I finally believe that I'm not. If it happens once, it's an accident, but twice...

"What's going on man?" Blake asks as I look around one more time. "You look—"

"I think you're right," I say.

He squints at me, but then his eyes go wide. "You're not saying..."

I nod quickly, wiping off sweat that's just dripped into my beard. "They called me a 'faggot' out there," I say, deadly quiet.

His eyes remain wide, and I see a vein throb just above his tapered sideburns.

"And this isn't the first time," I say, reassured that no one's listening.

"What are you saying?" Blake asks, his teeth gritted.

"That time I was tackled back in December," I say. "When my ACL was torn—they called me a 'faggot' then, too."

Blake's jaw drops, and he holds his stomach like I've just punched him in the gut. I bet that's exactly how he feels, too.

He closes his mouth and glares at me, about to speak, but that's when the reporters swarm us. We put on our best media façades and answer the questions as best we can. Yes, we've been strategizing as quarterback and tight end. Yes, we've been working on my passing. Yes, blocking's still important. And yes, we're hoping this will take us to the Championship Game this year.

Blake and I don't even look at each other until we're both showered and the locker room's mostly empty. We gotta make it to the bus soon, but we got time.

"So let me get this straight," Blake says, tossing down the bag full of his gear. "You're telling me that you getting your ACL torn was indeed a hate crime, and now you're—"

"It wasn't a hate crime," I say. "It was—"

"Wyatt," he says, spitting out the 't' in my name like it's venom. "They called you a faggot on the field just before that happened. And I saw that tackle. That was deliberate. They went after you." He shakes his head. "Fuck. This all makes sense."

I shift my weight on the bench, pulling on my beard. "It's not as bad—"

"Not as bad? Wyatt, you heard them call you a faggot on the field again tonight. And you think that's a coincidence or something?"

"I'm not saying it's a coin—"

"Yes you are!" he nearly shouts. And then he hushes himself, stepping closer. He sits down on the bench next to me.

"Look, I don't know why you keep downplaying this. And since this season had gone so well without any sort of incident, I began to believe you. But you're telling me you slept on the fact that they called you a faggot back in December, and they just did again tonight? Imagine what could have happened to you."

"I know," I grunt out. "I fucking know, alright? That's why I told you. Because hearing that word brought me back to that moment right before I got injured." I rub my knee, feeling a low ache deep in my bones. "It feels like parts of my body think the injury happened over again."

"Because it could have happened again," Blake says. "Or worse."

I drop my face into my hands and rub my eyes. "We have to get going. The bus is probably waiting for us."

"Not until we figure out what to do."

I lift my face and scowl at him. "What's there to figure out?"

"I don't know!" he says, throwing his hands in the air.

"Are you thinking we report this to the authorities or something?"

He runs his hand through his fuzzy black beard, still drying from the shower. "That's likely the only choice."

I push myself off the bench and grab my bag. "We can't do that."

"And why the hell not? Wyatt, you're clearly not safe."

I clench my fists and bite my lip, taking a deep breath to calm down. But it doesn't help much. "Because if I do, who would believe us? Sure, I heard the words spewed out at me on the field. But that narrows it down to eleven guys on the other team. And that doesn't even account for the guys on our own team."

He widens his eyes. "You think—" he shakes his head. "Fucking Christ, man. This is bad. What if it is someone on the Pioneers?"

"See?" I nearly shout. "My allegations are serious. This shit would take time to prove. Meanwhile, the media would focus on me like a hawk. But it wouldn't be about my playing. Remember Kyle Weaver a few years back when there was even a hint that he was gay? That's all that ran about him for months. He had to fucking find a girlfriend to silence it. And sure, I'm out now, but imagine the field day the media would have with me accusing someone else of a hate crime. This wouldn't just disrupt our team. It would disrupt the entire NFO. I'd probably put more targets on my back.

"I don't want any of that," I say, lowering my voice and shaking my head. "I just want to fucking play football. I want to go down as a memorialized tight end, not as some faggot who cried that some other players were beating him up."

Blake's jaw locks as he pushes himself up from the bench and approaches me. He stands just in front of me, several inches shorter, then looks both ways like he's crossing the street, making sure that no one's listening.

"And what about him?" he asks, his voice sharp and quiet. "What about Silas?"

Hearing Silas's name come out of Blake's mouth feels like a punch to the gut. I told Blake about him in confidence, and considering how skeptical he's been to me playing this year, I was surprised when I got his support. He said that after all that's said and done, we both deserve someone special, whether that's in secret or not. But I guess he's withdrawing that support now.

I grind my teeth, glaring down into Blake's eyes. "What about him?"

"For whatever reason," Blake says, talking quietly and enunciating every word. He's talked this way when upset ever since college. "You think that you're the only one affected by these threats. I've tried to tell you that this could affect me—"

"You're not out," I spit. "How could it affect you?"

"I've tried to tell you that this could affect me *and* other queer players. If you let this harsh treatment of you go on, what's to say it won't happen to the next out player? And so on?"

I stand there looking down at my best friend, my fists clenched and chest heaving. He's mentioned this before, but it never really clicked until now—not until I mentally went back to the time when I was injured. When I had been called a 'faggot', just like now.

"But now that you've got someone special," he says. "He's at risk, too—but that risk is so much greater."

I cross my arms. "What do you mean he's at more risk?"

"Think about it," Blake says, gesticulating with his hands between us. "You're a high-profile player, and that profile has only grown now that your catches have improved this season."

"Yeah," I say, shrugging. "So?"

"So," Blake says impatiently. "There's only so much that can happen to you. You can be injured on the field—purposefully, mind you—but no one would ever go as far as to try and hurt you outside of a game. But the same can't be said for Silas."

My entire body goes cold as I imagine these mysterious football bigots targeting the man that I love.

The man that I love.

What a fucking time to realize that.

"Whoever these guys are," Blake says. "Whether they're the Sparrows or Steeds or some mysterious faction made up of a bunch of players across the whole league—they could do a lot more to hurt Silas than they could you."

"Blake," I say, clenching my fists so tight I'm afraid I'll break my bones. "Stop it."

"So you need to finally wake up and realize that these *crimes* you're witnessing," he says. "Because they are *crimes*—and they extend beyond just you. They have repercussions for me, for other queer players, and for your little beloved."

I shake my head, feeling my eyes heat up with tears. "This is fucking stupid," I hiss. "*I'm* the one being targeted. Yet it's *my* responsibility to make it right?"

Blake softens a bit. "I know it's not fair, man, but—"

"You're right that it's not fucking fair," I say. "I just want to live a life like any other football player can live. I want to find someone I love, date him publicly, and be treated the same for it. But apparently that's too much to ask for."

Blake opens his mouth, but we hear a knock on the wall, and we both jump. We turn to see our running back standing at the entryway to the locker room. God, I hope he didn't hear anything.

"You guys coming to the bus?" he asks. "We're waiting on you."

I quickly wipe my eyes and glance at Blake. He's glaring at me with a mixture of reprimand and fear. I know I have no reason to be angry with him—in fact, this conversation alone is proof as to why he's one of my best friends. He always tells me as it is. Sometimes, I admit, I can be a little too naively positive about the world. And after our conversation, this is just one of those moments.

Blake and I hurry to the bus, not saying another word. Because there's nothing else to be said. It's clear now. I'm in danger, and it's not just me, but every queer person in my circle and involved with the NFO.

When we board the bus to the airport, I shimmy back to the open seat next to Silas. We've come up with a strategy for us to be together in discreet ways whenever we're with the whole team. When the bus lights go out, we hold hands underneath his jacket. And this time, I hold him a little tighter. Because now I'm so afraid of what could happen to him if I don't do something about my safety. But I have no idea what that should be.

Eventually, we reach the airport and board the plane. On our flight home, Silas and I don't get to sit together, and I instead sit with one of our linemen. But the entire time, my heart races, and I have to resist jumping at any one of his movements. Could he be the one who said 'faggot' out on the field? Or is he harmless? Or is he part of the mysterious faction out to get me? Is there even a faction?

I lean my head back against the seat and let out a deep sigh.

I'm in some deep shit.

When we finally land in Salt Lake, Silas and I drive back to my place in separate cars. Nobody can know we're together, so we take every precaution we can.

"Everything okay?" Silas asks when he shuts the door to my high-rise condo behind him.

I set my back down and prop myself up against granite kitchen counter.

When I don't answer, Silas comes up behind and wraps his arms around my belly. He kisses the back of my jacket, and the warmth of his body calms me.

I turn around and meet his lips with mine, noting each little square millimeter where our lips touch. It's like Silas is my drug. He calms and grounds me, which I definitely need after all that's just happened.

"You played really well today," he says, pulling away from me. "How's your leg?"

I nod and rest my forehead against his, clasping our hands together and holding them out like we're dancing. There are some dim lights coming from underneath my kitchen cabinets, but besides that, the only other light comes from the city outside. Beyond that, the large mountains loom.

"Was a little sore today," I admit. "I think I'll ask that you look at it tomorrow."

He nods, gently rubbing his forehead against mine. "Is that why you seem upset?"

I bite my lip, then kiss him gently. "Just... working with Blake to improve my catching has been harder than I thought," I say. "But I'll get through it."

He kisses me back. "I know you will."

I smile, then hold him against my chest as he leans into me, kissing the top of his head every now and then.

Blake is right. And he's been right this whole time. I'm in danger, and now Silas might be too. I have to say something to him.

But I can't yet.

Because I'm so scared of what could happen.

I've never had anyone like Silas in my life—ever. I've never met someone who thinks so deeply about music and the world like he does, and I've never met someone who can see me so plainly and easily. It's like he's wearing contacts that see right into my soul. And he feels the same about me. I'm afraid that if I tell him the risk that we're in, he might run away, or we might lose the effervescent intimacy that we have. But I don't want to give up football either, and I know that seeking protection from what is happening would disrupt everything.

All I want is to have my cake and eat it, too. Which is what all straight people get. They can date, fall in love, get married, and have a family—but they can also have a career, be public facing figures, and have adoring fans. All at the same time! But me? This society makes me choose one or the other.

But you know what? When I came out, I decided I wasn't going to let straight society decide what I could or couldn't choose. I decided to choose for myself—that I was going to get both. And that's a choice I'm sticking with.

I kiss Silas more aggressively, and he meets me with the same fervor.

"Wanna fuck tonight?" he asks. "I can get douched."

I nod, rubbing the tips of our noses together. "Only if it's not a hassle," I say, feeling my dick harden against his belly.

He's about to kiss me, then he just licks my lips and pulls away. "Nothing's a hassle for you," he says. "I'll be a minute."

And that's when he swiftly disappears into my bathroom. While he's preparing, I unpack both our bags and let my mind wander.

I know it's not the best idea for me to just keep my mouth shut. I'm not unaware that I should do something to ensure the safety of me and Silas, especially with our relationship as precarious as it already is with him being a PT on our team. But I deserve, at least for a little bit, to live the privileged life that any straight person gets to live—even if it's just an illusion. I deserve to feel safe *and* loved— not just safe.

By the time Silas leaves the bathroom, I'm laying on my bed with sweats and nothing underneath. Wearing nothing himself, Silas mounts me, and I get hard just from touching his body alone.

I lube us up and then he rides me. We switch to missionary, and I stick his huge feet in my face and sniff as I fuck him. Before, I was never really into smells, but seeing how much Silas is into it, I decided to give it a try, and now I'm a convert. Silas says any sort of musky man smell turns him on, and I feel similarly, but more than anything Silas's smell provides me comfort. They say that touching skin releases oxytocin, which calms the body down, especially when the touch is with the person we care about the most. But I feel the same with smell. Whenever we get intimate, if I've had a rough game or stressful day, just breathing Silas's natural scent in is enough to ease the tension in my shoulders and slow my heartrate. And I especially need that after today.

After I cum inside Silas, his feet rubbing against my face, we get into what Silas likes to call the throne position, the one where I sit on his face and pin his legs behind my shoulders. When I get to fingering him, he cums all over the both of us, and I happily clean us both up. And by the time we're cuddling—with me as the little spoon this time—I feel tired and content enough to sleep. This is the life I've been working for. Nothing is going to take this away from me.

Silas kisses my shoulder. "You sure everything's okay?" he asks.

Some of the tension Silas helped me shed off earlier returns to my shoulders. I adjust my body, and he holds me tight. "Yeah," I say, obviously lying. I kiss his hand to reassure him. "All good here."

"Alright," he says, burying his face into the crook of my neck. "You excited for Kyle and Michael's wedding?"

I smile, genuinely relieved to be talking about something else. "I am."

Just yesterday we received the official invitations for Kyle Weaver and Michael Cunningham's wedding next month, a couple weeks before Thanksgiving. Apparently, they've had a wild ride, and I don't doubt it. To be one of the biggest players of the century and to come out at the end of his career? To date a man who used to be a sex worker? Insane stuff. But I know they're happy, and I'm excited to celebrate their wedding with Silas. We're going as friends, of course, but those who need to know have all the details.

He grabs one of my hands and squeezes it. "It'll be nice to be home with someone I love," he says. "Oh fuck."

And my stomach leaps. "What did you say?"

"Love," he says. "Because I love—fuck, does this have to happen now?"

I untangle myself from his arms and turn around, his face barely visible from the light coming from the city. "Say what you want to say," I say.

"I love you, Wyatt," he says. "But you—"

"I love you, too," I say, recalling my thoughts while fighting with Blake. At least there was one good thing to come out of that conversation.

He wraps his hands around my head and pulls me close, and we kiss for what feels like an eternity of pleasure. When we finally release, I look into his brown eyes and smile.

"I'll say it again," I say. "I love you so much."

He kisses me on the lips, then turns around for me to spoon him. I press our hairy bodies together tightly.

"I love you, too," he says.

And that's when I know that I can't lose this man. I'd be devastated. There has to be some way to ensure both our safety if I say in the NFO. My first option is to tell Silas and take the necessary measures to make us safe. But that would cause all sorts of problems. First, I don't even know how Silas would react. He could be too afraid to continue our relationship, and that's on top of the fact that we really shouldn't be dating anyways considering he's staff on my team. And then then there's the media. They'd be all over this story, and I just know that all the attention and pressure would get in the way of my playing. I can't do any of this.

But I can't think of anything else to do. The only thing that comes to mind is continue on as is and hope I just don't get injured and then come out publicly as dating Silas either when one of us retires or we find some other reason to come clean. But this is so risky. Just today I almost got injured again, and the season isn't even close to being over, especially if we make it to the playoffs. I have no fucking clue what to do.

So I bury my face into my boyfriend's arms and shut my eyes, punting the solution to tomorrow. Or some other day. Maybe I'll know what to do then.

Chapter 17

Silas King

"Silas, dear," Linda says, wrapping her arms around me as I stand in her doorway. "Please, come in."

She lets me into her small house, and Miss Beautiful prances up to greet me. She sniffs my jeans, no doubt smelling Cheshire on me. She hisses, then scurries away.

"Hey, that's not nice," Linda says to her cat. "Silas is family."

I laugh. "How are you holding up?"

She lets out an exaggerated sigh. "I couldn't be happier. But it's been a stressful time. Sit down—let me tell you about it."

As Linda explains the woes of helping plan her son's wedding—helping Kyle with the design, since he's not aesthetically minded; dealing with questions from reporters asking how it feels to be the Mom of a gay former NFO player about to be married; and this is on top of the new hobbies that she's been exploring.

"I've been hiking a ton, too," she says.

"No way!" I say. "Me too. I'm actually hiking with Jimmy later." She raises her brow. "Where?"

"Turns out there's a trail right next to the lake."

"Oh, I love that trail," she says, pressing her hand against her sternum. "I joined a hiking club, and we..."

As she explains all the trails she's been on, I ease back into the couch, happy to be back home with Wyatt soon to join me. We've been official—well, secretly official—since the beginning of the football season, so a little over two months. But these two months have been amazing. We spend all our time together, and I hardly feel sad anymore—or so caught up in an emotional whirlwind. When we're apart for a while, I start to miss him, and I get worried that he's rethinking his feelings for me, or something worse, but that's all resolved when we're together again.

And I'm happy that that'll be very soon. I came down to Glamour Springs to help Michael out with some of the wedding details and see my friends. But I also came alone so that the wrong people wouldn't suspect that Wyatt and I were together. The important people know about us—Linda, Martha, Llewellyn, Jimmy, Tanner, Kyle, Michael. But the general public, which includes anyone on the Pioneers team, save for Blake, no nothing, and that has to stay that way. I don't know how Wyatt and I plan to handle this, especially since neither of our careers are ending any time soon. But we'll figure it out. I feel that our love is plenty strong.

"And you and Wyatt," Linda says. "Are you good?"

I smile, my chest warming. I may not have a mother I trust, but Linda is more than a sufficient substitute.

"We're great," I say. "I can't remember the last time I've felt this way for anyone. Or, quite frankly, when I've felt this good. Ever."

"Oh, that's wonderful," she says. "But do remember to focus on you sometimes. That way you both can show up to the relationship 100%. It's hard to depend on one person for everything. I would know."

I nod, feeling an uncomfortable pinch in my chest. "Of course." But I don't know why I feel this way. Wyatt and I are fine. I don't depend on him for everything. We have some days apart. They suck, but I live through them. I got nothing to worry about.

I glance at my phone. "Shoot," I say, grabbing my hat off the armrest of the couch. "I gotta go meetup with Michael. He wanted my help with the center pieces for the tables over at the Community Cabin."

"Oh, then you better go," she says with a quick flick of her wrist. "He's been stressing about every little detail, poor thing. He needs all the help he can get."

I laugh. "Don't worry," I say. "I'll keep him in check and calm him down as necessary."

"You're a saint," she says, standing up.

We hug goodbye, and then I decide to leave my car here and walk to the community center on the other side of the lake. It's a chilly, fall day here in Glamour Springs, wonderful for walking. And after I help Michael, I'm meeting up with Jimmy for our hike.

While walking the trail, I put on Wyatt's playlist that he made for us. I'm greeted with old German lieder composed by Strauss and sung by none other than Fischer-Dieskau. Halfway over, walking along the edge of the water with the multi-colored trees around me, I take a deep breath and relish what my life is. It couldn't be more perfect.

My phone rings, and I quickly answer, thinking it's Wyatt. But it's not. It's a voice I recognize but was definitely not expecting to hear.

"Brigham," I say. "How's it going?" My stomach clenches a bit. Does he know about me and Wyatt? Fuck. Is our relationship suddenly over?

"I've had better days," he says, and there's sadness dripping from his voice. Which is strange. Because he's usually one of the most chipper people I know. Hearing his voice so sad is like watching honey spoil under the rare conditions it does.

"What's going on?" I ask, afraid to find out.

He sighs. "I'm sorry to bother you on your vacation, but I've had something personal come up. When you get back to Salt Lake, I'm gonna be taking some time off, so you'll take on a bigger load for a bit. I just wanted to let you know."

I shift my phone to the other ear as the community center comes into sight, relieved that it's not me in trouble. But I'm still concerned.

"Oh, alright," I say. "I—I hope you're doing okay."

He sighs again, heavier this time. "I'll tell you because I think you'll understand as someone part of the LGBT community. My niece, who is trans just like my daughter—" his voice chokes. "She committed suicide."

I stop on the trail and stare out past the trees to the water, feeling my heart squeeze as if someone's trying to unscrew it like a twisty cap.

"Brigham," I say. "I'm so sorry. That's—"

"Our whole family's at a loss. See, this daughter—she's my sister's daughter, and my sister is the only one still in the Mormon Church. As her aunts and uncles, the rest of us have tried to extend a life raft to support her, but it hasn't been enough. And now my own daughter, Belle, is at a loss. She looked up to her older cousin. And to lose a mentor like that—someone who is trans just like her—I can't imagine."

Suddenly, I dissociate, and I see my body as if I'm staring down from above. I see myself wearing a jester's outfit with a big fat red nose as Brigham cries through the phone.

Who am I to console this man?

Is this how Linda would have reacted had I done the deed? Jimmy? Llewellyn?

Did Brigham's niece consider the ripples her suicide would leave in the lives of those around her? Did she care?

Does it even matter?"It's not your fault, Brigham," I say, which does come from a genuine place. The people I love in my life have nothing to do with my propensity for self-annihilation, even though it's clear to me how guilty they would feel if I did it.

"I just feel like—" he blows his nose. "There was something I could have done, you know? And now I'm scared for Belle. So scared. I'm wondering if I need to get out of the state or something. Go some place that's actually friendly toward trans people."

I open my mouth, but I'm at a loss for words. Because I know what that fear is like—to know that there are no guardrails between your loved one and the abyss, or in my case, myself and the abyss.

"I should say that my sister brought up an organization here in Utah—Affirm. It's an organization for LGBTQ+. She mentioned it to Belle. I think we'll have her give it a try."

"That should be good," I manage to choke out, but I otherwise feel useless. Here this man is, pouring is soul out to me, no more than a friendly coworker, and this is all I can say. I'm pathetic.

"Anyways," Brigham says, not sounding as sad as before. "I'm sorry to unload all of this on you. I really just wanted to let you know because I'll be taking off some work, but then I remembered that you're gay, and I know it's not the same as trans, but I wanted—"

"It's alright, Brigham," I say, fiddling with the end of my mustache. "I'm glad you called. It'll be alright. I promise." Even though I can promise no such thing. Not even for myself

"Thanks, man. I hope you enjoy the wedding. I'll see you soon."

"Thanks, alright," I say. "Take it easy."

And when I hang up, I feel forty pounds heavier. This is grief that he's going to live with for the rest of his life—the same kind of grief that I would inflict on those who I love if I chose to leave this earth.

But I don't need to worry about that anymore. I have Wyatt now. I haven't felt deep sadness in months. In fact, my old, slower music doesn't even hit as hard anymore. I'd rather listen to what Wyatt gives me.

By the time I reach the Community Cabin, I feel better, but my body feels cold, like a ghost has passed through me and I'm still processing the feeling.

When I walk into foyer, several doors open up into their main ballroom. It's filled with tables covered with white tablecloths. Around the room sit unlit lanterns, the very kind of lanterns we push into the lake for the Lantern Festival on Thanksgiving. During the reception, Kyle and Michael will host their own little festival for their guests. In front of one of the tables, I spot Michael, and he's carrying at least four door-stopping books in his hand.

"Need a hand?" I call out, jogging into the ballroom. As he turns, one of the books falls out of his hand, and I catch it just in time.

"So good to see you," he says, sounding both exasperated and exhausted. He sets the books down, and I give him a big hug.

"Happy to be here," I say, my hands on my hips.

"Okay, be honest: am I ridiculous for trying this out?"

I laugh and shake my head. "Absolutely not. The idea's genius."

"Alright," he says, setting down the four door stoppers in the center of the table. They're all different epic fantasy books.

A couple months ago, Michael called and asked to run by an idea he had for the reception. Each table would have a stack of books as the centerpiece, but they wouldn't just be random books. They'd be books in the genre or with similar tropes to match the vibe of the people sitting at the table. Then, at the end of the night, everyone at the table would be free to take whichever booked they liked home. They would just have to coordinate with their tablemates.

"You don't think that this will cause any fights, right?" he asks as we set down a stack of gay romances in the center of the next table.

"Maybe your friend Skye might fight someone for a paranormal romance," I say with a chuckle. I've met some of Michael's friends, and they're a hoot.

"But I think the rest of them will be tame."

"You're right," he says with a laugh. "Alright, let's get these set up."

I help him load the rest of the books up as we catch up. Apparently, Kyle's with Tanner up in Memphis picking up the suits for all the groomsmen. Michael's all finished up writing the second book of the series, so he's onto the third. And I catch him up about working as a PT in the NFO.

"How has it been?" he asks. "I know you've been wanting it for a while."

I set down a John Green science book on top of the stack on one table, then follow him to the next.

"Honestly," I say. "It's been nothing and everything I expected."

"Elaborate," Michael says, pulling out a stack of thrillers from his tub.

"It's just—" I bite my lip, thinking how I want to explain it. "It's everything I expected in that it's no different from working in the clinic at Miss U. You have your arrogant players, the players who don't trust you—which is especially true for me since I'm so new.

"And the schedule, man," I say, rolling my eyes. "This is definitely not something I anticipated. I mean, it's one thing to be an NFO player and have to travel all the time and be present for all these practices. But we gotta do that and more. Yet our pay is a small fraction of what they get. I will admit that it's nice making more than I ever have been, and I'm relieved to be paying down my loans. But I'd say that if I wasn't dating Wyatt, I'm not sure how worth it all this would be. Which is crazy considering we shouldn't even be dating."

"Damn," Michael says, flipping through a number of historical fiction novels before he sets them on a table. "I didn't realize how much you really weren't enjoying it. Do you think you'll stick with it?"

"Sheesh," I say. "Let me think about that."

I lean on the back of a chair as Michael finishes up the last of our tables. There's a giant glass wall at the end of the ballroom, showing the deck that leads out onto Glamour Springs Lake. A gust of wind blows by, carrying some brown, dead leaves into the air and dropping them on the surface of the water. The clouds part of a bit, revealing the autumn sun. I can't wait to go hiking later. I love fall weather.

But I'm not sure how to answer Michael's question. On one hand, working in the NFO is what I've been wanting my whole life. Yet at the same time, I don't know if this is *actually* what I've wanted deep down. Sure, now I have a more important job, proving my parents wrong. But I've never even really liked my line of work to begin with. The hours are long, and working with football players, most of the time, isn't as fun as I thought it would be. When I worked at the Miss U clinic, I got disillusioned with the whole thing, I convinced myself that the NFO would be different. But it's just a whole lotta the same shit, just amped up.

Plus, I've always been a sad guy, which has affected every aspect of life. And one of the ways it's done this is through my tolerance. Because of how down I've always been, I tolerated things that maybe now I wouldn't tolerate. For example, for years, I kept buying these shitty earbuds that would only last a few months before they got all quiet. But a month ago, I finally caved and bought a high-quality pair, and I can't believe I put up with such shit ones for so long. Another thing: the free streaming service that I've used to watch space videos? I never considered premium because I just figured it wasn't for me, even though I watch these videos like crazy. But a few weeks ago, I just bought it, and it feels like my quality of life has improved drastically. And why did I make all these changes so recently?

Wyatt.

I don't think I've ever felt this happy. And feeling this good, I think I'm starting to see my own worth and more of what I want and deserve. It's like I've been in Plato's cave my whole life. But now I've finally exited the cave, and I'm seeing all that life has to offer. So I'm taking advantage of that.

I fold my arms and sigh. "I just think that being in a relationship has changed me," I say. "At least the way I see things. I think I'm just getting to know myself a little better. And maybe this is helping me realize I never really wanted to do physical therapy to begin with. I just did it because I thought it would pay well, and I could spite my parents that way."

"Huh," Michael says, closing his empty bin. He walks over and sits down in a chair at the table across from me. "That's a pretty self-aware thing to say."

"I guess that's because I'm becoming more self-aware," I say. "Thanks to Wyatt."

Michael raises a brow. "Thanks to Wyatt? What do you mean?"

"I don't know," I say with a shrug, turning slightly to look out the back windows onto the lake. "He just gets me. He sees the good in me. And that's just really encouraging. I feel like he is helping me learn about myself."

"Do you see the good in you?"

I look at him with a furrowed brow. "Huh?"

Michael adjusts himself in his seat. "I mean to ask that if Wyatt weren't in your life, would you still think you'd be as happy as you are now?"

My chest tightens. "Those are two different questions."

Michael sucks on his teeth and rubs his forehead. "Sorry, not what I meant. I just think I'm concerned. I don't want you relying on Wyatt for your self-worth."

There's a sharp pain in my chest, and I remember what Linda said earlier—that I shouldn't depend on Wyatt for everything. And here Michael is, saying something similar.

"I know I can't depend on him or anyone for everything," I say.

Michael rubs the bridge of his nose. "It's not like he can't make you feel good. Kyle makes me feel good. But self-worth is different. Self-worth is the idea that you deserve to live and thrive despite what anyone else might say or do.

Inside, you know you're worth it. So you live your worth even if you don't have a partner."

My whole body goes cold again, and I dissociate. I see myself from above, wearing that goddamn clown uniform again.

My will to live didn't strengthen until Wyatt waltzed back into my life and took me up that summit. And it really got solid when we decided to have sex and go steady. If Wyatt were to walk away, I don't know what would happen to me. When even light falls into a black hole, it can't escape. And Wyatt's my blackhole. I can't pull away from him. I can't imagine life without him now.

"I don't think you need to worry," I say, tension in my voice. "I'm fine. I know my worth. Wyatt's just something nice to have on top of it all."

"Alright," Michael says. "Sorry—I didn't mean to step all over you there. I'm happy you're happy."

"Thanks," I say, but it doesn't come out very sincere.

"Well," Michael says, clapping his hands against his knees and standing up. "Kyle and Tanner are gonna be back soon with everyone's suits. I'll meet them at Tanner and Jimmy's cabin."

"I'm headed there, too," I say. "Meeting Jimmy to go on a hike."

"Cool! We can walk over together."

Michael hides the container in a storage closet, and we head out the front door. The afternoon, autumn sun is shining brightly now, and it's a little windier. We set on the path for Jimmy's cabin.

"What's it like in Salt Lake?" he asks me.

Pleasure swells in my chest as I think about my life there: hiking with Wyatt, getting takeout with Wyatt, going to museums and shows with Wyatt. It's nice working for same team because we have similar hours, which means we can spend our downtime together. And we usually do. I can't remember the last time I spent the night at my place alone.

But I can't say all this to Michael. After what he said to me earlier about having worth outside of Wyatt, he'll think I'm insane for spending so much time with him.

"Oh, it's a cool city," I say. "Not super diverse, but there's a lot to do. And the outdoor scene is wonderful. Wyatt and I—" I stop myself. "I wanna go see the national parks down South."

"Oh, Arches, right? And Zion? Heard those places are gorgeous."

I nod, happy he didn't catch me saying Wyatt's name. Which, I mean, I should be able to say. He's my boyfriend. But I still want to come off as independent as possible.

When we reach Jimmy and Tanner's place, we can plainly see that their car has yet to arrive.

"You wanna join us on the hike?" I ask.

"I need to wait for Kyle and Tanner to get back," he says, yawning. "And besides, I'm exhausted. I'll use this time to take a nap."

After we knock on their side door, Jimmy lets us in. He's wearing flannel, jeans, and some boots.

"You coming with us, Michael?" he asks.

"Nope," he says, headed straight for the couch. "I'm passing out."

"Alright then," Jimmy says with a laugh. "Make yourself at home."

As we walk out, I'm a little relieved. I love Michael, but I'd rather not have to censor how much I talk about my boyfriend around him.

"So where's this trail?" he asks, shutting the door behind him.

"Actually close by," I say. "I got this app in Utah that shows you trails all around the country. Apparently, there are a ton right here in Glamour Springs, and this one's walking distance from us."

He claps his hands. "Well let's get a move on, then."

I lead us onto the trail that connects all the houses, then we head toward the woods. Once inside, I take us on a side path.

"Apparently, this leads us up a hill that overlooks the lake, which I think is pretty cool," I say.

"Alright," Jimmy says, already out of breath. "Lead the way."

As we walk, my mind drifts to Wyatt like it always does. I mean, he's like my gravity, so of course my mind always goes to him like a ball rolling down a hill.

I can't wait until he gets here tomorrow. While I was able to take off work, he needed to stick around for a game happening this morning in Salt Lake. And with how good he's playing lately, the Pioneers really need him. He's been working hard, and his catching has dramatically improved. I wouldn't be surprised if they made it to the Championship Game.

"How's it going with Wyatt?" Jimmy asks in between breaths.

I hesitate answering. I don't want him to, like Michael, think I'm like too into Wyatt or whatever. But Jimmy and Tanner are also crazy close. Maybe he'll understand.

"Things are great, man," I say as we turn a corner. I check my phone. "We're about halfway there, by the way."

"Thank God," Jimmy groans. "Fuck, I need to do more cardio."

I laugh. "Well, this trail's pretty close to you. Imagine doing this every morning."

"Oh, the joy," Jimmy says flatly.

We continue on, and I'm almost expecting that Jimmy won't respond to what I said about Tanner. But that expectation goes unmet.

"Is he being good to you?"

I turn my head over my shoulder briefly as I walk, furrowing my brow at him. "Good to me? Of course he is."

"You guys are a secret, right?"

I scoff. "Yeah, but it's not like Michael and Kyle were a secret. We can't go public because I'm staff on the team."

"Alright," Jimmy says, still skeptical. "So when are you going to go public in your relationship?"

My chest tightens. It feels like I'm being interrogated, like if I say the wrong thing my relationship with Wyatt will crumble and slip right between my fingers.

"I don't know," I say quickly. "Not like it matters."

"Not like it matters?" Jimmy asks. "Silas, Wyatt being comfortable in the relationship definitely matters."

Now it feels like someone is wringing my heart out like a towel. "Wyatt is comfortable. And so am I. This isn't about his sexuality. He came out before I even met him."

"Okay, yeah, that's true," Jimmy says. "But—"

I stop and turn around. "What does it even matter? Why do you even care?"

Jimmy stops and puts his hands on his hips, breathing heavy with a pained expression on his face. "Because I care about you, man. I want you to be happy."

I resist a scoff.

Happy.

Not like I was ever happy before I met Wyatt, even with all of my 'loving' friends. Sure, I care about Jimmy, Michael, Linda, Llewellyn, and everyone else. But I still wanted to kill myself with them in my life. But with Wyatt? That desire's gone.

"Honestly, Jimmy," I say, turning around to continue our ascent. "I've never been happier."

Jimmy follows, and besides the leaves crunching underneath us, accompanied by both our heavy breathing, there's just silence.

Finally, we reach the summit, and it honestly takes my breath away. From our vantage point, we can see nearly all the cabins around the lake. Some have smoke coming out of the chimneys—including Jimmy and Tanner's, which means that Kyle and Tanner are back. And I swear every single tree is a different color from the one next to it, showcasing a stunning fall display. The sun is setting just beyond the tree line, and the scent of campfire lingers in the air.

And more than anything, I wish Wyatt were here. With him, the colors would be more vibrant, the scent of campfire stronger. We would sit as the sun dips beneath the horizon, talking about music, football, our families, and life. Man, I miss him. I can't wait for tomorrow when he arrives.

"Goddamn, that's beautiful," Jimmy says, standing next to me. He folds his arms and takes in the scene.

"It is," I say, my mind still on Wyatt.

He clasps my shoulder, and I turn to him.

"I couldn't be happier that you're happy," he says, giving me a big, bearded grin.

"Thanks," I say shyly.

He lets go of me and walks over to prop his leg on a boulder. I walk over and sit down next to him.

"I'm sorry if I gave you trouble," he says. "I just wanna make sure you don't get hurt."

"I'll be fine," I say. Sheesh. I feel like everyone's worried I can't fend for myself. But then I feel bad. I know Jimmy just cares about me.

"Thanks," I amend.

"Anytime," he says, setting his leg down. He sits right next to me. "I'll admit, I felt kinda bad when I got with Tanner."

I give him a funny look. "Why?"

He shrugs with a laugh. "You and I were always the single ones, and I left you behind."

"Oh, you're fine," I say. "I honestly didn't think I'd ever really be in a relationship. Never really found the one until now."

"Well, I'm glad you have," he says, wiping sweat from his brow. "Because now you're like the rest of us. Now all we need is for Linda to find a partner, then we'll all be saddled up."

His words prick my heart. Not the part about all of us having partners, but the other one—that I'll be like the rest of them.

I just don't feel like that's true.

Earlier, Linda talked to me about not depending on Wyatt for everything. Michael said that I should have a sense of worth outside my partner. And Jimmy just now wanted to make sure that Wyatt was in it for the right reasons—that he wasn't hiding anything by keeping us a secret.

All three of these friends of mine have one thing in common, and it's the one thing I lack.

A sense of self.

Sure, I could be skeptical of Wyatt being okay with keeping my relationship a secret. And Michael and Linda are right—it's important to have a solid relationship with myself outside of Wyatt. And I obviously know all these things. But what scares me is that I don't live them like my friends do.

Truthfully, I don't want to know if Wyatt has ulterior motives or if I'm too emotionally dependent on him. Because what would be the answer if I discovered something bad about him? That would mean I'd have to pull away from Wyatt in some way, and I can't do that. He's my everything. That day that he talked about my music with me after he listened to it on his own—when he said things about my music that I had only felt yet had never verbalized—I knew that I was falling head over heels for this man, and faster than I could control. Having been so used to my sadness, I was hesitant to let myself keep falling. But when Wyatt helped me see my relationship with my parents in a way where I no longer felt guilty, he changed my perspective, and he changed my life. I can't just push someone like that away. I feel like I'd crumble to pieces if I did that. I need Wyatt. I need him.

I feel like I'm a magnetar, spinning so fast with such a high charge that I'm tearing apart everything inside and around me—that I'm losing control of myself.

But if this puts me in denial or makes me emotionally dependent, then that's what I am. Because the alternative? It's going back to writing in that journal every night, counting down the days until I know it's time to end. And as comfortable as I was doing that before, I really, really don't want to go back to that place.

"You gonna show this to Wyatt when he gets here?" Jimmy asks.

And my chest soars hearing someone I care about saying his name so casually.

"I think I will," I say.

Jimmy pats me on the knee, then stands up. "Alright, let's get back to see the others. I already know my fiancé's itching to fuck."

"Gross," I say with a laugh.

He shrugs. "You could argue that I used to be addicted to sex, but I think that trophy goes to Tanner—sex with me, that is. That man is insatiable."

I roll my eyes and stand up. "Glad you found someone who suits your needs," I say. "Let's head back."

And as we do, I try to tell myself that maybe I'm not so crazy for needing Wyatt so much. Look at how much Jimmy and Tanner fuck, after all. They're connected at the hip.

But something tells me—as it always has—that I'm different. So different, in fact, that I should expire my life early before it gets out of hand.

I shake my body as chills run through it. Wyatt can't get here soon enough. Once I'm with him, I won't think such dark thoughts anymore.

Chapter 18

Wyatt Nelson

AFTER SILAS AND I have reunion sex at his place in Glamour Springs, I drive over to my mom's. In the car, I steel myself to put up with anything she might say about my gameplay or how me coming out has affected it. She doesn't know about Silas yet, and it's gonna stay that way, at least until after this season. I will not deal with her telling me to break up with the man I love.

When I arrive, I knock on the door, but there's no answer. Weird. My mom's not usually the one to slack when it comes to hosting, even if I'm family.

I let myself in. "Mom?" I call out.

"Come in here," she says forcefully, and immediately my stomach twists over itself. This is the voice she would use on me when I was a kid and did something she didn't like, which wasn't often. But when it did happen, it was memorable.

I slip off my shoes and take my time on my way to the family room, trying to delay whatever reprimand I'm about to receive. When I spot her, she's sitting on the couch already dressed for Kyle and Michael's wedding later.

"Where's Dad?" I ask. "I know he's invited—"

"Sit down, please," she says, pointing to the cushion opposite her.

I swallow what feels like lead. Here we go.

I make my way across from her and lean back. "So what's—"

"You didn't tell me," she says.

My mind immediately goes to Silas, and I lean forward. "Tell you what?"

"That day on the field," she says, her shoulders rigid. "When you were injured."

I let out a small sigh of relief. Okay, not about Silas. That's good.

Outside, it begins to rain, providing a steady patter on the roof of our cabin. Nearby, the fireplace burns.

Then I crinkle my brow. "What do you mean I didn't tell you? You knew—"

"Blake called me," she says. "And he told me everything."

I clench my fists. That son of a bitch. Homophobic, closeted—

"Were you ever going to tell me that someone called you a slur on the field?"

"Mom," I say with a sigh. "It's complicated. You don't—"

"Complicated? That was a hate crime. You were injured because of a hate crime. And you got back out on the field?" She shakes her head. "And Blake tells me it happened again."

Panic rises in my chest. The first time something happens, it's a coincidence. The second, it's a pattern and likely to occur again. I remember seeing the fury in the other team's eyes after I heard the gay slur for the second time. I can still sense the low fear in my gut. Because it will likely happen again. And again. And again. Unless I do something. Or stop playing.

"It did," I say. "And I'm trying to figure—"

"Trying to do what?"

"Mom," I say. "Stop interrupting."

She opens her mouth, then shuts it, then opens it again. She leans forward on her cushion, rubbing the makeup off her forehead.

"You have to understand how concerned I am," she says. "This is why I told you coming out was not going to be good for you."

"Yeah," I say, scoffing. "You and everyone else. Thanks for being supportive."

"I am being supportive," she says. "But I want you to be safe."

"So what?" I ask. "You're gonna tell me to stop playing?"

She shakes her head. "No. But you at least need to tell someone about this. You need to protect yourself."

And Silas, I think. At least Blake was bro enough not to spill that secret to my mom.

"Or what, Mom? It's not like someone will come to my house and shoot me."

She looks at me, horrified. "Jesus, Wyatt."

"What?" I ask. "You're acting like this could happen."

"No, I'm saying that someone could tear your ACL this time, or worse. Somebody's out to get you, and we need to do something about this."

Fear bubbles in my chest as I clasp my kneecaps.

These last couple weeks, I've held off doing anything about this situation. I just wanted to look forward to this wedding and my time with Silas. But talking to my mom about all of it is just bringing all the fear to the surface. And more than anything, I'm afraid for Silas. Because, unlike myself, much worse things can be done to him. And I'd rather die than see him get hurt.

"Like I was going to say," I say, grabbing the bridge of my nose. "I'm working on it."

"How?"

"That's my business," I say through gritted teeth.

"But is it?" she asks plaintively. Tears well in her eyes. "You're my son, Wyatt. I know a lot has happened between us, and I know I haven't been a perfect mom, even now. I can be controlling, I know, and I can be mean. But I can't see you get hurt." She wipes a tear from her eye. "I'd rather die."

Her words, the same as my own about Silas, give me chills.

The truth is, I still don't know what to do. If I come out with this, I just know that my football career will be derailed, maybe even for good. They might ask me to stop playing for my protection, or an even bigger target might be put on my back to silence me. The NFO might even ask me to stop playing altogether. And if any of this happens, the title of best tight end slips through my fingers, and the world proves that, yet again, gays can't do what straight people can.

Or I can just continue on, not only risking my own safety and the safety of the other players who might be queer, but Silas as well. My lovely Silas, the man who's helped me experience true, authentic connection—the man who sees me like no one else.

I don't know what to do, but I do know one thing: I have to protect him. And, just like my mom said about me, I'm willing to die trying to protect him. I will figure out how.

My phone buzzes, and I quickly pull it out to see. It's Silas. He's asking if I want to have sex before Michael and Kyle's wedding. Of course I do. Fuck. How am I going to keep this man safe?

"Wyatt," she says. "Tell me: what do you plan on doing? We have to do something."

I sigh and shake my head. I know my mom means well, but I can't have her involved with this. She doesn't know the NFO like I do, and this is truthfully none of her business, even though Blake yanked her into the conversation—fuck him. I don't see how she could be of any help here. She would just make me doubt whatever conclusion I come to, and I definitely can't have her knowing about Silas. I don't want to hear anything she has to say about how risky it is to date someone again. I'm tired of it.

"Mom," I say, standing up. "I appreciate the concern. But I have to go get ready for the wedding."

"Wyatt Nelson," she says, pushing herself off the couch. "You are not leaving until we—"

"Until we what?" I say, spinning around. She stands a couple feet from me, and I point my finger at her chest. "You have told me what I'm doing my whole life: my football career, my singing. And you know what? I'm fucking sick of it. Let me decide my future for once."

"But Wyatt," she says, her lips quivering. "This is your safety we're talking about."

And Silas's, I remind myself.

"I know, Mom," I say, my voice softening. "But you need to let me handle it on my own."

She closes her eyes and sighs. A tear runs down her face and leaves a streak in her makeup.

"Fine," she says. "But will you keep me updated? Please?"

I pause for a beat, then nod. "I'll tell you what I can."

She wipes her eyes. She nods. "I'll see you at the wedding," she says, her voice hoarse. She clears it.

"See you then," I say. And then I make my exit. I step out into the rain, and it creates a pleasant tapping sound against my jacket. I rush to my car, and once inside, I take a deep breath and assess the situation.

It's really not as bad as I think. I just panicked in there because my mom stresses me out. Really, the situation hasn't changed since I was called a faggot. There are no new updates. My game yesterday was completely fine, and we won because of a clutch pass I caught. No slurs. Maybe I'm overthinking. I'm fine. Silas is fine. For right now, at least.

Once I've left my heartrate drop a little more, I make my way back to the cabin Silas and I are renting. He's laying with Cheshire on the couch, who I didn't realize was here, and I look at him funny.

"You brought Cheshire for this small trip?" I ask.

He sits up, and Cheshire jumps to the floor.

"Cheshire likes to be with me," he says. "And he's actually a pretty good traveler."

He leans over the back of his couch and gestures for me to join him. Outside, it's still raining, and out his window I watch the rain patter against the surface of the lake.

I grab his hand and step over couch. He's about to kiss me, but then I pin him down. I rub my beard against his face, and he shivers.

"We got time for one round?" he asks, helpless as I hold his arms down.

I move his legs and insert myself between him. "Doesn't matter," I say. "I'd make the time regardless."

And I fuck him silly. I get him to cum, then cum inside him with plenty of time to spare. We both shower, then get in the car. We would walk on any other day, but it's raining as hard as ever. I know that Kyle and Michael were planning to do their own version of the Glamour Springs Lantern festival, but it looks like that might not happen.

Once we get there, my phone buzzes in my pocket, this time a call and not a text. I'm tempted to answer, but I don't want to do it in front of Silas. It could be related to my whole business being threatened, and I'm not ready to spill the beans there.

I grab our umbrella from the backseat, open Silas's door, then rush us both to the entrance. Inside, I can see guests smiling and greeting each other.

"You go on ahead," I say. "Gotta take a quick call."

He kisses me, and I can still smell my crotch and ass musk on his face. I smile. What a fucking pervert.

I step to the side of the front door, careful to stay on the concrete and not step into any mud. Rain falls off the roof and onto my umbrellas as I pull out my phone. Several wedding guests rush to the door as I see that my caller left a message, but I can't tell who it is. It just says 'Unknown Caller'. I lift the phone to my ear and listen.

"Wyatt Nelson," a creepy, AI voice says. And chills run down my spine. This isn't some automated response machine or whatever. This is something else. And I don't like it.

"You are an abomination to the world and the NFO," the creepy robotic voice continues. "Retire now, or face the consequences." I clench my shoulders. "If you do so now, you can go on and live your perverted life as you wish. But if you do not, we will come for you."

I picture the angry eyes of the players that looked like they wanted tear my limbs off my body. Because that's probably what they wanted to do.

"And we know about you and your relationship with Silas King."

My entire body goes cold, and I shiver, shaking the water off the umbrella.

"If you do not end your career now, we will target him as well. It will be much easier to hurt him than you. Choose wisely."

And then the message ends, and I'm left in the rain—cold, wet, and petrified.

"Wyatt," somebody says. And I turn to see Silas, the love of my life, standing in the doorway to the Community Cabin.

"The wedding's about to start. Hurry!"

Not knowing what else to do, I shove my phone in my pocket and rush inside. After I set my coat and umbrella aside, I take my seat at the very front table, and Silas joins the other groomsmen.

And then the wedding begins.

A young black woman walks Michael into the room while Kyle stands at the altar next to his mom, tears in his eyes. When Michael reaches the altar, they take hands. All the groomsmen and groomswomen smile. Linda, officiating the wedding, says a few words, but they go over my head. The words of that robot are still echoing in my mind. Outside, the rain pours even harder, applauding the couple about to be together forever—something I will probably never get to experience now.

Kyle and Michael say their vows, and they kiss. The whole room cheers, and I almost forget to cheer with them. Silas looks at me and asks silently if I'm okay.

Silas.

The love of my life.

The man whose very life is in danger just by being associated with me.

I give him a thumbs up, but that's definitely not how I'm feeling.

Once all the official wedding business is done, we seamlessly transition into the cutting of the wedding cake, which I hear that Jimmy baked with the help of the managers at his diner. Silas takes his seat next to me. Just as they're cutting the first slice together, the lights go out, and the only light we get comes from the angry glow of the storm clouds outside. For a moment, there's mild pandemonium, which briefly gives me the opportunity to reflect on what's just happened to me.

I'm officially being threatened. It's not a conjecture anymore. And I have my message to prove it. Yet I have no idea who it's from. I just know that if I continue to play this season, it's not just me who will pay the price. It's Silas, too.

And they know about Silas. How? Did they talk to Blake? That can't be true. Now, I'm pissed that he would tell my mom about all the threats, but I know he did that because he's concerned for my safety. And he's just as afraid of this secret faction as I am, if not more so. He would never give them my secret.

But it doesn't really matter how they know about us. Because they do, and now Silas is officially in danger. And I have no idea how to protect him.

Kyle jogs up to the microphone where they were married. "Everyone," he says, in a deep, calming voice. Now, I've never known Kyle super well, but it sounds like he would make a nice baritone.

"Instead of having our own little Lantern Festival, which we clearly can't have because of the rain," he says, pointing outside to the downpour. "We're gonna do something a little different. Everyone should have a lantern underneath their chair. Reach down and pull it out now."

Silas and I reach under our chairs and pull out a cloth lantern with a wick in the middle. Attached to the side is a small lighter.

"Now," Kyle continues. "If you all would like, detach the lighter and light the wick. But before you do, be sure to make a wish."

My hand shakes as I grab the lighter. A wish? Do I only get one? Because there's so much I want right now—that I need.

Next to me, Silas closes his eyes, then his lantern illuminates. Gradually, throughout the room, others light theirs up, and soon the entire hall is lit in the warm glow of the lanterns.

"Wonderful," Kyle says. "Now if you all could set some up at your tables—away from the books, if you could—and around the room. Let's get this reception going!"

Jimmy and Tanner walk off to set their lantern on a nearby table next to some food, while Silas and I set ours on the table. Once everyone has placed their lantern, it look like we're at a medieval ball or something. If I wasn't so distressed, I'd bask in the beauty.

"What'd you wish for?" Silas whispers to me.

I let out a shaky breath. "I—"

"That was some quick thinking," Jimmy says to Kyle as he approaches our table.

"Thanks," he says, wiping his forehead. Someone hugs him from behind, and he turns to see Michael looking up at him. They kiss tenderly, and a bitter pit forms in my stomach.

They're able to be happily together forever. Yet Silas and I can't be.

Pretty soon, the Glamour Springs quartet plays some music, and the dancing begins. Silas drags me out on the dance floor, and I try to be present with him, but I can't unhear that damn robot's voice in my head. 'It will be much easier to hurt him than you'. Fuck.

"Hey," Silas says, putting his hand on my cheek. "Are you okay?"

"Yeah," I say, shaking my head. I look around, worried my mom will see us, but it's too dark out here to really see anyone. Which is good. Before the wedding, I was worried someone would recognize me with Silas, but now my troubles are far greater.

As Silas and I slow dance, we glance over at Michael and Kyle. They're looking into the other's eyes like there's no one else in the room.

"I remember meeting both Kyle and Michael for the first time," Silas says. "Apparently, when Kyle introduced us to Michael, that was the first time he called him his boyfriend."

My stomach sinks to the floor. "Must have been a special moment."

"Yeah," Silas says, his arms around my neck. "Makes me wonder when you and I can go public."

Alright, now I feel like I'm gonna vomit.

"I, uh—"

"I've been thinking," Silas says. "I don't know if I really like being a physical therapist."

I tilt my head, thrown out of my fear momentarily. "Really?"

He nods. "It's just—it's always something I thought I wanted to do, but now that I'm in a happier place, I'm sorta thinking I settled with it. I think there's something better for me out there."

"And what's that?" I ask.

He frowns. "I'm not sure yet. But if I were to leave the NFO, we wouldn't have to hide anymore. We could go public."

My chest squeezes, and I have to scrunch my face hard to keep from crying. Of course, right as Silas and I could be public, he and I both get our lives threatened. Just as I catch a break, a new obstacle appears. It's like the universe doesn't want me to have genuine love.

"What?" Silas asks. "You're making a face."

"I'm sorry," I say, letting a tear slip through, but thankfully it's too dark for Silas to see. I look at Kyle and Michael, then Tanner and Jimmy. There are several lesbian couples here, too. And they all look happy—happy in a relationship that I'll never be able to have.

Not if I want to keep the man who I love safe.

"I can't do this," I say, letting go of Michael. I turn and make my way to the exit of this beautifully lit hall, rain dancing on the roof above.

"Wyatt," I hear someone hiss. I turn to see my mom glaring daggers at me.

"Were you dancing with that Silas boy?" She steps closer to me. "Are you really seeing him while you're going through all this?"

"Oh, quiet, Mom," I spit out. And then I rush out of the hall. The doors open behind me, and this time it's Silas.

"Wait, Wyatt," he says, following me out into the rain.

I fumble with my keys, trying to unlock my car. It's the kind of downpour where if you stand in the rain for more than three seconds, you're soaked. And we've both been out here for longer than three seconds now.

"Wyatt," Silas says, clearly crying now. He takes off his cowboy hat and holds it against his chest as the rain pelts him. "What's going on? Why are you running away? Tell me, please."

I finally unlock my car, and the flashing lights help me see where I'm stepping.

"Get in," I say, not even processing what I'm saying. He quickly obeys, getting into the passenger seat more quickly than I get into mine. We shut our doors, protecting us from the rain. But now we're both soaked, and we're both crying.

"Wyatt," he says. "What the hell just happened?"

I close my eyes and take a shaky breath.

I can't go on knowing that Silas is in danger. I have to protect him.

But I don't think the solution is as easy as just not playing football anymore. These goons, whoever they are, know about Silas. Which means they probably know where he works, and they may even know where he lives. Oh, my stomach twists over itself at that thought.

Sure, Silas has just said he may not want to continue on as a physical therapist. But he wouldn't just quit during the season. He would stay until the end of his probation. Which increases the chances that he can get hurt.

"Wyatt," he says. "What's—"

"I'm taking us home," I say. "I need to think."

"About what?" he asks, almost whimpering. "About us?"

I wince and bite my lip. "Just let me think, okay?"

He nods and turns to face the window as we drive. We pull into our own cabin in no time, which sucks because I wish we had more driving time for me to think of a solution. Without a word, I get out of the car into the rain, no doubt ruining the nice suit that Kyle bought for me.

I hear the door slam behind me as I walk onto our slippery porch.

"Okay," Silas says behind. "When we get inside, will you please tell me what's going on?"

I fumble with the key to unlock the door. "Fuck!" I shout.

"Here." Silas moves me out of the way and unlocks the door with ease. I slip inside and immediately throw off my wet suit jacket. I tear off my tie and immediately start unbuttoning my shirt. I want these wet clothes off me, and I want the terror of being threatened off me, too. But only one of these things will come off easily.

"Wyatt," Silas says, sitting down on the couch, still in his wet clothes. "Talk to me."

I sit down across from him, finishing the last of my buttons and starting on my cuffs.

"What the hell is going on?" he asks.

I slip off my shirt and wipe my hand down my sweaty, hairy torso. Then, I lean forward, rubbing the pulsing headache that is only just beginning.

I can't tell him everything. Because if I do, then he'll try to help, just like my mom. But he can't help. Because he's in more danger than me. He can't know about this.

"I—" I start, then I stop myself. Fuck. I really only think there's one way to do this where he's safe. There's nothing else I can think to do.

"Tell me," he says, his voice soft and earnest.

Which makes what I'm about to do so much harder.

Fuck me.

And Silas, I hope you can forgive me.

"We need to break up," I say.

He looks at me like I just smashed the table between us with a sledgehammer.

"What?" he asks, his voice hoarse.

"We can't do this anymore," I say, the words like bitter poison on my tongue. "It's not safe."

Silas clutches his chest, and he looks at like he's Alfredo and I'm Violetta in *La Traviata*. Of course, that opera ends in tragedy—with Violetta's death. But I'm doing this to prevent Silas from getting hurt. I'm doing this to help him. After this all blows over, we can try to salvage what was lost. This isn't truly the end. This is what I have to tell myself.

"Not safe?" he asks. "What do you mean?"

I'm tempted, more than ever, to tell him everything—that both he and I are under threat. But I can't. He'd insist on staying with me and solving the problem together, and I know I wouldn't have the strength to resist him then. I have to do it now.

"You—you're on staff with the Pioneers," I say. "If were caught, you could lose your career. Mine could be in jeopardy, too."

"But Wyatt," Silas says, standing up. "I just told you—I don't know if I want to stay a physical therapist. And this is all the more reason to quit. I can find other work."

"No," I growl, shaking my head. *Stop being so goddamn accommodating*, I want to say. But that will only make this worse.

"But that can work," Silas says, standing there, dripping water from his wet suit on the rug.

"Silas, you have bills to pay," I say.

"I can pay them another way," he says. "I'll figure it out."

I wipe the tears from my eyes. "This could hurt my career, too, you know. Playing is important to me. I want so show queers that—"

"I know that," Silas says. "Which is why I'll quit before any of this goes public." He rushes over and kneels next to me. "We can make this work. Don't do this to me. Please. I need you, Wyatt. You're the most important person to me. Ever."

I look into his deep, brown eyes, and it takes everything in me not to grab him and kiss him hard. Of course he'd be bending over backwards to make this work. In any other circumstance, I would, too. But his safety is on the line. And I will do absolutely nothing to jeopardize that. Even if that means walking away from him, the man who I love most. I just pray we can pick up the pieces when all is well.

I pick up my shirt and stand up.

"Wyatt, no," he says, standing up with me. He's ugly sobbing now.

I put all my focus on each step I'm taking, knowing that if I lose this focus, I'm turning around and wrapping my arms around the man I love. And we can't have that. Not if I don't want him to get hurt by these homophobic bigots.

I get to our bedroom and pack everything I can into my suitcase, doing my best to drown out Silas's crying and pleading at the bedroom door. But his wails are shattering my heart.

This shit is ridiculous. I feel disconnected from everyone my whole life, having needed to hide my authentic self from them. Then, when I finally come out, I meet someone perfect. And then we can't be together because of stupid fucking institutional barriers, not even because of anything homophobic. And now that Silas has proposed resolving the institutional barrier that has barred us from being officially together, both of our lives are at stake. I cannot fucking catch a break. Coming out was a bust. I should have never even bothered being authentic. Because I just got burned all the same.

I slip on a T-shirt, then zip-up the suitcase.

"Please," Silas moans. "Don't leave me. Don't do this."

I pick up the suitcase and make my way out of the bedroom. To my surprise, he doesn't try to stop me. He just steps out of the way. Which actually breaks my heart more than anything. Silas has given up.

I put my hand on the doorknob and dare to hesitate, the storm outside as intense as ever.

I tighten my grip. "I'm sorry."

"Wyatt," he says. "Pl—"

And I open and shut the door as fast I can, running out into the rain. I get in my rental car, and drive straight to Memphis. I'm headed back to Salt Lake where I can think about a way to stop all these threats from turning into reality. And I can rest assured that Silas will be safer by not being associated with me.

Chapter 19

Silas King

I STUMBLE AROUND THE cabin for God knows how long. Every now and then, I open the front door, hoping that Wyatt's somehow changed his mind and returned. With each passing silent moment, only accompanied by Cheshire occasionally scratching the living room rug, it dawns on me that he will never come back.

I plod to the kitchen to take out some liquor I bought to celebrate Michael and Kyle's wedding. Wyatt and I were supposed to drink some of it, relax, and fuck tonight before our hike tomorrow.

But he's gone. And he's not coming back.

I slump down in the kitchen, my clothes still soaking wet. I unscrew the bottle of top shelf whiskey and sip it carelessly. I grimace as the savory liquid slides down my throat. I don't like whiskey, or even alcohol in general. I just bought it because it's Wyatt's favorite.

My phone buzzes in my pocket, I reach down to grab it faster than the lightning striking outside. But my pants are still wet, so it's hard to get the pocket open. Truthfully, I don't know how my phone is still functioning with how wet I am.

I pull it out, hoping it's something from Wyatt. But my chest burns white hot when I see it's not him but instead Jimmy. In fact, Jimmy's sent me multiple texts.

"Hey, I saw you follow Wyatt out of the building. Is everything OK?"

Another one five minutes later. "Kyle's playing the banjo with the quartet, and it's awesome. Where are you?"

Then, ten minutes later. "Hey, Kyle wanted to give a speech addressed to the groomsmen. Are you coming back?"

I close my messages to see he's called me several times.

Then I get one last text from him.

"Silas, you're not answering. What's going on?"

And that's when I throw my phone. It hits the far wall so hard it shatters into pieces and sends Cheshire running into the other room.

I don't know what's possessed me. I'm never violent. But there are so many emotions pouring out of me that I just needed to do something. And that was it.

I pick up my bottle and make my way to the back porch. I open the door, the sky dark and rain falling hard. The handle's wetness makes it difficult for me to shut the door all the way, so I don't even bother. I leave it ajar, letting water blow onto the hardwood floor.

I walk to the edge of the dock, paying the rain no mind, and sit and let my legs dangle over the water. I take another swig of the whiskey, this time only wincing slightly. I can see why Jimmy used to drink. I think I may actually be feeling better. But then this night's events replay in my head, and I feel worse than I've ever.

Wyatt left me. He said that it was to protect both of our careers. But doesn't he see that I don't really care about any of that? I mean, sure, I wouldn't do anything to sabotage his career, but I said I was happy to leave my job for him. Physical therapy in the NFO is not where I want to spend the rest of my life, anyways. Sure, I don't know what I want to do next, but I could have figured that out. Wyatt didn't need to leave me.

Maybe there's something else I can say to remind him of this. Maybe I can still change his mind.

Having sipped a considerable amount of whiskey, I press against my pocket where my phone should be. Wind whips water into my face as I panic. It's not there.

"Fuck," I shout into the storm.

Right. I destroyed my phone. I destroyed the only fucking means of communication that Wyatt and I have now that he left. He's probably trying to reach me right now to tell me he's changed his mind—to apologize and ask for me back. And I've just burned that bridge.

I stand up and almost fall on my face. I'm not exactly sober now. I hobble over to the back door. Cheshire is sitting nearby, curiously watching the rain pelt the wood floor. I step inside, getting water everywhere, and angrily shut the door behind me. I spot my broken phone nearby, rush over to it, and pick up the biggest piece. A lot of the outer shell is gone, but it's still working.

Which means it can still make calls.

I immediately find Wyatt's contact and call him. It rings once, then goes straight to voicemail. I try calling again, but I get nothing. Frustrated, I nearly slam my phone down to finally destroy it, but then that would mean that he absolutely couldn't contact me. So, I press my back against the wall, fall to the floor, drop my face into my hands, and weep.

How could Wyatt do this to me? We loved each other. He just sprung this on me out of nowhere. And I'm lost. I have nothing.

Linda and Michael tried to tell me that I needed my own sense of self-worth. And I fucking know that, but when you've never had it your whole life, then somebody comes along and makes you feel like a million bucks, how the hell am I not supposed to take the offer? And how the hell, when he shatters my life to pieces, am I supposed to pick all of them up and continue on like nothing happened? To continue on like life still somehow has worth?I hear something buzzing, and I grab my phone like it's water in a desert. And I only scowl when I see it's Jimmy again. I deny the call. If I talk to him or anyone else, they're just gonna say that this was bound to happen, that I shouldn't have put all my emotional eggs into Wyatt's basket. But what else was I supposed to do? The man listened to my music and was able to describe my relationship with it flawlessly, hardly even knowing me at all. He sees me like no one else. And the sex—oh. My. God. I rub my mustache, which reactivates the scent of Wyatt's ass that I ate earlier and wafts it up to my nose.

And that's when the tears get harder.

I'll never smell him again. Taste him again. Kiss him again.

I'll never laugh with him or talk about music with him again. I'll never hear that gorgeous, rich voice again.

Finding myself splayed out on the wood floor, I grab my phone and lazily find the YouTube video of him singing "Che Gelida Manina". The opening words give me chills, and I break into another sob when I hear the voice I will never hear in real life again.

Throughout the song, I reflect on what he told me—how I was like Mimi when he met me, and he was like Rodolfo. Like it was love at first sight, and that more than anything he wanted to get to know me to see how I ticked.

And now, the more I think about it, the more I realize how apt this analogy is. Because the whole opera is a tragedy. Wyatt and I have watched a recording together. Mimi and Rodolfo fall in love, but then slowly drift apart until the very end when they are reunited. But Mimi is sick, and just as they are reflecting on their happiest days, she passes, leaving Rodolfo in misery.

Maybe Wyatt is right. Maybe I am just like Mimi. Except, instead of dying from consumption, I'll die in another way—a way where I'm in control.

I pick up my phone and stop Wyatt's video before it reaches the climax. I don't need to torture myself listening to him anymore. All the pain—not just from Wyatt, but from everything—stops tonight.

I make my way to my feet with my bottle still in hand, my broken phone in the other. I go back to the playlist that I made for Wyatt—the one completely devoid of his songs—and put it on shuffle. "Palemote" by *Slow Meadow* begins playing through the broken speakers, and I couldn't think of a better, more plaintive song to accompany me.

Slowly, like a march to the death, I make my way to the bedroom—the same one that Wyatt and I were going to share.

As I walk, Cheshire prances in between my legs, meowing loudly, nearly knocking me on my face.

"What do you want?" I ask after taking a sip of whiskey.

He meows for so long that he almost sobers me entirely. Never has Cheshire, in my entire life, meowed for so long or so loud. On some primal, psychic level, he must know what I'm about to do. He usually eats in the morning, but tomorrow I don't think he'll have anyone to feed him. Not if this goes right. So I'll give him one last supper.

As *Slow Meadow* plays, I break out a can of cat food from the fridge, and the second I click it open, Cheshire's right at my feet, wrapping his tail around my wet ankle like wants me to stay and eat with him.

My music stops, and I see I'm getting another call from Jimmy. I quickly hang up, this time feeling more guilty than angry. I remember Brigham calling me just yesterday, almost crying to me about the loss of his niece to suicide. He remarked how her death rippled throughout the whole family, and how he was scared for his daughter, too.

I can't help the guilt flaring in my chest as I imagine what similar effects my death will have on those who I love. Now, I could sit here and tell myself that these people don't really love me. I could try and say that I was alone until the end—that I'm not leaving anyone behind.

But that would be the biggest lie I've ever told.

In truth, I know I'm deeply, deeply loved.

And that just makes this so much harder.

People say that those who die by their own hand are selfish. But right now, it's my guilt for Cheshire that's delaying the inevitable, and it's Jimmy's love for me and my love for him that's delaying it further—not to mention all the other people I'd leave in my wake. Linda. Michael. Kyle. Tanner. Martha. Llewellyn.

But if self-worth comes from within, doesn't that mean I should make decisions based on what I want? That I shouldn't unnecessarily prolong my life just because others will be hurt?

The song resumes playing, eventually reaching its high point as I watch Cheshire eat. I think it's time to move on—to go elsewhere. Once I can see that Cheshire is happily distracted by his food, I make my way into the bedroom.

I kneel in front of the nightstand and pull out my travel bag. Inside, I have some over-the-counter medications, but at the very bottom are two bottles of pills that have been in my possession for a while. I double check to make sure they're not expired—even though I always know the state of my pills—and I'm relieved to see they're still potent. Just underneath them are a number of small shooters that I was able to take with me on the plane. "Palemote" is about to end, so I just restart it. When I go out, I want to listen to something beautiful.

I unscrew the cap of one of the bottles and pour about a dozen into my hands. This will be good to start with. But just as I lift them to my mouth, there's knock at the door. Thinking it's Wyatt, I'm about to jump to my feet, but then I hear who it is.

"Silas, buddy," I hear Jimmy say through the door. "Are you in there?"

I freeze, the pills still in my hand, and my heart pounds in my throat.

"Silas," he yells. "Are you OK? It's pouring out here. Can you let me in?"

I wince as I imagine how hurt he'll be to discover me tomorrow after this is all over. Luckily, my music is too quiet for him to hear, and there's nothing else to give me away.

I better do this quick.

I reach for the bottle of whiskey, but that's when I whack the neck with the back of my hand, and it spills all over the carpet.

"Fuck," I grunt.

"Silas?" Jimmy shouts. And then he starts fumbling with the door.

No. If he finds me, then I'll never go through with this. People will just say I'm overreacting, but I'm not. Wyatt was my everything, and I lost him. I lost everything. I can't go on longer.

I shove as many pills as I can into my mouth, then grab the bottle of remaining whiskey and wash it down. It burns especially hard. Just as I'm reaching for more pills, I hear the front door burst open, and I swear my heart stops.

"Silas?" he calls out, his voice deadly close. "Are you okay?"

"Palemote" continues playing as I put the pills into my mouth. And right when I grab the bottle of whiskey to wash them down, Jimmy appears at my bedroom doorway.

And, for a moment, time stops.

He stands and stares at me, his tie undone with his dress shirt untucked, completely soaked from the rain. His eyes widen when he sees the pill bottle on the bed and the liquor in my hand.

"Silas," he says. "You're not...?"

But I don't want to have to answer him.

I lift the bottle to my lips, and Jimmy charges at me faster than Wyatt on the field. He knocks it to the ground, and the rest of it spills onto the carpet.

He stands there, inches from me, complete horror on his face.

"What are you doing?" he asks, his voice hoarse. "Why?" My lips quiver, and I move around the pills in my mouth that I still haven't swallowed. I'm already starting to feel a bit strange, but I don't know if it's the alcohol or the pills or the grief or something else.

His face hardens. "Are they still in your mouth?"

And that's when I start crying again. I try to swallow, but Jimmy spins me around and manages to pin my arms behind my back with only one of his. With his other arm, he reaches around and tries to pry my mouth open with his thick fingers.

"Spit them out, Silas," he yells. "Spit them the fuck out."

I shake my head. "No!" I manage to say, but that gives him the chance to stick his finger in my open mouth and force it in. He fishes the pills out, and they fall to the ground like broken teeth. And that's how bad the pain feels. Because the more Jimmy tries to stop me, the more I know I'll have to live with the consequences of what I've just done.

I try to elbow Jimmy, but he keeps my arms firmly in place. He manages to get all the pills out, then he spins me around and pins me on the bed.

"How many pills have you already taken?" he asks, shouting from above me.

I shake my head, weeping again.

"Goddamnit, Silas," he says, breaking into a sob. "Goddamnit. How many did you already take?"

I shake my head and press my face into the comforter. "I need him," I say. "I need Wyatt, and he's gone. I want to be gone."

"No, Silas," he says, racked with sobs. "I can't let you do this. I can't let you leave me. I can't let you leave us. You're not going to be gone. I need you to stay right here. With us."

I shake my head, the comforter soaking up my tears. "Please, let me go."

"I'm doing no such thing," he says. "Fuck, you're freezing. We need you out of these wet clothes."

He flips me over onto my back while I weep. He manages to strip my wet clothes off me until I'm just in my underwear. He takes off his wet clothes, too. With the lights still on, "Palemote" finally coming to an end, he gets us both under the covers. He wraps his arms around me, and that's when I realize how cold I am. I'm shivering and nuzzling back into Jimmy's hairy body. He has my arms pinned to my sides, and I feel my eyes go heavy.

"Don't you fall asleep on me, Silas," he says. "Come on, Tanner, where are you..."

As if summoned, Tanner appears at the bedroom door, his outfit disheveled, though he looks like he's been dancing rather than out in the rain. He stares at me with just as much horror as Jimmy did when he first saw me.

"Call an ambulance," Jimmy says, his mouth right next to my ear.

Tanner nods, and just as he leaves, my eyelids grow too heavy for me to resist. So, despite Jimmy's admonition, I let my entire world go black.

Chapter 20

Wyatt Nelson

I PACE THROUGHOUT MY condo as heavy snow falls over Salt Lake City. I'm on the phone with Blake, determining whether or not I should play in tomorrow's game.

It's been two weeks since I ended things with Silas—since I walked out on him. And I've just been one big ball of nerves. Just before I ended things with him, I received that message, threatening me that if I didn't drop out of this season, it wasn't just me who was going to get hurt. It was Silas, too. So that's why I broke up with him, why I pushed him away so abruptly. I couldn't have him get hurt because of me.

Since then, I've played a couple games, and there have thankfully been no consequences. I haven't gotten another message, and nothing on the field has been particularly suspicious. I'm thinking it's because these teams we've played don't have players who are part of this mysterious faction out to get me. But tomorrow, we're playing against the Sparrows, and I know for a fact that team is against me.

"Do you want my honest opinion?" he asks.

"Well," I say. "You've never been one to hold your punches."

He sighs. "I would sit out."

I rub the bridge of my nose. Of course that's what he would say.

"But dude," I say. "This has been my best season yet. I've caught nearly 90% of my passes this season. That's unheard of. I can't just give that up. Besides, it's not like I can just decide on a whim when I can or can't play. Management wouldn't allow that."

"They would if you came clean about the threats," he says. "And what if you tear your ACL again? You heard that message. You or Silas *will* get hurt. It's a miracle that it hasn't happened yet with how confidently you've been playing."

I plop down in my lazy boy next to my window and watch the snow fall. It's not even Thanksgiving yet, and we're gonna get a foot of snow. Living in the mountains is wild.

"Well, we don't have to worry about Silas anymore."

He trills his lips. "I'm sorry about that man," he says, referring to our breakup. "But he's still at risk, right? Even if you aren't together."

"He would be if he was here," I say. "But I haven't seen Silas since we broke up. As far as I know, he hasn't come back to Salt Lake."

"Did he quit?"

I think back to him saying he was willing to give up his job as a PT so we could go public, and my chest tightens. "I don't know."

"Well regardless," Blake says. "I still don't think you should play."

I roll my eyes and fold my arms tightly. "I'll decide in the morning."

He sucks on his lips. "I'm telling you man: becoming the best isn't worth it. It just isn't."

I think about my high school self, feeling so ashamed for just liking the same sex. I remember getting the ideas that 'faggots' and 'sissies' were lesser hammered into my head.

"And I'm telling you," I say, standing up. "That it is. I'll see you tomorrow."

"Alright," he says, exasperated. "I'll see ya."

And as I lay in bed that night, my body craves the man I left behind. But in a way, I'm doing this for him, too. I'm doing this to protect him, and I'm here to show every queer person out there that we can excel, too.

The next morning, I decide: fuck it. I'm playing. I'm not going to let a bunch of homophobic goons stop me. And now that I know that Silas is safe, all I gotta worry about is myself. As long as I play well, then I have nothing to worry about.

Blake nearly glares at me when I walk into the locker room.

"So you haven't changed your mind about being an idiot," he says when I sit down next to him.

"Hush," I say. "I'll be fine. I've been safe enough so far."

He shakes his head. "Pride cometh before the fall."

I huff out a breath. "That's if I fall."

We both go start putting our gear on, and then my phone starts ringing. And suddenly, the protein shake I had this morning goes right to my gut.

I glance down and see a number I don't immediately recognize—not unknown, but unrecognizable. And my blood goes cold. This could be another threat message.

"Is that one of the...?" Blake asks.

"I don't know," I hiss, picking up my phone. "I'll be back."

I hurry out of the locker rooms to a private hallway, only wearing my game pants. I answer the phone just before it goes to voicemail.

"Hello?" I answer shakily.

"Wyatt Nelson," a familiar voice says. "You fucking son of a bitch."

I squint my eyes, confused. "Kyle Weaver?" I ask. That's why his number looked slightly familiar. It's Mississippi. I must have not saved his contact.

"You know, my wedding was a real special night," he says.

"Yeah," I say. "I'm glad I came. Sorry I had to leave early."

"Yeah, yeah," he says, ignoring my apology. "It was real nice until I discovered the next morning that one of my best friends was hospitalized."

My knees go weak. I fall against the wall and let myself slide to the cold, concrete floor. My forehead breaks into a sweat.

"Silas," I say, breathless. "Was he hurt? Who hurt him?"

"He hurt him," Kyle says.

"'He'," I say. "Who's 'he'?"

"Silas," Kyle spits out. "Silas hurt himself. Christ, Wyatt—he almost killed himself."

Alright, now it feels like I'm gonna throw up the shake I had this morning.

"K-killed himself?" I ask, my whole body shaking. "What do you mean?"

"I mean that the night of my wedding—the night that you broke up with Silas—my good buddy Jimmy goes back to your cabin and finds Silas with a mouth full of pills and a handful of liquor."

The hallways starts to spin around me. "What?"

"And we're lucky that Jimmy found him. Because if he was just a minute later Silas might be dead right now."

Tears well in my eyes. "You're kidding me."

"Kidding you?" Kyle asks, genuinely pissed. "You're the one kidding me, Wyatt. You break up with one of my best friends out of nowhere, and then he nearly kills himself. It would be an understatement to say I'm pissed at you."

I shake my head. "I—"

I see Blake poke his head out in the hallway, and I try to swat him away. But he stays right there.

"Now I know you're not really to blame for this. Apparently Silas has been dealing with depression for a long time now."

"Silas," I say, his name grounding me. "Where is he? Is he okay?"

"By the grace of God, he's okay now," Kyle says. "Tanner was able to call an ambulance. We got him to the Miss U hospital and got his stomach pumped. He's staying with Martha and Llewellyn now, where he used to live."

I breathe out the biggest sigh of relief. And that's when Blake comes out into the hallway with all his gear, save for his boots. He sits against the wall across from me. Around us, we can hear the Sparrow's stadium roar.

"I'm so glad he's okay," I say.

"Us too," Kyle says. "But it was real reckless of you to just walk away like that. Silas could have died."

"I know," I say. "I feel horrible."

"And imagine how much worse you would have felt if he did go through with it," he says, his voice shaky. I think Kyle Weaver is crying on the other line.

"I—I'm sorry, Kyle," I manage to say.

"He kept saying your name, too," Kyle says with a sniffle.

I grip my phone tighter. "What?"

"Apparently, when he was about to end his life, he couldn't stop talking about you, according to Jimmy. Kept saying he needed you."

Guilt pools in my stomach like a giant brick of shit. This entire time, I've sworn to protect Silas. And with what I did to him, I put him in more danger than ever. Yet it wasn't with these homophobic NFO goons. It was with himself.

"Oh, man," I say, pulling on my beard, tears streaming down my face. "I—" But I stop myself. I want to say how much I want to see him. But with how fragile Silas is, would that even be a good idea? And hell, I knew Silas wasn't the happiest person around. I could just tell by his demeanor. But he was happy around me.

"I swear, Kyle," I say. "I didn't know he was suicidal. If I had known, I wouldn't have done it the way that I did. I'm just—" I shake my head. "I'm in some deep shit right now."

"What do you mean 'deep shit'?" he asks. "Because if it's NFO deep shit, then I can relate. I can help you, man. Shit, I also broke up with Michael years back just as abruptly as you did Silas because I was too afraid of what being a gay man meant. You're not alone, dude."

My stomach jumps. Of course. Kyle was the first big NFO player to come out so publicly. And sure, he retired just after he did, but he set the precedent for everyone after him. Not only was he the greatest linebacker of the 21st century, but he was also the first gay one. If he was threatened, I don't know about it, but he and I are alike in more ways than I realize.

I glance up at Blake. He gives me a gesture that practically says 'what the hell's going on?', and I just rub my temple.

If I told Kyle the truth, then I know this story would slip out of my control fast. But I know now that the way I've handled things thus far is pure shit. I almost got the man I love killed. All because I was too afraid to talk.

"Hey, it's nothing, Kyle," I say. "Well, not nothing. I may need to talk to you about it. But not now."

"Okay," he says skeptically. "Just know I can help."

"Thank you."

There's silence between as the weight of all that's been said presses down on me. Silas almost died. Because of me. Despite everything I tried to do to keep him safe.

I clear my throat. "Is Silas okay—"

"I don't know if Silas would want to see you," he says. "He's stopped talking about you altogether."

It feels like Kyle just punched me in the stomach. "Alright." Guess that answers that.

"He's seeing a bunch of professionals right now, and they think he's in a safe place. But even then, I don't know if reaching out's a good idea. He's still fragile."

I sigh. "I get it."

"And Wyatt," Kyle says.

"Yeah?"

"Don't let the NFO control your fucking life," he says. "I don't know what you're going through, but if I could take a guess, I'd imagine that's what you're struggling with. I wasted too much of my life worried about my career and how the world would see me. Just fucking be yourself and let the world take care of the rest. You'll be alright."

For the first time during this conversation, I feel a little lighter.

"Alright. Thanks, Kyle. I'll be in touch."

"Take it easy." And then he hangs up.

"Who was that?" Blake asks. "And by the way, you need to get dressed if you're still playing. We're the only ones not practicing on the fields right now."

I rub my temples, trying to process everything I've just heard. I feel like Don Giovanni being dragged off to hell at the end of the opera, finally getting what he deserves.

Silas nearly killed himself. He's more stable now, but he's still fragile, and his mental state is more precarious than I ever could have imagined. I don't know if he wants to see me again, which is hard, but that might be for the best right now. Because he's not the only fragile thing. My life is still in danger, which means that his is, too.

"That was Kyle Weaver," I say.

Blake furrows his brow. "Kyle Weaver? Why'd he call?"

I rub my temples harder. I don't want to go all into it with Blake. I don't need another person to tell me how bad I've fucked up. Because it's plain now.

My indecision about handling my own safety led to Silas almost losing his life. Sure, it wasn't directly my fault, but I'd be idiotic to not see the connection. And now that we're playing the Sparrows, it seems so much more likely that I might get injured again—or that these homophobic NFO goons expand their efforts and start threatening Blake. Or newer gay players. It's all so in the realm of possibility, and I've been foolish to punt off doing anything about it for so long. I need to take action about these threats, or I know everything's going to get worse. But I can't do it alone. Because that's only how I've approached it so far, and all it's done is nearly take away the life of the man I love.

This whole time, I've held myself to an impossibly high standard, saying that gay men deserve and should achieve just as much as any straight man could. But that ignores the barriers set in our place, like homophobic NFO members who threaten violence just to keep queers from achieving greatness. Now that the love of my life has almost died, I see how foolish it is to ignore barriers like these. Because ignoring them won't make them go away. I'm not sure what will, but I know it can no longer be sticking my head in the sand.

"I'm not playing today," I say.

Blake leans forward. "Seriously?"

I nod. "I've delayed taking action about this for long enough. I need to get safe."

"So are you gonna go public?"

I imagine talking to reporters again about this, and I cringe. "I don't know yet. I—"

And then I remember Kyle.

He's dealt with shit like this before. And Tanner probably has, too. And they're both gay, former NFO players. If anyone would know my deal, they would.

"Then what are you gonna do?" Blake asks.

I pull on my beard and let out a deep sigh. "I think I'm gonna enlist the help of some others who might know what to do."

Chapter 21

Silas King

THERE'S A KNOCK AT my door—well, not my door. It's Martha and Llewellyn's guest bedroom door.

I don't say anything.

The door clicks open, and Llewellyn pokes her head in.

"Hey, chief," she says. I remain on my side facing away from her, looking out the bedroom window.

I hear her step in the room, and I tighten my body like a snake protecting itself. She walks in and sits down at the foot of the bed.

"You got therapy in a little bit," she says. "You ready to get up?"

I let out a deep sigh. "I don't know if I can today." My voice is scratchy. I think it's the first time I've spoken in at least a full day.

She doesn't respond or even stir. I glance down at her. She's scratching the quilt with her thumb.

"You need to go," she says. "Saying you'd go to therapy was the only way to get you out of inpatient. Unless you want to go there instead."

I grimace. Grippy socks, shoes without laces, and group therapy. Not that those things aren't good for some people. I just couldn't imagine myself in such an institution. I managed to convince the doctors, along with the help of my loved ones, that I was well enough to be released, as long as I started visiting with a therapist and psychiatrist. The meds are fine. But talking about everything has been the hard part. Which is why I don't want to go today.

"I don't want to do that," I say.

"Then it's that you get up," she says. "Or we take you to the inpatient clinic. Your choice."

Her voice is hard. Hurt. And I can't blame her. I almost decided to abandon her and everyone else.

And this is why I can't help but feel pissed at Jimmy. If he hadn't saved me, I wouldn't have had to deal with everyone else's grief and anger toward me.

"Fine," I say. I throw off the covers. All I'm wearing is some gym shorts, so I'll just throw a T-shirt on. I couldn't give a shit about my appearance right now. As I do, Llewellyn leans down to pet Cheshire who's just walked into the room. And I can't help but be angry with him, too. If he hadn't meowed up a storm, he wouldn't have delayed me. I would have completed the deed before Jimmy arrived. I've wanted to push him away, especially when he comes to sleep with me, but I haven't had the heart to do that.

Once I dress, I sigh. "Alright. Ready."

"Let's get some food in you first," she says.

I roll my eyes, but then I just nod. There's no point in fighting this. And I know that Llewellyn and Martha are just doing this because they care, even though they aren't even bothering to hide the pain on their faces.

I make way to the kitchen and sit down at the table. Martha's just finishing up some bacon, and Llewellyn hands me a plate of scrambled eggs. Without a word, I take a bite, and I try not to visibly wince, even though I'd rather eat cement than these eggs right now. Which is awful. I love breakfast food, and I love Martha's cooking even more. And my love for these women who took me in as their own when I moved here so many years ago knows no bounds.

But everything tastes like ash, and everything looks like it's covered in ash, too. I remember, as a kid, reading the Lemony Snicket books. In *The Series of Unfortunate Events*, he likens depression and grief unto ash after a big fire. It covers everything. It seeps into our food, into everything we smell. It covers everything in a thin film of black and white powder. So everything we do, touch, feel, taste, smell, see—it's corrupted by this ash. Nothing tastes good anymore. Everything looks a little off. It's almost like my senses are completely gone, even though the doctor assured me that my attempt on my own life will not have any lasting consequences on my health.

They say the vast majority of the people who attempt regret their decision. I can't say I'm part of that demographic. I regret that it didn't work, and I'm pissed everyone is grieving me as if it did. The only things that are really making me happy I'm still around are the stupid little things. I enjoy hearing Cheshire's purring. I enjoy hearing Martha and Llewellyn laugh in the other room. I like watching leaves fall from their backyard oak tree. As much as I wish I was successful, these are some of things I'm glad I didn't lose. And they're the only things getting me through right now.

Martha is sitting across from me, her laptop in front of her. She runs her fingers through her red hair and squints at the screen, mild frustration growing on her face.

"Honey, I'll handle that," Llewellyn says. "You can take Silas to therapy."

Martha's eyes linger on the screen, then she meets Llewellyn's gaze. "You sure?"

Llewellyn puts her hand on hers. "Positive. You've been working this whole morning. Let me take over."

Martha sighs and thanks her.

It turns out the adoption process is a little bit more difficult than they thought. Every time they've found a viable opportunity to adopt, something has fallen through, forcing them to reapply every six months. And they've been doing this for a while now. Honestly, if I were them, I would have given up. But they're as determined as ever.

Martha grabs the keys to their Subaru off the table. "You ready to go?" she asks me.

I force one last forkful of egg into my mouth and try not to gag. "Yep."

Llewellyn touches my arm before I can stand. "Good luck, okay?"

I nod. "Thanks."

I help Martha load the dishwasher, and then we're on our way. As we drive, the air in the car feels heavy. I feel that Martha wants to talk about so much, but she doesn't know what to say or if she even should say anything. Which is fine. Since that night, I've never really been in the mood to talk.

My therapist has his office right next to Miss U, and it's about a twenty-minute drive. Normally, I'd listen to music to pass the time. But I haven't really wanted to listen to music either. Before, it was like my life was a giant painting, filled with different colors depending on my mood. Most of the time, those colors were a variation of black and blue. With him, the colors became more vibrant. But after my attempt so many weeks ago, it's like all the colors have been erased, leaving me with a blank canvas. Like I've passed through the singularity of the black hole, and all the remains that formed my identity have been reduced to nothing.

So music doesn't sound as it once did. The only song I can think of to fit this mood is the solo piano version of "Boy in a Water Globe", this version completely stripped down to the bare bones of the original. But I can't listen to that. It reminds me of him, especially after he helped me see what the song really meant to me.

When we reach my therapist's office, Martha puts her hand on my knee just before I leave the car, and I freeze.

"I'm really glad you're still in our lives," she says, tears in her eyes.

I quickly look away. Emotion in others overwhelms me right now. Seeing it makes me feel so out of the ordinary for not feeling that way.

"Thanks," I say.

"If we never have a child," she says. "Know that we always considered you as our own."

I sigh and nod. I wish I could give her the response I know she wants. But I just have nothing to give.

I reach over the console and give her a lukewarm hug, and she holds her arms tight around me.

"I love you," she says.

"I love you too," I say flatly. "I'll see you in an hour." And then I hop out of that car before it can get any more emotional.

I enter a brick building in downtown Fordsville. I take the elevator up to the third floor—the highest level—and make my way to his clinic. After I check in, I'm quickly escorted back to his office. On the far side, there's a window that overlooks the downtown square of Fordsville, a mixture of restaurants owned by townies mixed with undergraduate bars. But it's mostly empty considering it's Thanksgiving break at Miss U.

"Have a seat," Damon says, sitting at his desk. He's a middle-aged black man with a fit build and graying hair.

I sit down on the couch, bracing myself for another session. If I'm counting correctly, this is the sixth one.

"Alright," he says, standing up. He makes his way over and sits right at the edge of his winged back chair across from me. He smiles. "How we doing today?"

"Well, I'm alive," I say with a shrug.

"And that's definitely a win."

I roll my eyes. I am so not in the mood to be grateful for my life right now.

We go through the normal routine. How I've felt since my last session. How I'm liking my psychiatrist, how the meds are working. How do I feel about killing myself—which, I don't really want to—it seems too rash now. But even if I did, I'm not even sure I would say it. That would just mean a straight ticket to inpatient. And I want my freedom.

"Great," he says, jotting something down on a clipboard in front of him. "Now, are we ready to talk about him?"

My breath quickens, and I grip my knees.

"Who?" I ask.

"You know who," Damon says, looking at me over his reading glasses like a scolding teacher.

I bite my lip and dig my fingers deeper into my knees.

"I know this is obviously not easy," Damon says, taking off his glasses. He leans forward onto his knees. "But we have to dig into this."

"I can't," I say. "It's hard."

"Working on ourselves is hard," he says. "But I can't help you unless this is something you really want to do. So if you want to come here and just talk surface level things until the hospital is convinced you're healthy—which, they won't for a while if you just do that—that's your choice. But if you really want to heal, you gotta talk. And I mean talk deep."

I grimace and look out the window. Down in the street, I see Martha load a shopping bag into the back of her car—a bag from a nearby store for baby apparel.

Despite all their setbacks, Martha and Llewellyn have striven to adopt, even when they could just artificially inseminate. But they are adamant on adopting. They say that they'd rather help the children that are already here than bring a new one into the world, and they've kept to this despite how hard it's been. If they can do something this hard, maybe I can, too.

"Wyatt's his name," I say, his name practically burning my tongue as I say it out loud.

"Wyatt," he says. "And in the past you mentioned he was in the NFO."

"I did," I say, gripping my knees again.

"Easy," he says. "We're going at a good pace."

I relax my fingers slightly.

"Now," he says, scratching his beard. He's about to ask a question, and I feel my heart begin to race.

Ever since he left me, I've given everyone as little detail as possible. Even Damon. Because I don't want to hear what they have to say.

Linda? She would say that I was too emotionally dependent on him. Michael would say I need to stay away from him until I develop my own self-worth. Kyle would say that gay NFO players are mostly bad news, even though he was one. Martha and Llewellyn would probably say to wait until I'm 100% healthy until I even consider a relationship again. Jimmy and Tanner? They're furious that Wyatt was so careless when he broke up with me. They think he's a bad guy.

But me? I still think about Wyatt every moment of every day.

I miss his smell.

I miss his bearded face.

I miss his rich tenor voice.

I miss the way we talked.

I miss the way he saw me like no one else did.

And the truth is, I love him.

I love him.

I love him.

And I love him.

"Let's back up, actually," Damon says, sitting back up in his chair. "Can you share with me why it's so hard to talk about him?"

Even though it's felt like years since I've listened to him, I picture the little shadowy figure that appears on nearly every single one of *Eluvium*'s album covers.

"Can I give you an analogy?" I ask.

Damon nods. "Go ahead."

I take a deep breath, bracing myself to speak longer than I have in weeks.

"There's this monster pursuing me in my head," I say, picturing the shadowy figure. "But the thing is, I don't really know if he's a monster."

"What does this monster look like?"

"Imagine he has the shape of me or you, but he's entirely made of pitch-black smoke," I say. "Like a walking black hole."

"Alright, got it."

"I imagine myself locked in a school. Alone. And there's this smoky monster I've described—let's call him the wraith—looking for me. And I have to keep hiding, but he always eventually finds me. So I have to keep running and hiding. And I have to do this over and over again."

"Why do you keep running from him?"

"Because he's grief," I say. "And he's love. And he's fear, and joy, and sadness, and anger. He's the emotions of life all bundled up into one entity made of smoke. If I touch him, these emotions overwhelm me. I get sucked into an emotional blackhole, and I can never escape of my own accord."

Damon nods solemnly. "I see."

"You asked why I'm afraid of talking about Wyatt," I say. "It's not Wyatt I'm afraid of but the emotions he makes me feel. This wraith represents these feelings."

"Interesting," he says, setting down his clipboard. "You have a real gift, you know."

"A gift?"

"I've never heard emotions described like that," he says. "And it makes perfect sense. Well done."

I shrug, feeling slightly proud of myself, even though I've never taken myself to good at emotions at all. In fact, his words are making me a bit emotional.

"Thanks."

"You're welcome," he says. "So why is the wraith something to be afraid of?"

I grimace, feeling tears heat my eyes for the first time in weeks. It must have been Damon's compliment that set them off.

"Because," I say, my voice shaky. "I'm a fucking freak."

Damon furrows his brow. "What do you mean you're a freak?"

"Because," I say, tears flowing freely, my emotional dam finally bursting. "Normal people don't remain single their whole lives unable to find a partner remotely interested in them. Normal people don't meet a handsome stranger and then fall head over heels for him. Normal people don't lose control of their emotions when this stranger listens to their music that nobody else understands and then perfectly explains back to them why the music is so lovable. Normal people don't break their professional boundaries to date a man in secret just because he helped assuage them of the guilt they have for estranging themselves from their parents.

"Normal people don't feel the way I do. They don't let their emotions for someone corrupt them so much that they try to end their lives when this person walks out of their life. Normal people then don't fall into catatonic depression just because this person is gone," I say. "I'm a fucking freak. Damon. I don't deserve to live. I'm not normal. I'm not fucking normal. I'm an emotionally dependent man with no self-worth who sees no reason to live outside of having a man to love me back. I'm better off fucking dead."

My chest heaves, and I grimace at the table between us as if it's carrying all my words in the form of vomit. And my face burns red hot from embarrassment. Now I'm definitely going to inpatient. Because I've finally said the quiet part out loud. I'm a fucking freak, and I deserve to be institutionalized, if not dead.

Damon just sits there nodding, almost taunting me with his nonchalance. I brace myself for the next things he says, knowing that he has the power to determine my treatment.

He starts playing with his wedding band, sliding it up and down his finger. "I don't think you're a fucking freak."

"What?" I ask as if he just called me something worse.

"I don't think you're a fucking freak," he says. "I don't."

"What do you mean?" I ask, genuinely perplexed.

"I mean exactly what I'm saying," he says. "I don't think you're a freak. I think you're much more normal than you realize."

I don't know if I should be relieved or offended. "How am I not a freak?"

"You've mentioned to me before your relationship with your family."

I huff a breath out. "Or lack thereof."

"Right," Damon says. "Your family didn't see you for who you were. So when you meet someone who sees right to your core, how could you not fall in love with him?" I squint at him, confused. "You're saying that falling in love with Wyatt isn't a bad thing?"

"How could love ever be a bad thing?"

I grimace. "It was love that led me to try and kill myself."

"That wasn't love, Silas. I would argue that it was mostly fear that led you to do that."

I chew on my lips.

"Let's go back to the analogy of this 'wraith'," he says. "Your entire life, you've run away from difficult emotions, many of which come with relationships. Per your analogy, you've been hiding around the school, avoiding the wraith at all costs. Which doesn't make you a freak. It means you're traumatized, sure, but there's nothing to be ashamed of with that. I don't blame you at all. In your upbringing, you never learned how to feel or process emotions. You were just shamed for them. So you learned to fear them as a coping mechanism. That's why you run away from the wraith. That's why you tried to end it all. Fear."

There's a burning in my chest, and I reach up to rub it. Echoes of the song "Know" by *Alaskan Tapes* reverberate in my head. 'They never taught you to know how', it sings. 'I know'.

"But you don't have to live that way anymore. You can let yourself feel your emotions. Enjoy them. Learn to live with them. Let them be a part of you. Let the wraith swallow you whole."

Chills run down my spine, but they're not from fear. What Damon is saying feels right.

"In the process," Damon continues. "Your emotions won't control you like they always have."

I bite my lip and sigh, trying to process everything that Damon's said. "So loving Wyatt isn't bad?"He shakes his head. "Of course it isn't. Like I said, how could you not fall in love with him if he saw you like no one else did?"

"But the love—well, fear as you say—is what led me to want to end my life."

"And learning how to live with these emotions will put you in a place where you will no longer consider suicide as an option to solve your problems," he says. "I can't make any specific promises about your future, but I can reassure you that it's possible for you to be in a place where you can live and love without thinking about ending it all. It will take work, but I think you deserve the outcome. As long as it's what you think you deserve, too."

I sit back against the couch and look out the window. Brown leaves flow across the deserted downtown, and I'm tempted to feel peace. But then an anxious thought comes to mind, throwing me into a near spiral.

"But Wyatt's left me," I say. "He said it was unprofessional for us to date, but I don't want to keep my PT job with the NFO. Hell, I doubt they'll even hire me on permanently after how long I've been gone. So we could date. But I don't know. It feels like there were other reasons for him ending things."Damon leans forward. "Why don't we spend the next couple weeks working on you?" he asks. "Then we can start thinking about love."

"Right," I say. "Nobody can love me until I love myself."

He grimaces and shakes his head.

"What?" I ask, almost laughing despite how exhausting this whole conversation has been.

"I think that saying is a little harsh and reductive. Even when you don't love yourself, people will always love you. Look at your friends who have been by your side at your lowest."

I think of Jimmy taking me to the hospital, Martha and Llewellyn housing me until I get on my feet. And all the love I've received in between. "Right."

"I think that loving yourself will make it easier for you to open up yourself to true love from others," he says. "And be able to reciprocate it. But never think you are unworthy of love just because you are struggling."

My chest warms, and it feels like Damon's opened my chest and inserted freshly baked bread inside. Everything feels right, and I feel cozy because of that.

"Alright," I say. "So what do I need to do?"

Damon shares some worksheets to help address codependency. He also shares resources for codependency support groups in the area and where to find them out of state. He encourages me to go to these groups to meet other people like me.

"Throw yourself into these things," he says. "And let's continue meeting. I'm really proud of the work you did today, Silas. I think we're really making some progress."

I nod and wipe my puffy eyes. "Yeah, thank you."

After we wrap up the session, I make my way out to Martha's Subaru. On the way, I realize I feel hope, which I haven't felt in a long time. With Wyatt, I felt hope, but it was more frenetic, completely dependent on him and the state of our relationship. But now the hope feels more grounded. More certain.

Of course, I love him, yet he's still gone. I don't know what to do about that.

So I guess I'll do what Damon suggests. I need to focus on myself for a bit anyways. And then maybe, just maybe, Wyatt and I will get the opportunity to talk, and I'll be healthy enough to handle it.

But it's time to get healthy first.

Chapter 22

Wyatt Nelson

THE DAY AFTER THANKSGIVING, I finally gather the courage to get the help I need. I arrive in Memphis and take a rental car down to Glamour Springs.

This is the city where I stayed for a few weeks during my ACL recovery. It's also where I met Silas, and it's where he is now.

When I found out it was me leaving him that caused him to spiral and try to take his own life, I nearly had a meltdown. I want to see him while I'm here—to know that he's alright. But I get a feeling I shouldn't. If it was me that sent him over the edge, I might be the last person he wants to see. Besides, Kyle said it wasn't a good idea.

And on top of all this, I'm still in danger, which means he is, too. I didn't play in that game against the Sparrows, but I've now played a few games since. Nothing's happened, which has got me real worried. Something's bound to happen soon, and I'll make sure that hell freezes over before Silas is the one affected. Once all this has blown over, there's nothing I want more than to reconnect. But now is not the time.

When I get to Glamour Springs, I head straight to my mom's cabin. Like always, Dad is out golfing, but the moment I arrive she gives me some leftover Thanksgiving food: stuffing, turkey, and cranberry sauce.

"Thanksgiving with Linda was spectacular," she says.

I nod as I eat the amalgamation of food that should be gross but is actually delectable. "No kidding. This is great."

"When are we meeting with the others?" she asks.

"In about thirty," I say. "We're meeting at Tanner's cabin."

"Thank God," she says, leaning back into the chair. "I'm glad you're finally doing something."

I remember the message I received just before Kyle's wedding, threatening me that something would happen to me or Silas if I kept playing, and I shiver. "Same here."

A few days after Kyle called me to share what had happened with Silas, I called him back. I told him that I was having some troubles with the NFO, but they were likely stranger than he imagined. And I asked for his help. So now I'm here in Glamour Springs. I've asked to meet with Kyle, Tanner, my mom, and anyone else they think could help us out. I'll even phone Blake in—and of course, I'll keep his sexuality a secret. There's no way in hell I'm delaying this any longer. I'm finally getting help. And there's no better person to help me than two of the biggest gay NFO players in history.

When it's time, my mom and I drive over to Tanner's cabin. There are a number of cars there, which means everyone else has already arrived. Jimmy lets us in through the front door, but he hardly looks me in the eyes. I know how close he and Silas are. If Kyle was pissed at me, then Jimmy's furious. Without a word, he leads us over to the couch where Tanner, Kyle, and Michael are already waiting. My mom sits down, but I decide to stay standing.

"First of all," I say. "I'd like to say thank you for having me. And I'm really sorry about what happened with Silas."

Jimmy huffs and rolls his eyes. "Right."

"I know you all are probably pissed," I say. "Especially since I kinda ruined the night of your wedding."

"You didn't," Michael says. "We found out the next day."

"I mean," Kyle says. "I'm still pissed."

I sigh. "Well, regardless—I'm sorry. But I wanted to share with you all what's going on with me. Then you might understand why I did what I did."

I pull out my phone and set it down on the coffee table sandwiched in between the U-shaped couch. I press play on the message I received right before

Kyle's wedding, then stand up and turn around. As it's playing, I walk toward the window and look out onto the lake. It's a cloudy day, a bit chilly, and I can barely hear the message from here, which is good. I'd prefer not to relive the feelings I experienced when I first heard that message. And everything that came after.

When it's finally done, I turn around to retrieve my phone, and the room is horrified. My mother is covering her mouth with her hand and shaking her head. Michael has his jaw dropped, while Kyle's staring down at the table with a deadly serious expression. Jimmy has the most disgusted grimace on his face, while Tanner's rubbing his forehead and staring at the floor.

"Wyatt," Kyle says, his voice sounding deeply Southern right now. "Your life was being threatened? And you said nothing?"

Jimmy glares up at me, his jaw locked. "And not just your life—Silas's, too."

"Oh my God," my mom says. "This was so much worse than I thought."

"And there's more," I say.

Everyone looks up at me with wide eyes, and I let out a shaky sigh. I knew this conversation wouldn't be easy, but it's definitely harder than I expected.

"When I got my ACL torn a year ago," I say. "I think it was a hate crime."

"Hate crime?" Tanner asks. "How?"

"Just before the play," I say. "I was called a faggot."

Half the room gasps, and the other half remains deadly silent.

My mom grips the couch armrest. "They called you what?"

"Faggot, mom," I say, annoyed. "They called me a faggot."

"See, this is why I told you not to come out," she says.

I grind my teeth.

"And you were injured right after," Tanner says. "You were thinking that was the hate crime?"

"It all makes sense," Kyle says, shaking his head. "I remember seeing that tackle and thinking that there was something off about it. But the refs didn't say anything, so I didn't think further. But of course. You had just come out. And knowing they called you a faggot just before that happened..."

Michael rubs his temples. "How did this not happen to you?" he asks Kyle. "Or you?" he asks Tanner.

"We came out right as we were retiring," Tanner says.

"And Wyatt's just hitting his prime," Kyle says.

I can't help blushing at that. If I didn't have to worry about all this, I could be celebrating the fact that I'm on track to be in the NFO hall of fame as one of the best tight ends of the century. But instead, I'm strategizing how to protect myself from being hate-crimed again.

Kyle turns to me. "Why didn't you say anything when that happened?"

I suck on my teeth. I could say the whole truth—that I wanted to live in denial about what it means to be out in the NFO. But saying it in front of Kyle and Tanner would be weird. They know what it's like to be a gay player. They would judge me.

"I just didn't see it as a big deal," I say. "Not until I was called a faggot again on the field earlier this season."

"Christ," Tanner says, shaking his head. "You played the Sparrows the first time, right? When you were injured?"

I nod. "And then it happened with the Steeds."

"Do we have any idea who the message is from?" Michael asks.

I shake my head. "No clue."

"Wyatt," Kyle says, annoyed. "Why are you asking for help now? Why not earlier before things escalated?"

I close my eyes and sigh. There's no point in delaying it any further. I pull over a chair by the porch door and plop it down in front of all of them.

"I was so fucking tired of living inauthentically," I say. I point to Kyle and Tanner. "Sure, I met other gay guys at Miss U, but none of y'all wanted to come out. And so I just went along with the party. But last year, I decided enough was enough. I wanted to come out so I could finally connect with people as the real me. It's so lonely going through life as somebody besides yourself."

Kyle shrugs. "Right."

"It's true," Tanner says with a sigh.

"And after I came out," I continue, reassured by Kyle and Tanner. "I wanted to prove that I could be just as good as any straight player." I turn to Kyle. "You were actually a big inspiration there."

He nods.

"But I guess I was naïve. I guess I supposed I could strong-arm reality into being what I wanted it to be. I just hoped that the NFO and the world would be nice to me as a gay man. But I think I'm learning that just 'cause I believe something is right doesn't mean it will happen.

"I thought that if I could just ignore all these signs that something bad was happening, they would go away. But as they ratcheted up in intensity, I knew something had to be done. Getting this message and hearing them threaten Silas was the last straw." I trill my lips. "I broke up with him so I could push him away and keep him safe from the threat."

"You realize you could have kept him safe if you just came clean about this earlier, right?" Jimmy asks. "Instead of getting him to fucking kill himself."

"Jimmy," Tanner says, putting his arm on his leg. "Let's not—"

"No," he says, removing Tanner's hand. "I'm fucking pissed. You know what would have happened if I didn't come to your cabin that day? Silas would have been fucking dead." Jimmy starts to cry. "It was me who had to pin my best friend's arms so he wouldn't do anything else to hurt himself."

I shake my head, feeling my own eyes heat up. "I'm sorry."

"Are you? Because you were dating Silas, and I feel like if you had known him better, then this wouldn't have happened."

I scowl at him. "That's not how depression or any of that works," I say. "Silas probably knew how to hide it. And aren't you his best friend? Shouldn't you have known too? You've known him for so much longer."

"You asshole," Jimmy says. "I swear—"

"Guys!" Kyle shouts.

Jimmy and I silence ourselves, properly reprimanded.

"Fighting won't help," he says.

Tanner puts his hand back on Jimmy's leg, and Jimmy sighs. Then he looks at me.

"Sorry, man," he says. He sighs and wipes his eyes. "I know it's not really your fault. I was just so scared that I almost lost my friend. And that fear hasn't really gone away."

I nod. "I know—I get it. I'm sorry."

The room is silent, giving me a chance to clarify myself more.

"My whole life, me not being myself has made it hard for me to connect to others. And I think a result of that is not understanding how my actions might affect another person. This entire time, I kept all these threats a secret because I thought they only affected me. And even as they escalated, I tried to keep them in this little box, and it backfired. For that, I'm sorry."

Kyle and Tanner nod, while the rest just look like they're stewing in their thoughts.

"We get it, man," Kyle says. "And I'll say I think you're brave for coming out when you did."

"Seriously," Tanner says. He squeezes Jimmy's leg. "If I had your bravery, I could have come out and made my relationship with Jimmy a lot easier." He kisses Jimmy on the cheek, and my stomach sinks. I wish I could have what they have—with Silas, right now. But there's so much holding us apart.

"I don't feel brave," I say. "I haven't done anything about the threats."

"Until now," Kyle says. "Isn't that why you've gathered us?"

"I guess that's true," I say with a shrug.

Finally breaking her silence, my mom leans forward. "I know I haven't been the best Mom," she says, wiping her nose. "But I love you, Wyatt. And I'm happy you feel confident enough to be yourself. I'm sorry you didn't feel that way when you were in our home."

"Thanks, Mom," I say.

She wipes a tear from her left eye. "And I just want you to be safe. So can you please tell me what you're doing about this?"

I pull out my phone. "Let me call Blake. I need to get all the perspectives I can."

"Blake Farmer?" Kyle asks as the phone rings.

"Yep," I say as Blake answers. "Quarterback for the Salt Lake Pioneers."

"Hello," Blake says through the phone.

"Blake," I say. "You're one the phone with Kyle Weaver, Tanner Bash, and some friends."

"Oh man!" he says. "So you're finally getting help?"

"Yep," I say with a sigh.

Everyone says their greetings.

"I told them everything," I say. "And now I need your help."

"Okay," Kyle, Blake, and Tanner say in unison.

I sigh. "I have no idea what to do. I want to come out and talk about the threats, but I'm worried this will ruin my reputation. If I just came out alone, I'm afraid people wouldn't believe me. I'd be the gay man who cried wolf. And I don't want the NFO barring me from games under the guise that they're trying to 'protect me'. I don't want to be silenced, and I don't want to be barred from playing. I just want to be genuinely protected, or I want the harassment to stop."

Kyle strokes his beard. "I see. Yeah, just coming out straight about it might get you bad press."

Tanner shakes his head. "With that message? That's direct proof that he's being targeted. That's threatening violence. Whoever sent that should be arrested."

"But Wyatt needs to come out with support," Kyle says. He leans back into the couch and folds his arms. "And I think you and I should be the ones to do it."

Tanner squints, then widens his eyes. "Oh, I have an idea for what we can do."And that's when the magic happens. We spend the next hours planning how I should report these threats of abuse. In a way, it feels like I'm coming out all over again. Except this time, I know my wellbeing—as well as Silas's are at stake.

"Are we sure this will work?" I ask after we've laid out most of our plans.

Kyle thins his lips. "Honestly? I don't know. I've never had to deal with any of this before, and neither has Tanner. But we're gonna do all that we can to make sure that everything turns out okay. And that you and Silas are safe."

I nod and let out a deep, shaky breath. "Alright."

Once everyone in the room knows what they need to do, we wrap up and exchange contact info. And this week, I'm finally coming clean to the NFO about what's happening. Kyle and Tanner will then step in and talk to the people they know so I get the support I need.

As we say our goodbyes, folks are still a little standoffish with me, and I don't blame them. I still can't fucking believe what Silas did to himself—all because I broke up with him. I want to see him and know that he's alright. I just want to hear his voice. But he's unstable, and so is our safety. I need to wait.

I make my way to my car. It's now late morning, and the fog from earlier is fading away due to the heat of the sun. It looks like it'll be a bright one today.

"Wyatt," my mom calls out. I turn to see her standing in front of her car, her hand rubbing her elbow.

I turn around to fully face her. "Hey, Mom."

She closes the distance between us, and I lean against the trunk of my car. Without stopping, she wraps her arms around my waist and squeezes me tight. I hesitate for a minute, and then I melt into her embrace. After all that's happened between us, it still feels nice to hug.

She pulls away and wipes her nose. "I'm really proud of what you did in there," she says. "That was very brave."

I shrug. "What other option did I have? You were always on my ass about it, too."

She folds her arms. "I know, but you still could have done nothing. You could have let yourself get hurt."

I sigh. "I guess."

"Wyatt," she says. "I—" she shakes her head. "How do I say this?"

I look up at her, squinting. I've never really seen her so unsure of herself.

She rubs a spot between her brows, then runs her hands through her gray hair. "Since I retired, I've been going through a lot."

I lean back against the car, my arms folded. "Like what?"

She looks out toward the lake covered in fog, her fingers resting against her chin. Then she looks at me. "You guys have been my whole life. You and your siblings, that is."

I think back to her in high school pushing me to do football. At the time, she just seemed like she wanted me to succeed. But looking back, it's almost like there was something else to her motivations.

She leans against my car next to me. The only thing that would make this more picturesque would be if we shared a cigarette.

"But now I've realized how I've never really been close to any of you. Dad always had Rachel. And Maddie and Tyler have been on their own ever since sixteen. And you—" she shakes her head. "I don't know, you were always a kind kid. You always shared what was on your mind. You were always so open."

I let out a sharp laugh. "Sure, I was open enough to come out to you—but I still didn't officially come out until I was twenty-seven."

She gives me a nasty side eye, reprimanding me with her face alone. Then she shakes her head. "Imagine what would have happened if you came out at a younger age. Would you have even made it to the NFO?"

"Maybe not," I say. "But I probably would have lived a more authentic life."

"But you wouldn't be one of the best tight ends, either," she says. "You probably wouldn't even have been drafted."

I kick some gravel and watch the rocks skitter along the road. "I guess it is cool that I'm doing this. As a gay man, too."

"I think it's cool, too," she says. "I think things happen for a reason. But I could have been a better mother about it all. When you told me you were gay in high school, I was worried for all the wrong reasons."

I raise a brow at her. "How so?"

She adjusts herself, clearly uncomfortable. "I told myself it was for your safety, but now I realize it was more born of fear that you wouldn't get the same opportunities and how your sexuality would reflect on the family." She turns to face me squarely. "I feel bad admitting it, but of all my children, I've felt closest to you. And so I felt I had a personal stake in your career. I didn't want it to be all thrown away because you were gay, but this was my own prejudice speaking. I was afraid what other people would think about us having a gay son who lost out on a career in the NFO because of it. In a way, I was embarrassed."

I look out to the lake. "Well that makes me feel better."

She puts her hand on my arm, and I look at her.

"And I'm here to say now that I was wrong, and I'm sorry," I say. "I saw back there what a brave man you are and what a brave man you've had to be to come out when you did." She shakes her head. "I'm sorry that you've had to deal with these threats all on your own, and I'm sorry I haven't been kinder to you about them. I can't imagine what you've been feeling about all this."

I feel the backs of my eyes heat up. "Yeah, hasn't been easy."

She squeezes my arm. "So I want to support you. I want to be your mother again, but for real this time. You can share as much or as little with me as you like, but I want you to know that you can trust me." She laughs. "Even if that means you quit your NFO career to become an opera singer."

I wipe a tear from my eye and laugh. "I still like football. I wouldn't quit now."

"Well once you retire, then," she says with a laugh. She leans back against the car. "But I you to know that I accept you as you are. And I love you so much."Those words make the tears flow freely. And they make me realize how much I've needed to hear them.

Growing up, my mom was also the person I felt closest to, but there always felt like there was a barrier between us. I see now that this was fear that I wouldn't be the boy she wanted me to be. So she molded me.

But here she is now telling me that she'll remove her hold on me and love me as I am. This is the mother I've been asking for my whole life.

Crying, I reach around my mom's shoulders and pull her against me. She's crying, too, and I hold her as I watch geese fly into the lake, dispelling the last of the fog.

"I'd love to have you in my life again," I say.

She pulls away and smiles at me. "There's nothing I would want more."

With my arm over her shoulder, we watch as the geese swim through the water, the sun gradually warming us up.

"I'm sorry to hear about Silas," she says.

Hearing his name almost undoes the satisfaction I just got from the conversation. "Me too."

She pulls away and shoves her hands in her jacket pockets. "So you two were really dating?"

"I loved him, mom," I say, trying to hold back more tears. "I love him, I should say. I've never felt so seen by anyone. He's told me he never felt so seen by anyone."

She sighs. "That's likely why he was so devastated."

I grimace as fresh tears fall. "I know. I really fucked up. I just wanted to keep him safe."

My mom reaches out to rub my back. "At least's he's still with us."

I scoff, still unable to fathom how close I was to losing him.

"Can we still make it, Mom?" I ask with a sniffle. I sound as unsure as a fucking child.

She sighs. "I think you both have things to work on," she says. "And I'm not saying that because I think he's a distraction or whatever. I want you to find love and be happy. But you need to get safe, and he needs to heal."

I nod and wipe my eyes. "Yeah."

"But who knows," she says, putting her hand back in her pocket. "Maybe since you both see each other so well, you'll see each other after this thing. As better, stronger people."

I blink away the last tears in my eyes and watch the geese fly elsewhere. "I hope you're right," I say. I trill my lips. "But first, it's time to come clean about the threats."

My mom turns to me, stands up on her tippy toes, then kisses me on the cheek, rubbing my back all the way. "I'm here for you," she says. "No matter what."

I reach down and give her a side hug, then kiss her cheek. "I know."

Chapter 23

Silas King

As I PULL UP to Jimmy's diner in my rental, my stomach feels like it's in knots, and I'm wondering if agreeing to get breakfast with Linda, Kyle's mother who's basically my own, was a good idea.

I take a deep breath, then remove the keys from the ignition.

After my attempt, everyone I cared about in town came to see me. But I had the privilege of saying I was too tired or generally unwell to talk for long. This included when Michael came to see me, as well as Kyle and Jimmy. And Linda, too.

But my therapist Damon has encouraged me to get back out there, to reconnect with the people who I love and who love me unconditionally. He's said that one of the best ways to learn how to love ourselves. And Linda is one of the first people I thought of when I imagined unconditional love. So, I'm getting breakfast with her now, and then I'm visiting Michael and Kyle later.

With another deep breath, I open my car door and make my way to the diner entrance.

I have no reason to be afraid. Linda loves me like her own son. She only wants the best for me.

Which means she was devastated when she discovered I had attempted. I could hardly look her in the eyes when she came to visit me in the hospital after it happened. I couldn't bear the pain of seeing the same kind of grief she would have had had I been successful. It was too much.

And I'm embarrassed. It was Linda herself who said that I couldn't depend on Wyatt for my emotional stability. And that's exactly what I did, which is mostly what led to that awful night where Jimmy had to pin me down to make sure I didn't try to kill myself again. I'm afraid she'll judge me, or worse: never look at me the same again.

The diner door jingles as I walk myself in. Jimmy, behind the counter, spots me and comes to greet me. He wraps his hairy arms around me and pulls me in tight.

"How we doin' today?" he asks, still holding my arms.

"Okay," I say.

Since Jimmy found me that night, he's actually been a little easier to talk to. After seeing me so low, it's hard to really feel ashamed around him. Especially since he's been so unconditionally supportive. But I still feel bad. I wish I could repay him somehow. I feel like I need to after he literally saved my life.

He pats me on the elbow. "Well, Linda's in a booth over there waiting for me. And don't worry about paying. Breakfast is on me."

"Jimmy," I say. "You don't need to—"

"I know," he says, standing tall and folding his arms. "But I'm just happy to have you around."

My face reddening, I scratch the back of my head. "Well, thanks."

"My pleasure," he says. "Now go see Linda. She's so excited to see you."

He pats me on the back as he disappears into the kitchen. When I spot Linda, she raises her hand and waves. By the time I walk over, she's already standing and nearly jumping out of her shoes. She hugs me, and for some reason my eyes are watering. The work and support groups that my therapist is making me do, along with a medication adjustment, have made me more emotional lately. And Jimmy's outpouring of love, only matched by Linda's, isn't helping me keep my eyes dry.

I wipe them quickly as I sit down, not wanting Linda to see.

"How are you?" she asks, beaming.

"Alright," I say with a small laugh. I take off my cowboy hat and scratch my head, then replace it.

Jimmy quickly takes our order, then reassures us it's on the house. Linda tries to protest, but he shoots her down quicker than she can argue.

Linda asks me about harmless things: how Cheshire is doing, if I've been enjoying the chilly December weather we're having, if I've been reading any good books lately.

"Haven't been reading that much as of late," I say. "I've been watching a lot of videos. About space, mostly."

"Oh, fascinating," she says genuinely.

Our food arrives, and she asks me how I'm liking my eggs. And then I feel bad. The conversation's mostly been about me.

I ask her how Thanksgiving went, which I chose not to attend this year so I could just be by myself. She tells me about this new running club she's joined and how she's gotten into solving jigsaw puzzles as a hobby. After she divorced her husband Brian, Linda just decided that she was happier on her own. And it shows. She is living her best life.

"Now," she says, her tone becoming more serious. I tense up a bit.

"How are you doing?" she asks. "Today."

I move around some eggs on the plate with my fork. Jimmy's food is great, but my appetite's still all wonky. Occasionally, I still taste ash and just want to stop eating. And I'm not sure why. The suicide attempt? Medicine? Grief from losing Wyatt? Who knows.

"I'm doing alright," I say. "Working with Damon, my therapist, to explore some of my past."

"That's good," she says with a nod. And she hesitates, as if she's afraid to ask more or that if she doesn't, she'll miss something important.

"I'm just trying to take things one day at a time," I say. "It doesn't help that I miss Wyatt so much."

And I shut my mouth so quickly I'm afraid I'll crack my teeth while Linda stares at me with thinned lips. But it's too late. I've already said how I feel.

This had been going so well. Linda's not made me feel bad at all for my attempt, and the conversation is nice and easy, even talking about my mental state. But Wyatt? I still miss him. And after what Linda's said about self-worth,

I'm afraid she'll reprimand me for still loving him after leaving me and leading me to try to kill myself.

Damon has helped me not only see that it's okay to love someone, even while hurting, but also that falling in love with Wyatt was a good thing. He's working with me to help manage my emotions, and so far I think it's been working well.

So I feel that it's okay for me to still love Wyatt, especially now that I'm putting myself first. But I'm afraid that Linda won't think so.

"Wyatt is still on your mind?" she asks. But I can't tell if she's concerned or just curious.

I curl my fist tighter around my fork, feeling like a turtle retreating into its shell. I'm comfortable acknowledging my feelings to Damon. He's on my side with how I feel about everything. But I don't know about Linda.

"He is," I say, unable to lie to her. "And I think I still love him."

Damon's also said to open myself back up to the people I love. No point in holding back now.

Linda swallows. "You're focusing on yourself, though, right?"

"Yes," I say, my voice tense. "That's what I've been doing ever since the attempt."She winces at the word, and I lock my jaw. I don't know why I'm feeling so defensive. This is just Linda. I know she loves me.

But, per Damon's suggestion, I let the wraith swallow me whole. And now all the feelings I'm letting myself experience, without trying to bury or control them, make me feel so raw and uncomfortable. No wonder I'm crying so easily. I'm sensitive as hell. And I don't want someone else, not even Linda, to tell me what I should or shouldn't feel.

"Silas, honey," she says, putting her hand on mine. "What's wrong?"

"I know what you're gonna say," I say, my voice shaky. "That I'm too fucking codependent or whatever. Still. And that I just need to let Wyatt go. So just say it."

I start crying uncontrollably, my bottom lip quivering too much for me to say more. Linda still has on her hands on mine, so I drop the fork in the other and grab a napkin. Nearby I see Jimmy watching us. Goddamnit. I hate being such a goddamn spectacle. I want to go back to my room and sleep and not wake—no,

I'm fine with waking up. But I just really don't want to be conscious or perceived right now.

"Silas," she says, her voice soft.

I look up at her, not even bothering to stop my tears.

"Can I tell you something? Honest?"

I look around, uncomfortable. Jimmy's no longer watching us, and there aren't that many patrons in the diner.

So I nod.

She squeezes her hand, then sighs. "To this day, I still love Brian."

I furrow my brow. "You what?"

She nods. She pulls back her hand and rests both in her lap.

I shake my head, my tears stopping for now. "But you—you divorced him, right? He was too set in his ways, you said. He—"

"All that's true," she says. "But he was funny. Resourceful. He always knew when I was sad or uneasy. He knew how to hold me. And when he was in the right mood, the sex was better than anything I've ever felt."

I let out a small laugh, trying to resist a grimace. I can't imagine Linda, my mother of choice, having sex.

She sighs and looks out the window. "You're right. I did say he was too set in his ways. And that ultimately made it too hard for us to continue. I wanted to change with the world becoming more tolerant, and he didn't. But even after he left, I still missed him. And I still loved him. And after his death I had to deal with this grief all over again."

"But now—" I say, shaking my head. "Still?"

"Feelings aren't convenient, Silas. They don't fit into the neat boxes we try to put them in. You can remember an ex that was supposedly 'bad' and smile. You can remember an argument with an old friend in college and be angry that they were ever your friend, then remember a positive memory and wish they were back in your life. You can still love somebody even though they weren't the right person for you. Society will say that emotions have to fit perfectly into neat little categories. But they don't. So we shouldn't try to place them. We just have to feel them."

I try to smile at that, but I can't. It's bittersweet—and a little too bitter.

"But I—" I hesitate, scared to share my hope with her and have her pop it like a balloon. Yet I feel like I need to. I need to get it out of me.

"What is it?" she asks.

"I still want Wyatt and I to be together. I still *love* love him. I want us to have another chance." I sigh, embarrassed. "Even after everything, I still think he's good for me. In therapy I've been learning how to embrace these emotions without trying to control or push them down.""And you shouldn't try to suppress them," she says. "Because they are what they are. I'm not telling you what the future holds. I'm just reassuring you that you're normal for what you're feeling. You're just like everyone else."

I sigh, feeling like a ton of weight has been lifted off my shoulders.

"But I do encourage you," she says, adjusting in her seat. "Live a life beyond these feelings you have for Wyatt. Be yourself. Discover your own worthiness. Find what you love."

"Like what?" I ask. I was anticipating this message before, but now that it's prefaced with the idea that my emotions are what they are, it's really resonating with me. There's nothing I should feel or be. I just am.

"That's something you have to discover for yourself," she says. "After Brian and I parted, I let my feelings overwhelm me. I was sorry for myself for a couple years. But then I realized that while it was okay to feel what I felt, I needed to do things for myself. I needed to live my life outside of him. So I get into embroidery and reading. And I keep discovering new things, like running and puzzles. My life is full and rich now. There might come a time when I meet someone, but I'm not really looking for that. I have myself, and I'm pretty damn good company. That's enough for now."

Her words burn brightly in my chest. Because they feel true.

"So self-worth is finding things you like?" I ask.

"That's part of it," she says. "I think self-worth and happiness are one in the same. You invest in yourself, and then you feel good about yourself and the world around you. This can't come from a partner or career or anything else. It comes from within."

"Within," I say. "But you're doing external things like puzzles and running to develop self-worth. Those are external things. That doesn't make sense."

Linda laughs. "Confusing, I know. But it's not the external things themselves that give me contentment. It's me listening to my own thoughts, feelings, and body to determine what I need from the outside world. And self-worth comes from seeking those things out and reaping the benefits. Then, like dew on a foggy morning, you'll wake up and realize how happy you are with yourself. How happy you are in general. It can surprise you when you realize you have self-worth. I know I was."

I look over to the dew in the grass outside. "If it's like dew, it does seem like it would come out of nowhere."

"But it does come," she says. "So let yourself love Wyatt. Things may even work out between you two. I hope they do. But invest in Silas first. Because he's the longest lasting thing you have." She reaches out to hold my hand. "And I'm so glad he's still with us."

I wipe a fresh tear from my eye, and this time I squeeze her hand back. "Thank you," I say, genuinely refreshed from this conversation.

Jimmy comes by to take our plates, and when Linda tries to pay, he scurries away before she can even get some cash out.

"Asshole," she says to him, but he just ignores her. And I laugh.

Man, this morning I've both cried *and* laughed. I'm feeling again. And I'm not so overwhelmed by this either.

When we step outside, Linda gives me the warmest hug she can. I hug her tightly back, so happy I took my therapist's advice.

"My therapist gave me some good counsel," I say, pulling away. "He said I can learn how to love myself by looking at others who love me. And I think I have a better idea how to do that after this conversation."

Linda wraps her arms around me again, then pulls back to look me in the eye, her hands on my shoulders.

"I can always be that example for you," she says. "Even if I'm the only one."

Before she makes me burst into tears again, I thank her and hug her goodbye. Then I hop in my car and make my way to Michael and Kyle's cabin.

When I arrive, I'm not as nervous as I thought I would be. After our conversation before the wedding, I was worried that Michael would be like Linda and make me feel bad for my emotions for Wyatt. But after my conversation with Linda, I have a feeling that won't be the case.

And I'm correct.

Michael, Kyle and I catch up. They're a bit skittish at first, probably worried they'll say something to trigger me or whatever. But soon our conversation is filled with joking and laughter, just like it used to be. Michael and I talk about books, including the one he's writing, as well as how Kyle joined a bluegrass group. Hearing the story about how Michael got a banjo for Kyle is just too dang cute.

And when the conversation turns to me, I tell them how I'm doing. Candidly. I mention my feelings toward Wyatt and what my therapist has me doing, and they are nothing but supportive. Michael even echoes what Linda said earlier, that emotions are what they are and I should honor them—and that investing in my own worth is the best thing for me and whatever relationship I decide to have, whether it's with Wyatt or not. Toward the tail end of our conversation, I'm so glad I took my therapist's suggestion to do this that I lament the alternative reality version of me that didn't. Because I feel so much farther along in my growth than that guy. I swear I can even hear *Slow Meadow's* hopeful song, "Pareidolia", playing in my head, reminding me that we can always find new patterns out of old things—that we can change. That I can change.

"By the way," Kyle says, leaning back against the couch. Michael's leaning forward, and Kyle's scratching his back. "Have you heard about Wyatt and what's going on?"

Michael looks back him, his brow forming a deep V.

"What?" Kyle asks. "Silas said he still had feelings for the man. I figured he had reached to Wyatt by now."

I sit forward on the edge of the couch, my heart beginning to race. "What's going on with Wyatt?"

Michael rubs his forehead, and Kyle's wearing a guilty expression.

"Guys," I say. "What's going on?"

Michael puts his hand on Kyle's knee and sighs. "We didn't want to say anything. We didn't know how stable you were, or about your feelings toward Wyatt."

"Well I'm more stable now," I say, my heart racing faster. "And I'm a big boy. I can handle it. What's wrong with Wyatt? Is he okay?"

Michael sucks on his teeth, and Kyle leans forward.

"I'm sorry—I didn't mean to complicate things, it's just—" Kyle says. "Man, you really don't know."

"Guys, come on," I say. "You're scaring me, and you're making it worse by not telling me."

Michael sighs. "Last year, when Wyatt tore his ACL, we have overwhelming evidence suggesting it was a hate crime."

And they tell me everything: what they called Wyatt on the field that day, his injury, him being called the same slur back in October. And then the message.

"I hate to be the one to tell you this," Kyle says, resting his elbows on his knees. "But Wyatt broke up with you because he was afraid for your safety. He wanted to distance himself from you so you wouldn't be at risk anymore."

I feel like my stomach has jumped to where my heart is supposed to be, and my heart is now in my throat.

Wyatt didn't want to break up with me. He broke up with me to protect me. Because we were both at risk.

"And what now?" I ask. "Are the threats still active?"

"We can't be sure," Kyle says. "Wyatt spoke with the Salt Lake Police Department along with the NFO's conduct team. They assured him that they would get to the bottom of the threats."

I shake my head. "Why don't I know about this? Why haven't I heard?"

"Because it's not public," Kyle says. "Wyatt specifically said, for his own safety—"

"And Silas's," Michael adds.

"That too," Kyle says. "For both of your safety, he didn't want the accusation to go public. He wanted the investigation to be private."

I trill my lips, trying to take it all in.

"I'm sorry," Kyle says. "I just assumed you would have known.""I didn't," I say. "But I'm glad you told me."

Wyatt didn't break up with me because he wanted to. That may mean he still wants me.

"Your mind looks busy," Michael says to me. "What are you thinking?"

I wipe my face and lean back into the couch. I grab my hat and rub the material with my thumb.

After my suicide, I took a leave of absence from work. Since Brigham, our head PT, trusts me so much, he let me. So my whole time here at home was temporary, whether or not I'm sticking with my NFO job or not. I still want to see the season through.

"I think I'm gonna go back to Salt Lake," I say. I stand up and put on my hat.

"No," Michael says, standing up as well. "You're not well, Silas. And it wasn't just Wyatt that's being threatened. You are, too."

I step closer to Michael. "You're not my therapist. I know you mean well, but I do know myself best. I won't leave now, but I have unfinished business in Utah, Wyatt aside. And it doesn't seem like I'm under threat so much now that the case is being investigated."

"It's still unknown," Kyle says, standing up to join us. "They could just be laying low until the investigation is done."

I shake my head. "I know you guys are worried for me, but I'm in a better place, and I'm growing every day. I'm gonna consult with my therapist, and we'll ultimately decide if this is the best idea together. You may have your opinions, and that's fine. But I expect your support as my friends no matter what I do."

Both of them stand there, silently looking at the floor. Then Kyle raises his head.

He puts his hand on my shoulder. "You know yourself best," he says. "I'm on your side."

Then we both look at Michael.

He sighs, then folds his arms, meeting my gaze. "I'm just worried about you. As long as this isn't just some desperate attempt to get Wyatt back, then I might not think this is a horrible idea."

"It isn't," I say. And I mean that honestly. I do want to see Wyatt. That's important. But I have my job out there. My apartment. It was a matter of time for me to get back out there, and now seems like the right time, especially now that I know Wyatt's true situation.

"Then you have my support," Michael says.

I hug the both of them goodbye, and then I make my way home to Martha and Llewellyn's. On the way, I think about what might be best. I need to take the time to make sure I'm doing this for the right reasons, and I need to make sure I'm in a good space mentally to do this. I'll talk to Damon and my psychiatrist. Then, once I feel it's right, I'm headed to Salt Lake. I'm going to figure out whether or not I continue my career in the NFO, and then I can hopefully see Wyatt. I just hope he's safe. And I hope that I'll be safe, too.

Chapter 24

Wyatt Nelson

I sit on the bench in the locker room of the Salt Lake Stadium, bouncing my leg nervously. I'm fully dressed for the first playoff game. And as luck would have it, we're playing against the Arizona Sparrows—the team with the players who called me a faggot and destroyed my ACL.

Blake sits down next to me. "You're already dressed," he says. "When did you get here?"

"A while ago," I say, still bouncing my leg, staring straight ahead at nothing. "Didn't want to be nervous while getting ready."

"Well, fuck, man," he says, opening his locker. "You look stressed now."

I finally break eye contact with the wall and look at him. "It's the fucking Sparrows today. I could be fucking injured again."

"The NFO knows about this," Blake says. "All teams are under investigation, especially the Sparrows. It would be crazy for them to do something." I shake my head, bouncing my leg as fast as ever.

Blake puts his hand on my leg to stop it. "You're gonna be fine, man," he says. "We've done all that we can. Tanner and Kyle have talked to all the players they know to tell them to report any suspicious behavior. I really think you're safe."

I sigh, unable to believe that Blake's the calm one now. "I don't know, man. We just haven't heard anything. Maybe—"

"No news is good news," he says.

I nearly scowl at him. "When we're trying to catch the people threatening me? I feel like news by now would be very helpful."

"Maybe they've just decided to lay low," Blake says. "Either way, we're good. Let's just go out there and play well." He reaches out for me to bump his fist. I return it lukewarmly.

"Let's make it to the Championship Game, alright?"

"Alright," I say with a sigh.

Pretty soon, other players arrive. We practice on the field, and before I know it, the game begins.

The game starts out in our favor. I catch a pass and score us a touchdown in the first five minutes. After our kicker scores us an extra point, we're in the lead 7 – 0. But that only makes me nervous. I don't want to give the Sparrows anymore reason to be angry with me.

But I can't think this way. I'm a gay man, and I've made it this far as one of the country's best tight ends. I can't let my fear of what people might do stop me.

So I lock in.

Just before half-time, I manage to score for us again just after the Sparrows's touchdown, putting the score at 14 – 7 with us in the lead. As we rush into the locker room, I stock up on calories and Gatorade. I'm gonna need all the fuel I can get for our second half.

"Killing it out there," Blake says, patting me on the shoulder.

I take a bite of my protein bar and wipe the sweat from my forehead. "You too, man," I say. "Let's keep it up."

He looks around, then leans in close to me. "Heard anything?"

I shake my head. "No slurs," I say.

"Good man," he says with another pat. "Glad you're safe."

"Don't say anything too soon," I say, knocking on our wooden bench. "We still have the rest of the game."

"Don't worry," he says. "Just focus on playing. You'll be fine."

But a strong feeling in my gut tells me to worry. At least a little bit.

When we get back out there, the Sparrows manage to score twice, and our wide receiver scores for us once, putting us at 21 – 21. Now, we're at the last two minutes.

As the Sparrows use the rest of their timeout, I'm tempted to relax. To think that I'll get through this game unscathed. But something still feels off. Even though I have no evidence of anything being off. It's a sunny winter day here in Salt Lake. The fans have been great. Sparrows have played clean. No objectionable calls.

But I still sense something off, like animals knowing it will rain when there isn't a cloud in the sky.

We get into position, and Blake and I give a subtle nod to one another, our agreed upon sign. I'm about to catch the ball and win us the game.

As long as everything goes well.

For a moment, in that short time just before our center snaps the ball, everything feels fine. Like we're about to win this game. Like my life isn't being threatened. Like I didn't have to end things with the man I love to protect him. Like this man didn't almost kill himself.

But then I hear it.

"Faggot," someone says. But it sounds like it's coming in at all angles.

My body tenses up, as if it has a memory and fear of what's happened of its own. My heart starts racing, and my body produces a fresh layer of sweat. The center snaps the ball to Blake, and he gets into position to throw it.

The linebacker charges toward me with the same intensity I've seen before. Except this time, I don't see fury. I see coldness in his eyes. He's calculated. Focused.

But I'm not gonna let myself get hurt this time.

Drawing on strength from every cell in my body, I face forward to where I know Blake will throw the ball. By now, I know he's chucked it, so I just have to get in position and catch it. Then run.

I manage to evade the Sparrows linebacker—very likely the man who just called me a slur—and head to where the ball will land. I turn upward and see it barreling toward me. With a jump, I manage to catch it. Nearby, I feel the heat of bodies—bodies who want to hurt me. Who have wanted to hurt me for months and now finally have a chance.

When I land, sharp pain shoots up my ankle, but this is absolutely not the time to be stopping. I run forward, feeling pain shoot up my right foot with each step. But the pain I'm feeling now is nothing to the pain I could be feeling if I let myself slow down.

From behind, a hand reaches out, and I push myself even harder, tears welling in my eyes from the pain in my ankle. But I don't fucking stop.

Eventually, I'm in the clear with no guys around me, but I don't even slow down. I keep my speed up until I cross the touchdown line. My players reach me and cheer around me, but I remind them it isn't over yet. After our kicker scores us an extra point, I limp to the sidelines and ask to sit out, my ankle on fire. My backup replaces me, and I relish the safety of the sidelines. There's no way anyone can injure me out here.

After we kick off to the Sparrows, they try to score to put us into timeout, but they run out of time. We win 28 – 21. In the locker rooms, I'm congratulated by my teammates, and Blake is over the moon—so over the moon that he doesn't even ask me if anything happened.

Yet I just sit there on the bench, grimacing at the pain in my ankle. And now I'm afraid what's going to happen next. Because we at least have one more game after this. And with how I just defied the people who want me out of football, I think they're even more pissed off.

Which means two things.

The NFO isn't doing shit to protect me.

And I'm going to be targeted again.

Everyone around me is ecstatic, thrilled that we have a chance at making it to the Championship Game. But I'm just hoping I can make it to end of the next game in one piece.

And I have no fucking idea how.

Chapter 25

Silas King

WALKING BACK INTO THE Pioneers stadium feels like a dream. Even though it's only been a couple months, it feels like ages. And that's probably because I'm a completely different person.

After I discovered that Wyatt was in danger—that he really broke up with me to keep me safe—I knew I had to go back to Salt Lake. But it wasn't just to desperately win him back. I'm still miraculously employed by the Pioneers as a PT, and I want to finish out the season just like I said I would, even though these last couple months have shown me that I no longer want to continue in this profession. But there is something dignifying about keeping a promise. And hearing the news about Wyatt only made it seem like the right time to return. After bumping up my sessions with Damon, he and I finally felt like I was ready to go. So now, in the middle of frigid January, I find myself back in Salt Lake in the training room for the Pioneers.

I walk past all the machinery, and my stomach flops all over itself. Everything in here reminds me of Wyatt. Even listening to my own music reminds me of Wyatt. When I spot Brigham through the glass wall sitting at his desk, I put my earbuds away, approach the doorway, and knock.

He turns and gives me a small, yet genuine smile. He stands up to shake my hand, and I return it with as much vigor as I can muster. There are bags under his eyes, and it looks like he's gained a little weight. Right. He lost his trans niece to suicide. He was worried how this would affect his own trans daughter, too.

"Are you feeling better?" he asks, putting his hands on his hips.

I nod. I told him I had a serious health scare, but I kept it at that. Saying it was an attempt on my own life seemed like too much unnecessary information, especially since that's how he lost his own family member.

"Thanks for seeing me," I say as he sits down. I sit down in a chair across from him. "I'm honestly surprised you would."

"Well, I won't lie," he says with a shrug. "You've been one of the most cooperative and liked therapists we've ever had. Everyone loves you here. Wyatt made a good call recommending you."

I blush, thinking about him. I heard they won their first playoff game yesterday. Yet he's being threatened by other football players. Kyle and Michael said the NFO was investigating these threats, but I still wonder if he's really safe.

"Thank you. It's been a great experience," I say, not necessarily lying. "I have learned a lot while working here."

"And you can continue this learning," Brigham says, his hands clasped in his lap. "If you want to stay on with the team permanently, you can. We'd love to have you."

My stomach jumps. "Seriously? Even though I was gone for the last two months?" Brigham nods. "You communicated with us, and we understand emergencies. But we really think you'd be a valuable asset to the team."

I look down at the turf that covers the floor of this office.

This is what I've always wanted—a legitimate, professional job. One that no one from back home could ever dream of having. One that would prove that I made it.

But I don't know if this is actually what I want anymore. Sure, this job makes a lot of money, and I still have loans to pay. I just don't know if I'm happy here. The schedule is a bit erratic, and even though I'm well-liked, I don't really love the patients. The athletes, just as they were at Miss U, have been difficult. Working with such a good team is cool, but the only thing I really enjoyed was being in such close proximity to Wyatt. But that was a double-edged sword because being a therapist posed an institutional barrier to our relationship—not that that still exists. But still. It's something to consider. I don't know how much

I'd like to be in a secret relationship again. Especially since this was the reason that Wyatt used to break up with me.

"Can I get back to you?" I ask.

"Of course," Brigham leaning forward. "But can I ask—is there another team that's trying to hire you? Because if so—"

"Oh, God no," I say. "I'm flattered you would think so. If I continued with this line of work, it would be here with you all."

Brigham smiles. "That's what I like to hear."

I chuckle. "I'll let you know," I say. "Definitely before the Championship Game."

"Perfect," he says. "And we'll need you. Because actually…"

He pulls up his tablet. "Wyatt Nelson's coming in today. He rolled his ankle in the game yesterday. Said it hurt bad, but we're lucky that it's just a grade one sprain. Just stretched his muscles a bit. He's coming in tomorrow if you want to help him out."

My stomach jumps to my throat. "Wyatt—is he okay?" I blurt out.

Brigham gives me a quizzical look. "Yeah," he says. "Just needs to stretch it out a bit. We don't want it to turn into something worse. We need to make sure he can play in the Championship Game if we reach it, fingers crossed."

I clear my throat. "Of course. Uh, sure, I can do that."

"Great," he says. "I know you guys have worked well in the past. I have some other guys to work with, so this will be perfect. Glad to have you back."

I nod nervously. Man, does he not know the half of it.

But this is fine. I can help Wyatt out—in a professional setting. And that will give us a chance to talk about everything. I just want to see him again. I want to make sure he's okay.

"Wonderful," he says, clicking on his tablet one more time before setting it down. He claps his thighs with his hands. "Well, anything else?"

I shove down my anxious thoughts regarding Wyatt. I don't have to see him until tomorrow. So I'd rather talk about something completely unrelated.

"How have you been doing?" I ask. "Regarding your family and all—your daughter."

His face goes from light to pensive, and he folds his arms. "You know, I was worried—after our nieces passing—that my daughter Belle would be devastated."

I nod. "How is she doing?"

"She's—" he shakes his head, a smile forming on his face. "I told you how she joined Affirm, right?""You did," I say. "But I don't quite remember what it is."

"It's wonderful," he says, leaning forward on his elbows. "It's this non-profit organization literally designed for LGBTQ+ youth in Utah. I'm sure you know how high the suicide rate is in this state, especially for queer folk."

I nod, my stomach feeling uneasy. This still isn't the easiest topic for me.

"Well this organization has safe houses all over the state. They have volunteers who help make the kids feel at home, and they also have paid staff—therapists, vocal coaches for trans kids specifically, and tutors. I think they even have some physical therapists for kids in sports or working out more generally."

My stomach jumps, but it's from excitement this time. "Really? Like trained PTs?"

"And athletic trainers," he says. "My daughter's always been way into sports, so it's cool to see these interests affirmed by others in her community."

I nod, feeling the bubbles of excitement in my chest.

It's not that I don't really like physical therapy—it's that I don't like the hours and who I'm usually working with. But working with troubled queer kids? That's like working with my younger self. That could be so rewarding.

"That's sweet," I say. "Cool as hell."

He nods. "It really is—" he pauses to look up at something behind me.

There's a knock on the glass door, when I turn around to see who's here, I nearly collapse onto the floor from nerves alone. I may have better control of my emotions now, but they still find ways to sneak up on me.

He stares at me like a ghost, which at this point isn't an invalid description of me. In some ways, I have come back from the dead. And I wonder if he knows that.

"Wyatt," Brigham says. "What brings you in? We didn't have an appointment, did we?" He picks up his tablet again. "I have you marked down for—"

"No, I know—we had one for tomorrow," Wyatt says. And his rich, tenor voice reaches all the way down to the core of my soul. God, I've missed him. "I just—my ankle was hurting, so I thought I'd come in today. Are you available?"

Brigham glances at his watch. "I have to go meet my wife," he says. "Maybe we can—"

"I can help out," I say. Wyatt looks at me, his jaw tight.

"You sure?" Brigham asks. "That would be a big help, and I know you just got back."

"It's all good," I say. "Happy to."

"Alright," Brigham says, standing up. He takes a sip from his water bottle, then closes and grabs his laptop. "I'll leave you both to it then. Have a good one."

And then Brigham leaves, leaving me alone with the ex who led me to try to end my life.

Chapter 26

Wyatt Nelson

"WHAT ARE YOU DOING here?" I ask, my voice hoarse. I can't believe I'm looking at him now. He's lost a little bit of weight, but he's otherwise looking healthy. And he looks slightly happier, too.

"I came back because—" he clears his throat. "I still work here."

"But you said you wanted to quit the NFO," I say.

Silas winces, like he's offended. "I said I could leave, but I haven't yet."

"Sorry," I say, shaking my head. I eye him head to toe, my entire stomach in knots. "It's just so good to see you again. I didn't know—" I thin my lips. But this is so risky. I got called a slur again yesterday. I've been more on edge than ever. And now that Silas is back, him getting hurt is a stark reality.

Silas leans back in his chair. "You found out what happened?"

I nod.

He trills his lips. "Well, I know everything, too."

I tighten my jaw and shift my weight to my right leg. I wince from the pain. "Then you know it isn't safe for you here."

"Kyle told me that you guys told the NFO conduct team," he says. "You were getting it taken care of."

I lean against the glass wall and fold my arms, shaking my head the whole way. "That's what I thought too. But it almost happened again yesterday."

Silas widens his eyes. "What almost happened?" His jaw slowly drops. "You're saying you were called a slur on the field again?"

I nod, feeling the backs of my eyes heat. It's so nice to have Silas know all this. It killed me keeping it back from him, even when I knew it was for his own good. It's just so nice to finally have the man I love the most on my side.

"And if I had let myself get tackled, I'm suspecting I would have received another injury." I point to my ankle. "I got this because I pushed myself too hard trying to avoid getting hurt again."

"But—" Silas shakes his head. "That can't be. You told the NFO what's going on. There's an investigation, right?"

"Supposedly," I say, annoyed. "But it looks like they're not taking it seriously. Because nothing's happened, and I'm still being targeted."

Silas takes off his hat and runs his hand through his short hair. I loved it when he'd take off his hat in front of me, like a turtle coming out of its shell. And after hearing the story of why he wore the hat, it just made me love him more. He's trying to be the open-minded person his family could never be. And that makes him a paragon on strength to me.

But no matter what I think about it, I can't let us get close again. Not with his life at stake.

"There has to be something," he says. Then his brow furrows. "Wait—why are you still not going public with this?"

I grind my teeth. "Because I don't want everyone knowing."

He looks at me like I swore at him. "Not knowing—what do you mean? Are you embarrassed about this or something?"

I clench my fists. "No. Well—I don't know. Fuck, I don't know, Silas."

"Wyatt," he says in that soft voice that I miss so much. "Talk to me."

I press my back against the glass wall and sigh. "I've told you I wanted to be the gay person who could do anything a straight person can do. I already feel like I've compromised that by getting the NFO organization involved."

"But they're not doing shit," Silas says. "And they're probably not doing shit because they only have to be accountable to you. But if this was public—all hell would break loose. Players targeting and injuring a gay player? That would be madness. The NFO would be in hot water."

I glare at him. "It *would* be madness. Because you know what else would happen? People would say I'm the gay who cried wolf. They would say I'm too scared, too much of a sissy. Or worse—that I deserve this. It's best that as few people as possible know."

Silas shakes his head. "No, I don't think that's true."

Heat burns in my chest, and that's when the tears flow. "What would you know? You're the one who tried to leave us. To leave me."

And then the dam of my tears bursts. I start weeping. I expect Silas to walk away. To slap me. But he does what I'd least expect. He stands up and wraps his arms around me.

For a moment, I do nothing. I don't deserve this. I don't deserve his love after what I called him. But then I let myself melt into him. Because I've missed him so goddamn much.

"I'm sorry," I say, weeping down into his shoulder. "I'm so sorry. I shouldn't have said—God, that was horrible. I'm just so happy you're here. I've needed you. And I pushed you away because I was so terrified that you'd get hurt. And now I'm so worried you will get hurt." I sob into him. "Please forgive me."

Silas holds me tight, but he says nothing. He just lets me cry it out. Finally, he pulls away and looks up at me. He wipes the tears a falling tear from my cheek.

"I've been going to therapy since I tried to end it all," he says. He steps back and leans against the edge of a desk across from me. "And I've been learning a whole lot—how to process my emotions, how to navigate relationships. But one of the most important things I've learned is how to lean on people's love."

I wipe my snotty nose. "Talk to me about it."

"When we don't know how to love ourselves, we can often learn by example from those who love us."

I raise a brow. "But there's the—"

"Yeah, sure, there's the saying that no one will love us until we love our-selves," Silas says with the roll of his eyes. "But that's grossly over-simplified and over-used. Even when we don't love ourselves, we still deserve to love and be loved. And we usually are."

"Alright," I say, leaning back against the glass, my eyes puffy. "I can buy this."

"From what it sounds like, you came out because you wanted to be who you are. But you're still afraid of what the public thinks of you. You still have in your head all the negative things that people say about gay people."

"Because people do think those things," I say. "Exhibit A: the people targeting me."

"Sure," Silas says with the shake of his head. "But what about everyone else? Surely not everyone is against you now."

I pause, thinking. Then I nod. "When I came out, there was a lot of public support."

"Exactly," Silas says. "And how do you think these people would react if they discovered that one of the biggest gay players of our days was being hatecrimed?"

"They'd go ballistic," I say.

"And they'd likely pressure the NFO to do something about it. And the authorities." Silas stands up. "You have people, who though may know you personally, love you—the people who supported you coming out publicly. Let these people love you by advocating for you."

I chew on my lips, thinking.

"And when you do that, maybe you'll see that the world isn't as hostile a place as you think it is," I say. "By seeing their example, you'll see yourself as more lovable than before."

Silas stands only a couple feet from me. I reach out and grab one of his hands. He freezes.

"Is this okay?" I ask.

He unfreezes himself and nods. I push myself off the wall and hold both his hands between us. I rest my forehead against his.

"I've still loved you all this time," he says. "Even when I had to break up with you."

Silas's lips hover dangerously close to mine. "Me too," he says. "I know."

I pull away before we can kiss and look him in his brown eyes. "You're right," I say. "I think I should get the public involved. But until this blows over, we can't see each other."

He nods. "I'm in danger."

"And you're on staff," I say. "I don't want to compromise your career any more than I have. It's selfish of me."

"And if I choose to quit," Silas says. "And when we're both safe. What then?"

I press my forehead against his again and take a deep breath, breathing in his scent that I've missed so much. "Then I hope you'll take me back," I say. "Despite all I've done."

He wraps his arms around my neck and starts rubbing my back, sending me into a deadly state of relaxation. Then he stops, unwraps his arms, and pulls away from me.

"Sounds like a deal," he says. "But I want to help you divulge this to the public.""Alright," I say. "We can get the others involved, too. I know they'll be eager to help, especially now that I've been threatened again." I point to my ankle. "And I'll still need help with this."Silas kneels down in front of me, and I'm afraid he's gonna that slutty thing where he takes my dick and presses his nose against it, nearly getting me to cum without even using his tongue. But he just puts his gentle hand on my ankle.

I wince as he presses into it, but it's not as bad as it was yesterday. I just came here so that I could recover as quickly as possible.

"Grade one sprain," he says. "You should be good to play by the Championship Game. So long as you guys make it."

"I hope to hell that we do," I say. "One more game, and I'll solidify my record of being one of the best tight ends of the century."

Silas stands up and smiles at me, melting my heart. God, I hate that I have to wait for this man. But it's the best for both of us.

"Alright, he says. "Let's get you healed, and let's get you safe."

Chapter 27

Silas King

I stand on the sidelines of the Vanguards' stadium in Kansas. It's Championship Game day, and Wyatt's finally healed from his ankle sprain. He's out on the field right now. The Pioneers have just kicked the ball to the Vanguards, and I couldn't be more nervous.

In the past month, Wyatt has gone public with all the threats. He first told a reporter, and then the news spread like wildfire. It's been all over every social media platform, and there have been a number of vocal critics calling out the NFO for their mistreatment of this abuse towards Wyatt. And the NFO has been insultingly quiet.

They haven't been completely silent, though. They've said that they acknowledge what's going on and are investigating it, but they're doing surprisingly little. There have been influencers on YouTube and TikTok dissecting different teams, using the little evidence they have to piece together who is threatening Wyatt Nelson for being gay. And even they're coming up with more compelling leads than the NFO, or even the cops. It's fucking ridiculous that Wyatt still isn't safe.

Brigham comes over and nudges my shoulder after the first down. "Think he's alright out there?"

I let out a heavy sigh. Brigham's been nothing but supportive toward me during my time with the Pioneers, and he's just as supportive toward Wyatt now that he's come out about the threats.

"I don't know," I say.

"Despicable," Brigham says. "You think with all the pressure the NFO would be on this."

"Not so loud," I warn him.

"What?" Brigham asks, pissed. "It's not like they care."

I shrug and shake my head. "True."

I take another deep breath, then focus on the game. I'm praying that Wyatt doesn't get injured out there. I expressed my concern for him playing in the game, but he says needs to do it for all the other queer people out there. And for himself. He said he won't let some bullies stop him. And I admire him for that, but that still doesn't erase the fear that he could be brutally injured out there.

Or worse.

Wyatt gets tackled, and I panic. But soon he's up and about, and he looks fine.

"We're good," Brigham says. "He's good."

I nod. "Just gotta get through the game," I say. "Please be safe, Wyatt."

Chapter 28

Wyatt Nelson

I SHOULD BE ON my knees thanking God right now. Because the game against the Vanguards is almost over, and I've almost made it through the entire game.

Or maybe I shouldn't throw in the towel just yet.

The Vanguards are up 27 – 21, having missed one extra point. If we score a touchdown and get our extra point, we win, and the game's over. I'll have won a Championship Game, which will solidify my position in the NFO hall of fame.

Even as we end one of our plays, the crowd is still as wild as they were at the start of the game. And I swear I can hear them calling my name.

Ever since I decided to go public with the threats toward me, I've received an overwhelming amount of support—even more than when I came out. Sure, there was some of what I feared, people saying that I'm just crying and whining for more attention. But otherwise, I'm surprised with all the love I'm receiving, and all this love has made me feel more confident that out in the field is right where I belong.

Silas was right. Feeling other people's love does make it easier to love myself.

We make our way to our positions for the next play. We've got less than thirty seconds on the clock, but Blake stops me on the way to my place.

"I'm gonna throw it to you," he says. "That's what coach wants to do."

My stomach churns. Nothing bad has happened this game so far, but that's how it always been. The threats don't come until the very end, and I swear it's to catch me off my game—to distract me from doing my best.

I bite my lip. "I don't know, man," I say out of earshot from the mic in his helmet. I don't want coaches hearing this. "I'm worried."

Blake pulls me in close. "I know I've kinda been a shit friend to you," he says. "But I'm proud of you. And you've been right this whole time. You deserve to play, regardless of who's out to get you. This is our sport, too."

I widen my eyes. He just insinuated that he was gay. And I'm pretty sure the coaches can hear him.

"We've done all that we can," he says. "I doubt they'll try with the public on our side. But if they do, I'll fucking run out there and get them before they can get you. But it's up to you. What's your call?"

I take a deep breath and chew on my mouth guard. I glance over at Silas on the sidelines. He's watching me with anticipation. I think about all he's told me—how he held me in his arms despite what I said and told me I was worthy of being loved—and I resolve to do my best out there to show how much that love means to me. Not just everyone out there supporting me, but his love, too.

I nod and slap his shoulder pads. "Let's do it."

I jog into place, and then the play's about to begin.

And I hear it again.

But this time it's different.

"Hey, faggot," a voice calls out. "We warned you."

We warned you.

The message.

The same one that this cabal of homophobic NFO players left me just before Kyle's wedding.

They warned that they would hurt me.

But I wasn't the only one.

They said they would hurt Silas, too.

Before I can process anything beyond that, our center snaps the ball to Blake. And now it's showtime.

I rush forward, expecting to see fury in the linebacker's eyes, or the same cold, calculated stare that I saw in the Sparrows last time.

But what I see is far worse.

The linebacker looks at me. But his gaze also flickers back to someone on the sidelines.

Silas.

"Oh no," I say to myself.

As I rush forward, I look up at the ball to make sure I'm gonna catch it. And I'm right on target.

But when I look back to where I'm running, my stomach leaps to my throat. The linebacker isn't headed for me.

He's headed straight for Silas.

The next moments feel like slow motion.

Instead of jumping to catch the ball, I run faster. I watch Silas's eyes widen as he realizes he's about to be tackled by a man strong enough to crush him into a coma.

Not on my watch.

Just as the linebacker puts his hand on Silas—the man that I love—my arms wrap around his waist. Instead of crashing into Silas, he crashes into the empty turf next to him with me on top.

"Dirty faggot," he says, shoving me off him.

I jump up, then stand between him and Silas. He rises to his feet, his lips bloodied and uniform disheveled with cameras and staff all around us. He has blood, short hair—almost bald—with a clean-shaven face.

He snarls. "You fucking—"

And that's when the stadium breaks into a deafening roar. An angry one. People around us are angry. They've seen everything.

Suddenly, several security guards come from behind me and take the linebacker by the arms. They usher him off the field and into the stadium, leaving the rest of us bewildered on the field with a crowd going wild.

I turn and rush to Silas. "Are you okay?" I ask, wanting to hug him, to kiss him, to hold him. But I can't right now. Not yet at least.

He nods. "Yeah, thanks." He exhales. "Thank you."

He hugs me, and the stadium bursts into applause. Then they start chanting something. Silas pulls away from, a puzzled expression on their face.

"What are they saying?" he asks.

"Redo," Brigham says. "They want us to redo the play."

I turn to our coach who's talking to the head ref. "Can we do that?"

He looks around at the stadium filled with patrons. Some are even trying to jump out of their seats down into the field, and the rest of the security guards are busy keeping them in check.

When coach looks back at the ref, the ref just shrugs, turns, and makes his way out to the field.

"What's going on?" Silas asks.

"I think he's calling the play," I say.

Once he's in the middle of the field, the ref turns his mic on. "Redo of the play," he says with a wide gesture of his arms. "Interruption by the Vanguards. Ball goes back to the Pioneers."

The crowd goes ballistic, but this time they sound happy. I look down at Silas, and I can see my smile mirrored on his face.

He slaps my back. "Get back out there!"

"Alright, alright," I say. And I jog back out onto the field.

"Dude," Blake says to me when I reach him.

"We can talk about it later," I say. "Same play?"

"You sure?" Blake asks.

I nod. "They'll have their backup linebacker out there. It'll be easy."

"Alright," he says. He relays it back to the coaches, and they agree. It's my time to shine. For real this time.

We get into position, but this time I feel completely energized. Ready to go.

The play begins, and I confidently bolt out to where I need to be. Around me, the crowd cheers—the people I was afraid wouldn't like me for my authentic self. Yet my fear couldn't have been more incorrect. I'm loved in more ways than I can comprehend.

When I'm in place, I jump to catch the ball and then hit the ground running. I leave their backup linebacker in the dust. Ironically, if they hadn't been so worried about hurting Silas and instead focused on me, they could have tackled me and won the game. But I guess you don't think straight when you're so full of hating other people.

Predictably, I score the touchdown, cementing my reputation as one of the best tight ends of the 21st century. And right after, we score an extra point, putting us in the lead. Shortly after, the timer runs out, and we win over the Vanguards with a tight score of 28 – 27. With all the cheering from my fellow teammates around me, paired with the ear-splitting cheers from the stadium, I'm afraid I'll go deaf. But honestly, that feels like it would be worth it after all I've been through.

At the after party, I finally spot Silas. I hand him a glass of champagne and gesture for us to go out on the balcony. Alone.

On the rooftops in chilly, snowy Kansas, we sip our drinks and look up at the stary sky. I look around, and when the coast is clear, we both set down our glasses. I wrap my arms around his waist, and he slips his arms around my neck. And we dance.

"I spoke with Brigham," he says. "I told him I decided I didn't want to keep working for the Pioneers."

"What are you going to do instead?"

"There's this organization called Affirm in Utah," he says. "For queer youth, often mentally unwell. Apparently, they hire physical therapists. And Brigham even said he'd put in a good word."

"That sounds perfect for you," I say. "Like really perfect."

"I think so, too," he says.

I raise my brow. "So does this mean...?"

Silas untangles himself from me and holds my hands between us. "Why don't you ask me out when we get back to Salt Lake?" he asks. "We can talk then."

"I can do that," I say as Silas runs his thumbs across my knuckles.

"Great," he says. "I'm gonna head back to the hotel. Feeling exhausted."

And without another word, he kisses me on the cheek and disappears back into the party. As I watch him go, I count down the moments when I can see him again. And finally call him my boyfriend.

Chapter 29

Silas King

WHEN WE BOTH ARRIVE back in Salt Lake, Wyatt does not delay in the slightest. A couple days after the Championship Game, after all the culprits for the threats toward him have been discovered thanks to the public putting pressure on the NFO, the world is finally calm enough for us to finally be together.

Wyatt picks me up in his Jeep Wrangler. He's wearing a navy suit, which makes his ginger beard look perfect. I'm wearing a black suit and a cowboy hat, and Wyatt tells me I look like the most handsome man on the planet.

He takes me to some fancy restaurant where the lights are dim and romantic. Halfway through the dinner, other patrons notice that Wyatt Nelson is eating at the same restaurant as them, but luckily no one bothers us.

We talk about everything. I mention therapy, how I've grown since we last saw each other. I mention how much I've already heard back from Affirm and how they want to interview me next week. I can't wait for that.

I also tell him how I finally started listening to his music again. I missed the sound of classical voice. And I mention how now that I'll have more free time with my new job, I want to get into music production. It turns out that my favorite artists—*Jónsi, Eluvium, Slow Meadow, Alaskan Tapes*—all use software that I could easily download and learn on my laptop. Sure, they also use instruments like the piano and the guitar, which I don't know how to play, but maybe this would be a good place to start to learn how to make the same kind of music that has inspired me so deeply. Linda said it'll be good to find things outside of Wyatt, and this is definitely one of them.

Wyatt tells me how the NFO, thanks to the pressure of the public, finally found the players threatening our lives. Turns out it was a collection of players all over the NFO, but most were part of the Sparrows. He mentions how his relationship with his mom has improved, how she's much more willing to see where he's coming from instead of imposing her own desires on him. He also says that he wants to get back into singing, and I tell him that I would love to hear his voice in real time, which I still never have.

"I guess this means you'll take me back," he says, smiling over the candle in the center of our table.

I smile and blush. "I think I could tolerate that."

His smile falters a little, and his face gets more serious. "Is that—is a relationship something healthy for you? After all that's happened?"

I take a long exhale out of my nose and rest my elbows on the table, having finished eating. "I'm in a much better place than I was when you broke up with me."

He nods. "I promise that if I have an issue, I won't bottle it up like I did with this whole threat thing. I'll tell you. I won't try to solve everything on my own."

"I appreciate it," I say. "And you know what? I think I am ready for a partner."

He raises his brow. "Is that so?"

"It is," I say. "With my therapist, I've been working on processing my emotions on knowing where my worth lies. I feel like enough of a person now to depend on myself for worth, not on anyone or anything else. Even you."

"That's good," Wyatt says. "Because I don't think I'd be very reliable for that."

"No one is," I say. "And no one should be. Only I can know my deepest needs and desires. So I should be the one to seek to fulfill them. It's unfair for me to put that on anyone else."

Wyatt leans forward onto the table. "You sound like a sage."

I blush again. "I don't really feel like one. I feel like I'm just wading through fog trying to figure all this shit out."

"But you're trying," Wyatt says. "And it shows."

He stares at me, the flame of the candle shining in his eyes. I feel drawn to him again, like he's a black hole. Except this time, I have a stable orbit. I can still admire him, but I won't fall in and lose myself.

"So, Silas King," he says. "Will you do me the honor of being my boyfriend?"

I chew on my lips, butterflies swarming in my stomach. "I think I will."

He gives me a wide smile, then takes a drink of his water. "I hope you still have energy for tonight."

I lean back, relishing the thought of having sex with Wyatt again. But then I realize that he may not be talking about taking me back to his place. Everyone around us is dressed nice, but we're dressed nicer, like we have somewhere else to be.

The waiter comes with our check, and Wyatt gives him our card.

"Tonight?" I ask. "You had more planned?"

"I do," he says. "If you're still up for it."

"I mean, I'd go anywhere with you. But what is it?"

He puts his finger to his lips. "It's a surprise."

I chuckle. "Alright."

The waiter returns with our card, and we make our way to Wyatt's car. And instead of heading in the direction of either of our places, he's heading right into downtown. Soon, we found ourselves in the parking lot of the Salt Lake opera house.

"An opera?" I ask as we park. "Which one?"

Wyatt can't contain his smile. "You'll see."

But as we walk inside, it becomes alarmingly clear.

"La Boheme," I say, looking up at all the posters on the wall. The theatre vestibule is dressed in maroon and gold, illuminated in dim light. It's a cozy scene. If I wasn't so excited, I could probably fall asleep in here after all that I just ate.

The greeter scans Wyatt's tickets, and before I know it, were in the theatre itself. The walls look liked their adorned in gold, and the roof stretches so high

I feel like I'm in an Italian opera house or something of the like. It's majestic, grander than life—kinda like opera itself.

We take our seats, and Wyatt puts his hand on my knee. I turn to him, and he plants a confident kiss on my lips, even as the lights are up and people can clearly see us.

This is perfect. Before I met Wyatt, I would have never thought that I would have found someone who's able to see me so well. And I would have never thought that someone to be in the NFO. But I have. And I feel so blessed for it.

"I brought you here," Wyatt says, stroking my thigh with his big, muscular hand. "Because, I don't know—this opera reminds me of you. It's what I thought of in those early days where we hung out. Our meeting just felt so electric, just like Mimi and Rodolfo, which you'll soon see in the flesh. And like, I don't know—you saw me in ways no one else had. You didn't see me as a football player who liked music, or a football player who was gay. You saw me as Wyatt, and then everything else came second."

I put my hand on his and squeeze it. "And I still see you that way."

He quickly leans over and kisses me on the lips. Then the lights dim, and the show begins.

We watch Rodolfo and his friends lament being poor, and then there's the scintillating encounter between Rodolfo is Mimi. I get chills during "Che Gelida Manina", and when I glance at Wyatt, I think he may even be crying. I reach my hand over and squeeze his leg, and he puts his hand on mine.

Eventually, the tragedy ensues. Rodolfo grows jealous of Mimi, and they part. And just when you think their love could never happen again, Mimi shows up again. But she's sick. And on her deathbed, she and Rodolfo recount their love together. But it's too late.

She's dead.

As we're all clapping, I find myself in tears, and they just keep coming.

Wyatt stops clapping. "Are you okay?" he asks.

"Yeah," I say, nodding. But honestly, I'm not sure.

On our way back home, I still feel uneasy, so I go through one of the exercises that Damon has recommended to me. I first identify the physical feeling—a tightness in the chest and a lightness in the head—and then trace it back to what emotion this might be coming from. In the past, the tightening of the chest has typically come from anxiety, anger, or fear. But this lightness of the head—it's not really lightness. More like clarity. And I've never really had the two of these together before. Hell, I'm not even sure if I've had this light clarity before either.

"You wanna come back to my place?" Wyatt asks, stealing a glance at me.

I bite my lip. With how I'm feeling, I'm not sure if that's a great idea. Yet I want to be with Wyatt still. Is this me using him to make me feel better?

"We don't have to do anything," he says. "We can just go to sleep, or cuddle. Or I can take you back home. I won't object to any of it. And regardless, you'll still be my boyfriend. I'll always be happy to call you mine."

His words warm my heart, and they make me feel slightly less uneasy. If we're just going to sleep, that would be good. I'm pretty tired. And in the morning, maybe I'll be able to process what I'm feeling a little bit better.

"That sounds good," I say. "I'll come over, but I'm pretty tired. Sleep would be good."

He nods. "Sounds perfect to me."

We arrive at his place and take the elevator up to his floor. Inside, the lights underneath his kitchen cabinets are dim, and the only other light comes from the city outside his windows.

"Before we do anything else," Wyatt says. He takes my cowboy hat off and puts his hands on my cheeks. He plants the most tender kiss he can on my lips and holds it there. And it feels like this connection is charging me up with life like a phone battery.

Which worries me. My worth should come from myself, not Wyatt.

Eventually, he breaks the connection, then looks into my eyes. "I just had to do that," he says, his hands still on my face. "I've just missed you. And I love you. So much."

I take a deep breath and reach up one of my hands to his. I feel love for him too. Strong love.

And I don't feel tired anymore, either. It's like his kiss not only gave me life, but also energy. So I can process this strange emotion a little bit more inside me.

I feel now that it's not a negative one, which reassures me that I'm not looking for Wyatt to solve my problems.

But it does make me want to get even closer to him.

"Wyatt," I say.

He tries to lower his hands from my face, but I make him keep them there.

"I want to fall into you tonight," I say, not necessarily knowing why, but knowing it's what I need to do.

"Fall into me?" he asks. "What do you mean?"

"I want to get lost in you. I want to explore you. Worship you. I want to take in everything about your body. Make love with you." I swallow. "And I know this sounds weird, but I want you to do nothing in return."

Wyatt furrows his brow. "Are you sure?"

I nod. "I just want you to let me fall into you. Don't try to control me or do anything. Please. I know that sounds weird, but I think that's what I want right now."

Wyatt kisses me on the forehead, his beard tickling my face, then pulls back and lowers his hands.

"I would be happy to do anything with you," he says. "So I want nothing more than for you to worship me."

I nod, still embarrassed at my request. I still don't know what the hell is going on with me.

He starts undoing his tie, then nods to his bedroom. "Shall we?"

I grab his tie, stopping him. "Let me handle it, okay?"

He removes his hands from his clothes. "My body is yours, Silas."

And then sends warm chills down my spine. "Thank you." He leads us to his bed, and then I take off his clothes. I start with his tie, then his suit coat. I run my hands up his fit torso, his body so hairy that I can feel it all through his shirt. I unbutton that, then remove it, and I marvel at the man he is. He's gotten more muscular since I've last seen him, and my mouth practically salivates at the sight of his hairy torso.

I remove his belt, then pull his pants and underwear down. Once he removes those from his ankles, he's wearing only socks, which is just how I want him. His cock pokes me in the belly, and I can see its veins from where I'm standing.

I start removing my clothes, which gives Wyatt time to kiss me. By the time I'm naked, I'm just as hard, and I'm worried I'll cum to soon.

But that's fine. Because it's Wyatt's body I want to focus on.

"Lay down," I say. "On your stomach."

Wyatt obeys. He wraps his arms around a pillow, and then he spreads his legs slightly. The moon illuminates his hairy ass, and I swear that one of his cheeks is bigger than my head alone.

And that's when I mount him. I rest my dick right atop his huge ass cheeks, like a hot dog in a bun, then lower my torso. I press my nose right against his upper back, just below his neck, and smell.

I swear it's better than anything else.

Because it's him. It's not rank, but it's not good either. It's just him, and it makes me want to get closer to him.

I wrap my arms under his and move down his spine, rubbing my face into his skin and getting the natural smell of him all over me. I don't know this before, but this is what I was looking for when I said I wanted to worship him. And I want more of this.

When I reach his ass, the scent of him becomes more potent, and I breathe in deeper. Gently, I nuzzle my face between his cheeks until my lips are touching his furry hole. I take in another deep breath of him, making my own dick twitch.

And then I start fucking him with my tongue.

I stick my tongue into him over and over again, using my hands to press his huge, hairy cheeks into my face. Occasionally, I stop to run my tongue around his hole, but then I get right back to tongue fucking him. The entire time, Wyatt moans deeply, and occasionally he'll squeeze his hole, making me work harder to tongue fuck him.

Wanting to get a better look, I pull my head out of his ass and pull his cheeks wide. His hairy, pink hole almost smiles up at me. Salivating, I gather the spit in my mouth and drop it on his hole. It lands right on it with soft plop, and as Wyatt flexes his hole, my spit makes his way inside him.

And the sight makes me go feral. "God, I've missed your tight end."

Wyatt chuckles, and I go back to munching on his hole, pulling his cheeks wide so I can get deeper. I lick him thirstily, desperate to taste him deeper and deeper. I even go so crazy as to press my tongue against his hole and suck, creating sucking and slurping sounds.

"You are a fucking slut," Wyatt says. "Goddamn."I kiss his hole, then smell it. "I'm your fucking slut."

"Yeah you are," he says. "You want me to fuck you?"

I nod. "When I'm done worshipping you. But let me do the work. It's so hot that way."

"Have at it then, Silas."And I do.

By the time I'm done eating his ass, I've left handprint marks on it.

"God, I needed that," I say, breathing in his scent lingering on my face. "Will you turn over for me?"

He rolls over, his huge, hairy, muscular body flexing as he does. And when I see his erect dick, I nearly short-circuit.

"Fuck, I need that inside me," I say.

But then I take in everything else—his forearms, his biceps, his chest, his abs, his dick, his thighs, his calves. And, oh Jesus, his feet.

"Fuck," I say. I lift one of his feet to my nose and smell. And I moan, chills running down my spine. "God, I've missed you so much."Wyatt puts his arms behind his head. "I've missed you too, babe."

I lower his foot, then straddle him. The head of his dick lightly presses against my hole. This afternoon, just before he arrived, I made sure I was douched. I had a feeling this was all going to happen, and I'm so glad I did.

I lower to his face and kiss him hungrily, and he meets my kiss with the same fervor.

I still feel that weird, light feeling in my head. But I know it's positive, which is why I agreed to all this sex in the first place. And this feeling has only grown the more I worship Wyatt. God, I can't even begin to describe the pleasure that comes from not only worshipping a sexy man, but worshipping a sexy man who I deeply love and trust? It's like nourishment for the soul.

"You want me to fuck you?" he asks. "I got lube over here." He reaches for his nightstand.

But then I stop him.

He looks up at me. "Do you not want to do this?" I shake my head. "No, I do," I say. "But I don't want you to use lube."

Wyatt raises his brow. "Are you sure?"

I nod. "I remember when you first stuck your fingers in me."

He laughs. "Right. In the Miss U PT clinic."

I shake my head, laughing as well. "I can't believe we did that."

"We were desperate, horny little fuckers," Wyatt says, reaching up to rub my pecs.

"I mean, that's true, but you also described my music back to me in a way that no one else would," I say. "So of course I wanted to fuck you." "You were stunning," Wyatt says. "And so was your music. I was just being honest."

"And that's why I love you, Wyatt," I say.

He pulls me down and kisses me.

"So you really wanna do no lube?" he asks.

I nod. "I do. Can you?"

He sighs through his teeth. "I'll try for you, but I don't know. Not sure how good it will feel."

"We can always use lube if it doesn't work."

"True," Wyatt says, tapping his dick against my hole. "But I'm a try-hard. I wanna find a way to make it work."

"Okay," I say. "How about—ahh—"

Somehow he manages to get just the head inside me. My entire asshole stretches, but the pain—the pain makes the light, clear feeling in my head even more exquisite.

"Fuck," I say. "Yes." Then Wyatt frowns at me. "You haven't given my feet that much attention."

I raise my brow. "I definitely—"

"Turn around and let me fuck you that way," he says.

I slip his dick out of me, already missing the painful pleasure. I stand up and turn around, then lower myself onto his dick. He presses his head back into me, then keeps going.

"Worship my feet while I fuck you," he says. "Like the slut you are."

"Yes, sir," I say as he slowly presses his dick into me. I lower my face to his foot and press it against my face. I breathe in his manly scent and keep my ass upright for him. Once he's all the way in, he flexes his deck, which makes my entire body jolt, almost as if he's controlling me via probe now. I can feel my hole stretching open, and it hurts in that exquisitely pleasurable kind of way.

And then he starts thrusting.

It's a little chaotic and rough since we're not using lube, but every movement lights up my entire body. And with thrust, it becomes a little less painful and a little more pleasurable. Which makes me want more and more.

I lower myself and press both of his feet against my face. But that isn't enough. I pull off his socks as he increases his thrusting speed. I put one of his socks in my mouth, sniffing the other one as deeply as I can, then put that one in my mouth. Only able to breathe through my nose now, I lower to his feet again make sure I stick my nose in between each of his toes, ensuring that the only air I'm breathing is his scent and his scent alone.

Wyatt's fucking grows more aggressive, and it takes all my strength to keep my body still for him. No lube makes every sensation a lot sharper, including that light, clear feeling in my head, but I love it. It makes me feel alive. And I really like being alive now.

"Here," Wyatt says. He slowly pulls out of me, and I already find myself craving him again.

I turn to him and question him with my brow. I can't speak with his socks in my mouth.

"Take those out and get me wet," he says. "I need some spit to fuck you right."

I take the socks out of his mouth and place them gently next to us like they're made of gold—which they practically are for touching Wyatt's feet. After gathering all the saliva I can, I open my mouth and let it slowly fall on the gorgeous sexual architecture that is Wyatt's dick. The spit hits the tip, then cascades down at all sides, and I watch it fall as more saliva pools in my mouth. Once some of the spit reaches the bottom, I let the second glob fall. But this time I don't just let myself watch. After it lands, I meet his dick with my mouth and massage his divine manhood as tenderly as I can with my mouth alone.

"Oh my God, Silas," he says. "This is the best—fuck."

I gently press my tongue against the bottom side of his dick, each time massaging a new part of his dick. With my lips, I form a strong suction, and every now and then I flutter my tongue all around his dick, then just as quickly return to pressing my tongue against him. Occasionally, I suction my cheeks against the sides of his dick, and he moans every time. I don't bother using my hand because I don't want him to cum yet. His first load is going straight into my un-lubed ass.

"Enough," he says, and I release my hold of him. There isn't one inch of his dick that isn't covered in my shiny spit.

"Sit on me," he says. "But face me. I want to look you in the eyes when I cum inside you."

He grabs his socks and hands them to me. He gestures for me to put them back in my mouth, and I eagerly obey. Then I situate myself on top of him again. With much more ease this time, he slips his spit-covered dick into me, and I grab his hairy pecs as I experience that white hot painful pleasure of him entering me again.

And he gets right to fucking.

"I know how you like it," he says, fucking me deep and hard. "I could never forget. I know you like I do myself, Silas."

I want to pause and bask in his words, but he's fucking me too gloriously hard. I moan as I dig my fingers into his thick, hairy chest, trying to keep myself still, but he's too strong. I'm at his complete mercy, and he's giving me none of it. God, this hurts so fucking good.

And then he puts hands around my neck.

"Can I?" he asks as he drills me.

I nod so hard I think my head will fall off as I hold his hands against my neck.

And when he squeezes, that light, clear, happy feeling in my head somehow expands.

There was always a thought in the back of my head that pain during sex was just another way of me being suicidal—me choosing pain over pleasure. But this isn't just pain. Sure, yeah, it hurts, but it makes the pain just so, so much more exquisite, like I'm testing the boundaries of what my body is capable of and finding that it can take more and more. It's like I'm strong. Capable. Resilient.

Wyatt somehow fucks me harder, and I hold his solid, hairy arms to keep my balance. My head grows lighter, and a smile forms on my face. You know what? Maybe I did really die. And maybe I'm in heaven. Because this has to be how good it feels. I've never felt anything better.

Until he releases one of his hands and spanks me so hard I know I'll have a mark.

"Sorry," Wyatt says, slowing down. "That was—"

But I give him a deadly glare. I grab his hand and gesture for him to do it harder.

"You sure?" he asks.

I nod as much as I can with his hand tight around my neck.

"Alright," Wyatt says. "I'm not holding back anymore."

And then I can definitely say I know what heaven feels like.

Wyatt wasn't kidding when he said he wasn't gonna hold back.

He thrusts harder into me than he ever has before. Sweat drips down his hot, bearded face as his hand clasps tightly around my throat. He spanks me hard and at unpredictable intervals, forcing me to bite down into his sweaty socks every time he does, which only makes me taste and smell more of his perfect manliness.

And that's when I realize I'm going to cum without even trying.

"I'm gonna fucking cum," Wyatt says. And as he goes harder, letting out an inhuman groan in the process, I can't help but spill my seed all over his hairy torso—all without touching myself. He moans as his body convulses, pushing himself into me over and over with deadly, sharp thrusts. Each one injects a spike of pleasure into me as I come down, and pretty soon I find myself slipping his socks out of my mouth, lowering myself to him, and kissing him lazily, all while his dick is still inside me. As we wrap our arms around each other, I focus on the feeling of his dick softening inside me, taking note of every nerve losing its pain and pleasure with the decrease of his size. And soon enough, I find myself laying to his side in the crook of his arms, my eyelids growing heavy. And then, we're both fast asleep.

An unknown amount of time later, I find myself wide awake. That's been pretty normal lately, though I'm not sure why. When I was super depressed, sleep came easily. But I guess my mind is processing more, so it's more awake. Who knows. I just try to honor it as it is.

I kiss Wyatt on the cheek, and he stirs slightly, but he doesn't wake up. I get out of bed, grab one of Wyatt's fuzzy robes, then make my way to the kitchen. My ass is wonderfully sore, especially since we used no lube, so I walk slowly. On the kitchen counter, I find my phone and earbuds. Outside, it's begun to snow. So, I slip on some shoes, put my earbuds in, and walk out onto Wyatt's balcony.

I press shuffle on our playlist, and the first song to come up is "Happiness", but it's not the one by *Eluvium*. It's the one by *Jónsi* and *Alex Somers*. I stand there in the frigid cold as I watch the snow fall, the strong tones of the song gradually fading in.

To me, this song "Happiness" has three parts. The first part is like the echoes of what's to come, which foreshadows how the middle will sound. The middle is like a stronger, more pronounced sound of the beginning. And the end is an echo of all that's happened, but to me this is the most distinct of all three parts.

And that's when I realize the whole thing is a metaphor.

Happiness is something we all want. But it can be elusive. Yet on my mental health journey, I think I've been learning that self-worth begets happiness. Like once I feel worthy in myself and no longer need other people or things to give me worth, happiness naturally comes.

But finding self-worth is hard, especially at first. You have to do things that feel hard but you know are right for you, like being vulnerable with those you love. This happened after I finally opened up to Damon, which gave me the courage to be open with Linda and Michael. This was like the first third of the song. I heard echoes of what was to come, but I still had no idea what the result would be. And then the second part of the song is when you see how worth it was to do these hard things. I feared that Michael and Linda were going to judge me for still having feelings for Wyatt, but they loved me where I was at. And their love helped me see the love I could have for myself. I also feel like this is where I came back to Utah and decided to no longer continue my job with the NFO, along with getting back together with Wyatt. It's me doing the grand actions that lead to a greater sense of self-worth. Yet I've never felt a true payoff of these things—that is, felt true happiness.

Until now.

So often, we can get caught up in exciting actions and decisions that we forget to sit with ourselves and see how we feel, which I'm doing now. And I'm finally seeing where all of my actions born of desiring self-worth have led me.

To happiness.

This lightheaded feeling? This joyful clarity I've been feeling that grew while Wyatt was fucking me?

It's happiness.

It's joy. Satisfaction with life. Satisfaction with self. Hope for tomorrow. A feeling of lightheartedness.

A knowledge that life is worth living. Every second of it.

When I watched Mimi die in *La Boheme*, I wept not because I saw myself in her or even who I used to be. No. I wept because I recognized I *wasn't* her—that I wasn't going to die. Since my attempt, I haven't even touched my old journal. And I don't plan on it. Because, unlike Mimi, God rest her soul, I plan to live my life happily for as long as humanly possible.

"Silas?"

I turn to see Wyatt at the door to the balcony in one of his other robes.

"What are—oh God, you're crying," he says, joining me on the porch. He puts his arm on my back. "Are you okay?"

I take out my earbuds just as the song is ending and put them in the robe pocket. "Yeah," I say, wiping my eyes.

Wyatt looks around, and his eyes snags on the railing of the balcony. And then they widen. "Are you—"

I put my hand on his arm. "Wyatt, I'm fine," I say. "I really am."

He grips my arm back. "Are you sure?"

"Positive," I say. "I'm just so damn happy." He gives me a small smile, then wraps his arms around me.

"Are you sure you want to be out here?" he asks. "It's freezing."

"Yeah, I just wanted to listen to music and think," I say. "But I can come in."

I put my phone and earbuds back in the kitchen, and I make my way to Wyatt's room.

"Wyatt," I say, just as he's getting under the covers.

"Yeah?" he asks, gesturing me to get in bed after him. I do, and he spoons me from behind, wrapping his strong arms around me and warming my cold self up after being outside. A year ago, I would panic, having forgotten to write in my journal. But I don't need to do that anymore.

"I love you so much," I say.

He squeezes me tight, then relaxes. "I love you too."

And I drift off happily, knowing now that happiness is indeed what I'm feeling.

Epilogue One—Six Months Later

Wyatt Nelson

I WAKE TO LIPS around my dick in a cabin bed. And I let out a contented sigh. I open my eyes to see Silas with my cock balls deep in his mouth.

"Happy birthday, greedy boy," I say, stretching. Today's Silas's thirtieth, and we're visiting Glamour Springs to celebrate.

He presses his tongue against my dick, then releases his hold for just a moment. "You just taste so good," he says, rubbing my dick against his face.

"Then get back to it," I say. "Make me feel good."

"Yes, sir."

And I close my eyes and relax as he worships my cock.

This is part one of my little birthday present to him. I told him last night that he could do anything he wanted to my body all night, and he took advantage of the gift. I woke to him eating my ass a couple times, and he even got two loads out of me.

I've never met someone as subservient as Silas, and I honestly never saw myself as such a dom until him. But it just feels perfect between us. He says he loves body worship and the power play involved. Using all his energy just for me really gets him off, and seeing how much he loves it—paired with how much I get out of it—makes it an obvious yes for me. Even him getting off on my most rancid smells is hot as hell to me. It's like I'm a god and he's a mere mortal, hoping that by worshipping the least parts of me he'll get just a glimpse of my glory. I used to worry that all this was a result of him not thinking he's worthy enough to have pleasure of his own, but that's when he helped me see that this *is* his pleasure.

So what better gift to give him than free reign over my body for twelve hours?

With my dick in the back of his throat, he can't contain himself. He cums all over our sheets and just starts sucking me harder.

"Good boy," I say, stroking his hair as he presses his nose into my crotch with my dick still rock-hard in his mouth. "But it's time we give your other hole some attention."

He looks up at me then releases my dick from his mouth. He gently strokes it with his hand. "No lube?"

"It's your birthday," I say with a smirk. "Of course."

And that's when I put him in missionary. I pound him fast and hard, already 'lubed' up with the ton of spit he left on my dick. To give him a little more pleasure, I lean down and put my armpit in his face. He wraps his arms and legs tight around me as he buries his nose in my pit, and this just makes me stroke him harder. Sooner than I know it, I've bred him, and my lips are on his as I greedily tongue his mouth.

I was initially skeptical of using no lube. You need something to ease the friction. But there's something about Silas's hole. There's just enough tightness for it to feel good, but it's loose enough for me to thrust in and out easily. And no lube just provides more friction, which feels good as hell. Whenever we go no lube, I find myself cumming so much faster than usual. It also helps that Silas is both a gorgeous man and a sex god.

After we've both satisfied our carnal desires, I hold Silas in my arms a bit. Then I check the time and realize that I need to get both of us out of bed and down to Jimmy and Tanner's cabin in the next thirty.

"I'm gonna shower," I say. "You keep resting."

Silas stretches and yawns. Dude must be tired, and I don't blame him. He was up all night playing with me.

"I'll go after," he says, curling up under our blanket.

I kiss him on the lips. "Take your time. Rest," I say, really meaning it. Because I want to make sure that everything's in order for his surprise.

In the bathroom, I check my messages to make sure that everything is right. My mom and Linda worked with Jimmy to get the food all ready. Martha and Llewellyn worked with Jimmy's assistant managers to get a nice cake prepared. Kyle and Michael got all the decorations set up, and Tanner managed to get the upright piano into their cabin. And when I receive a text from Blake, I almost forget that he's here, too.

"Thanks for inviting me again."

And I can't help but smile at that. Blake's had a hard time accepting who he is, so I thought to invite him out here to queer friendly Glamour Springs for Silas's birthday. I hope he feels a little bit more at home here. Oh, and he's an excellent piano player. I couldn't think of anyone else to accompany me.

I hop in the shower, and I can't help but think how grateful I am. When I first came out, I feared that I would have to do it all alone, that the world barely tolerated me coming out as an NFO player, so I wouldn't be able to expect any more mercy coming my way. Yet not only did the American public support me when I opened up about the threats, but all these folks in Glamour Springs forgave me for my rash actions in keeping everything silent and for hurting Silas the way I did. They're starting to feel like my own family, and now that I'm on better terms with my mom, I feel like my entire social life is overflowing. I'm not sure I've ever felt this loved before.

When I'm done, I tell Silas to get ready. He thinks we're meeting Martha and Llewellyn at breakfast for Jimmy's diner and that we'll have a relaxing day, maybe go on a hike. Little does he know...

"I'll be downstairs," I say. "Come down when you're ready."

"Alright," he says, plodding into the bathroom.

In the living room, I pull out the sheet music I've hidden in one of the side cabinets. I make sure to brush up on the lyrics to Ralph Vaughan Williams's *Songs of Travel*, and I do some quick vocal warmups to get my voice ready. I want only the best for Silas.

When I hear Silas shut the bedroom door upstairs, I quickly hide the books again and try to sit nonchalantly at the table. Once Silas appears on the stairs, he gives me a skeptical look.

"What?" I ask, trying to hold in a laugh.

"You seem like you're hiding something."

"What would I have to hide?"Silas shrugs. He's wearing a tank top that shows off his wide, hairy shoulders, and I'm tempted to pin him down and fuck him all over again. But we've got something more pressing to attend to.

"Let's go meet Martha and Llewellyn," he says. "I'm starving."

I'm about to give him a puzzled look, then remember that that's indeed what he thinks is going on. We get in my car, and once we turn right to head down to Jimmy's cabin instead of left to the center of town, Silas turns to me and gives me a puzzled look.

"Where are—"

"Just the scenic route," I say.

Then Silas quiets, and I think he has an idea of what's going on. Eventually, we pull into Jimmy's cabin lot—well, to the side of his cabin. His lot is completely full.

"What's going on?" Silas asks, observing all the cars.

I chuckle. "You'll see."

He follows me up to the door, and I enter without knocking. Silas follows after me, and as soon as we reach Jimmy's living room, everyone bursts out of their hiding places.

They yell.

There's a look of pure shock on Silas's face at first, and then it melts into raw joy. A wide smile sticks on his face as every one of his friends comes up to hug him. I swear I even see a tear in his eye.

And then we eat.

Silas loves breakfast food, so we prepared a lavish buffet style brunch. Jimmy, my mom, and Linda prepared a ton of eggs, bacon, sausage, pancakes, and more. As we eat, Linda goes around the table and has everyone say something they love about Silas.

And this is where Silas really cries.

Silas told me once how his attempt went, and we never really talked about it again—not because we were afraid to, but because it didn't seem necessary.

He has, however, gone into great detail about how much his life has changed since then. He feels lighter, more carefree, and he says he his healing forward by helping the queer kids at as part of the Affirm organization.

So I thought this to be the perfect gift for his thirtieth. He says he relishes every day that he has to live now, and I saw no better way to celebrate his life than getting together the people that love him most. He deserves to be reminded how blessed we know we are to have him still around.

When all that's done, Martha and Llewellyn take out the cake while Silas wipes his eyes, and I take this distraction as a way to get Blake and I situated with the piano. I push it from behind the couch, and he sets a binder down with all my sheet music in it.

"You ready to play?" I ask.

He trills his lips. "It's been a minute, but it'll be nice to get back out there."

I pat him on the back. "Good," I say. "So glad to have you here."

"Glad to be here."

We get back to our seats just as Jimmy finishes lighting the thirtieth candle on the flat Texas sheet cake, which Jimmy assured me was Silas's favorite. Silas didn't even know we were gone. As they wish him a happy birthday, I put my hand on his knee and squeeze it, and he squeezes me back. Then, he blows out the candles, and Jimmy starts cutting the cake for everyone.

Now's my time to shine.

Blake and I sneak over to the piano, and once everyone has their cake, I get their attention. Everyone looks at me expectantly—except for Silas. He stares at me with wide eyes and dropped jaw. He did not see this coming.

"Everyone," I say. "This is the second to last gift I'm giving to Silas. For the past few months, I've been brushing up on my singing. And today's the first time I'm really doing it since college."

My mom whoops and claps loudly, and I have to stop to chuckle. Glad she's finally supporting me in what I want to do.

I announce Blake as my accompanist, what I'm singing, and then I get to it.

The selection today is short. I didn't want to bore my audience, and honestly, that was my greatest fear. Yet as I go through the *Songs of Travel*, everyone listens with rapt attention. Especially Silas. He reacts to every song. He sits on the edge of his seat during "The Vagabond". During "The Roadside Fire" and "Youth and Love", he has his hands clasped in front of his chest. "The Infinite Shining Heavens" and "Whither Must I Wander?" put him in tears. And he stands up clapping when the whole thing is done, followed by the others.

"And one last song," I say, surprised by how well my voice is doing. I glance down at Blake, and he nods and turns the pages. The piano accompaniment for "Che Gelida Manina" begins, and Silas lets out an audible gasp.

I focus on him as I sing it. Because he, after all, is my Mimi. Except instead of losing him to consumption—or suicide—I pray I have him for the rest of my days. And that's what it's looking like. When I'm all done, everyone claps like crazy, and I approach Silas. He gives me a strong kiss on the lips and hugs me.

Then he gives me a puzzled expression. "You said that was your second to last gift," he says. "What else could you possibly have?"

I smirk and pull out an envelope from my back pocket. "You of course don't have to accept it," I say. "But I offer it all the same."

Epilogue Two

Silas King

I TAKE THE ENVELOPE from Wyatt, my hand shaking. I don't know why I'm so nervous. Nothing bad can happen. Wyatt won't run away from me again. And I know he's not being threatened anymore.

But I'm still nervous as hell.

I take a deep breath, accepting my emotions as they are as my therapist has taught me. And then I open the envelope in front of everyone. Inside is a typical birthday card. When I open it, I smile at his note. But then my eyes widen when I see what's written just below it.

"No," I say, shaking my head. "You can't."

Wyatt nods with a smile on his face. "I can."

I read it again, then again, unable to believe my eyes.

When I took the job as a physical therapist for Affirm, I took a steep pay cut. While working for the NFO, I actually had a realistic timeline for paying off my student loans. But not currently. I know it wasn't the smartest idea to take the cut, but it was what I needed to do. I wasn't happy in the NFO, and I loved Wyatt. And working with children in Affirm has proven to be everything I hoped it would be. I get to help struggling queer teens learn how exercise, play sports, and take care of their bodies. It is more rewarding than I could have imagined. Yet the pay isn't the greatest, and I've wondered for a while how I was to pay off the rest of my loans.

Until now.

"Alright, you're killing us," Jimmy says. "What does the card say?"

I look up at him, tears in my eyes. "Wyatt's offered to pay the rest of my student loans."

Half the room gasps, and the rest of them smile.

I turn to Wyatt. "Are you serious?"

He nods. "If you'll let me."

"But my loans aren't small."

"I know. You've told me," he says. "But I'm one of the best tight ends in the country. I make a lot of money. I can handle it."

"Are you sure?"

"Yes," he says emphatically. "We can talk more about it later, and you can always turn it down. But I want you to spend the rest of the day believing that you're student-debt free."

I do for a minute, and just the thought makes me dizzy.

I wrap my arms around the man I love. "Thank you."

The rest of the party is wonderful. Everyone chats with one another, and Blake turns out to be the unexpected star of the show. His piano skills were just as impressive as Wyatt's singing, and I didn't know that one of the best quarterbacks in the country had such use of his fingers. I mean, I know what Wyatt can do, but still.

As the party wraps up, I insist on helping clean up, despite the protests. When I say it's because I want to spend more time with everyone, they relent. I chat with Linda, Michael, Joan, Llewellyn, and everyone else. It's just perfect. This day is perfect.

And then I find myself alone with Jimmy washing some dishes. And it dawns on me that ever since he found me in that cabin about to die, he and I have never spoken about what's happened directly. We've danced around it, and we've talked about my mental state, yet I haven't even expressed gratitude. Not once.

"Jimmy," I say, setting a plate down. "I don't think I've ever thanked you."

He grins at me. "For all this? Oh, it was a pleasure setting it up. Wyatt actually—"

"No," I say. "Though I am so grateful for this."

"What is it?" he asks, turning off the sink.

"Thank you for finding me," I say. "The night of Kyle and Michael's wedding. I, uh—" I clear my throat. "I wouldn't be here without you."

He frowns down at the sink. "Of course," he says. "It gives me chills to think what would have happened if I arrived just a little later."

We both sit there in silence, and then I can't take it anymore. I wrap my arms around his wide shoulders, and he holds me tight in return.

"Thank you so much," I say, tears in my eyes.

He tightens his grip around me. "The pleasure is all mine."

We hold each other for as long as we both need, then let go.

"I'm really glad you're here, Silas," he says. "I mean it." I sigh, then smile. "Me too."

* * *

When Wyatt and I get back to Utah, life continues on as it normally would. The football season officially begins for Wyatt, and work picks up for me as well. Thankfully, he feels safe playing now. School has started, and a bunch of kids are trying out for their sports teams, so I'm helping them out at Affirm.

After a particularly rewarding day of helping a young transman work on throwing a football, I make my way home to my apartment. Wyatt's already there. I finally accepted his offer to pay my loans, and today we're working out the logistics to make that happen. And I'm so grateful for him. Wyatt would have never had to do this. I'm beyond touched and thrilled. I'm so excited not to have to give up an exorbitant amount of my paycheck each month.

When I walk into my apartment, Wyatt is freshly sweaty after working out, so I know the sex we're about to have will be fire. But when I shut the door, he stands up, and there's worry plastered all over his face.

"What's wrong?" I ask.

He walks over to the counter. He sifts through the mail he collected for me, then pulls out an off-white envelope.

"It's from Alabama," he says. "Your hometown." My stomach lurches, and I shake my head. "But who—" and then I remember. When I officially moved to

Salt Lake, I sent a letter to my family informing them of my new address. In the rare chance that they would try to reach out to me.

And it looks like they did.

Wyatt hands me the envelope, and my stomach lurches when I see the name for myself. The letter is addressed to me, Silas King, from a Deborah King—the same name as my mother.

My heart racing, I tear the envelope open. I need to see what it says. Inside, there's a short hand-written letter. I read it once, then twice, and finally a third time.

"What does it say?" Wyatt asks.

"My mom," I say, setting the letter down on the counter. I keep my eyes on it, afraid that if I look away it mind change or disappear completely. Then I finally look at my boyfriend.

"She says she's happy to see I'm with someone," I say.

"Okay," Wyatt says skeptically. "So she watches the news."

"And she says that if I want, I can visit. She said she'd like to meet my boyfriend."

Wyatt folds his arms and frowns.

"What?" I ask. I glance back at the letter. I can't believe that after all these years, I've finally heard from my family. Damon, my therapist, has said that I should be careful about thinking I need to feel certain things at certain times. Right now, I feel like I should be shocked or angry that after all these years my parents finally reach out to me when I'm dating a celebrity. But I just feel happy.

"I don't know," Wyatt says, pulling on his beard. "This just sounds fishy. They reach out after all these years after you're dating me?"

"I know," I say, shaking my head. "But the letter—" I pick it up and scan over the words. "She says she's sorry, too. And the vibe of it all—it doesn't seem like she's using me."

Wyatt thins his lips, his bulging arms still folded. "So what are you going to do?" I reflect on what he said when we hiked together that one night. They were the ones who missed out on a relationship with me. I was the open one. So wouldn't I be missing out on something if I rejected them now?

"I want to go see them," I say.

Wyatt runs his hand over his bearded mouth. "Are you sure?"

"I am," I say. "I have a good feeling about this."

Wyatt puts his arm around me, takes off my cowboy hat, and pulls me in, allowing me to breathe in his musk. My shoulders relax as he squeezes me against him, and he kisses me on the top of my head.

"Do you want me to come with you?" he asks.

I think about a recent virtual session I had with Damon. It's important for me to not depend on others, especially Wyatt, for complete emotional support. But he's also said that I shouldn't do hard things alone. And this might be the hardest thing I have to do.

I pull away and look up at him. "I do."

He leans down and kisses me. "Then let's work something out," he says. "After I pay off your loans."

I laugh. "Thank you again."

He brushes my mustache with his thumb, then kisses me again. "I love you," he says. "I love you too."

And so, that night, Wyatt helps me pay off the rest of my loans, and it feels like I've been freed from the ball chained to my ankle. After that, we look at our schedules to see when a good time to visit my parents ranch down in Alabama would be, and I prepare a letter to send back to my mom.

But I wait until the morning to send it. Because now, Wyatt and I just want to make love, and after we both get off twice, I fall asleep in his arms, happily knowing that making myself open to a relationship with my family has finally paid off. And that, for the first time in my life, I'm sustainably happy. I no longer have to check a box, saying that today won't be the day I'll end my life. Because I know that life will always be too good to give up.

What's Next?

Thank you for reading *Winning Wyatt*! If you'd like, please leave a review!

Still want to read about Silas and Wyatt? <u>Sign up for my newsletter</u> (https://dl.bookfunnel.com/bp0xm1ngn4) and receive a free bonus short story! Silas decides to go visit his mother back in Alabama with Wyatt by his side, and he couldn't be more nervous.

Want more football lovers? Check out the Football Heartthrobs prequel *<u>Downing Dominic</u>*!